Downfall
Jeff Abbott

sphere

SPHERE

First published in the United States in 2013 by Grand Central,
a division of Hachette Book Group US
First published in Great Britain in 2013 by Sphere

A CIP catalogue record for this book
is available from the British Library.

ISBN 978-1-84744-517-9

Printed and bound in Great Britain by
Clays Ltd, St Ives plc

Papers used by Sphere are from well-managed forests
and other responsible sources.

MIX
Paper from
responsible sources
FSC
www.fsc.org   FSC® C104740

Sphere
An imprint of
Little, Brown Book Group
100 Victoria Embankment
London EC4Y 0DY

An Hachette UK Company
www.hachette.co.uk

www.littlebrown.co.uk

For Mitch Hoffman

Corruptio optimi pessima.
The corruption of the best is the worst.

Latin proverb

PART ONE

WEDNESDAY, NOVEMBER 3

I

---◦◉◦---

Wednesday, November 3, afternoon

San Francisco, California

THE SIMPLEST BEGINNINGS can unravel a life. A family. A world.

In this case, chewing gum.

Diana Keene reached into her mom's ugly new purse in the middle of their argument to snatch a slice of spearmint. She saw three cell phones hidden at the bottom of the purse.

One pink, one blue, one green. Cheap models she'd never seen before, not like the smartphone Mom kept glued to her side at all times, befitting a public relations executive.

"And since you'll be running the company while I'm gone," Mom was saying, her back to her daughter while she stuffed a sweater into her luggage, "no sauntering into the office at nine, Diana. Be there by seven thirty. Give yourself time to scan the news feeds from the East Coast."

Diana grabbed the gum, stepped away from the purse, and considered whether or not to confront her mother in her little white lie. She decided to dance around the edges.

"I don't think it's healthy to go without a cell phone for two weeks." Diana crossed her arms, staring at her mother's back. She unwrapped the gum, slid the stick into her mouth. "What if I need you?"

"You'll survive." Her mother, Janice, zipped up her small suitcase, turned to face her daughter with a smile.

"What if a client throws a fit? Or I do something wrong?"

"Deal with it. You'll survive." Janice straightened up and smiled at her daughter.

"Mom—what if I need—" and then Diana broke off, ashamed. She stared past her mother's shoulder, out at the stunning view of San Francisco Bay, the hump of Alcatraz, the distant stretch of the Golden Gate. It was a cloudless day, the early haze burned away, the blue of the sky bright. *Need what? Need you to keep running my life for me?*

"Need money?" Mom, as she often did, finished the sentence for her but misinterpreted what she meant. "Diana, you're a grown woman with a good job. You can survive for two weeks without any"—and here Mom did her air quotes, bending her fingers—"emergency loans."

"You're right." *Why are you lying to me, Mom?* she thought. "Where is this no-contact retreat again?"

"New Mexico."

"And I have no way to contact you—none at all?" *Like on these three cheap phones?*

"Cell phones are forbidden. You could call the lodge and leave a message, I suppose," Janice said, but in a tone that made it clear that she didn't want her Bikram yoga or her bird-watching or her organic lunch interrupted. "The whole point is to get away from the world, sweetheart."

Mom stuck with the lie, and Diana felt her stomach twist. "This just isn't like you, withdrawing so completely from the world. And from your work. And from me."

"Yes, I'm a workaholic, sweetheart, and it's made me tired and sick. I'm ready for a break, and I'm ready for you to be fine with it."

Diana thought, *Confront her with the lie. And then she knows you snooped in her purse like a kid would, and you're twenty-three, not thirteen, and…maybe Mom has a good reason.* She thought of the hours her mother had worked, everything she'd done for Diana. In the car. She'd ask her about the phones in the car.

"I'm ready."

Diana jingled her keys. "Fine, let's go."

Mom's town house was the entire top floor of the building. They took the elevator down and walked across the building's small lawn (a rarity in San Francisco), through the heavy metal gate to Green Street. Diana put her mother's bag in the back of the Jaguar that Janice had bought her for her last birthday. Diana drove out of the lovely neighborhood of Russian Hill. Janice talked about what needed to be done at work while she was gone: account reviews, pitching stories on clients to the leading business publications, preparing for client product launches in January. Diana kept waiting for her mom to stop lying.

They were ten minutes from the airport and Diana said, "Why are you taking three, yes three, cell phones to a place that forbids them?"

Her mother looked straight ahead and said, "So when they confiscate one, I'll have extras hidden away."

Diana laughed. "You troublemaker. Give me the numbers and I'll call you or text you."

"No. Don't call me." She looked out the window. "Just let me go do what I need to do and don't call me."

Her tone was far too serious. "Mom…"

"Do not call me, Diana, and frankly, I don't appreciate you rooting around in my purse. Stay out of my business."

The words were like knives, sharp, and to Diana's ears not like Mom.

The drive turned into a painful silence as Diana took the exit for the airport.

"I don't want this to be our good-bye, honey," Janice said.

"Are you really going on this retreat?" Diana pulled up to the curbside drop-off.

"Of course I am." Steel returned to Mom's voice. "I'll see you in two weeks. Maybe sooner if I get bored." Janice leaned over and gave Diana a kiss on the cheek, an awkward sideways hug.

You're still lying to me, Diana thought. *I don't believe you.*

"Love you, honey," Mom said. "More than you can know."

"Love you, too, Mom. I hope you have a great time at your *retreat*."

Mom glanced at her. "Two weeks will let you make a splash at the office while I'm gone. Be smart, show everyone you deserve to be my successor. You'll be running it when I'm dead and gone." Janice's voice nearly broke on the last words, like she needed to clear her throat. She squeezed Diana's hand.

Diana didn't care for talk like that—for any suggestion of a Mom-free world. "I'll keep everything running smoothly."

Then Mom stepped out of the car, grabbed her small suitcase, and walked toward the terminal entrance.

Diana thought of jumping out of the car, running to her for one more hug, and thought, *No, I won't, because you're clearly lying to me and I want to know why.*

Her mother had never lied to her. The reason had to be big. Two weeks where Mom didn't want anyone to know where she was. She headed back toward the city. But not to her own apartment. Back to Russian Hill, back to Mom's.

Diana felt a cold tapping of terror down her spine, her imagination dancing with the possibilities behind her mother's lie.

Janice Keene watched her daughter, the only true good thing she had done in her life, drive away until Diana was gone from sight in the eddying swarm of cars, cabs, and limos.

Inside her purse the pink phone rang. She answered it.

A voice of a man, with a soft mixed accent of an American who'd spent much time in London, said, "You'll be traveling under the name Marian Atkins. Inside the lining of your purse is an appropriate ID. There'll be a package for you at your hotel when you arrive with what you need. Call me on this phone when the first job is done, and then destroy the phone. I'll call you then on the green phone. The blue phone for the last job."

"I understand."

"Remember you're doing it all for your daughter, Janice. And then you can rest easy."

"I know."

The man hung up. Janice Keene went to the ladies' room and tore open the lining of the purse and yes, there was a California driver's license and a credit card in the name of Marian Atkins. Attached was a sticky note with an airline and a confirmation number and a hotel name with another confirmation number. The purse had been delivered to her house yesterday via an overnight courier, from an address in New York.

Janice walked to one of the airline's self-service kiosks and tapped in the first number. The screen brought up an itinerary that informed her she was booked on a flight to Portland, Oregon. It spat out a boarding pass for Marian Atkins.

She collected the pass and walked with resolve toward the security lines.

Janice Keene was going to do what she must to ensure the world—that uncertain, awful, wonderful place—could never hurt her Diana. To be sure her daughter had a perfect life, just as perfect as the last seven years had been for her mother.

No matter who had to die.

2

Wednesday, November 3, afternoon

Sam! I want to get married here!"

"Of course you do, darling," I said. I smiled at the venue's event planner as we walked through the large marble atrium of the Conover House, one of the grander spots to host a wedding or conference in San Francisco. The romantic grin on my face was the kind I'd worn when I got married for the first time. Mila's hand was clenched in mine, and her smile was dazzling. Pure bridal joy.

"Well, let me give you a tour," the planner said. She was a tall woman, fortyish, in a smart gray suit. She'd sized us up the moment we arrived—sans appointment with that hurried disregard of the truly moneyed—and we were dressed to kill. No pun intended.

"One thing first," I said.

"She will show us a cost estimate later, darling," Mila said, ever the impatient bride. She leaned in close to me, her hair smelling of lavender, her eyes dancing with mischief. "Whatever it is, I'm sure it will be worth it."

"My question isn't cost. It's security," I said. "You have security here, yes, during events?"

"Yes, of course, if that is a concern."

"It is." I didn't elaborate on a reason. I just kept my fake smile in place.

"We have a contract with a topflight security firm here. And a system of monitors and cameras throughout the building." She gestured up at a small camera in the top corner of the atrium. I flexed the smile for the camera's benefit.

"He is such the worrywart." Mila looked stunning in her dark, snug dress, every inch the giddy bride. She wore a ring on her hand, a lovely diamond, that sparkled grandly on her finger. "Now the building."

"One more question," I said. "You have cameras monitored, yes?"

"Yes. Our on-site team can respond. Or they're happy to work with your own security team, if you should have one."

"That's very reassuring," I said, and off we went on the tour of the beautiful old building, which had once been a very grand bank, the planner pointing out the venue's features and facilities.

"I am thinking," Mila exclaimed as we walked along the marble floors, "of a 1920s theme for the wedding. Sam, is that not brilliant?"

"Brilliant," I said. The architecture and decor certainly fit her idea. We were on the second floor by now, and I spotted a men's room as we headed toward a grand staircase leading to the third floor. "I'm feeling a bit unwell, please excuse me. You all go on, I'll catch up."

"He is so nervous to marry me," Mila said to the planner as I went through the men's room doors. "We have been through so much together, you see."

That was true. The door shut behind me. No cameras in here. I went into a stall, counted to sixty, and then I walked out and headed downstairs. The planner had already told us that most of the food service and administrative offices were on the first floor.

I assumed security was there as well. There might be a guard on duty, but there were no events being hosted right now, one conference having ended at noon. I tested the door marked SECURITY, lockpick at the ready.

But the door was unlocked.

I stepped inside. A small chamber, because they needed the real estate for food and rentals. Nine monitors set up to show various rooms and entrances of the Conover House. But no guard. Bathroom break?

One monitor was tuned to a cable news channel. The vice president of the United States had died last week from a sudden stroke, and conjecture about who the president would appoint as his successor was rampant. To me it sounded like a festival of endless talking heads. On the security monitors I saw Mila and the planner strolling on the third floor, and Mila pantomimed excitement to keep the planner focused on her, not on wondering where I was at or why I was taking so long in the bathroom.

A stack of DVDs stood on the rack, each in a jewel box, with a date and time range written on it, tied to a particular camera. The dates went back for a week. Liability issues, I thought. The venue wanted to protect itself. Because even among a well-heeled crowd, fights break out, people get drunk, tumbles happen down the stairs.

Or someone tries to commit a murder and fails.

I pulled one disc out of its jewel box for an evening three nights ago, from 8:00 p.m. to 10:00 p.m., for the main ballroom. I replaced it with a similar disc. The discs got reused, I figured, at the end of the week. I slid the jewel box home and slipped the original video disc into the small of my back, against my belt. My jacket hid it.

On the screen, Mila bounced on the tiptoes of her elegantly shod feet, enraptured with the thoughts of the perfect wedding reception.

The door opened. A guard, midtwenties, about my age, stepped in. He looked annoyed but not angry to see me. "Sir, you're not supposed to be in here."

"Sorry. I was getting a tour with my fiancée"—I pointed toward Mila on the screen—"and I had a security question that I didn't wish to ask in front of her while we're getting the tour for our wedding reception. The door was unlocked."

"Yes, sir?"

"Are your people armed?"

The guard blinked. "No. We've never needed to be."

"Thank you." I didn't explain my question. I knew my intrusion would be mentioned to the planner, and they'd wonder why I was so obsessed with security. I didn't need to give an answer since Mila and I wouldn't return here. I nodded and I walked past him, and I was entirely sure that as I went up the two flights of stairs he watched me on the screen. I rejoined Mila and the planner and made sure to give Mila a convincing kiss for the benefit of the security guard. Her mouth was tight under mine, firm and warm.

We finished the tour, discussed possible booking dates eight months from now, and promised to call back soon.

Then we headed out into the busy Financial District, walked to the car, and drove back toward my bar in the Haight. I told Mila what I'd found, handed her the stolen disc.

"You asked if their guards were armed? I suspect every date I mention to the planner now, the venue will be booked," Mila said. "I am so disappointed."

"I could kill you," I said.

"What, the wedding is off?" she said in mock surprise.

"I got caught. I had to talk my way out."

"You have gotten lazy and sloppy," she said. She slipped off the diamond engagement ring—I had no idea where she'd gotten it—and put it in her pocket.

"I told you I didn't want to do...*this* anymore."

"Do what?"

"Be your spy, your thief, your hired gun." I kept my hands steady on the wheel. "I have a son now."

"And the reason you have him back is me," she said. "I've given you much and asked for little."

"Mila..."

"Fine. Let's go see your son. And"—she held up the disc I'd stolen—"let's see who our would-be killer is."

My bar in San Francisco—one of thirty plus I own around the world—was called The Select and it wasn't open yet; I'd decided while my son Daniel was here not to open until five in the afternoon. It gave me more time with him. I parked behind the bar in a shared lot and opened the door with a key. The bar itself was silent. Upstairs, I could hear laughter and music and my heart melted a bit. Call me sentimental. I'd fought far too hard to get my son back to ever feel embarrassed by emotion.

Upstairs, in the office/apartment above The Select, my son

Daniel, ten months old, was on a blanket, crawling and laughing, while Leonie played with him. I'd been lucky. Leonie hadn't en-rolled yet in art school, so she had the time to travel with me, bring Daniel along as I went to several of my bars over the past two weeks: New York, Austin, Boston. We'd flown down from my bar in Vancouver yesterday, at Mila's insistence, because there was a problem.

Mila knelt to tickle Daniel's nose, earned a giggle from him, and then she completely ignored Leonie. Leonie ignored her back. They don't like each other and I'm not entirely sure why. Leonie is not Daniel's mother; she is, well, a nanny of sorts, an art student-turned-forger. She'd lost a lot in her life, and I'd saved Leonie from a criminal syndicate called the Nine Suns. The same syndicate that kidnapped Daniel and his mother, even before he was born, and de-stroyed my CIA career. Leonie had been good to Daniel and taken care of him when no one else would. She was deeply attached to my son, and so I'd asked her to stay in his life. We'd had a brief fling—under highly stressful circumstances—and were back to be-ing just friends. Leonie had been nothing but perfect with Daniel, but I knew Mila thought I'd made a mistake, asking a former crim-inal to watch over my son.

I hoped Mila was wrong.

Mila slid the disc into a laptop on the desk.

"Here he is." She pointed. "Dalton Monroe." She clicked with the mouse and a red dot appeared on Monroe, a tall, rangy man in his sixties. He wore a suit and seemed determined to meet and greet everyone in the room, which was at least two hundred people.

In his right hand was a glass of bourbon.

"It's no easy thing to poison a man in front of two hundred wit-nesses," Mila said. "I admire the nerve."

I picked up Daniel and sat next to her. He squirmed a little on my lap, eager to watch the red dot, like it was a game. Leonie stretched out on Daniel's blanket and began to sketch in a pad aimlessly.

"Two hundred people, but it gets pared down pretty fast," I said. "Look. He has a bodyguard near him. Maybe five admirers in a knot around him. Beyond that, a few people watching him directly, angling for their chance to talk to him. Maybe fifteen, at any given second, looking at him. And looking at that same moment at the poisoner."

She accelerated the feed; forty minutes into the video, Dalton Monroe stumbled badly, clearly ill. He dropped the bourbon glass. The bodyguard hurried him out, Monroe smiling, waving off concerns from the other guests. He had then been taken to a private medical clinic, where it was diagnosed that he'd ingested a nonfatal dose of digitalis. The press were told he'd simply become ill at the party and had to leave. Dalton Monroe was worth a billion dollars and did not care to have it known that someone tried to poison him at a reception celebrating his latest business acquisition, a local software company he'd bought to fold into his empire.

"He's Round Table, right?" I asked Mila. The Round Table. My secret benefactors. A network of resource-rich and powerful people who want to be a force for good in the world, behind the scenes. They have Mila as their face to me; they gave me the bars to run, a web of safe houses around the world.

They helped me get back my son. I know little about them, except that they started off as a CIA experiment that finally broke free to pursue their own agenda.

"Yes," Mila said. "Someone tried to kill a Round Table member. I want you to find out who."

"I said I'd run the bars for you all. Nothing more." I settled Daniel on my knee.

"Sam, perhaps Leonie wouldn't mind taking Daniel for a walk," Mila said. "The day is so lovely."

"I don't mind." Leonie was normally chatty with me, but always quiet around Mila.

"No, would you leave him, please?" I got down on the blanket with him, wriggled fingers at him. I felt like I never got to see him enough, even when he was traveling with me.

"Fine," Leonie said. "I'll go get an iced coffee." I thought she already had the ice in her voice. She left. Mila stood at the window while I played and made bubbling noises at Daniel, and I figured she waited until she saw Leonie on the street below.

"You need to be nicer to her," I said. "You can trust her to keep her mouth shut about the Round Table." And I knew we could—we'd given Leonie a far safer, brighter new life.

"I will never trust her."

"I do, end of discussion."

"I understand you want to be with your son," Mila said. "I do. But the bars, a very good livelihood for you, were not free. There was a price attached."

"I'm not ungrateful. But I'm also not a police detective."

"The Round Table never wants the police involved. If this poisoning attempt on Monroe was because he is a member of the Table, then we must know without involving the police. Felix will help you." Felix was the manager of The Select. The senior managers of my bars know about the Round Table and were recruited to help with their work.

"What about you?"

Daniel grabbed my wiggling fingers and laughed. Sweetest sound ever.

"I have to return to Los Angeles tomorrow on other business. I'm sure you can handle this."

"And what do I do when I find out who tried to poison Monroe?"

"Give me their name. Then the Round Table will decide how to proceed." She got up from the laptop, gave me a smile dimmer than her fake bridal one. "Don't pretend you're not itching for some action. A man like you doesn't like to sit and play with a baby on a blanket for long."

"Actually, I like nothing better." I made a face at Daniel. "Don't we? Don't we like playing on the blanket?" Daniel concurred with laughter but then gave me a rather serious frown, as though a more detailed answer required thought.

Mila didn't smile. "I know you love Daniel. But I also know you, Sam. You cannot sit at a desk; you cannot play on a floor. You need something more."

I looked up at her. "No, I don't."

"Sam. Send Leonie and Daniel home to New Orleans. They've

been traveling with you for two weeks; a baby needs routine and order, not bars and airplanes. I'll even give Leonie and Daniel a ride to the airport, get them their tickets. Then you go home when you've cleared up this little case for me, yes?"

I was a former undercover CIA agent, not a detective, but I nodded. Anything to get her to go. If I found Monroe's poisoner, fine. If I didn't, then maybe I could make a new deal with the Round Table. One that kept me out of trouble. One that let me play on blankets. Then I could go home to New Orleans for a while. I had to find a way to make this balance work.

"That planner will be so disappointed that we're not getting married there," I said. I don't even know why I mentioned it. The words felt odd in my mouth, and I was glad Leonie wasn't there, even though we were just friends now.

Mila crooked a smile at me. "Maybe if you find our poisoner," she said, "I'll throw you a big party."

3

Wednesday, November 3, afternoon

DIANA STOOD ALONE in her mother's town house, trying to decide, *Do I search on her computer? Go through her mail, what? Listen to her messages?*

She went to the cordless phone, neat in its cradle. She pressed the message button. Heard first her own voice calling two days ago, then the failed pitch of a telemarketer trying to upgrade Mom's cable TV package, a friend from an art museum calling to ask if Mom would serve on a committee for a fund-raiser. A man's voice, smoky and a bit gruff: "Janice? It's Felix. Just calling to see if you'd like to have a drink tomorrow night at The Select after the meeting. Let me know. Okay, good night." Then nothing.

Felix, oh yes. Mom's new friend. A bartender down in the Haight, she'd met him once. An odd friend for Mom to have, he wasn't exactly the corporate suit type. She wondered what meeting he meant.

A stack of mail by the computer. Diana flipped through it, feeling more and more like a thief. No letters from secret lovers, no flyers from the Cell Phone–Free Yoga Hippie Institute, either. Just bills and invitations, mostly to charity events. People wanted Mom involved. She was connected; she got things done.

And what "thing" is she doing for the next two weeks? Because it's not yoga.

The cordless phone rang. Diana reached for it, then stopped. Let the machine pick up. Her open hand, reaching for the cordless nestled in its cradle, clenched into a fist.

Three rings, and the machine clicked on.

"Ms. Keene? This is Inez with the San Francisco Bay Cancer Center. You had canceled your meetings with Dr. Devendra to discuss your treatment options, and we wanted to see if we could reschedule. You can call me at 555-9896. Thank you." The message ended.

Diana sat still as stone. She replayed the message.

"No," she said while Inez repeated the words of doom. "No."

Cancer. Treatment options.

Maybe she'd gone some place for treatment. But why lie about it?

She dialed the phone, trying to stifle the shaking in her hands.

"San Francisco Bay Cancer Center."

"Inez in Dr. Devendra's office, please."

She waited and the chirpy voice came on the line.

"This is Janice Keene." Diana closed her eyes, tried to make her voice a shade lower, like Mom's. "Returning your call."

"Okay, Ms. Keene, thanks, your appointment…"

"Uh, yes, I was going to be in and out of town over the next two weeks…"

"I think he very much wanted to see you before then, Ms. Keene. I have some cancellations next Monday."

Diana felt she might shove her fist into her mouth to stifle the scream.

"I have 2:00 p.m. available."

"Okay." *Get tricky*, Diana thought. "Listen, can I bring my daughter with me? I want her to understand what I'm facing."

"Of course."

"And…" Diana decided to press her luck. "Dr. Devendra told me the technical name of my cancer, but I was forgetful, I didn't write it down…Can you tell me?"

"I'm sorry, I can't. I only make the appointments. E-mail Dr. Devendra if you like."

"Yes, of course. Thank you." Diana clicked off the phone, and then she dropped it to the floor, where it clattered and the battery cover sprung loose and skittered under the table. The grief was sudden, an earthquake to her core. This couldn't be happening. It couldn't.

If her mother was so sick, where had she gone? So sick the doctor didn't want to wait two weeks to see her. Good Lord, Diana thought, maybe Mom was chewing on apricot seeds in Mexico or had gone to a holistic healer or something else way too alternative when she needed a doctor...

She started to dial the number for Keene Global, the giant public relations firm her mother had built from nothing. She paused. What was she going to say? *I know my mother—I mean, your CEO—has cancer; tell me where she is?* She was halfway through keying in the number when she thought, What if Mom hadn't told the senior management at Keene Global? In trying to help, she might do more damage to Mom's business relationships.

She clicked the phone off. The tears came—tears of shuddering grief for the mom she loved beyond all reason. She cried herself out. It took a long while.

Then she sat up, dried her face. Her mother kept a home office; she hurried down the hallway to it. An old, elegant desk, bookshelves behind. Under the shelves were drawers that disguised file cabinets.

Diana tried the cabinets. Locked. She couldn't find a key in the desk. She found a small toolbox beneath the kitchen sink, fished out a screwdriver and a hammer. Every blow of the blunt end into the lock scored and splintered the clean cherrywood.

The doctor doesn't want to wait two weeks.

The lock broke with a satisfying *clunk*. Diana yanked out the tray, heavy with a neat, tidy rainbow of hanging files.

She found the papers in a manila file marked MEDICAL. She read the records of the initial visits and the amassed tests. Breast cancer, aggressive. Spreading into lymph nodes, lungs.

"Why didn't you tell me?" she asked the empty room. She looked up at the walls. Framed articles about her mother as a mover and shaker in the public relations world, pictures of her mom with famous people at her New York office, her Washington office, her Los Angeles office. A perfect life, and now it might end.

She felt an odd shape, taped in the back of the heavy manila folder.

A brown envelope. Marked in her mother's blocky handwriting TO BE OPENED IN THE EVENT OF MY DEATH BY MY DAUGHTER ONLY.

ONLY was underlined three times, in thick black ink.

Through the envelope, Diana could feel a cylindrical object inside. She sat back down among the stacked files on the floor and the wood splinters and the dented and broken lock.

Weighing the envelope in her hand. Open. Don't open.

BY MY DAUGHTER ONLY.

She tore open the envelope. If Mom complained, she could say, *Well, you didn't tell me about the cancer, so don't be mad I stuck my nose in your business.*

Into her hand fell a silver, ornate cylinder.

Diana stared in disbelief.

It was a lipstick case.

Why…why would Mom leave her a lipstick case?

Diana opened it.

It didn't contain lipstick. It was a memory stick, the kind you slot into a computer port. She went to her mother's computer and inserted it. On the screen it showed up as a drive marked FOR DIANA ONLY. The sole file on the drive was a video. She clicked it.

Her mother appeared on the screen. Not smiling. Looking serious.

"My darling Diana. If you are seeing this, I have died. I've spent my life making sure you had the best life I could give you. And now that I am gone, you must understand what I've done. I have to explain a difficult choice I made. I must trust you with my greatest secret…"

The neighbors were all at work or out enjoying the gorgeous day, so no one heard Diana's loud screams of anguish, of denial, of shock. Or her soft moan of "This can't be true."

PART TWO

THURSDAY, NOVEMBER 4

4

Thursday, November 4, early evening

San Francisco, the Haight

*H*ELP ME.*"

At first, over the noise of the bar I wasn't sure I heard her correctly. I was filling in for a bartender who hadn't bothered to show, and I was sick with missing my son, Daniel. Mila had taken him and Leonie to the airport an hour ago.

"Help me," she said again.

She'd hurried into the bar as if she was late for a meeting, panic bright in her eyes. Noise—conversations, the swirling beats of the chill electronica/Asian fusion music, the clink of glasses—washed over us. It was a Thursday night, when most bars like The Select got more groups and fewer quiet drinkers, the start of the weekend.

I blinked and leaned forward, turning my ear toward her to catch her words over the pluck of the electric sitar, rising violins, and thrumming drums from the speakers. Other customers weren't crowding the young woman at the bar; most of The Select's crowd lounged at tables scattered around the back. Most bars in the Haight are small and narrow, but mine is one of the roomier ones. Couples or small groups sat at the tables, drinking beers or cocktails or wine kept in coolers in the centers of the tables. A lot of the artistic crowd in the neighborhood, a smattering of tourists come to see the Haight hippies (but not getting too close), a few people who thought casual Friday at work meant a little bit of a hangover.

"What would you like?" I said, thinking she wanted service, not assistance.

Then her eyes widened, looking past my shoulder into the depths of the mirrored bar, and she turned and she ran, hurrying past the crowd getting drinks, past the clumps of people chatting about the post-workday.

Bars are a magnet for odd behavior. But a woman whispering a plea for help and then fleeing, that was a new one. I glanced over my right shoulder toward the entrance, where the woman's gaze had gone, and saw two men entering, hurrying, walking with purpose, pushing past a clump of young homeless dudes sitting on the sidewalk. One was a broad-shouldered man, wearing eyeglasses, in his late thirties, short haired. Wearing a blazer and jeans. The other was a mobile mountain, heavy with muscle, head shaved bald, ice eyed, and I saw this mountain assessing the room with the same measuring gaze I would have taken back in my CIA days, evaluating where the dangers were, gauging who was a threat, finding an escape route.

Daniel was on my mind and my first thought was *I don't want trouble*. But I couldn't ignore the situation, so I went to deal with the threat. I stepped down the bar to the mountain, who had stepped much closer to the bar as he surveyed the room, my gaze locked on his hands. His hands would give away more than his eyes did. His stare was flat and cold.

"Drink, sir?" I asked loudly, thinking, *Look at me. Not the woman. Look me in the eyes and let me see what kind of trouble you are.*

The mountain turned to glance at me. He shook his head no and then stormed out onto the floor. The young woman—pretty, African American, hair cut short, tall and dressed in a black shirt and jeans—had hidden in a corner behind a pair of chatting women and was now bolting toward the back door, under the red glow of the EXIT sign. She had her hand in a small, dark purse, clutching it close to her chest.

The mountain started barreling through the crowd, shoving a few people. Making a beeline for the woman.

I vaulted over the bar, surprising a woman sitting on a stool, sipping her Dos Equis. The dance pulse of the Bombay Dub Orchestra tune was loud and booming enough to cover the sound of my feet hitting the hardwood floor, so the two men did not turn around.

They hurried toward the back of the bar, free of the restraints of the crowd in the front.

The young woman screamed.

They each grabbed one of her arms, and she tried to wrench free and bolt. They manhandled her back toward the one red EXIT sign.

Four steps and I grabbed for the older guy's shoulder; he looked to me like a suburban dad type. He tried to shrug free of me, but I'm stronger than I look. He sneered at me—navy suit, my normally short hair styled into a fauxhawk (being a bar owner, I thought I'd try to look a little more hip than I actually am), an inch shorter than he was.

"What's this about?" I asked.

The woman broke away from the mountain. She stumbled into a couple who'd risen from their small table, wanting to avoid being drawn into the confrontation. They stepped back from her like she might be a wayward drunk.

"She's a thief," the mountain said loudly. I could hear the Russian accent in his voice.

"Then we'll call the police—" My innocent choice of words acted like a lit fuse.

"No police," the woman said. "None!" She held the purse up, close to her chest again.

The men turned to me, the suburban dad raising an eyebrow as if to say, *See?* I let the dad type go and the mountain said, "Back off."

"Excuse me?" I said.

"Back off. We're leaving your bar—we don't want trouble—but she's coming with us. She stole something of mine, and I just want it back."

The woman's gaze met mine, and the plea again: "Help me."

I grabbed the mountain's shoulder just as the suburban dad again closed a grip on the woman's arm and her purse as she tried to pull away from him. "We just want it back. No one wants to hurt you. Best for you and your mom," I heard the suburban dad say.

Instinct made me glance downward when my brain registered the flick of the mountain's wrist. He held a blade, finely carved, the silver edge a sheen in the dim light of the bar. Now pointing at me.

Eight inches of steel. The knife lashed up toward my outstretched fingers and I dodged the upward swing. In the second he had the knife raised, I hammered a kick into the man's knee.

I have a policy of ending fights quickly when some jerk brings a knife into one of my bars.

And I run. A lot. Sometimes over rooftops. My legs are strong. Guys like the mountain always underestimate me. This amuses me, after the fight.

The mountain didn't crumple. He gasped but smiled at me. But it was a smile of a man who didn't fear or flinch from the threat of pain the way ordinary people do.

"You are an idiot," he told me in Russian.

"You are quite correct," I answered in Russian.

It surprised him. For all of two seconds. He didn't expect it of me and the stupidest reaction can make you pause on the verge of a fight. His moment of indecision let me launch a repeat of the kick; but that wasn't the best move, because the mountain was ready. He blocked the kick, pivoted, and struck my throat with the flat of his hand.

Suddenly I was on my back, the ceiling's waves of steel undulating along the wall. I heard shouts and screams, but they sounded distant, people rushing out of the building.

And then the mountain leaned over me, the knife pivoting in his grip to point downward, fingers now a fist around the polished pearl handle. I heard screaming and feet stampeding on the concrete floor.

He raised the blade and plunged it toward my chest. No hesitation, because he did not have time for me. Even as he stabbed I saw his gaze dart toward the woman; I was just a speed bump. I couldn't die; my brain filled with thoughts of my son. I blocked the big man's descending wrist with my forearm, the tip of the steel hovering above the lapel of my suit. For two beats, two seconds, the knife stayed still in its arc. It caught the lights from the retro disco ball moving in a lazy turn (still hanging from Wednesday's seventies night), the bits of broken light like snow against the steel.

Surprise for those two frozen seconds. I powered a knee hard into the mountain's groin, hooked my fingers, and jabbed his eyes. He staggered, off-balance, the knife's edge skimming the floor as he swung downward at me in rage and missed, and I scrambled to my feet.

Then gunfire. I saw the woman. She'd fired at the suburban dad through her purse, tattering the fabric. The dad type ducked for a moment, then charged at her, grabbed the purse, aiming it upward. After another shot, a bourbon bottle shattered against the mirrored bar. The gunfire cleared a path among the terrified club goers. A river of people surged toward the front exit.

I delivered a hammer fist to the face of the mountain, twice, faster than he expected. I pressed, grabbing the knife handle. I pivoted so he and I were facing the same direction. This needed to end. I tried to wrench his arm up and across my chest, to break it. He tried to kick out my foot, failed, and instead launched us both into the wall. The air whooshed out of my lungs. But I headbutted him without a lot of momentum, and as we staggered back, the knife fell from his grip, clattering on the floor.

I wrenched free, sending him crashing into a table of abandoned cocktails.

The suburban dad dragged the woman toward the back exit, pulling on her purse. They slammed into a cart holding a plastic bin of empty beer bottles, used glasses, and wadded napkins. I saw the suburban dad's mouth moving, whispering into the woman's ear. She screamed again, wrenched free from him, swinging a beer bottle at his head. He ducked and staggered away from her.

The mountain lumbered up, threw himself into me, rage purpling his face.

I saw the woman grab a drink from the nearest table—an abandoned pint of lager sitting between a couple of purses. She smashed the glass hard into the mountain's face, beer spraying, the glass cracking. Trying to help me.

It didn't slow him.

The knife was in my hand, but his fist covered mine and the blade stayed steady between us. He caught my leg with his own, sending me crashing to the floor, trying to aim the knife toward my throat. But he lost his balance as I tugged hard on his wrist, fighting for control, and the mountain fell.

Onto the blade.

Bad luck. There are places in the chest that can survive a bad stabbing. He didn't land that way. He collapsed, eyes fading of life, just enough to see my face and the wicked blade too close to his heart.

A man I didn't know, who'd tried to kill me and now lay dying on my floor.

Everything going bad for me, in less than a minute. My life was supposed to be calm now. So I could be a father to my son. I wasn't supposed to be a weapon anymore.

"Stop her!" I yelled, but nearly everyone was gone, flooding the entrance out onto the sidewalks of the Haight.

5

Thursday, November 4, early evening

The dead man—not dead yet, dying—glanced at me. Surprise in his eyes at the turn of fate, the embrace of the unforeseen. He pulled out the knife from his chest and stared at his own blood on the blade, turned over on his side, legs curling, emptying life on the stone floor, red seeping along the broken glasses and bottles.

I saw the woman under the dim light of The Select's soft Asian lamps, running into the hallway that led to the back exit.

The suburban dad ran after the woman, scooping up the gun from the mountain's back holster. If he needed the mountain's gun, then he hadn't gotten the gun inside her purse away from the woman.

Her I could still help.

I ran after the suburban dad as he hit the back door where the woman had fled. He turned, gun raised, and fired at me. He did it running; there was no bracing his stance or aiming.

He missed and I didn't know if it was by a foot or by an inch. I kept on him and the man made his choice.

Go after the woman.

The Select's back door exited into a small courtyard, a narrow parking area for a business behind us and an apartment above it. Pallets of wood and junk lay stacked along the edge. She stumbled out into the night and the man hit the door ten seconds after her.

He said, "Give it to me and we'll leave you alone"—I could hear the woman's hard sobbing of freaked-out terror—and I hit him. I knocked him hard into the side of a recycling bin that was fragrant with the sweet-sour smell of discarded liquor bottles. The front of his shirt tore in my grip and in the streetlight I saw a silver gleam: an odd symbol of lines and spaces hanging on a small necklace.

I couldn't see the woman but he could hear her screaming, "Don't, please, don't."

The suburban dad levered his elbow back hard into my jaw. It hurt and I was surprised; I didn't think he was much of a threat. The man whirled back, launched another punch at my head. It caught me hard, and I fell back heavily against the metal.

He put me down with another kick to the throat. Unlike the mountain he moved fast and didn't try to psych me out of fighting. Then he steadied the gun at my head as I fought to breathe. Bracing himself to shoot another human being point-blank in the face. I could see the hesitation in his eyes as I tried to scramble back.

She'd pried the board loose from a pallet next to the bin, and she swung it with a crushing force. She connected. He dropped. The suburban dad made a gagging noise, as though his stomach was wrenched instead of his head, and she dropped the plank to the ground. A twisted nail lay bent in the wood, and a fresh flower of dark hair and blood bloomed on it.

On his knees the suburban dad grabbed at his head with his hand. Making a low humming noise of surprised agony. Stunned.

The woman picked up his gun.

Aimed it at the man.

Her hand shook. I could see her purse with the hole in it, dangling now from her shoulder.

"Don't shoot him! The police will be here," I said. "They'll help you—"

And the woman looked at me again, her eyes meeting mine for the first time since she'd leaned across my bar and whispered, *Help me*. "No police, no!"

"What's your name? I can help you." I raised a hand toward her, trying to calm her.

"You can't. They'll kill you, too."

"Who are you?"

The gun wavered and the man said, "Don't, please..." his voice unsteady as he stared down the gun.

"You're just like my mom," she said to him, her voice breaking, and it was perhaps the single strangest comment she could have made.

She looked at me, then at the man, and she decided not to kill anyone that night; then she turned and ran out onto the side street, still holding the man's gun. A hard left into the thin curling light rain of the night, away from Haight Street.

A car screeched to a stop close to the alleyway—an Audi, it looked like—and the suburban dad bolted toward it, holding his bloodied head.

I was torn for a second, and it cost me—which one did I chase? So I chased him. I threw myself at the car as he slammed the passenger side door and the Audi roared forward.

I landed on the roof, fingers scrabbling for purchase. I tried to hammer my foot against the back window but the Audi swerved hard, barely kissing the steel of the cars parked along the road. I saw a flash of blonde hair at the wheel, a blur of a face, nothing more.

I was thrown. I slid off the Audi, landing on the trunk of one of the parked cars. I rolled, my parkour training taking over, spreading the impact along my backside, landing on my feet on the sidewalk.

The car roared off into the dark, vanishing with a hard right, as the cry of the police sirens grew.

But I saw the license plate before it made the swerving turn, caught in the garish glow of the grow lights seller's display on the corner. I memorized it.

Where was the woman? I jerked around, trying to find her. Vanished. The crowd at the intersection had cleared, some of the homeless regulars screaming and pointing.

I stumbled back into the bar. And there was a dead man lying on my bar's floor, some of The Select's employees milling by the bar, in shock. Felix, the bar's manager, stood near them, studying the body with a calm eye. Felix was fortyish, balding, thin and strong like wire.

"Are you all right?" he said.

"Yes." I knelt by the body and told Felix, "Go to the front door, keep everyone out. Meet the police there."

"Sam…we have to know who he is, who he's from…"

Like this wasn't random. Like it was an attack on me. My past catching up with me. He didn't know about the woman asking for help.

"Now. Get them out."

But as Felix herded everyone onto the street, I positioned myself between the mountain's body and The Select's security camera. I stuck my hand in the dead mountain's pocket.

I needed to know something. Before the police arrived and I lost all control of the situation.

6

Thursday, November 4, early evening

I'M TAKING YOU TO THE DOCTOR." Holly kept one hand on the steering wheel, put the other hand on Glenn's bleeding head. He was hurt badly.

"No doctor. You know the rules."

"Screw the rules. I'm taking you to the hospital over on Parnassus..."

"Absolutely not."

"Glenn! Must you argue with me?"

"I don't need a doctor."

Holly took the next corner hard, barely making the light before it glowed red. She glanced in the rearview. She could hear a distant cry of sirens.

"Holly! If we get pulled over for running a light, how do I explain a head wound? Think!"

"I am thinking. I am the only one thinking. I am thinking we go straight to the hospital."

"We can't. He's dead. The Russian. He's dead."

Holly gripped the steering wheel harder. "She killed him? That little...nothing?"

"A bartender killed him."

"What, he had a gun behind the bar?"

"He took the Russian's knife from him and he killed him with it."

Holly hit her hand against the steering wheel. "You said this guy was former freaking Russian Special Forces."

"He was. Once." He winced. He clutched at the silver symbol on the necklace, hanging loose from his shirt. "The bartender was better."

"I *told* you you'd made a mistake hiring him." Her voice rose hard and fast. A dead body left behind. How would they explain this mess to Belias? "I *told* you it was a bad idea; we could have grabbed her…"

"I'm going to vomit," Glenn said, like he was reading a bullet point off a presentation, and Holly wheeled to the side of the road and he was sick on the curb, the few pedestrians walking by averting their eyes.

While he puked she pulled out the prepaid phone and called the one number programmed into it.

The voice came on—"I am expecting nothing but good news"—and she thought as always how Belias could sound both like silk and steel.

"It went badly."

She heard a click of disapproval in his throat and terror seized her chest. "Badly like you were caught? Because you better not be calling me."

"No. Glenn's hurt. Blow to the head. She got away."

"And where exactly have you two geniuses taken yourselves?"

"He needs a doctor. I'm taking him to UCSF…"

"No." Then a long pause that stretched her nerves taut. "Bring him to me. I have a safe house in the Mission District, off Valencia." He gave her directions.

She glanced at Glenn. His skin was pale, the blood bright against it. "He needs a doctor," she repeated.

"Roger is here and he can tend to him." Roger. This was getting worse. If she had a broken leg, she wouldn't want Roger for her impromptu medic. He'd give her aspirin and tell her to do fifty push-ups, to take her mind off the pain.

"Why is Roger in town?"

"Get here." Belias hung up.

Holly threw the phone out onto the sidewalk—now useless to her—and pulled away from the curb, and at the next light she looked at Glenn. His eyes were half-open.

"Who's the president?" Holly asked.

Glenn answered correctly.

"What year is it?"

Glenn mumbled the answer, but he had to pause and think about it, and that scared her.

"When is my birthday?"

"The day I met you," he said. "You asked if I was your present."

She swallowed past the steel in her throat. "That was a long time ago, stupid."

"It was?" He blinked at her, the blood running in his face. "Holly? Are we still married?"

"No."

"We're not?" he said. "Baby, it hurts."

Baby? How long had it been since he called her that? She told herself she had no time for sentiment; Belias might kill them both for this mistake. "It was a long time ago," she said, and she veered the Audi through the light. "Listen to me. Our lives depend on this. You cannot tell him about the Russian. You can't."

"Whatever you say." His words slurred.

She said, "I'm serious, Glenn. You let me do the talking."

"It's fine." He tried to give her a reassuring smile. "I'll handle him. So who am I married to now?"

The apartment was on a quiet side street, not far from the intersection of Valencia and 16th Street. Most of the entrances were gated—not for grandeur, but for security—and several featured decorative barbed wire or spikes in the spaces above the gates. Holly pulled the Audi in front of a DON'T EVEN THINK ABOUT PARKING HERE sign that correlated to the house number Belias had given her. Faded graffiti looped beneath the sign. The street itself was dark, a few windows lit, the bright glow one street over coming from the funky shops and restaurants of the Mission District. She could smell food cooking, a heady mix of Korean and Indian, and under it the sharp tang of brewing coffee. She heard the laughter of young people. She felt her heart twist as she hurried around the side of the car and opened the door to pull Glenn out.

Belias emerged from the doorway and hurried down the steps to help her. He was dressed, as always, in his jet-black suit: black pants, jacket, shirt. She thought crazily that Glenn's blood wouldn't show on the dark fabric.

An older man, in his fifties, came down the wooden stairs. He was shaved bald, thickly muscled. He had long been a soldier and he looked like it. Roger. Normally he greeted her with that cruel flexing of his thin-lipped mouth he thought was a smile. Roger carefully eased his hand under Glenn's shoulder and steadied him.

The two men got Glenn past the front door and into a back bedroom. A bed was already covered with sterile paper.

"Didn't exactly show management skills today, did you, Glenn?" Belias asked Glenn, in a falsely hearty voice, who didn't answer as he eased onto the bed. Holly stood back, arms crossed, her heart heavy.

Roger pulled on latex gloves and began to inspect Glenn with brisk efficiency. Belias waved fingers over the injury on the side of Glenn's head. "Do everything you can for him."

"Is he going to be okay?" Holly said. Then she noticed what else was in the room. A chair with straps. Plastic spread on the floor. A tray of surgical tools. *Because we were going to bring them Diana Keene. They would strap her in that chair. With plastic so it wouldn't make a mess. That poor girl.* Holly's stomach somersaulted again.

"Holly, let's get out of the way. You come in here with me," Belias said.

Holly said, "I can help..."

"Roger trained as a field medic. He can handle his injuries." His tone didn't brook argument.

Roger was no doctor. Roger knew far more about inflicting pain than relieving it. For a moment Holly thought of taking Glenn back out to the car and finding him a real doctor. But Belias wouldn't let her, she knew that. Now she bitterly regretted not going to the hospital. So Holly said, "All right." And she followed him into a small den. It was clean and neat, but there was a city of bottles on one table, bourbon and vodka and whiskey, and Holly stared at the glass.

"Those were for Diana in case we needed to calm her down. Roger's sober, no worries."

Holly sank down into the chair. "Great. Sobriety is something I look for in my medical professionals."

"What I look for in my people," Belias said, "is the ability to grab and capture an unarmed, untrained little idiot off the street."

She looked up at his face and wondered how far she could stretch her lies. He was a bit older than her, midthirties, sleek with muscle under the suit, with two premature graying streaks through the dark of his hair. Eyes blue as the sea, almost an unnatural blue. She wondered if he wore contacts to disguise his real eye color. It would be like him to wear a lie on his eyes, to keep a constant mask in place. Even his voice—American but with a British accent trying to work its way through the top. She knew nothing about him except that she feared him.

Be calm. Save Glenn. Fix this mess. Holly said, "We checked her mother's usual hangouts; we spotted her near a bar her mom frequented in the Haight. She'd gone to the bar last night and used her credit card before she realized we could track her. Glenn followed her into the bar, and I brought the Audi around so he could inject her with the sedative, pretend to be her friend helping her after she'd drunk too much, get her out the back. Then we'd force her into the car."

"What a nice, simple plan." His tone was mocking. He folded his hands in his lap. "How'd he get hurt?"

"She ran out into the alley; the bartender came after her, Glenn said. One of them hit Glenn. It must have been the bartender."

"This bartender was protecting her?"

"I guess."

"And you let her get away."

"You know we can't be caught."

Now he knelt before her. He had a sharp, angular face, all lines and cheekbones and chin, and it broke into a smile that made her think of graves. She'd wondered if Belias's smile would one day be the last sight in her eyes. "Holly. Haven't I always been fair with you and"—he waved his fingers in the direction of the other room—"Glenn?"

"Yes." She was afraid to give any other answer.

"I give so much. I ask so little."

"I know."

"But I do ask for the truth." A pain crossed his face, as if a memory of a lie lingered.

Holly stared at him, then her lap.

"It's very touching that you're worried about Glenn. You are really the better person, after all he's done to you. It's not like he's shown you loyalty and consideration. You need not lie for him." Belias took her hand in his. His skin was always so dry, so cold. His fingers so pale. Once she had dreamed of those pale hands with strings attached to his fingers, strings that led back to her shoulders, her wrists, her brain, her heart.

"Lie?" She hated how he always knew.

"I listen to the police dispatch. There's a dead man on that bar's floor. Who is he?"

She listened to five loud ticks from the red clock on the wall. "Some bystander."

"Glenn killed a bystander. That is unusually…reckless."

"Yes. The bystander interfered."

"The police dispatch report is saying that there were *two* men attacking a woman in The Select. Two men." He raised a pale finger on each hand and pushed them together. "Who was the other man, Holly?"

You're a great liar, she told herself. *Lie like you never have before. For Glenn. For your kids.* "The news reports are wrong. It was chaos. So Glenn said." Holly pulled her hand from his cool grip.

He let her; he folded his hands before him in the gentle pose you might see with a saint's statue. The silver ring he wore was a match for the symbol on her husband's necklace, and she stared at it like it was a mark of the devil. She was suddenly very frightened, a terror that touched her bones. She stared at those folded hands. *Your life has been in this man's hands for how long? And now it's come to this. Your ability to sell one little lie.* "How are the kids, Holly?"

She looked up at his face. "What? They're fine."

"Isn't that why you do what I ask you to do? So your children have a 'better life'?" He smiled the smile a knife might give if it suddenly came to life. "Who was the other man, Holly?"

"A bystander, maybe he intervened in the fight."

"And Diana?"

"Ran out into the night. The cops were coming, we had to go." She kept her gaze steady. "We...we had to protect your investment in us."

Belias smiled and she knew her lies hadn't worked. He touched the tip of her jaw with his finger. "You make me sound mercenary when all I care about is your well-being." He got up, poured her a glass of ice water. She drank it silently while he watched. "Let's see how Glenn is doing."

Roger, with his typical efficiency, had cleaned Glenn's wound, shaved the hair away, and butterfly bandaged the wound. "How is he?" Holly asked. He looked bad. So pale. But his breathing was steadier.

"Blood loss, concussion. He could have a hairline skull fracture," Roger said. His accent was rural, English, thick. "When did he last have a tetanus booster?"

Holly wanted to say, *It's not my business anymore to keep up with his medical records*, but she found herself trying to recall what Glenn's file at home said...Did she still have one for him? Wouldn't he have taken it when he moved out?

But Glenn answered for her, as though cogency were returning to him. Roger went to a fridge and checked supplies and gave Glenn an injection. *Lord only knows what's in that fridge*, Holly thought. *Truth serum?*

"We have to find Diana," Belias said.

"She'll go to the police now," Holly said.

"No, she won't. She won't send her own mother to prison. I've profiled this young woman. Her mom is everything to her." Belias glanced at Glenn. "You're off the job, Glenn. She knows your face. And this dead bystander's face."

She wanted to say, *Be smart, Glenn*. But he was hurt, disoriented, and in pain.

Roger said, "The police dispatch say another man at this bar was stabbed. I thought you were strictly a gun man. You never did that well when I trained you with the knife, Glenn."

"I thought the knife would be better," Glenn said. "I needed a way to scare her, to get her into the car. But she had a gun. She fired it at us through the purse."

"I've underestimated her," Belias said, more to Roger than anyone else.

"Bring her mother back to deal with her. Her mother calls her and tells her to meet us, she'll come straight out of hiding," Holly said.

"Would you do that to your own child, Holly?"

Holly looked at the floor. "If I needed to make my child understand…" But she knew it was a lie. *Please don't let my kids ever know about Belias. Don't let them know what I've done.*

"Her mother is busy on a very important job for me. For us. Busy, busy bee." Belias wiggled pale fingers in front of his face.

"Well, Glenn could have been killed," Holly snapped. "She's not that busy."

"And you two are screwing up so bad we have collateral damage on the bar floor. Do you think the police will ignore a customer killed inside a Haight-Ashbury bar, where tourists frequent? Well. They. Won't." Belias crossed his arms.

Glenn said, "I didn't kill him. The bartender did."

Holly's heart sank.

"Again the bartender. Explain?" Roger asked.

"You said we had to get this woman. Bring her to you." Glenn licked his lips. He spoke with what Holly thought of as his negotiating voice—firm, calm, reasonable. Same voice he'd used when he told her just because he was leaving her and the kids, she didn't need to make a scene. "I didn't want to put Holly at risk. We've never done a kidnapping before. This is in fact the riskiest job you've ever asked us to do."

Holly stepped behind Belias and Roger, and over their shoulders, she shook her head at Glenn.

Glenn ignored her. "So I hired a guy to help us. Big man, used to be Russian Special Forces."

"And you and he went into the bar together to grab Diana," Roger said.

"She made a scene. The bartender confronted him and the Russian went for his knife."

Roger inspected his fingernails. "Why did I bother training you and Holly? Seriously. It's good we never needed candy stolen from a baby."

"She had a gun, so I was right. You said she was the biggest threat we ever faced. I wasn't going to take chances, even if you were." Defiance armored Glenn's tone.

"And this...bartender killed your hired thug." Roger always wanting to understand the tactics of the situation.

"Yes."

"You didn't make a very good investment this time, Glenn," Belias said. "I thought you had a perfect record."

"I wanted to protect Holly, and I wanted to be one hundred percent sure we got your so very important target."

"Glenn," Holly said, "calm down, please."

Belias didn't appear to be bothered by his tone. "You broke a rule, Glenn. We do not involve outsiders. Did you mention my name?"

"Of course not."

"Can anyone connect me to this dead, useless Russian?"

"No. Never."

"Only you and Holly."

"Only me," Glenn said. "He didn't know Holly. He had no contact with her until tonight. I never told him her name."

"What did you tell the useless Russian was your reason for finding Diana?"

"He didn't ask for a reason. He didn't care as long as he got his cash." Glenn's words came out in staccato bursts.

"What was his name?" Roger asked.

"Grigori Rostov," Glenn said. "It wasn't a bad decision; he should have been able to grab Diana with efficiency and deal with any random threat like a do-gooder bartender."

"A Rostov." Roger glanced at Belias. "There's a Russian crime family in New York by that name. Notably disciplined and vicious."

Holly watched Belias. She'd thought Glenn's plan stupid, even patronizing to her, but he'd already hired the Russian when she met him at the rendezvous point in Golden Gate Park, and they'd set out, trying to track Diana from where she'd gone before she realized they were tracking her movements and abandoned her car. The Russian was an impulsive decision by Glenn, and she thought, with a blaze of anger, that he made too many of those. Like when he divorced her. *We're over. I'm sorry, Holly. We had good years. Let's concentrate on that and the children.*

"I hate Russians, but this is just spilt milk," Belias said in a light tone. "I think we can wipe it up with a rag. Holly, why don't you go home? Nothing more to be done tonight."

"I don't understand why you don't tell Diana's mom to call her…"

He put his hands on Holly's arms. "Because Mama doesn't need to know Diana's running. Mama's working on something that will take us to the next level, to borrow a cliché from Glenn's world."

"Whatever her mother's doing won't be so important if we get exposed," Holly said.

"If our merry band cannot capture a ditzy, spoiled twenty-three-year-old, we deserve to lose," Roger said.

Belias looked at her with a gaze that was supposed to be sympathetic but instead just made her cringe. She hoped her flesh wouldn't goose pimple under his cool grip.

"We build each other up, Holly. Brick by brick. But we'll have to come up with another strategy. So go home. Tuck in the kiddies, watch some TV," Belias said.

She patted Glenn on the shoulder. "C'mon, you. I'll take you home."

"No," Belias said. "I think it best he not go home to the new wife, not with an unexplained injury. Not to mention he should be under medical observation, isn't that right, Roger?"

Roger nodded.

"Audrey will worry about me…" Glenn began.

"Send her a text," Belias said. "You can talk to your wife without really talking to her. Should have been invented right after the wheel."

"She'll freak out if I don't come home."

"Tell her you have an emergency meeting. May run all night." He put a hand on Glenn's shoulder. "You're injured, Glenn. You go home and collapse, you get taken to the hospital, you have to answer questions. Let Roger take care of you."

A cold itch worked its way at the base of Holly's spine. "He can come home with me. The kids would love to see him."

"And explain a head injury?"

Holly said, "He fell down some stairs."

Belias said, "If the police are looking for an injured man, better he lay low. Someone might have seen him get into your car. This bartender, perhaps."

"But…" Holly started.

"It's a good idea, Holly," Glenn interrupted her. His voice was soft. "I'll be fine."

Shielding me again, she thought. "Please don't be upset with him."

"He's just trying to protect you, Holly. I would do the same." Belias flicked her a smile. He made her think of a grinning crow.

Holly said, "I don't need protection."

"You never have," Belias said. He never underestimated her the way Glenn did, and for a second she felt terrible, thinking better of him than she did of Glenn. But Belias had never hurt her the way Glenn had.

"Give the kids a kiss for me," Glenn said.

She ruffled his hair, the way she always had, careful now not to touch the bandage. Old habit. She had to stop caring. But how did you turn love off? She thought when he left her she'd grow to hate him and instead she missed him. She glanced at Roger. "Take good care of him."

And Roger, who could teach you how to kill with a knife or a gun or the ballpoint pen on the desk, smiled at her. "He'll be fine."

"Holly?" Belias said as she reached the door.

"Yes?"

"Don't lie to me again. It's hard for me to make proper, reasoned decisions if I don't have complete information."

"Of course." She looked at Glenn again, and he gave her a weak smile and a nod, and she went downstairs.

She got back into the car. The blood dotted the leather, but it wasn't on the carpet pad. His jacket had soaked up most of the flow. She stopped on the way home and bought cleanser, and she wiped up the blood.

We could have died tonight, she thought. *Is this all worth what Belias gives us?*

Instinct told her to avoid the stretch of Haight where The Select was, but she could not help herself. Only one lane was open, an officer letting the traffic take turns. She eased the car past the police lights, the silent red-and-blues throwing shadow and light like cards across a table. She saw a cop talking to homeless people outside the bar, a small fleet of cop cars in the front. Had anyone seen her, noticed her in the Audi before all hell broke loose? But no cop stopped her car as she inched by; no one had reported the vehicle's license plate. She wondered what she would have done if they had. The nightmare would be over but at a terrible price. She shivered, and then she drove the Audi back to the rendezvous point, a parking lot off Stanyan. Several other cars sat in the lot, and she wondered if one was the Russian's. Did you take a bus or your own car when you were hired to kidnap someone, when you didn't have to worry about the transportation? She felt ill. She'd seen the terror in the young woman's face, in a momentary gleam of a car's headlights, as she ran away from the bar. She shoved it to the back of her mind, out of the light.

She wiped the prints off the car. Glenn had another key; he would pick it up tomorrow, assuming he could drive, or Belias would take care of it. She walked out of the lot. A homeless man ten feet away entreated her for loose change, and she tossed him a five-dollar bill she had tucked into her jeans pocket. She didn't know why she did it; she never gave to bums. He looked too young to be a bum. She could never figure out the young homeless in the Haight; what were they looking for, sitting around, doing nothing, playing drums? It scared her to think that her kids could ever make that choice; that was why you had to do everything right for them, everything you could to give them every advantage. So they didn't make a grand mistake.

She walked the four blocks to her own car and she drove home, wondering who had made the bigger mistake tonight: Glenn in hiring the Russian or her leaving Glenn with Belias.

7

Thursday, November 4, evening

YOU'RE MINT TO ME. So valuable," Belias said. "I know I shouldn't have sent you on a kidnap job, but...I trust you and Holly so. You were my first. My best."

Glenn's voice was sluggish with painkillers. "I'm sorry we failed."

"Because of this bartender."

"You think she knew the bartender?" Roger asked.

"He was certainly the right guy at the right place for her," Glenn said. "You're sure she won't go to the police?"

"Diana Keene doesn't want her mother in jail," Belias said. "I've erased several rather panicked voice mails she's left for Janice where she's said she won't go to the cops until she talks to her mom."

"You seem very sure," Glenn said.

"It's what I do," Belias said. "Understand the way people program themselves to behave in certain ways. Describe this bartender."

"About six feet, very lean build. Midtwenties unless he's got a boyish face. Dark blond hair, wearing a fitted suit. At one point Rostov spoke to him in Russian and he spoke back."

Belias's gaze narrowed. "Did they know each other?"

"I don't think so. But the bartender clearly knew how to fight. The Russian was bigger than him, by four inches and fifty pounds, but the bartender took him down. I was fighting with Diana then, trying to get her purse..."

Belias laughed at him. "You couldn't even snatch her purse, Glenn? You're so handy at wresting money from people on a good day."

Glenn stared at him, and Belias saw a flash of anger in the dulled gaze, cutting through the painkillers. "You and Roger go find her, then. It's not my fault we're in trouble. If there's a problem, it's yours to fix."

"You do what I tell you to do. You were supposed to be the fix."

"I can't be kidnapping women on the streets of San Francisco. A career, a reputation. Children. A wife. I shouldn't have agreed to do your dirty work."

"And you have Holly to consider."

"Yes. I have everything; you only have the little world you've built for yourself."

"*I am a little world made cunningly*," Belias said.

"What?"

"John Donne. You lack a poetical soul, Glenn; read a book now and then. You're right. But you have benefited tremendously from my little world."

"Have I?" Glenn's stare was steady. "When you ask me to risk everything I've earned, I wonder."

Belias smiled. "Earned?"

Roger laughed.

Belias touched Glenn's jaw. "You have nothing without me."

"It's occurred to me you have nothing without *me*. Without *us*. All of us."

Belias let ten seconds tick by. "Did Diana call the bartender by name? Was he wearing a name tag?"

"No. But if he works at that bar, then we know where to find him, and he has no idea where to find us."

"But he could have seen your car."

"I'm sure he didn't."

Roger made an unconvinced noise in his throat.

Glenn closed his eyes, and Belias reached down and opened one of Glenn's eyes with his fingertips.

"Look at me. Him helping her to the point of killing the Russian would suggest he *did* know her."

Glenn was silent.

"So we have an unknown in the equation now."

"The bartender was just some guy who interfered."

"Oh no, I don't just mean him." Belias nearly laughed. "I mean *you*. You hiring thugs, you and Holly lying to me, you failing to follow my incredibly simple orders regarding Diana."

"Can we speak privately?" Glenn's gaze slid to Roger.

"Roger. Give us a moment, would you?"

Roger left, shutting the door behind him.

"I sense honesty is about to break out all over," Belias said.

"I don't think your orders make sense anymore."

"Mutiny. Of the bountiful." Belias sat down. "You must still love Holly, breaking my most important rule to be sure you did the job and she didn't risk a broken nail."

"Holly's a good thief and good shot. A kidnapping is different." Glenn closed his eyes.

"You're still in love with her." Belias patted his heart. "Very touching. I'm getting misty."

"Could we not discuss her?"

Belias tapped his finger against his own lip. "And you seem more worried about Holly now than when you were married to her. That's psychologically very telling, Glenn."

"What are you now, my therapist?"

"I don't need to see into your soul. I own it."

Glenn started to speak and Belias shushed him. "I want to know where this Rostov lived."

"I...I don't know."

Belias sat down at the computer. "It won't take me long to find him. Try to rest, Glenn. I want that brain of yours functioning at peak capacity tomorrow. You know how I rely on your advice."

Roger came back into the room, and Belias gestured him toward Glenn.

"John...I'm sorry." Glenn spoke in a tone that made Belias wonder if he were apologizing for more than one mistake. He started to sit up, and Belias nodded at Roger, who grabbed Glenn's arm and slid the needle home—using the syringe Glenn had meant to use on Diana.

Glenn closed his eyes and fell into a regular, drowsy pattern of breathing.

"He needs to be in a hospital," Roger said.

"When I say so," Belias said, eyes locked on the laptop's screen. "He's never disobeyed me before. I want to know what's special about today."

8

I HAVE KILLED BEFORE NOW.

I have killed to save my son, to save myself.

But I have never killed before in public. With witnesses.

It changes everything.

I'd just gotten my life back to seminormal, and now I might lose it all again.

I sat in the still quiet of the police interview room. The video camera lens watched me. This is what happens when you show yourself as not fitting inside the borders of everyday life, such as taking out two armed assailants.

My jaw felt bruised; my shoulder and my ribs hurt from the hits I'd taken. The paramedics had checked me out outside The Select, pronounced me battered but okay.

I thought of what would happen if the police started looking too hard at me. The CIA Special Projects division, my former employer, would not be happy if the police started excavating my history. And as for my current employers? Mila would be gritting her teeth at the thought of a death inside one of the bars and me answering a police interrogation.

I waited for the cops to come talk to me some more. I'd told the patrol cops who'd arrived first exactly what happened. I only left out…a couple of details. Minor, really, but I had my reasons.

Maybe this had nothing to do with my past. Fine. It would be the police's problem.

But people like the dead Russian? They have friends. They don't like their own getting knifed in a bar. I needed to know the why of what had happened, the who of what had happened. I needed to know what brought the woman to The Select, to me.

So I could protect myself and protect Daniel from whatever came our way.

I was probably going to be the lead story on the San Francisco news, the plucky bar owner who foiled a robbery/crime/whatever it was.

The media loves stories like this. I did not love stories like this. Not at all.

My lovely, quiet new life, all at risk now for a woman I didn't even know. I nearly laughed at the thought, *Of all the gin joints in all the towns in all the world, she walks into mine.* That line from my favorite movie worked, even when you had never seen the woman before.

Note how I try not to think too much about having killed a man tonight? I could still feel the shudder of the blade parting his flesh as he fell wrong onto it. It made a weird little ripple against the steel, and I could remember how it felt.

The door to the questioning room opened, the detective holding it open, speaking softly to someone in the corridor. I could hear her voice, but I couldn't see her until she stepped into the room.

"Mr. Capra. I'm Anitra DeSoto."

I remembered DeSoto was a conqueror's name; it fit her. She was fierce and resolved—tall, strong, like she might slip into Joan of Arc's armor with more ease than a cocktail dress. High cheekbones, olive skin, narrow lips that she shaped into a hard, practiced frown on her face, one that she must have sported so long and consistently that lines marred an otherwise striking face.

"Hello," I said.

Detective DeSoto sat across from me.

"Can I go now?" I asked. No point in answering questions if I didn't have to.

"I just want to clarify a couple of things on your statement you gave at the scene. But you're not under arrest, if that's what you mean."

"There is nothing to clarify. I own a bar. These men came into that bar and threatened a woman. They tried to grab her; they said they were taking her with them. She clearly did not want to go with them. They threatened me and the woman with a knife."

"From the beginning, please, again, everything."

I glanced at the camera. I told the story. I only left out the details that might give the police answers before I got them.

She didn't interrupt or ask questions during my statement. "None of that is questioned. Witnesses support your account." DeSoto folded her hands with a schoolteacher's formality. "But."

"But."

"You unarmed a man a good four inches taller than you, with fifty pounds of muscle on you, and you killed him with his own knife."

"Adrenaline," I said.

"Where did you learn to fight with a knife?"

"Kenya."

She waited for the rest of the story, but I felt I'd answered the question. She tapped her pen against the worn tabletop and asked, in a tone of false patience, "What were you doing in Kenya?"

"Learning how to fight with knives."

The thinning line of her mouth told me that perhaps this wasn't the best approach. I opened my palms in surrender. "My parents worked for a global aid agency and were on the move every few months. I grew up in a lot of exotic spots around the world. A guy in Kenya taught me knife fighting when I was sixteen." I didn't add that an instructor in CIA Special Projects gave me pointers, too.

"And that was, what, ten years ago? You've stayed in practice."

"Like riding a bike."

"That's very handy."

"Not until now. It's not like I do it at children's parties."

She tapped out a beat with the edge of her pencil against the table. "You own The Select, true?"

"Yes, I own it. What else? I have had the snot beaten out of me tonight. Are you arresting me?"

She hesitated. "Given you have a number of witnesses who support your story of self-defense, I spoke with the district attorney's office, and they don't seem inclined to have you arrested."

I tried not to sag in relief.

"But…the case could go to the grand jury, and they might make a different decision."

"May I go home now?"

"Just a couple more questions. You don't reside here in San Francisco?"

"I own bars all over the world, and I travel, visiting all of them," I said. "It keeps me moving around fairly steadily. New Orleans is my home base, though."

"How many bars?"

"Thirty-two at last count."

She raised an eyebrow and the scowl deepened. "Wow, and you're what, twenty-six? Entrepreneurial, aren't you? How lucrative. You're like a cocktail tycoon."

"It can be a moneymaker. Unless you have customers being attacked and you stand there and do nothing. Then the customers tend to sit on some other stools at some other tavern."

"Do you own any bars in Russia?"

"Yes. One in Moscow." I hadn't visited it yet. I blinked, wondering why she cared. And then, mental rewind, I saw where this was going.

Uh-oh.

"One of the witnesses in the bar said you spoke Russian to the dead man after he spoke it to you."

"I speak several languages. As I mentioned, I grew up all over the world."

"But what a coincidence that you and this attacker both speak Russian."

"Three hundred million people do, actually."

"Perhaps in Russia. It's a rarer skill in America. Did you know him?"

I already knew his name—Grigori Rostov—as I'd searched his pockets and found a driver's license in his wallet. And his cell phone. I slipped his ID under mine in my wallet and put his phone in my pocket. So when the police officers searched me and found wallet and phone, it didn't occur to them that there was a second ID wedged in my wallet or that the cell phone in my suit jacket wasn't my own. You have to think creatively in these situations.

"I don't know him. I had never seen him or the other man before."

"What did he say to you in Russian?"

"He called me an idiot. I agreed with him." I could feel the conversation move in a direction I dreaded. Maybe this wasn't about a woman in trouble. Maybe a man who owned thirty-two bars around the world had enemies. I could imagine the thought inching across her brain.

She made a note on her pad.

I kept my voice calm. "Let's review who the actual bad guys are. One pulled a knife, one pulled a gun, in my place of business."

I knew it was a trump card and it shut her up. She glanced back at her tightly written notes. I didn't wait for her to ask a question again. I wanted a new normal: just running the bars and taking care of my kid. The bars were the safe houses for Mila's team, but that didn't mean I had to play spy anymore. I could just be like Rick Blaine in *Casablanca* (well, how he wanted to be before Ilsa showed up) and run the bar and not get involved in the world's troubles. The only trouble I wanted came from mixing drinks too strong. So I cut her off.

"My bar, my customers, my responsibility. I suppose it's a practically medieval idea—my protection offered under my roof."

"I suppose this woman you don't know owes you her life."

And I owe her mine, I thought, but I kept that thought to myself. I hadn't mentioned she'd saved my life. I hadn't yet decided what I was going to do about settling that particular debt. "I suppose."

"This woman, she's not a regular?"

"No, apparently not."

"You wouldn't know, though, as you're not here often."

"No. But ask the staff if they recognized her."

"We have. No one mentioned having seen her before…She didn't ask you to call the police."

"No."

"She fired a gun, you say? Through her purse?"

"Yes."

"The other witnesses weren't quite clear on that."

"People were panicking, running."

"So. An African American woman chased by a Russian and a guy you said, I quote, 'looks like a suburban dad.'"

"That's about it," I agreed.

"One of the officers said you were looking at the Russian's arm as they came in."

"I was trying to find a pulse."

Well, yes, but I'd also looked for a tattoo marking him with a nine, with a sunburst in its center. Nine Suns. The people who'd taken my wife, framed me for murder, destroyed my CIA career, stolen my baby—all because I had gotten too close to their criminal operations. I'd gotten my son back and I'd exacted a heavy price against Nine Suns. We'd all retreated to our respective corners. Their people wore a small tattoo as a marker. I hadn't seen one on the dead man's arms.

Anitra DeSoto drummed a pencil against the tabletop. She didn't like me. She didn't like my answers. "How much longer are you staying in town?"

"I don't know. If we're done—"

"Mr. Capra."

If she asked me one more question, I was going to stop this and phone a lawyer. I was tired and sore and aching and wanted to go curl up in a bed. The bar was a wreck. And I needed to find out exactly who this Russian was and why he'd come into my bar.

Before someone else came looking to avenge him.

"Usually when someone kills another person, they are real broken up about it."

I let five, then ten seconds pass. "Who says I'm not?"

"You don't seem upset."

I leaned forward. "These guys tried to kill me. I defended myself and my customers. I am not at all happy that it ended the way that it did, and when I'm alone, I'll have a reaction, which I will keep private." I stood. "But if you want to see me emotional, I'll be back in the morning with tears in my eyes and a cup held by my attorney to catch them."

She doodled on her notepad. Arrows circling back on themselves. She was trying to connect me as more than an innocent bystander because of me speaking Russian. I was supposed to be just a guy who owned some bars. I had better start acting like it right now.

"I'm sorry," I said. "I don't like the suggestion that I did something wrong."

"If we find there's any connection between you and these men, I will not appreciate your lack of honesty." Now she leaned forward. "I'm not convinced, Mr. Capra, that you are entirely an innocent bystander."

"Is this one of those 'last chance' moments?"

"Interpret how you like."

"Then it's a wasted chance. I did not know them."

"Or her."

"Or her."

"You're free to go, Mr. Capra. But don't leave San Francisco in a hurry."

If she wasn't arresting me, it was an idle request. I went to the door. "Come by and have a drink some time, on the house. Good night, Detective."

I walked out into the night. The police car had brought me to the Hall of Justice on Bryant Street, where the SFPD homicide detail worked. I saw some people from the bar on the corner, awaiting a ride back to their cars. All the witnesses had been brought here to give statements.

"Hey!" one of the guys said, recognizing me. "Bar guy! Man, you were amazing!"

"Oh," I said. Saying thanks sounded wrong. Him being excited about what he'd seen sounded wrong, too. A man was dead. One of the women nudged him, and he shut up, as though realization had settled into his bones.

"Do you need a ride back?" one of the women asked. "They're bringing around cars to take us back to the Haight."

"Thanks." I stood off a bit from them. I didn't want to discuss the case. Three police cars came around and we all piled in, three at a time into the backseats, and they drove us back to The Select.

"They're not filing charges against you, are they?" the young woman asked me. She'd ended up sitting next to me, with the excited guy on the opposite side.

"Not yet," I said. "I don't think I'm supposed to discuss it." I nodded toward the officer who was kindly giving us a ride back.

That resulted in silence, and I looked out the window as we headed back to the bar. I used the time to think.

My kid. Leonie. They should have been on a plane by the time the attack occurred. Mila would be sure they were fine. But I hadn't heard from Mila.

This violence had to be random. It *had* to be. But there'd been a poisoning attempt on a Round Table member, and now this…

The police detail was still working the bar. In the back an investigator was digging through the recycling bins. He'd probably find the bloodied plank soon enough. I walked around to the front of The Select, the crime scene tape decorating the door. It would be a few more hours before I could go back into the bar, one of the investigators told me. I could see they had cut out part of the mirror where a bullet had gone. A tech was taking photos of the bar and of the dead Russian from several different angles. The dead man's hands had been bagged. Had I caused a defensive wound on his hands? I couldn't remember.

"I have an apartment above the bar," I told the officer. "It has a separate entrance in the back. Is it all right if I go up there?"

"Yes, sir."

"Thank you." I moved away from the crowd that was watching the police—a mix of tourists and neighborhood regulars; of the homeless who'd made this neighborhood their home; of employees of the vintage music shops, the clothing stores, the other bars, the fancy grocery at the end of the street.

I went up to the apartment. I opened the door and saw a man tapping furiously at a keyboard. He had a bald head; wore a graying goatee and old-fashioned eyeglasses, narrow and black like my grandfather's, and was in his late forties with a spare, lean build.

"Hello, Felix."

Felix Neare—The Select's manager—stood up from the computer. "Are you all right?"

"Yes. I didn't know you were here."

"I thought it best to make sure everything up here was safe. The cops didn't search up here."

I breathed a sigh of relief.

"Mila called. They're safe; they're away from…whatever this is."

"They headed back to New Orleans?"

"Well, via Los Angeles. Mila wanted to keep Daniel and Leonie with her until we knew more information about tonight."

"That's a relief," I said.

"What the hell happened? Is this tied to the poisoning of Monroe?"

"I don't know."

"He's part of the Round Table, and now our bar's attacked. No way is that a coincidence."

I felt sick.

"I've been busy cleaning any incriminating Round Table evidence off the computers. Just in case you didn't get released."

"They didn't arrest me yet, but they could decide to charge me." I explained how speaking Russian to Rostov had been part of the eyewitness accounts and how it had raised DeSoto's suspicions.

"Good thing I've also found the blueprints for each county jail," Felix said. "In case I need to break you out tomorrow."

"Wow, you're prepared." I managed a smile.

"I even have a shovel."

Felix Neare. I'd read a file on him Mila sent me when I arrived in San Francisco. Felix had moved four months ago to San Francisco. He'd worked for the Round Table for seven years, starting up bars/safe houses as a manager, then moving on once the bar was established. Like most of the other bar managers, he had a crime in his past that he'd been wrongly accused of and cleared through the subtle influence of the Round Table. Mila's report simply said he'd been wrongly tied to embezzlement from his employer. He'd eventually proven his innocence, but the scandal had ruined him; his wife had committed suicide over it. A tragedy. The Round Table had given him a new, fresh start far away from his old life. I hadn't broached his past; he hadn't asked about mine.

It was the same story, I had found, with the managers of my bars in London, New York, Amsterdam, Brussels, and more; the manager's life had been saved by this group in the shadows, and in return they were willing to help the Round Table fight its own war for justice in the world. They'd helped me find my kidnapped infant son. You cannot buy gratitude like that.

"This... I don't see how this connects to Dalton Monroe's case."

"Maybe it doesn't. But we have to know." He didn't look at me. "Can I ask you a question?"

"What?"

"You joined the CIA, right? Because of your brother."

I supposed Mila had filled Felix in on my history. My older brother Danny, a relief worker, had been slaughtered by extremists. He was trying to follow in our parents' footsteps, and he'd wanted me to go with him to Afghanistan. I'd stayed at Harvard instead, and after he was killed I joined the CIA two days after graduation. "Yes."

"Did you do that because you wanted justice or revenge? They're different things."

His questions surprised me. "Why do you ask?"

"Because I think we're in danger, and I want to know if you make decisions out of emotion."

I stared at him.

"You don't want the Monroe incident and tonight's attack to be related. And I'm worried you'll blind yourself to a possible danger, just because you don't want there to be danger. You just want to serve drinks and run the bars."

Felix was right. Dead right. I couldn't dodge this now.

I picked up my phone. "I want to talk to Leonie," I said quietly. But her phone was off. So was Mila's. They might be in the air still, depending on when they'd been able to get on a flight.

I stripped off the bloodied shirt, the ruined suit jacket. I washed down the fauxhawk, combed my hair smooth. I put on a black turtleneck and black jeans.

First stop: find out more about the man with the knife. I pulled Grigori Rostov's ID from my wallet. The address was in Outer Richmond.

"Wait, where are you going?" Felix asked as I headed down the back stairs.

"You're right. We have to make sure this isn't an attack on us specifically. I want to make sure this is a coincidence. And if it is, then it's not going to be my problem."

9

Thursday, November 4, late evening

It had taken John Belias a while to decide he was willing to risk breaking into Grigori Rostov's house, after what he'd learned about Rostov in a few hours on his computer. Glenn might leap before he looked, but not John Belias.

Finally, he decided it was a necessary risk. Roger wanted to go, but this was an information issue — what did the Russian really know about him and his operation? And what might the police find once they identified the dead man? So Belias went instead.

Grigori Rostov's house was in Outer Richmond; it was on 35th Street, off Geary, north of Golden Gate Park. The street was on a gentle slope (for San Francisco) and Rostov, according to an online address search, resided on the top floor of the house. The front of the house had been redone in a modern look and featured a large metal trellis that led up to a small open patio. No cars were parked in the small driveway. Only the light by the door glowed. He walked up the driveway, up the stairs to the top-floor apartment. The lower apartment had a FOR LEASE sign in it, which would make it easier for him if there were no neighbors to overhear his searching.

The lock wasn't sophisticated and Belias worked the picks with practiced ease. He felt the little odd rush he felt whenever he invaded another's private space, whether physical or online or mental. He closed the door behind him and drew the gun from his black jacket, listening for sounds of occupancy.

But there was only darkness and silence, and he risked turning on a small penlight. He drew all the curtains. If Rostov lived alone, this would be so much easier. He searched the apartment quickly.

An empty vodka bottle on the counter; magazines from the mother country, including a Cyrillic edition of *Playboy*; a CD by the Moscow rap group Centr.

Russians. He frowned. For a moment he thought of Svetlana, the clear purity of her voice ringing in his ears; and then his brain went silent, like he'd slammed a door. Focus. Two bedrooms, one cluttered, one neat.

That meant a roommate. And the police might arrive at any time; if you ended up on a slab, they tended to come look for family to tell. He might only have minutes to see exactly what Grigori Rostov knew about him.

Or perhaps the police had already been here. Which meant a grieving roommate, returning from identifying the body, might be back at any moment.

Two men shared this apartment; he could see photos of both of them on the stereo, toasting the camera with small clear glasses while a tropical sunset gloried the sky behind them. They looked enough alike to be brothers. At the safe house, he'd hacked his way into the California driver's license database and found a picture of Grigori Rostov. Here on the shelves there were photos of Grigori with a young blonde woman and a smiling lady who might be his mother in the messy room. Lovers and parents were nothing but a way to tie you down, keep you from your potential. Except Svetlana, she'd been his muse. Belias pushed her out of his thoughts again. He could not be distracted.

There was a laptop on the desk. It wasn't even passworded. Laziness disappointed Belias but it was a constant among the stupid. Holding the penlight in his mouth, he searched the hard drive for his name.

And found matches.

He read the e-mails between Rostov and what he guessed was an anonymous account set up by Glenn. And his face began to burn with horror and shame.

His name is John Belias—not his real name, but when we've got him, we'll force him to tell us who he truly is . . . So when we've caught the young woman, we'll bring her to him. He may have a man named Roger with him, and Roger you'll have to kill immediately. He is highly trained and dangerous. And then you will subdue Belias and take him to the address I gave you . . . You don't let him near a weapon or near a computer. He can kill you with either. He doesn't look like much of a threat, but you don't ever underestimate him. He must be kept bound. Do not kill him. I need him alive. I need his brain working.

He can tell us who all the others are.

Betrayal.

Betrayal was the darkest poison, the hottest acid.

After all I've done for you, Belias thought. *I made you, Glenn Marchbanks. I made you.* He deleted the e-mails from the server and wiped Grigori Rostov's account clean. He turned off the laptop, and he flipped the laptop on its back. He cracked the chassis open with a small tool. He carefully pulled the hard drive free of its moorings, cradling it in his gloved hands, slipping it into his coat pocket. No backup hard drive.

And heard someone at the door. Not the scrape of a key.

He tongued off the penlight and drew his suppressor-capped gun, stepping back into the shadows of the bedroom. He waited. A physical confrontation was more Roger's kind of problem to solve, but Roger had taught him self-defense, both armed and unarmed. And Belias thought he'd been a better pupil than Glenn Marchbanks.

The door opened and closed.

Whoever came inside was very still. Listening.

I hear you, Belias thought. *Do you hear me?*

A flashlight came on, swept across the den. Belias stayed still, hidden in the darkness.

From his vantage point he could see part of the den, the entrance to the other bedroom. He remained very still. He saw the light move from the den into the other bedroom, on the opposite side of the condo. Stealthily. Not walking like he belonged. Not turning on lights.

Then a moment later, the intruder came into the bedroom.

"Hello." Belias leveled the gun at him.

The man froze.

"Turn on the light," Belias said.

The man did. Six feet tall, dressed in a dark turtleneck and black jeans, dark blondish hair, blue eyes. Glenn's description of the bartender who'd killed the Russian.

"Well, this is awkward," the bartender said.

Aren't you a cool little customer? Belias thought. "I know who you are. Your reputation precedes you."

The bartender tilted his head.

"I like a vodka martini, three olives. Go make me one."

The bartender said nothing.

"I normally prefer gin but I bet our Russian friends here have vodka on hand," Belias said. "Are you a Russian, too?"

"No, I'm not." Clearly an American.

"That's a start as I don't much care for Russians," Belias said in Russian.

"Bigotry is ugly," the bartender answered in English.

"It's a mutual dislike," Belias said, switching back to English. "What exactly are you, because I think you're not just a bartender?"

"You've committed brain surgery on his computer." The bartender glanced toward the Russian's upended laptop. "I don't think you're Mr. Rostov's roomie."

Belias nearly laughed. "You always call someone you kill mister?"

"We weren't introduced."

"You are a mystery, and I hate those, but you are interesting. Curious about the man you killed?"

The bartender shrugged.

"You seem to think I won't actually shoot you," Belias said. Most people cowered in front of a gun. This man didn't.

"You don't want to shoot me because you have questions and you correctly assume I have answers."

The bartender's calm began to work under Belias's skin. "You kill a man and then you come to his house? Really? That's kind of creepy. What are you?"

The bartender studied him. "I wanted to know who he was. Who sent him."

A cold bolt ran through Belias's arm. "What does that mean?"

"I know hired muscle when I see it. The whole way he acted toward the young woman. She was a stranger to him and him to her. He was just doing a job."

"Is that normally a bartending skill? Classification of thuggery?"

"Did you send him?"

Belias laughed. "This is an interesting collision between you and me. Now. Tell me who you are or I'm going to start shooting you in delicate areas." He gestured vaguely with the gun. "It will be gross and bloody and I am not optimistic these guys own a mop."

And this made Belias's heart sing, because the bartender didn't blink. "It sounds terrible. Here's the problem. You're connected to this dead Russian but the police don't know that. I am not connected to this dead Russian but they think I am. I have friends stashed outside who will kill you if you kill me."

"Bluffing."

The bartender studied the gutted laptop. "Is that why you wanted to clean off his laptop? Because he had proof you sent him after the woman."

"I didn't send this loser after anyone," Belias said. The bartender's lack of visible fear impressed Belias. Fear was the best, most potent weapon. Fear was golden. He needed to know who this man was. Glenn had already betrayed him by trying to seize power and he had no sense how deep the damage was. "You did me a favor killing the Russian, bartender. The evening has been most, um, instructive."

"Monroe."

"Is that your name?"

"No."

"Well, it's not mine, either."

"Monroe," the bartender said again.

"Monroe? Marilyn? President James? What?"

"I think you've answered my question. Tonight was a random encounter. We don't need to dance together."

"You mean did I send those guys to your bar?" Belias said. "Do you mean was I targeting you? No. But we have collided now, and what are we going to do about that?"

"Your ring. It's like the charm the suburban dad wore on a necklace." He pointed at Belias's finger, at the delicate silver band marked with spaces and bars. "Interesting symbol. Are you two engaged?"

Belias smiled. "Are you telling me you don't know the woman you risked your life to save?"

"I don't know her."

"Well. You could be lying. I can't decide." Belias tilted his head. "I find you interestingly capable. That's not random."

"I don't have a beef with you if you don't have one with me," the bartender said. "Just stay away from me and my bar and we're out of each other's business. Oh, one thing more."

"What?"

"Give up on hurting the woman."

"I have the gun yet you're telling me what I'm going to do. Very nice. I like that. I want to have a drink at your bar with you, friend."

"I'm not your friend," the bartender said.

"Not yet. But I'm an optimist. So why did you come here?"

"I want to know who Rostov is."

"Why?"

"In case he has friends who want revenge against me."

"Now that I do believe. Back up slowly."

The bartender obeyed, moving back into the den, standing by the couch. Using his elbow, Belias flicked on a ceiling light. "Let's sit, talk. I'm facing a challenge, so are you. Maybe we can work together."

"I don't think so."

"I'm impressed by a…bartender who can take down a Russian Special Forces veteran. I don't want to hurt your girlfriend. Truly, I don't. What has happened between us was a misunderstanding. You get her to talk to me, let me explain. We can talk to her mom to-gether. You get me that video she has and I'll make it worth your while. And I can protect you from the Russian's friends. And he has friends. A whole, bitter violent family of them, more than a barten-der can handle. They will kill you. I can protect you."

"I'm not interested. I don't know her. This has nothing to do with me."

"You're in this now," Belias said simply. "You know too much…" And then the front door opened and a thick-necked man entered the apartment.

Belias swung the gun toward the man.

10

---◦◉◦---

I'D KILLED ONE MAN TONIGHT; maybe I could save a second one.

I threw myself at the man in black, slamming into him, trying to get a hand on the gun. It spit fire, and the hiss of a suppressor is always louder than you think it is. I heard screaming in Russian from the man who'd just arrived—I presumed it was Rostov's roommate. He was built big like Rostov—they could be brothers. I'd knocked the man in black to the couch and was intent on breaking his grip on the gun. He was stronger than he looked. He grunted as I wrested it from him, slamming my knee into his throat.

I levered free the gun, and then the Russian swung a heavy backpack that had been on his shoulder hard into my hand. You'd think he'd run for the street but he didn't. I didn't have a tight grip on the gun, and it flew over the couch and landed on the carpet toward a corner of the room. The big Russian swung the backpack again and this time I caught it and pulled hard. It brought him into the heel of my hand.

I needed to take him out of the fight to save him.

The man in black ran over the sofa, springing for the gun. I kicked out, caught his shin, sent him sprawling over the edge of the couch.

I guess the Russian believed muscle paved every road, made life easier. He tried to seize my throat in one big hand while grabbing at the man in black with the other.

He missed.

"Idiot!" I screamed. In English. The Russian started strangling me with one hand while dragging me along in pursuit of the man in black.

"Let go—*hurk*, I'll help—*hurk*." I believe these were the noises I made.

The man in black reached the gun, spun, fired at the Russian. He missed but I felt the heat of the bullet pass between me and the Russian. The Russian surged forward, propelling me along with him, using me like a shield as I tried to pull away, his arms locked over mine. Only my feet were free. I powered a sideways kick into the man in black's arm and he fired again as I did. It all happened within three seconds. I'd used my left leg and the shot went right into the Russian's chest, just missing my ear. The poor guy screamed and he let go and sank.

I pulled free and the man in black was running out the door.

The door slammed.

The Rostov brother—I assumed from the photos in the room—looked up at me as I knelt beside him, pulling out my phone to dial 911, and he stared at me and he drew a shuddering breath and then released it; his last. And me, a stranger, his last sight on earth.

Just like his brother, he looked confused, surprised. Life can end in a snap; we wrap ourselves in all sorts of blankets to hide that cruel fact.

What would Detective DeSoto make of two brothers dead the same night, one in a bar fight, one in his home?

She would be looking very, very hard at me.

My situation had reached a new level of disaster by an order of magnitude. If she found a print of mine here—a strand of hair even…I wiped, carefully, the front door, the light switch, trying to think of any surface my hand might have landed on during the fight. A bit of fiber from my clothes, a stray print, and I could no longer deny that I had any previous connection to Grigori Rostov.

"I'm sorry," I said to him when I was done. How weird is that? Sorry for having killed his brother, who tried to kill me? Sorry he came home and died because two strangers were having a stare down? He was midtwenties, about my age. I was alive. He was dead and gone and soon he'd be cold.

I hurried out to the street, hoping my life wasn't about to collapse. In trying to make sure I was safe, I'd just put myself in far greater danger.

You're in this now... You know too much.

Because there was no way the man in black would let me walk now, would let us be ships that passed in the night. Now I was a threat to him.

II

---===•((●))•===---

Thursday, November 4, late evening

W AKE UP."

Belias tapped the edge of the hard drive against Glenn's head. "I have a bit of wisdom to share with you, knowing the value you put on information, Glenn."

Glenn opened his eyes, bleary, bloodshot, the bruising darkening on his temple. "What?"

Belias put his face close to Glenn's. "People teach you who they are under pressure. That's when you see all their failings, all their weaknesses. I visited Grigori Rostov's humble abode." He dangled the hard drive above Glenn's face. "I read your e-mails to him. He needed to use a spell-checker."

Glenn's eyes widened.

"You want to take over from me, Glenn. In you I created a monster. You're like a zombie of ambition. Ravenous but brainless."

"I...I..."

"Please. Don't deny it."

Glenn shifted his voice to low and reasonable. "Let me help you. You can't run our network alone, John. It's too much power, too much responsibility. If I knew who all the others were..."

"You could use them!"

"No. I could help you protect them. What if something happens to you? We would have no peace of mind...not knowing if anyone else was going to find out about the network."

"Only I know the names of everyone. That's how I protect you, Glenn. And I'm really bad at sharing. Always have been. Ask my dad." He couldn't contain a bitter laugh.

"I could help you. Find new people. New ways for us to rise."

"I don't appreciate a succession plan being forced on me, Glenn. You were using our moment of greatest danger for your own advantage."

Glenn's mouth narrowed. "Isn't that what you do every day?"

"For your own good, Glenn! I made you!" Belias cupped his hands as though a potter's wheel spun beneath them. "I shaped you from the clay of failure."

"Don't sound so full of yourself," Glenn said. "You know you need me."

"You want to play the need card? Come on, didn't you need Holly once? Roger." And Roger, standing close, brought up the knife where Glenn could see it. "I should go chat with Holly about your little rebellion."

The panic flared hot in Glenn's eyes. "Holly didn't know about the takeover. She thought I just hired the Russian to grab Diana Keene. Please…leave her alone."

"And I should believe you why?"

"It's the truth. Holly's done everything you've ever asked. I swear, she knew nothing about this."

"You only had a few more years to pay out the debt, Glenn. This was really poor judgment." Belias set down the hard drive. "I think we must dissolve our business relationship."

Glenn stared at him, the beginning of a disbelieving grin cracking his face. "You can't replace me. Not in what I provide to you."

"Glenn, you don't get to plead once you've buried the knife in my back." He turned away from Glenn. "Roger, put down the knife and get the tools. Have him tell me who else is involved in his little revolt against me."

"It's just me. Not Holly. I swear!"

"Make him talk. You know how I like it done," Belias said. He went and got a glass of water while Roger began.

It took eighteen minutes. Roger probed with knife and scalpel and the soft sound of his voice, asking questions. Flecks of blood dotted the wall at one point. Glenn confessed that no one else knew, he was afraid anyone he approached would have told Belias, and finally Roger said, "I really think he might have acted alone."

"Is that true, Glenn?" Belias brushed back Glenn's hair from his pale, sweaty, bloodied forehead.

"Yes," Glenn whispered. "Just stop, please stop, don't let him hurt me any more…"

"Don't hurt him any more, Roger. End it."

Roger took the necklace off Glenn, handed it to Belias. And then Roger slammed the knife into Glenn's heart.

"I'm sorry," Roger said when either felt like speaking, "for the mess. A bit of blood on the walls." Roger poured himself a bourbon, neat. "I'll clean it in the morning."

"Paint over the blood. Holly will be back here tomorrow."

"Means a quick trip to the paint store," Roger said. "We'll have to kill Holly?"

"I hope not," Belias said. "What a bad evening." The only bright spot was the bartender. A bartender who was far more than a bartender. Belias could not resist the not knowing. The mystery of it. What you could not have you wanted to possess. He saw this truth constantly in other people but so rarely in himself; he felt a surge of heat rise along his arms, just like when he had a brilliant idea. The bartender who could give him Diana Keene and maybe be a new ally in his moment of need.

He went and washed his pale hands. He wanted a bourbon like Roger was enjoying, but it was vital to not lose control.

"Glenn was my first recruit," he said as he rinsed his hands. "Feeling a little sad. I hate when they leave me."

"No, you're not sorry." Roger took another tiny sip of the bourbon. "You like the ex-wife."

Belias dried his hands with a paper towel and he glanced toward Roger with a flash of ice in his gaze. "I respect Holly."

"You'd respect her right into your bed." Roger put Glenn's cell phone on the table, next to his drink.

"You don't mind cleaning up?" Belias asked. "I need to figure out what to do about this bartender." He dangled Glenn's necklace before his own eyes as if wondering whose throat it might decorate next.

"I live to serve. And I want things nice and neat when you bring in Diana Keene." Roger took another sip of his bourbon. "Are you mourning out of sentiment or because Glenn was very valuable to you?"

"He planned a takeover. I—and you—built this private empire. Not him. He'd be selling penny stocks over the phone to senile grandfathers if I hadn't made his life easier. Did he think I would ever tell him who all the others are? This is a relationship built on trust and it would have betrayed the whole network for him to know them all. After I gave Glenn the good life."

"People are natural ingrates," Roger said. "It's like a law of nature."

"You'll get rid of the body," Belias told him. "I know this was unexpected work for you. What can I give you? Stock information, per usual?"

Roger nodded.

"And anyone bothering you?"

"I'd like my daughter to be valedictorian." Belias knew Roger's ex-wife had his teenage daughter in a fine school in Boston.

"I can't work a miracle."

"She's in second place. Barely a point-zero-eight behind."

"I'll see what I can do."

"The current valedictorian plays soccer."

"An injury can be so distracting," Belias said. "Or a parent's unemployment."

"Thank you. I can dump Glenn in the bay. How will you tell Holly?"

"He died in his sleep tonight, brain injury. The blow he took was too severe."

"She might want to see the body."

"I'll tell her we couldn't leave a body around for hours. Get it out of here before she comes back tomorrow."

"His wife will be upset."

"Holly's not his wife anymore."

"Very funny," Roger said. "He's going to be a man that people miss. You'll need an explanation for the new wife. And quick."

"I can make it look like he left town for good reason. The press and the police will first think he's kidnapped. Then they'll think maybe he was crooked—it's what they'll always think of a businessman—then Holly will do exactly what I ask. She won't put her children's future at risk. The story we build around Glenn will ensure she stays loyal. I have plans for Holly now."

Glenn's cell phone began to ring.

PART THREE

FRIDAY, NOVEMBER 5

12

Friday, November 5, very early morning

THE FOG—I would have been disappointed if I hadn't seen it during my stay in San Francisco—began to snake its way through the city. I drove my rental car back toward the Haight, watching my rearview mirror. No sign I was being followed.

What had DeSoto said? *Most people are affected by killing.* Like I wasn't. She was wrong. A long shuddering took hold of me; a life ended at my hands, and I was powerless to save another. I felt like I'd taken a double-punch to the chest.

And I knew I could have died, on the wrong side of the knife, the tumble of the bullet. I could have been taken away from my son I'd fought so hard to get back. A heavy, aching need to hold Daniel in my arms took me. Had I only held him hours ago? I told myself not to worry. Daniel was safe now.

I didn't need to be involved in this nightmare. I wasn't a secret soldier anymore, right?

My life was not killing bad guys with knives or breaking into people's houses and getting involved in three-way fights that ended in death.

But I was going to have to fight. The man in black had made sure of that now. I'd have no peace until this was resolved, and I was at a serious disadvantage; he knew I worked at The Select.

He could find me and I couldn't find him.

I put my hand on the phone I'd taken from Grigori Rostov.

Time to find out who you were and what business you had in my bar.

I unlocked the gated parking area behind the bar, pulled in close to the back door. The police appeared to be finished with processing the outside of the bar in their search for evidence. I wondered what they had found. There were still techs inside the bar, talking quietly. I peered through the front window; Rostov's body was gone.

I went up the back steps. Felix was waiting inside the apartment.

"What happened?" he asked.

I told him.

"Oh, Sam," Felix said. "I just thought we should know who we were up against..." He sat suddenly. "I didn't mean to get a man killed," he whispered, as though the police techs a floor below could hear us.

"I've made a new enemy. We need to prepare."

He raised an eyebrow. "How?"

"We need to find out who Rostov is and who the man in black is." I felt weird simply coming in and giving orders; I was an absentee boss, and Felix did all the hard, daily work of keeping The Select running and in the black. And he was older than me, if not quite old enough to be my dad, at least my really much older brother. "And then we need to clean up the mess downstairs." I think better while doing physical work or running.

"It would be a bigger mess," Felix said, "if the police decided to look hard at you and wanted to know more about you or the bar and subpoenaed our business records. I've finished uploading everything to a secure server, wiped the hard drives, and put in a fake set of business records. You're clean as a whistle."

"Thank you. I want to look at the security feed. I want to see if we can find out who this young woman is. She's the key."

"Of course, we gave a copy of the feed to the police, but I kept a copy." Felix kicked up the security video feed, watched the woman enter, talk to me, run away from the bar. The angle didn't give the best view of her face.

"I want to review the feed from the past few days. See if she ever came in before," I said.

Felix slowed the video, ran it again, studied it. Ran it again. "I know her," he said. "Diana Keene. Her mother is a friend of mine."

"Friend?"

"Friend." He rubbed his fingers along his face. "We...we're not dating. Exactly."

"How exactly then do you know her?"

Felix swallowed. "I need you to swear not to tell Mila."

"I won't tell."

Felix took his time. "I have cancer. In my lung. I know Diana's mom—her name is Janice—from a cancer support group I'm in."

I am bad at this stuff. Comfort. Reassurance. "Felix, I'm sorry."

He didn't know what to say, either. Presumably if he'd wanted me or Mila to know this, he would have told us earlier. He was only telling me because it was relevant to the disaster we were in right now. "It's okay."

It wasn't, but like me he didn't know what else to say. "How bad is it?"

"Small, caught early." He swallowed. "I start chemo soon. But I want to keep working. Mila doesn't know. Please don't tell her. The higher-ups at the Round Table know; they take care of my health insurance."

"Higher-ups."

"Jimmy. Mila reports to him. He knows."

Mila had told me Jimmy recruited her into the Round Table after she'd taken revenge against the leader of an international criminal ring who'd hurt her sister. She'd had a million-dollar bounty put on her head; Jimmy kept her safe. I'd never met him. I'm not sure I wanted to—Mila told me we'd either be close as brothers or we'd kill each other.

"What can I do for you, Felix? Whatever you need, whatever you want."

"What I need is to be helpful to you. To stay busy. I'm okay, Sam. Please. I'm not an invalid."

I'm all for staying busy rather than talk about the unpleasant and overly personal. "So Diana Keene came in looking for you."

"I don't know why she would need help. She works for her

mother. Janice is a public relations guru, one of the best in the country. Big name clients."

"Maybe they found out something unsavory about one of those clients."

"Then Janice would go to the police. She's totally respectable."

No police, Diana Keene had said. "Maybe her mother's involved in a bad way."

Felix shook his head emphatically. "No. No, Janice is a solid citizen."

"Okay. Tell me about Diana being here."

"She came in Wednesday night. I was down at the bar, you were upstairs reviewing the business accounts."

I didn't recall seeing her. "Looking for you or for her mom?"

"Her mom, but I told her that her mom wasn't here. I've only met Diana once. Janice did not want her to know she had cancer. She was going to tell her, but she hadn't yet, I guess."

"How bad is her mom's cancer?"

"Bad."

"Terminal?"

"No, but she is starting treatment soon. I guess she was going to tell her daughter then." Felix coughed, took a sip of water. "Diana said her mom had gone out of town and did I have a way to reach her. She was extremely nervous, upset." Felix scratched at the trace of gray in his goatee. "She ordered a glass of pinot noir. And have you ever seen someone, they think about getting drunk when the drink first arrives and then they decide not to? That was Diana. A couple of guys tried to buy her wine and she shot them down. She sat and she waited and she didn't finish her glass." Felix frowned.

"Did you talk much with her?" Felix, I had noticed, was very social whenever he was in the bar; he was great with customers.

"She didn't stay long. I told her I didn't even know her mom was out of town. It was news to me. She said, 'Well, maybe she isn't.' I said, 'Why would she lie to you?' She said something about a retreat with no cell phones, she can't reach her mom. She wanted to know if her mom came in, or if she called me, could she leave a message for her. I said yes." His eyes widened. "I haven't thought about it again since because I hadn't seen Janice this week...but I thought it very odd that Janice wouldn't be in touch with her daughter."

"Where's the message?"

"I put it by the cash register. She asked me to give it to her mom if she came in, but otherwise not to open it."

"I hope the police don't find it," I said. Okay, that could wait until the police let us back downstairs. No way I could go downstairs now and retrieve it. Next problem. I pulled the Russian's cell phone out of my pocket.

"What's that?"

"Grigori Rostov's phone."

"Robbing the dead, Sam. Have some shame."

"Clearly I'm going to hell. Why would a Russian thug be after your friends?"

"I literally can think of no reason." Felix raised an eyebrow and pointed at the phone. "Clearly you're going to need to wipe it off for prints before we say we found it in the mess downstairs and give it to the police."

"I'm not giving it to the police. I want to know why he came here. I want to know who the man in black is. They know I'm connected to the bar, and I know nothing about them. I'm a loose end who needs to be eliminated." I studied the phone. It was a cheap phone, the kind with few features, bought with prepaid minutes. Hard to trace and easy to trash.

First, I checked the call log. Two numbers were listed. I pressed the first number in the call log.

A slurred voice. "Yeah?"

"Who is this?" I said.

"Finders, keepers, jerk," the voice said. "She threw it out on the street and now it's mine, and all the minutes. Possession nine-tenths, baby."

Someone using the first number in Rostov's call log had tossed that phone. "You're welcome to the phone, sir," I said. "But do you mind telling me where you found it?"

"It's mine now."

"Who is she?"

"The stupid lady. This phone still works."

"What did she look like?"

"Blonde and clean. Stop chewing up my minutes." The charmer hung up.

"Enjoy the phone, sir," I said to the silence.

I tried the second number. Then the ringing stopped, and I heard a click. Someone on the other end of the line.

I listened to silence. The silence listened to me. Finally a voice said, "Hello."

The man in black's voice. That odd mix of British and American accent.

"You left in such a hurry," I said.

"I guess you're not dead." He sounded cool, collected. "The young man…?"

"Dead."

"Poor guy. You shouldn't have kicked the gun into him as I fired."

"You shouldn't have pulled the trigger."

"But I wasn't trying to hurt you, bartender. Do you think the poor fool would have treated you gently if he'd known you killed his brother? I did you a favor."

I said nothing.

"How did you get this number?" he asked.

"I took Grigori Rostov's phone off his body before the police arrived."

The voice took a moment to digest this news and all it implied. "You are so clearly not just a bartender."

"Well, I also collect stamps." Don't get me wrong; I was not in a joking mood. I wanted him off-balance. Let him slip, let him tell me more than he meant to say.

"What do you want?" he asked again.

That was an excellent question. "I want to know who you are."

"If you're protecting Diana, then you know who we are. The question is, who are you, bartender? You, we can find. But you can't find us."

I hate a threat, especially when it is true. I could've quoted the

Audi's license plate to him. I didn't. "How's your guy who took the blow to the head? Has he forgotten me?"

"Just give Diana to my safekeeping, and I'll make it worth your while. I might have an offer that interests you."

"I told you, I don't know her. But even if I did, I don't think your safekeeping sounds very safe."

He gave a bitter laugh. "What is it you want, interesting bartender? And I don't mean in terms of information for this scintillating conversation. I mean…what in your heart of hearts do you want?"

I misunderstood. What did I want? I wasn't in a position to make demands. Only threats that maybe I couldn't carry out. And as long as he knew where I could be found, he was more threatening than I could hope to be.

His voice slipped into a whisper. "You must have something you want."

"World peace," I said.

"Now, peace would bore a man like you. I can say that even after our slight acquaintance."

I said nothing.

"No matter how big your dream, your ambition, bartender, I can give it to you. I make dreams happen. I'm like a computer hacker—but I hack human lives."

Um, creepy. "I'm sure you can't. Otherwise, you'd be able to afford competent help."

"Grigori Rostov was less than nothing to me; in fact, I didn't hire him and I needed him dead. You did me a favor. Thank you."

"You're not welcome."

"You cannot hope to win. You're one against many. Keep breathing and just give the woman to me."

"I told you, I don't know her."

He ignored my assertion. "I only want to talk to her; I don't wish to harm her. Her mother is a friend of mine. A good friend. In fact, I'm trying to protect her. And I'll make it so worth your while." And then again he asked, "What is it you want?"

The question started to unsettle me. It was a crazy question to ask, and yet he asked it with a startling confidence that he could deliver.

"What do you care?" I asked.

"How hard is your life about to get?" he said. "You didn't tell the cops you came to the Russian's house. You stole evidence in a death case. Now the Rostovs are both dead, and maybe there's a stray hair or a fingerprint of yours…just waiting to tell the cops you were at the scene of both crimes tonight." He laughed. "I think you're about to have some really bad days, bartender. So. Maybe we can help each other. What do you want more than anything else in the world?"

I decided to ignore his constant question, threat, whatever it was. "If you send people after me, I'll kill them like the Russian. You understand me?"

"And next you'll claim that's not a threat, that's a promise. Whatever. I am the best in the world at making and keeping promises."

"I want you to stay away from me."

"But, see, you're interesting, bartender. I like interesting people. I—"

"I presume you like breathing better," I said, and I hung up.

I leaned over the desk. Declaration of war against an unseen enemy.

A knock at the door. The police techs. They told us they were done and we could clean up the bar. I stepped into the dim lighting and surveyed the mess in the expanse of the bar: the spilled drinks, the tumbled furniture, the chalked circle where a bullet's casing had been found, a hole in the wall where they'd recovered the bullet from Diana Keene's gun. There were probably two dozen walked checks from the melee; I'd have to see about charging the cards, seeing if any were declined, and returning cards to customers who hadn't picked them up after they were questioned. Bloodstains on the concrete. I'd have to find something to remove the blood.

We watched the techs leave. Then Felix fumbled along the edge of the register. He pulled out a sealed envelope with The Select's logo and return address preprinted in the corner and handed it to me. I opened the envelope and slid out a piece of paper. Felix read it over my shoulder.

Mom: If you get this, please call me ASAP. Why are you not returning my messages, where are you really? Why did you lie to me? I am worried about you and I found what you left me. In case you died. We have to talk!!!!!! Please, I'm scared. D.

"What you left me in case you died?" Felix said. "Like a will?"

"She didn't say it was urgent she find her mom?"

"No." Felix leaned against the bar. "I didn't really chat with her. It was busy. And I like Janice, and I didn't want to get in the middle of a fight between her and her daughter."

Felix dug in a cooler and produced two icy bottles of Abita Amber lager; I had developed a liking for it, living in New Orleans, and I made sure my bars stocked it if they could get it from a local distributor.

"I made a new friend," I said after I sipped the cold beer. I told him about the man in black's offer.

"Okay, don't call him the man in black because that is and always will be Johnny Cash," Felix said. "Secondly, call him back and tell him you'll stay out of his way. You don't want trouble."

"They'll find Diana."

"Wrong. We'll find her first," Felix said. "And why keep him on guard? Make him think he's scared you away. Be the threat he doesn't see coming."

I considered this wisdom.

"Why would he keep offering you whatever you wanted? That just sounds weird. And I love San Francisco, but it can be a crash course in weird."

"For Diana. He thinks I know where she is."

"Then we assume she's not at her mom's or her own place. She's hiding."

"She's running."

"Presumably." Felix took a small sip of beer. "So. What now?"

I had a number of options. "First, we clean up the bar so I can think. Second, we find the getaway car, the Audi, and see who was driving and what they can tell us. Third, we find Janice and Diana."

"Shouldn't we find them first?"

"I saw the getaway car's license. It's our only thread to follow right now."

"We should find Diana and Janice first," he said. "Get them to safety."

"Easier to find one man than two missing people. If we stop him as a threat, that puts your friends into safety, even if we haven't found them yet."

Felix let several seconds tick away, thinking. "You said Diana yelled at you not to call the police. She might not welcome our help." He set down his beer.

"If we can help her without involving the police, I think she'll welcome us."

"There is a chance that Mila will pull you out," he said.

"No, this guy won't let up. It's like leaving the playground to the bully. I end this now."

"She may not see it that way."

"She wants me working on the Monroe poisoning attempt. She can think that's what I'm doing."

"Then let's get started." I fed the Audi's license plate to him, and he typed again on his laptop. The Round Table manages to have access to all sorts of interesting databases, either through illegal access or backdoor entries that can't be traced. I don't judge.

"The car is registered to a Vivienne Duchamp. She lives in Tiburon." Felix raised an eyebrow. "That's in Marin County, other side of the Golden Gate Bridge. Rich people territory."

Rich people? "Rich people commit crimes."

"Yes. Or maybe her car was stolen. Or the car was registered in her name and she's a victim of identity theft. Or she affords her super-expensive house by being a getaway driver for Russian thugs. I really like option three."

I took another long swig of beer. "So now we clean up the bar. I don't want to leave it a mess overnight."

"We don't go to the Duchamp place tonight?"

"I already got someone killed trespassing tonight," I said.

"Not your fault. The man in black would have killed Rostov's brother just for walking in."

"Yet he didn't kill me. Let's clean the bar. Work will clear my mind."

"I was afraid you'd say that." Felix stood. "No sleep for the wicked."

"Could you sleep anyway?" I'd forgotten, stupidly, that he was sick. "Wait. You need your rest."

"I don't do sick," Felix said. "Are you afraid they'll come back here?"

"Not right now. Maybe they'll come back in a day or so. He might wait to see if I give him Diana, like he hopes."

Felix looked unsettled. I didn't blame him. "But I think they don't want any more trouble. They want Diana, and they'll only come here if they think she's here or I know where she is."

"You told them you'd protect her from now on."

"Yes," I said. "I did."

The phone rang. I picked it up.

"It's me," Mila said. "Are you all right?"

"Yes." I decided not to tell her about the encounter at Rostov's. Not yet. "Are my son and Leonie safe?"

"Yes. They're both asleep. I told Leonie to call you in the morning. We'll keep them in Los Angeles until this is settled. I want to know all details."

"I'm up against a very bad guy," I said. "And let me handle it, and I'll call you when I know more."

"Sam..."

"Mila, this is my problem now. Just keep my family safe." I hung up.

13

Friday, November 5, very early morning

Felix and I swept the floor, mopped up the spilled vodka and juice and pinot grigio and pale ale and gathered broken barware. With the dual shocks and horrors of the night, cleaning felt like therapy, a bit of calm that let my mind ponder my new set of problems. The work didn't clear my mind, but it kept me from thinking constantly about two men looking into my eyes as they died tonight. Death is always a lot to process.

There were coats left behind, two purses, a BlackBerry phone, a well-thumbed guidebook to San Francisco. Welcome, tourist. Did you leave your heart here? Gunshots do add that special ambience. Most of the witnesses had gotten their stuff back after they'd given their statements, but these had decided not to come back or would come back tomorrow. Felix got a cardboard box that had once held bottles of Napa Valley pinot noir, and we put all the abandoned belongings into it.

I swept up the broken bottles and glasses by a spilled bin and table near the back hallway. I stepped on something as I swept up the glass. An ornate silver lipstick case, fancy enough I thought it might be valuable or antique. I tossed the lipstick into the box with the other stuff. I wrote SHOOTING LOST & FOUND on it with a Sharpie pen. Felix put the box under the bar while I finished sweeping up broken glass.

We got everything cleaned. Exhaustion, emotional and physical, crept up on us. I just wanted to collapse into bed.

"Go home, get some sleep," I said.

"I'll be back early," Felix said. "Sleep seems like a waste of time when you're sick."

And I wondered how bad his cancer really was. If just a blot on his lung, couldn't he just tell Mila? Maybe he didn't want to spend what limited time he had asleep. If my clock was down to its last ticks, I'd want every second with my loved ones. But Felix had made no mention of family. I remembered his wife had been a suicide. The bar and the Round Table were his life.

But then, we all have limited time, don't we? The awful truth we never want to acknowledge. The Rostov brothers probably had food in their fridge they'd never eat, phone calls and e-mails they'd never return, plans for this coming weekend. All gone, all to dust.

"Don't come in tomorrow, I mean today; we're not going to open. And if our new friend comes back...I don't want you in danger. This isn't your fight, Felix."

"Sam, Diana and Janice are my concern. They brought this on you, and I'm sorry...and so it's my fight, too."

"Thank you." His loyalty touched me.

"Good night, Sam."

"Good night." To be safe, in case there were angry, revenge-minded Russians waiting outside, I walked with Felix to his car parked in the small lot behind the bar's building. I opened the locked gate. He got in and waved, and I watched his car vanish into the curtain of early morning fog.

I closed up the gate, locked it. Then realized—it hadn't been locked when the woman ran out the back. Maybe someone had left it unlocked. Or someone had picked the lock.

An Audi ready to get the suburban dad—clearly the idea had been to force Diana out the back of the bar and into the waiting car. So perhaps the driver had gotten out and picked the lock. I examined the lock. I could see the scratches of picks against the edge of the mechanism.

Who exactly was I dealing with? Grigori Rostov might have been

a run-of-the-mill thug, but the suburban dad and the man in black
were not what I expected. Neither was the connection to a prominent businesswoman like Janice Keene.

I went back inside the bar. There is no place quite so lonely as an
emptied bar. It is built for socialization, for civilization, and when
it is empty, it's like a stage bereft of actors. I walked upstairs and
stripped and fell into the bed, the adrenaline of the night draining
from my body. I shuddered under the blanket and cool, clean sheet.

I wondered if anyone had found the Rostov brother's body yet.
I wondered how soon I would be hearing again from Detective
Anitra DeSoto.

I had killed before, and there is nothing glorious or honorable
or cathartic about it, even when it's done to save another or in self-
defense. It's an awful thing, an echo that takes too long to fade.
This did not feel good. It felt lousy, horrible, all the things that
DeSoto expected me to show on my face and that I didn't. It made
me feel like I had stepped further away from the regular life that I
still craved. I was supposed to have a new normal: no more fighting, no more killing. Just traveling like a civilized man, making sure
the bars ran well and made a strong profit, coming home to my
son. Playing with him on the floor, watching his face light up with a
smile, changing his diapers, rolling a ball to him, singing along with
the Wiggles, or watching old Mickey Mouse cartoons.

That life of normalcy.

Normalcy might be on vacation. I turned and stared up at the
ceiling and wondered what the cool-voiced man on the phone
thought he could offer me, in my heart of hearts.

14

Friday, November 5, very early morning

OMG two whole weeks vacay in the Med! Gonna soak up
some sun Corfu style! Thanks Grams you rock LOL!!!!!

Diana had told Lily that sharing your travel plans on a social networking site was tantamount to stenciling PLEASE ROB THIS HOUSE
WHILE I'M GONE on your front door, so Lily deleted the status, but
now Diana was grateful for her friend's indiscretion. As of tonight
Lily still had ten days to soak up her Corfu sun, and now Diana unlocked the gate to the front door and closed it behind her. Lily had
given Diana a key when Lily was given the town house in the Marina District for graduating from Oregon (Lily finishing college had
never been a Sure Thing) because Lily needed plants watered during her frequent Grams-funded holidays. Diana hadn't thought of
staying here earlier, simply because she didn't want to get Lily involved. But it had all gotten much, much more dangerous, and she
needed a shelter beyond the backseat of her mother's car—an old,
classic BMW that lacked GPS, which she was driving as it couldn't
be tracked—or a cheap motel room south of the city, which had
been her previous night's bed.

She let herself in. Her heart jumped into her throat at the warning
buzz of an alarm, and for a moment her mind went blank as to the
correct code. She scurried toward the soft glow of the pad, studied

the keyboard, remembered. She keyed in L-I-L-Y. The alarm went silent, the red light switching to green.

Diana nearly doubled over in relief. The air tasted a bit warm and stale. She listened to the silence; it was as welcoming as a blanket on a cold night.

If they knew she and Lily were friends...but they'd have no way to know that she was here. Maybe they could identify her friends, but even if they drove by—her mother's car was parked four blocks away. Could they guess she was here?

But she had no place else to go.

She went into the kitchen, dropped her purse on the floor. She felt exhausted. She didn't turn on a light. In the refrigerator she found orange juice, and she drank a glass, happy to feel the cool sting against her throat. Lily had a little flat-screen TV on the counter. Diana remembered the two of them trying to cook along with a Food Network show, a complete disaster; they'd laughed so hard, sipping wine—that seemed a thousand years ago. She turned on the television, finding the all-local news channel. She wanted to know what the police were saying. The news feed was talking about the weather. She huddled against the cabinets on the floor and drank her juice and closed her eyes.

She'd been running for one day and it felt like forever. It was not like how it was in those innocent-person-on-the-run movies. No. Not at all. It was frightening and mind-numbing and she constantly felt like she was going to vomit.

And her mother was gone and not returning her calls. Holistic retreat, right.

Her mom's whole life had been a lie. A lie of proportions so gigantic it made her bones hurt to think about it. She didn't even know her mother and now maybe she shouldn't even try. Her mother was a stranger. A liar.

I did it all for you, baby, she'd said on the video. *Please understand. It made everything so much...easier. I wanted you to have a better life. And he offered this to me. If I did things for him. To help him, and it helped us.*

And now she'd vanished on purpose, and these people were trying to find Diana. Either her own mother had told them that she'd called about what she'd found, or...they had bugged her phone. Or bugged her mother's phone. Diana left increasingly panicked voice mails for her mother, and that's when the two men began to show up at the Keene Global office, at her condo, at the places where she hung out. And finally showing up at The Select. They knew about her mother's life. Maybe they'd killed Mom for telling about them in the video.

You will think I did bad things. But I did them for good reasons. Every advantage you have had is because I made this choice. You need not fear him, Diana. The man in charge—his name is John Belias—he has made our wonderful lives possible. He can help you, too. I want you to have as easy a road as I did. Don't judge me, and remember, I did it all for you, all for you.

All for you? Why would her mother do this to her? Sure, parents sacrificed for their kids. But didn't they work so they had a nice life as well? She was grateful to her mother, but...not for this. Not for living a lie.

She opened her eyes as a car commercial ended and the newscaster said, "Violence erupted at a bar in the Haight this evening, claiming one life." Diana crept close to the TV, crawling across the kitchen floor. One man dead, killed by a bar employee during an attempted robbery of another customer. Is that what people thought this was? She'd said, *Help me*, to the bartender—because Mom's friend Felix was nowhere to be seen and Felix was over forty, you know, *old*. There was something about the young bartender—he was cute, but beyond the nice face he had a...solidity about him. He was in a suit so he looked like he was in charge. Intelligence and power together. He just looked like the kind of guy who could and would help. This had gone through her mind in two seconds, because she'd sensed from most people those invisible shields that say, *Don't ask me for help; I don't want to get involved, this is not my problem.* It was an awareness that had come into her head the moment she needed help. She knew most people were good. But if she asked for help, people would want to know why, and if she said why, her mother would go to prison.

She listened to the news reporter and it didn't sound like the bartender had been arrested; it sounded like self-defense. The dead man had not been identified. Witnesses said both the woman who was the alleged target (to Diana the word felt like a prod in her spine every time the reporter used it) and the second alleged attacker had escaped.

Escaped? That meant he was still out there, looking for her.

So now what would they do? She'd gotten one of her pursuers killed. These people owned her mother, and if she could never find Mom again—a possibility that kept creeping around her brain and she kept shoving away—then what? She couldn't run much farther. She could hide here at Lily's, and if the neighbors asked, she was house-sitting; they knew she was Lily's friend. But then Lily would be home, in the bubble of her perfect life, in ten days and then what would she do? Where would she go?

She couldn't join this...little private Mafia Mom was part of. No, not an option. She wasn't going to sell her soul like her mother had.

Maybe she should go to the police. Explain. Show them the video.

And watch them arrest her mother.

Then the solution hit her. She could edit the video. Mom's confession meant only for her eyes after Mom's passing. Lily had a nice computer, the latest Apple laptop, because she remembered Lily didn't know squat about buying a computer and she'd gone along to help her pick out a model. Lily had pointed to the most expensive one and said, *Ooh, that one*. Of course.

Take out the parts where Mom confessed to doing such terrible crimes, all in the interest of giving Diana a perfect life. Where she explained to Diana that the man who had made her life simpler and easier would perform the same miracle for Diana now. Just leave in the parts about the bad guys, make it sound so Mom had found out about them but wasn't part of them. She played the video in her head; maybe it would work. At least it would give her another option. If someone questioned the herky-jerky nature of the video—well, they could probably tell the digital file had been edited. That was a worry for later. She'd think of an explanation.

This could be her weapon, a way to fight back, to get them to leave her alone…

She dug in the purse.

Her mother's silver lipstick case wasn't there.

No.

She emptied the purse. The small gun Mom usually kept in the BMW's glove compartment, supposedly for protection. Diana's own cell phone, turned off in case they were tracking her. Her own lipstick. Her wallet with its thinning amount of money. Her compact red notebook. Old ticket stubs to a movie from last week.

But not the silver lipstick case.

No. She turned the purse inside out, inspected the pockets. It wasn't there. She hurried back to her car. She searched the seats, the floor, her breath growing raspy. It wasn't there. The ragged hole the bullet had torn in the purse…the lipstick case must have fallen out as she fled the bar.

She nearly cried. What if the police had found it? It would be all over the news.

Diana replayed the scene in her head. The bar had turned into a battlefield. What if…it was still there? In the mess. In her mind's eye she'd seen people running, leaving behind coats and purses and cell phones left beside their beers…Gunfire tended to prompt a stampede. She hadn't made a copy of the video—to her it was like copying a nuclear bomb, or scanning and saving a murder confession. No, she didn't know a great deal about computers; she used them at work and to surf the Web, like everyone else. How could she be sure people who could hack her phone, listen to her mother's phone messages and delete them—how could she be sure any copy she made on any computer she could easily access was safe from her pursuers or from an accidental discovery?

And how exactly was she going to get back into The Select? She would hardly be welcome. Mom's friend Felix hadn't been there, but would he realize she was the young woman in trouble? He could call the police. The bar would surely be closed for a couple of days. It was just a lipstick case on the outside. What if it got thrown away? Then it might be in the trash bin. Just waiting for her.

She put her face in her hands, torn with indecision. She had to have the video. She had to have it, because if anyone else had it, then Mom was done. Going to jail and maybe dying there instead of being someplace where they could cure her.

Maybe the young bartender and Felix would help her.

Or maybe they'd call the cops the moment they laid eyes on her.

The bartender had killed the big man. He probably wasn't going to thank her for putting that burden on his heart. Did bars have security cameras? With a shiver, she realized they must. Would the police put up film of her on TV now? Her friends, who would start to wonder where she was—no social networking updates, no calling anyone, no e-mails, and phoning in sick at work—they would see her. Had the camera caught her face clearly enough to recognize? She shared every detail of her life online, but no, she didn't want this known. That her mother, her idol, her shining example was a Bad Person. A criminal.

She had to get back inside that bar. She started to think it through and the exhaustion crept into her brain, and she knew she needed sleep. She needed a plan. To simply show up there would never work.

She crawled into Lily's bed and she pulled the covers over her head. She wondered if the bartender was managing to sleep, and she wished she could tell him she was sorry. And she wished she could tell him thank you. He was her ray of hope after her bank accounts had been locked, her e-mails hacked, her GPS in her beloved Jaguar a beacon for them to find her. She was running, and she was running out of time. Her last thought before welcome, merciful sleep took her, heavy and hard, was *Mom, where are you and what are you doing?*

15

Friday, November 5, morning

One hundred miles east of Portland, Oregon

THE BEST-SELLING BOOKS had paid for the quiet, big house in the woods, for the horse idling in the sunshine, for the privacy. Janice Keene parked the rental car a half mile away, in the heavy, thick shade of the pines, and started to hike through the woods. She kept the backpack squarely on her shoulders.

She'd worn jeans, boots with the imprints sanded so any lifted prints would confuse the brand identification by the forensics people, and a heavy shirt and sleeveless vest. The backpack carried the eyedropper bottle of poison, her suppressor-capped Glock, a bottle of water. She kept the water bottle in a separate compartment in the backpack; she didn't want it near the poison.

The best-selling books. Janice had read them all. She could see the woman's house now, nestled in a curve of creek, sentinel pines standing tall. The air felt fresh and cool against her skin. *Diana would like a walk in these woods*, she thought, *as long as she had her designer pants and her fancy boots and a cute guy and a hot latte at the end of the hike.*

Janice shoved Diana out of her thoughts; there was no room for her daughter in her brain right now. She stopped a quarter mile away from the house. She felt winded and sick. When she got home, she'd have to rest more. She could feel the snake of the cancer in her, she imagined, twining around muscles and nerves and bones, settling into its dark roost. Two serpents in her life: Belias and this cancer. She leaned against rough bark.

The stone house, a thin curl of smoke rising from its chimney. The house that truth built, Barbara Scott had claimed in a cover interview in *Vanity Fair*.

Janice headed down the hill toward the house.

There were no visitors as of late yesterday evening, no one else living at the house. She'd watched the famous author entertaining a pair of old college friends for the past two days, hoping they'd be gone by the weekend. But now Barbara Scott was alone. She'd even seen the woman come out a half hour ago in the dark of the predawn, tend to the horse, walk it for exercise, her lips moving through the lenses of Janice's binoculars, either chatting to herself or to her horse.

Barbara Scott was one of those authors who looked exactly like their photos on the book jackets or in the electronic end pages: long black hair, a narrow face, toffee-brown eyes. She looked taller than Janice; she wore a plaid shirt, untucked, and faded jeans. On her book jackets she wore a suit that made her look intimidating, like she might fire you ten seconds after she hired you because you were already lagging. She'd written on her blog that she was behind schedule on her next book, and Janice thought an author running late on a book would probably tend to isolate herself so she could finish the project and get it to impatient editors.

So she would be alone. That would make this so much easier. She wondered what the new book was about. She wondered if the new book was why Barbara Scott had come to Belias's attention.

She assumed there was an alarm system in the house. Probably, with a wealthy and somewhat famous woman living out here alone (she'd researched her target; Barbara Scott's kids were grown, the husband long buried, and no steady boyfriend in the picture).

She reached the porch. She'd come in on the south side of the house, as Barbara Scott had posted pictures on her blog of her view from her writing office, and Janice therefore knew it was on the north side of the house. Amazing what little details people shared with the world, without ever realizing their importance.

She stepped onto the porch. She moved to the front door, and the wind rose and a rocking chair, caught in the gust, creaked. Janice felt her heart jump into her mouth.

This never got easier. Never. *Do it for Diana. Do it for a good life for your child.*

She tried the door. Locked. She knelt and she slipped two lock-picks into the knob. Forty seconds later the lock gave. Then she worked on the dead bolt's lock, adding a long hook to the picking arsenal. Three more minutes and she heard the bolt slide back into its unlocked position.

Deep breath. Her hand closed on the gun's grip. She would only use the gun if forced. She needed to make it look like natural causes; the poison would take care of that. She didn't know where Barbara Scott was in the house, and she didn't know if she was armed. Surely, with the enemies the woman had made in her writing career, she was prepared for trouble. Janice had heard of crime fiction authors who kept guns in their offices. Always best to assume the worst.

She opened the door, she slipped inside. No pinging noise of an alarm system, but she could see a system's keypad. So Barbara Scott didn't keep it activated when she was home.

The entrance foyer had a rich hardwood floor. The left side opened into a large den, with a stunning river rock fireplace, walls lined with bookshelves, the shelves full of hardbacks. Their even rows were broken by photographs: Barbara Scott with her grown kids or with famous people. Not the ones she'd made her fortunes savaging, of course.

Gun out and leveled, Janice stepped into the den. She heard nothing in the house, but she knew Barbara Scott was here. The car was still in the parkway, a grand red Suburban.

The photos of Barbara Scott with movie stars, with senators, with leaders of industry. They all looked slightly frightened, their smiles forced, as if hoping Barbara Scott wasn't going to turn the force of her pen against them. Like having a photo with her was a totem of protection.

Janice thought, *There's only one protection in this world, and his name's Belias.*

She stopped, listened. She could still hear the calm whisper of the wind; windows were open somewhere. It was a clear and pleasant morning and no reason not to let in the fresh air.

But she didn't hear Barbara Scott.

Silently, on her sanded boots, she moved through the den, into a small hallway that led to a guest room, empty, and then to a kitchen. The kitchen was large, granite countertops, a high-end steel refrigerator. Remains of breakfast in the sink. A coffeemaker, with the warming light lit red, the pot empty and cooling on the counter. Next to it a saucer filled with torn pink packets of artificial sweetener, a stained spoon, little dried puddles of coffee. Looked like the coffee setup of a writer blasting toward a deadline.

The view out the kitchen window was very similar to the view Barbara Scott posted on her blog of the inspiring view from her office. Janice glanced upward toward the ceiling. She almost imagined she could hear fingers striking a keyboard, the clicking march of words appearing on a screen.

She turned and she went up the stairs. The stairs were steep; a fall down them would be a suitable accident. If not, then the poison. If there was still coffee in the pot, she could have dosed it and hid in the house and waited for the woman to drink the fatal cup. She had to be sure the job was done. You did not fail Belias, since he did not fail you.

On the staircase were framed jackets, blown up, of Barbara Scott's brutal best sellers. *The Unmaking of a President*, the book that had elevated her from an academic at a small liberal arts college and rocketed her into the national spotlight. *The Hollow Men*, her incisive follow-up that dissected the incompetency of three American business leaders, leading to their downfall. *Unkind*, her correctly titled exposé of the country's foremost tabloid publisher and online gossip site owner, who had to face his own mortifying embarrassments when Barbara Scott was through with him. And more. Six books in eight years—all lauded, all huge best sellers, all using research and dirt that went far deeper than what most writers could manage.

The innermost secrets of the powerful.

The supposedly untouchable.

But Barbara Scott prodded them, dragged them, wrenched them into the light from the deepest shadows.

Janice wondered what she had found out about Belias. Why else would he want her dead?

At the top of the stairs, the hallway ran left and right.

She went to the right. An open door that showed another guest room. A closed door down the hall from it.

Janice moved to the door. Listened. She could barely hear the soft, infrequent click of a keyboard.

Would the desk face the window? Yes. What had Barbara Scott confessed on her writer's blog: *The book is late because I keep looking at the mountains.* So the desk would face the window. The littlest things people confessed online could be helpful to a knowing eye like Janice's.

Janice slowly eased open the door.

The study was big and comfortable. More bookshelves jammed casually with hardcovers and paperbacks shoved in pell-mell, stacks of printed manuscripts, awards on the top shelves. Colored sticky notes stuck out from the pages of books like captured rainbows. A huge window lay directly in front of her, and in front of the window and its stunning view sat a broad oak desk, with an open laptop attached to a huge screen, and a woman—Barbara Scott, her long trademark black hair down past her shoulders. She wore a denim shirt and her hands, for a moment, weren't typing.

Janice raised the gun and centered it on the back of the woman's head.

She told herself, *Maybe this is why Belias wants her dead. Maybe she's writing about him. About one of us. About all of us. Maybe she knows about the network. Just put the gun to her head and force her to drink the poison, and you're done.*

The hesitation changed everything for Janice Keene, because then Barbara Scott said, "Well, I do understand your point, Nina. I do. But I'm trying to do what's right for the structure of the book."

Janice froze. No one else in the room. Barbara Scott wasn't holding a phone.

Then Barbara's head tilted slightly, she typed a few keystrokes. "Well, yes, I could move the section on the financial investors up a few chapters...yes...but maybe we could break it into two shorter chapters...I don't want to give away too much too early..."

Janice couldn't shoot her while she was on the phone. She wondered if Barbara Scott could see her, standing absolutely still, in the window's reflection, a ghost against the mountain looming in the distance.

"Yes...ha, that's why you're such a good editor. Uh-huh..." And Barbara got up, brushing her hair back, and turning her head slightly as she studied a chapter printout on the corner of the desk, scribbled a note in red pen. Janice could see the silver of an earpiece in her ear, the soft gleam of its lit blue light.

And Barbara Scott sensed her presence and turned. She looked at Janice, her eyes going wide, her mouth a cold, wide O of surprise.

Janice fired. The suppressor hissed. The bullet caught Barbara Scott in the center of her forehead, and she didn't scream, but she collapsed onto the soft throw rug in front of her desk. She lay still.

Janice knelt by the body and she pushed the lit blue light on the earpiece with her gloved hand. The light faded, the call ended. Like Barbara Scott's life. She checked the wrist, the throat, felt the silence.

She looked at the laptop screen. A document front and center, red boxes of comments and annotations in the right margin. Barbara Scott's latest book. It appeared to be about the financiers of Wall Street. She untethered the laptop from the cords of printers and monitor and tucked it under her arm. She dug out the prepaid pink phone Belias had given her and dialed.

He answered immediately. But he sounded as if she'd woken him. It was strange to think of him...sleeping. Or eating. Or performing human activities.

"It's me," Janice said. "She's done."

"Very good." He sounded exhausted. Not that pleased. Maybe he was having an off day.

"I had to shoot her when she was on the phone with her editor; she spotted me. But she didn't scream."

Barbara Scott's cell phone began to ring; it played a sample of the Rolling Stones' "You Can't Always Get What You Want." Nausea gripped Janice; she and the woman she just killed shared a favorite band. The phone's screen announced NINA ROSENBERG and a number with a New York area code.

"Her editor's calling back."

"Don't answer. Don't worry."

"Do you want me to take her laptop?"

"Why would I want that?" He gave off a crazy little snicker that made her blood chill. He was either insane or brilliant, and she could never decide which. Could you be both?

"Because…because I thought you must want her dead because of the book she's writing."

"Oh. No. Thank you. Thoughtful of you."

So why did you make me kill one of my favorite authors, Belias? she wondered. "What do you want me to do?"

"Well, since you had to kill her with a bullet, burn the house down, Janice."

"I don't understand."

"I think my instructions were fairly plain."

"All right."

Barbara Scott's cell phone quit ringing. Pausing to leave a voice mail, Janice guessed.

"Call me when that's done."

"All right," she said, and she clicked off the pink phone.

She picked up the dead woman's cell phone and listened to Nina Rosenberg's voice mail: "Hey, Barbara, I think we got disconnected. Give me a call back. I'm in my office." She did not sound worried or anxious. Janice left that phone on the floor next to Barbara Scott's body. No more arguments over the structure of the book. Nina could do what she liked.

In the garage she found two gallon jugs of gasoline. When she went back inside the house, the main house phone was ringing, the answering machine kicking in, and as she splashed gasoline on the books and the wooden floors, she heard a voice say, "Hey, Barbara, it's Nina. Is everything okay? We got disconnected, but I guess you know that, and I thought I'd try you back in case it was your cell phone that died." *No, it wasn't the cell phone that died*, Janice thought. "Hope I didn't make you mad with the suggestions. Call me."

Janice spread the gasoline throughout the downstairs and heavily in Barbara Scott's study. She threw a match she found in the bathroom down in the puddle in the study, and the gas-soaked rug burst upward in a fiery fist. She ran downstairs and did the same in the den. The *whomp* of fire was so intense she felt the heat like a slap. She ran on to the kitchen and turned on the gas stove. Then she crawled through the closest open window. It was a wide, broad porch and she started to run, and she was holding the horse's reins when the blast heaved the roof into the air, collapsing back onto the burning innards.

This was an isolated area, but soon enough the neighbors would see the curl of smoke in the sky.

Janice staggered, ran. The horse whinnied, wide-eyed, the ancient fear of fire holding him in a grip. She opened the gate, and the horse cantered out, nervous.

Janice ran. The weakness from the cancer gripped her muscles by the time she reached the car. She leaned against the door, suddenly fighting for breath, fighting for energy. She couldn't dawdle. Diana's face swam up through her exhaustion and she got into the car and she tore onto the road. She drove past Barbara Scott's refuge. Flames exploded from every window, from the broken roof, from the shattered doorway.

She drove, cranking the oldies radio station high and loud, a Doors song, "The End," blaring in her ears. She got back on the highway to Portland. Her hands shook. She wished she could call her daughter but then she didn't; she didn't want to hear Diana's sweet voice when her head was crammed with murder and arson.

Belias didn't want Barbara Scott's book. He didn't want her notes. It made sense; this book was already written, already read and commented upon and in Nina Rosenberg's editorial hands, so there was a copy in New York and on her backup servers, and so…the book didn't matter.

Maybe.

She pulled Barbara Scott's laptop out of her backpack. She'd disobeyed orders by bringing it; surely it would be missed in the wreckage of the fire; a writer without a laptop was like a painter without a brush.

But she had it now, and maybe it held the answer to why Belias wanted her to kill three people in three different cities.

Why do you need to know? she asked herself. *You don't need insurance.*

Maybe Diana will. He's being forced to help Diana once I'm gone; he didn't pick her the way he normally chooses those he helps and who help him. He's…inheriting her. It wasn't the same. Diana might need every advantage.

Janice aimed the car west and drove to a Portland airport hotel, where she had checked in on Wednesday. The long drive calmed her. She parked and she wondered if her clothes smelled of smoke. She kept sniffing herself and started to imagine she reeked of fuel. She worried about the horse, running free.

She went into her room and undressed. In the shower the reaction hit her, and she sank to the porcelain, the hot water spattering on her, the tile hard against her back. She didn't cry but she felt sick, remembering the surprised glance of Barbara Scott, the blank realization that her life, her dreams, her hopes, her fears were all drawing to an immediate and nonnegotiable close.

If not you to do it, someone else. Barbara Scott was dead the moment Belias decided she was dead. His decision was what fired the bullet, not her finger on the trigger. *Diana will never know a real trouble in life. You did it for her. It had to be done.*

She told herself this four or five times, and she felt the strength return to her limbs. She stood and rinsed out the hotel's gloppy shampoo and dried off. She dressed, hurried downstairs, and put her smoky clothes in the washer. Then she came back upstairs and called him on the pink phone.

"I'm back in Portland."

"Well done. You need to get on a flight to Las Vegas."

"But…" She could hardly say, *I just put in my post-kill laundry, I have to finish it.*

"The second target is in Las Vegas, Janice. You just took the first step for Diana's safety." He coughed. "Get on the first flight you can. It's not like either of us has a lot of time. Destroy the pink phone; I'll call you later on the blue one."

Janice was silent for a moment. "She seemed very surprised. Like she didn't see danger coming at her."

"I'm sure she was," Belias said.

The laptop lay on her bed. If she confessed to taking it, now was the time. He would tell her what he wanted her to do with it. She wiped her lip with the back of her hand.

"This one was easy," he said. "The next one won't be. Bring your A game."

They're never easy, Janice thought. *Never.*

16

Friday, November 5, morning

THE PHONE JARRED ME AWAKE. Not my cell phone, the bar's phone, which had a line feeding up to the apartment. I clutched at it. I thought I could smell food cooking. My body ached and a headache pounded. You always feel a fight more the next morning; the bruises blush in the dawn. "Yes?"

"Hello, is this Sam Capra?"

"Maybe," I said.

"This is Louisa Alcazar with the *Chronicle*. I'd like to interview you about last night's death…"

"No comment."

"Did you have a connection to the victim?" she asked and I hung up. I wondered if I should have just said no. The phone rang again seven seconds later. I answered. It was a television station. I repeated the no comment and hung up. I pulled myself with reluctance from the warm sheets and looked out the narrow window. Two news crews were filming on the street. A self-defense death in a nicer bar in Haight-Ashbury was news. A new day after a dreadful night. Sleep had given me a momentary peace. Then I thought of the Rostov brothers, dead on two different floors, a man in black who seemed determined to make an unholy deal with me, a young woman running for her life with me as her impromptu protector.

Life, messed up in one second.

I called Leonie on her cell.

"Sam," she said, answering after one ring.

"Are you all right?"

"Yes."

"Daniel? I didn't call last night because I didn't want to wake him or you…"

"I hardly slept."

"You'll be safe there, and this will be over soon."

"What happened?"

I gave her the edited version.

"You said you'd just run the bars for them," she said after a moment.

"I don't have a choice. I've made an enemy and the guy won't let it go."

"Or you don't want him to let it go, Sam. You're back in your element."

"Is that really what you think of me?" I said.

"Yes. Right now. Because I'm hiding in a hotel in Los Angeles with a cranky, tired baby." I could have handled Leonie's words better if she yelled them. But she was quiet, stony, and that was more effective.

"Mila will watch over you."

"You mean Jimmy. He said it was better we stay close to him. He's here in town. He is down the hall from us."

Jimmy, Mila's English boss in the Round Table, a man I'd never met. "All right. It's only a precaution. This guy may not come after me."

"You don't believe that. I can tell it in your voice."

"If he does, I'll deal with him and you and Daniel can go home."

Her unusual silence made me worry. I knew she was upset. I knew she wanted to go home.

"Kiss Daniel for me," I said to break the silence.

"I will."

"Will you put the phone up to his ear and let me talk to him?"

"He's asleep, Sam."

"Okay. I'll talk to you later, then."

"Good luck," Leonie said and hung up.

I would have to talk to my, um, boss. Handler. Better angel. Queen of pain. Call her what you will.

I dialed her number, and when she answered, I was at first unsure it was Mila, her voice a sleepy, languorous growl.

"Yes?"

"It's Sam. The press wants to talk to me."

I heard a rustling of sheets as she sat up. She muttered something in Romanian. I'm fairly sure it was a string of curses.

I was not supposed to attract attention. I was not supposed to be noticed by the authorities. "Details. All of them. Leave nothing out."

I told her the story. She said nothing for thirty long seconds.

"Are you still there?" I asked.

"If this is simply friends of Felix who have gotten in trouble," Mila said, "then it's not about the Round Table, and we pull you out."

"Felix said you would say that."

"Felix is a smart man although I am questioning his taste in friends."

"She asked me for help," I said. "Then she helped me."

"Then you are even. How sad that you lack basic math skills." Her voice hardened. "You have other concerns."

I'd already decided on my angle with Mila. "I can't sit here or go home and wait for retaliation. The man in black sees me as a threat. I'm going to find out what this is about—for my sake, for your sake."

Mila's accent thickened in anger. "No, you are not."

I lowered my voice. "You wanted me to find out who poisoned Dalton."

"Too much heat now."

"Fine. But I didn't save Diana so they could just kill her today or tomorrow. Aren't we supposed to be the good guys?"

"I am standing with the ovation. Tomorrow is Official Sam Day. How much news are you on?" Rarely, when she got flustered, Mila's usually impeccable English got tangled.

"Reporters are calling me. News vans are filming outside. I'm not sure I can vanish."

"One moment, Sam."

She put her hand over the phone, but before she did, I could hear the barest tinge of a man's voice. Soft, quiet. I heard the words, "Let him sort it out if he feels he must. He's a big boy, he can stay out of trouble surely." A man's voice, a husky baritone, with a refined British accent.

It must be Jimmy...

Well, it was none of my business. But I felt an odd tug in my chest. And then I ignored it. I waited. Whatever conversation she was having with Jimmy stretched into three long minutes before she came back onto the phone.

"Sam? Very well. Identify who this man in black is so we can evaluate him as a threat. Daniel and that useless nanny woman are staying here in Los Angeles. No one will find them."

"Thank you." *That nanny woman.* Mila loathed Leonie. I think Mila thought attachments would distract me from work, but Leonie and I were just friends. We'd briefly been more than that, in a time of great stress, but now we weren't—it was too soon after Lucy. My ex-wife. "You know I have to help this woman, and I'm going to. With or without your approval."

"Find out who this man in black is and nothing more. Do you understand me?"

"I understand you," I lied. "The CIA took care of scrubbing my job history. The press won't break my background, neither will the police."

She sighed. "I will get on a plane to come help you."

"I can handle it, Mila."

"Sam."

"Yes?"

"It is never an easy thing to kill a person. Ever. Even a bad person who wants to kill you. Ending a life, it always sticks with you."

I cleared my throat. "He looked me in the eyes when he died. Like maybe I was going to change my mind and unstab him."

"Ah, Sam. I am sorry." And she sounded it. That was Mila. Tough as nails until you didn't want her to be.

"I'll call you later."

"All right, Sam." She put the phone down, and I could hear before she clicked off, her starting to say, "Darling, he said that..." and then silence.

Darling? It felt strange to picture Mila romantically involved with Jimmy; I'd always assumed their relationship was strictly professional. Actually, it felt weird to picture Mila with anyone. She didn't seem the relationship type at all. More a loner, like me, because we'd lost too much in life at too young an age.

I ignored the ringing bar phone.

Felix came up the stairs, having arrived already and fought the press gauntlet. He thoughtfully had a tray of breakfast food—eggs, toast, and coffee.

"Thank you so much," I said. "You're here early,"

"I sleep like a gnat," he said. "Sleep for one day, and then they're up for a week. Sleeping Gnat would be a good rock band name." Felix tried a smile, putting on a brave face in the aftermath of the night's events.

"I have a feeling I'm going to have the sleeping habits of a gnat this week." I ate and turned on the television to a local station, and five minutes in they went to the reporter standing across the street from The Select. The account so far was that two men had opened fire in an altercation involving a woman, one man had been knifed and killed by "Sam Capra, who is allegedly the owner of the bar."

Great. My name was out there now. The dead man was not identified pending notification of family. Harder to do when the family died the same night.

The next story was that a body had been discovered in a home in Outer Richmond by police. Shot to death. A police statement said that the dead man at the home was connected to the dead man at The Select, but didn't provide more details.

Which made it a lot less likely my involvement in the story would suddenly be forgotten. I felt sick. Yesterday I was so happy that I was living the new life I'd earned, running the bars, my biggest worry being that I would have to spend time away from Daniel.

Now this. If there was evidence of my presence at the Rostov house, I'd be arrested. I couldn't let that happen. I'd have to vanish again, with Mila's help, and live elsewhere under a new name. I'd lose my identity. The bars. It wasn't what I wanted for my son.

I finished breakfast while the news moved onto the wider world. The pundits remained in full pontificating bloom about who the president would select as a new vice president, that no candidate had yet been selected had tongues wagging. I knew I should pay attention, but I had weightier concerns on my mind. An earthquake off the coast of New Zealand, but no injuries, no tsunami. A fire at the house of a famous author near Portland, the author missing and feared dead in the flames. So rarely is there good news. I could use some.

"So. What now?" Felix said.

"I go see the lady who owns the Audi," I said. "That's my one thread to pull." I crossed my arms. "I don't want you here alone in case the man in black comes to play."

"I've been working for the Round Table longer than you have. There are reporters outside. Right now this is the safest place in the city. I won't let in anyone I don't know."

"Felix…"

Felix crossed his arms. "Look, the Round Table saved my life. And Janice and her kid are clearly in serious trouble. Now you go find the Audi, and I'm going to see if I can track down information on Janice and her daughter and this Rostov guy."

I went out the back door. The plank Diana had used to strike the suburban dad was gone. The police had taken it, no doubt for evidence. I knew the forensics people could summon fingerprints off untreated wood with a chemical process. I didn't know if her prints were anywhere on record, but if she was identified by the security tape, it meant I might not have much time to find her.

The press wasn't lingering around the back alley of the bar, so I walked to my rental car and tapped the rental's GPS with the Tiburon address of Vivienne Duchamp, who owned the Audi I'd seen racing away, and studied the map. Felix had found nothing useful on any Vivienne Duchamp in San Francisco or Tiburon via online engines last night.

I drove carefully, cutting back and forth in San Francisco's labyrinth of streets, heading north toward the Golden Gate Bridge, making sure no one was following me. The poor confused voice from the GPS, that of a famous British comedian, kept announcing he was recalculating and telling me a new route until I'd decided no one was following me.

I thought about Diana Keene. Wondering where the young woman was. She was pretty, now that I thought about it in the silence of the car, and she was brave to take on the gunman the way she did.

I tried to enjoy the view as I went across the Golden Gate Bridge, because it's incredible but the traffic is such that you don't want to be distracted. I love the bridge. But I could not shake the instinct that I was driving straight into bad trouble.

And yet I wanted to go. Risk it. Go back to my old life. When the Golden Gate Bridge was behind me, as the Redwood Highway began its climb into Marin, I felt like I'd truly passed through a gate that I couldn't close.

17

Friday, November 5, morning

I DROVE IN THE OPPOSITE DIRECTION of the commuter traffic toward Tiburon, the hills and trees a sudden shock from the packed citification of San Francisco proper, and the rental's GPS informed me how to proceed.

The hard truth I hadn't said to Mila was I might need to give the police the man in black, not just to stop him but to save my future. If I was facing arrest, if I got physically tied to the Rostov house, then I needed leverage. The man in black was my only hope at the moment. If the police tied me to the murder there, I could argue that my CIA past made me afraid an old enemy had sent Rostov after me. And that was why I'd gone to his home. The problem would be convincing anyone that I was innocent of the Rostov brother's death. And whether the CIA would back me—there was no guarantee.

The GPS led me through Tiburon, a lovely small town with schools and a shopping center, a library, a police station that looked more like a home than a law enforcement hub. The cop cars here were Dodge Chargers. It's good to know where the police station is when you're contemplating breaking and entering. An actual Rolls-Royce went by me in the other lane.

The houses started grand and kept getting grander as I followed the street's labyrinthine turns and twists and climbed a hill. Ahead of me a Mercedes crept along and I tried not to crowd it; I didn't want to be remembered. The cars parked along inlets of the road were high dollar. It felt like a slow drive up a tiered wedding cake, the road a spiral. Lots of people here, I figured, who had made their fortunes on the very real nonreality of the Internet. Or the banking or legal services required to make those on-fire companies function. At one house I saw a mom in a Volvo, backing out, a dad holding two well-scrubbed toddlers, waving good-bye for the day.

American dreams. What I was supposed to have with Lucy and Daniel. This, or a more modest version of it, should have been my life. When me and my wife's overseas tour of duty was done, we should have landed in a suburb—a Langley, an Alexandria—with the nice home and the quiet green lawn and tasteful flowers that stirred in the gentle breeze and the calm, resolute air of success and earned comfort. The cocoon woven to keep you safe. Now Lucy breathed because machines helped air push in and out of her lungs; wires were her wrapping. Now I was a single father to Daniel, and I sort of had Leonie, although we weren't a couple and she was there solely because of her deep attachment to Daniel. Her attachment to me seemed a very uncertain thing. We didn't have a suburban mansion; we had a small house with a pale red door and a porch, not too far from my New Orleans bar.

This—the quiet, the calm, the comfort; wow, it made my chest hurt—could have been my life. Should have been. The life I was on track for when I was an unlikely undergrad at Harvard, before my brother Danny got slaughtered on a terrorist's video and I decided to join a secret group within the CIA.

Because I was going to fix the world.

I hadn't. You might have noticed.

The Mercedes ahead of me turned in at the address I wanted. Stone and iron fencing surrounded the house; a gate slid open for the sedan. I drove past as the gate closed. I couldn't see the house except for a grand slate roof.

I continued down the road, the British comedian's voice chiding me that I had gone past my address. On the GPS I studied the curves and bulges of the surrounding streets. I traced my finger along the screen, looking for an access point—maybe the home behind the grand house that was the Vivienne Duchamp address. Then

I switched off the system and the comedian's lame joke about me missing my turn.

I parked on the street the next over; a FOR SALE sign was mounted where you might normally see a DON'T PARK HERE sign. A risky but quick glance in the windows told me the house was empty of furniture and people. A heavy stone wall divided the property from the address for Vivienne Duchamp. The rocks looked plucked for their worn perfection from a riverbed. I vaulted over the wall and dropped onto the back driveway of the house.

It was striking, lovely, two wings and a separate garage with a gray slate roof, charming with the look of a French Norman farmhouse. A range of toys lay scattered along the edge of the driveway, where the black Mercedes I'd followed stood parked. I never had many toys. Not complaining—my relief worker parents and I were often on the move every year, and toys were expensive to haul from Tanzania to Haiti to Suriname. My family kept it basic: trucks, little green soldiers, crayons, and sketchpads. My brother and I had to rely on our imaginations more than plastic. When we moved on to the next devastated region, my brother and I left our toys for the kids we'd left behind, who often had less than nothing. The kids at this house had toys to spare: bikes, balls, foam bullets scattered across the stones like a child's battle had been waged and won. A soccer ball, caught by the breeze, rolled toward me and I stopped it with my foot.

San Francisco's not cheap. This house was worth *millions*.

I thought, *This* has *to be a stolen identity—why would a multimillionaire be the getaway driver for a hired thug?* Who were these people? That kids were here made me uneasy; I'd have to be sure not to create a dangerous situation.

I stayed out of the view of the windows as much as I could as I hurried to the edge of the garage. I tried the door. I went inside.

In the garage was parked a silver Mercedes, a Range Rover. A sticker with a soccer ball with the name EMMA above it adorned the Rover's back window; above it was another sticker for Blaircraft Academy. The third slot in the garage was empty. No sign of the Audi that I'd seen roaring away with the suburban dad in the night.

I tried the door on the opposite side of the garage. It led to the back of the house, across a stone path and a large stone patio with a built-in grill and guarded with dozens of potted plants. A fountain quietly gurgled. It looked like an outdoor setting from an architectural magazine. I started thinking, *I've made a huge mistake*. But three years of undercover work with the CIA teaches you that things are often not as they seem.

I carefully crept up to the windows on the patio. In the distance I could hear a television, the bright burble of a morning talk show.

I leaned back from the window as a girl, around seven, walked into the large den, holding a bowl of cereal, screaming up at the stairs, "Peter Marchbanks please hurry up!"

Marchbanks?

I would be seen when they came out of the back of the house, presumably to drive to the Blaircraft Academy.

"Mom? Nana? We have to leave in a minute!" I heard the girl bellow again.

I heard a distant, indistinct answer.

Emma—I presumed—vanished into what looked like a large kitchen. I heard feet against stone, and then a boy, a year or so younger than Emma, hurried across the room to the kitchen. He was dressed in a school uniform and making machine-gun noises.

A noisy, argumentative breakfast was consumed. They talked, and I risked a hurried run across the patio (neither saw me) because kids say the most interesting things.

Emma: Well, I don't know why she's here. She was crying. Maybe she and Dad are getting a divorce.
Peter: Daddy will move home?
Emma: Don't get your hopes up. Why would Audrey cry to Mom?
Peter (*chewing*): I cry to Mom.
Emma: That is so different and don't be dumb.

Silence, I counted eight beats.

Emma: So, maybe Mom and Dad will get back together.

Silence, and I felt like I was eavesdropping on these children's fond-est wish. Not a proud moment.

> Peter: Or maybe Dad's just being mean to Audrey.
> Emma: Dad's not mean.
> (*Peter chewing, making a noise of disagreement*)
> Emma: Whatever. Nana! We're ready.

I heard the clang of a bowl hastily dropped into the steel sink. Then I heard another voice, a woman's, older. Yelling toward another part of the house. "I'm going to bridge club and lunch with the ladies and then the grocery store after I drop the kids off, anything not on the list you want?"

I could now see the older woman. Sixtyish. Trying to be stylish and trying too hard. The decor in the house was impeccable and the older woman was dressed in a look that didn't match the elegance. Pink leggings, an oversized peacock-inspired tunic of sorts, gaudy earrings that hung past her shoulders. Nana looked like she'd be a lot of fun, frankly, as a grandmother, but she did not match the studied, cool formality of this house. If this house was money, Nana was a stranger in a strange land. Or she was a wealthy eccentric.

And the kids answered, a litany of asking for certain breakfast ce-reals, chips, sodas, a red pepper hummus. What adventurous eaters.

"Hummus, gag me. Go kiss your mom good-bye," Nana in-structed, and the two kids vanished toward the front of the house and were back within thirty seconds. They pulled backpacks onto their thin little shoulders.

"What's wrong with Audrey and Mom?" I heard Peter ask. "Why is Audrey even here?"

"Ah," Nana said, "I shouldn't say anything." Clearly Nana was dying to say something.

"Tell us if we guess right," Emma said.

Nana's voice went lower. "It's grown-up business."

"I am more grown-up today than I was yesterday," Emma said, negotiating.

"We'll talk in the car," Nana said in a conspiratorial whisper.

I moved away from the window, easing between the brick wall facing the garage and a dense growth of box hedges that needed trimming. I heard a door ten feet away shut, and Nana and the two children walked to the SUV.

Nana and the children got into the Range Rover. Nana backed out, coming perilously close to the Mercedes I'd followed, as though considering putting a dent into it. The wooden gate slid back automatically for them and they drove off. After a moment the gate slid closed. I pulled myself free of the bushes and went to the back door.

Emma and Peter hadn't locked it. Either because they were forgetful or because their mother (I assumed that was Vivienne Duchamp or that was possibly Nana's name; I couldn't know yet) and this woman named Audrey were here, and Audrey would be leaving soon.

I stood in the doorway. Listened. I could still hear the television's newsy drone in the next room, and beyond that, in a front room, raised voices. Two of them, female.

I stepped inside. The back den that looked out onto the patio was beautiful: old brick walls; stone floors; wooden, lofty ceilings. I moved into the huge kitchen. On the marble island was a high-end coffee brewer. The air was heavy with the sharp, delicious aroma of French roast.

I moved quietly back into the large den, which might have been larger than my first apartment. It was elegantly furnished—leather couches; fancy, dark, rich fabrics; tables and chairs that looked expensive. I'd never lived this way, not with nomadic parents wandering the world or with my and Lucy's agency salaries.

Photos—all in silver frames—covered one table and lined the fireplace mantel. Emma and Peter at a kaleidoscope of ages. In more recent photos of the kids, they were posed with a tall, attractive woman in her early thirties with ash-blonde hair and a warm, strong face. I picked up one photo that was propped against a tall, heavy iron candlestick.

One picture with the dad. It was the man from the bar. Suburban dad. I'd been right.

Still holding the framed picture, I crept toward the end of the den, toward a stone hallway that carried voices from an entryway. I could hear their words clearly now.

"Holly, can we stop dancing around this?" A younger woman's voice, closer to the front windows. "You can tell me the truth."

Holly? Uh, excuse me ladies, I thought, *I'm looking for Vivienne.*

The second woman's voice—Holly's, I presumed—was smokier, tired, like she hadn't slept well. "I do not know where Glenn is and he's not here. Do you think I'd let him spend the night here? He's your problem now, not mine."

"Don't pretend that you don't want him back."

"I truly don't." Holly made a heavy sighing sound of cracking impatience. "He texted you that he had meetings and then, what, an emergency trip? There's your answer. Business trumps all. Don't act like you didn't know what you were getting, Audrey."

So, Audrey and Holly. I appeared to have misplaced a Vivienne.

"But what if something has happened to him? He hasn't called in hours. I thought he'd have to be here…with the kids maybe. I know he misses them…"

For a moment Holly sounded sympathetic. "I know you are worried. But coming over here and making a scene in front of my kids…his kids. No."

"I wouldn't ever worry the kids." Now Audrey sounded a bit pouty, slightly wounded. "I'm just shocked at how cavalier you are about him vanishing."

"If he tells you he has to leave town, that does not count as vanishing," Holly said, and she sounded weary of this drama. "You knew when you married him his work matters more than your feelings."

First wife and second wife of this Glenn guy. Peter's last name was Marchbanks. Glenn Marchbanks? The name sounded vaguely familiar, a breeze in the back door of my memory. I put my hand against the cool stone.

"I just thought he'd treat me with a bit more respect and consideration."

"It's disappointing when those we love decide we're not worth their time." I heard a bite in Holly's tone.

"You can't resist the stab, can you?"

"Audrey, he's yours now. You won the prize." Now I heard a harder edge in Holly's voice. "If he had a negotiation that ran late and then he made a trip this morning, he does it. He's going to send you a message and assume you've got your big-girl panties on and not throw a tantrum befitting a reality show."

"He's never done this before."

"You've only been married a year. He keeps a change of clothes and a packed bag in his car. He has access to a private jet."

"Yes." Audrey sounded uncertain.

"Then he's off to conduct business. Okay? Don't worry. Go shopping, spend his money, make yourself even prettier. He'll be happy you did."

And I heard the younger woman's voice rip with a sob. "I think sometimes he lies to me about what he does with his time. When he's out of town. Or even...I just don't think he's telling me the truth." The words broke as she spoke them.

A long, telling pause. "What do you mean?" Holly's voice was cold.

"I think he's lied to me. Maybe the way he lied to you. I don't think every business trip he makes is, you know, a business trip."

"Oh, Audrey. Please. I have a busy day ahead of me, so if you'll excuse me..."

"I always thought if he left me, he'd just come here. Back to you. He still cares about you."

"He cares about Emma and Peter, yes. Me, no."

"You'll always be the first wife. The first love."

"Audrey, the first love is Glenn himself, and the second is success. I'm sure he'll call you soon."

"Shouldn't I call the police? He hasn't texted me or called me since after midnight."

"Did he say specifically where he was going?"

"No."

"He could still be in flight. Japan or Sydney or Europe. Do you really want to humiliate him by calling the police?"

"Couldn't you call the police for me? So he won't get mad at me?" Now slightly coy, like she was playing a part and playing it rather badly. I nearly laughed. I wondered if Holly would just toss her at this point, but instead Holly said, "No, I won't. But I would advise you strongly to wait a bit longer before you freak out."

The women had moved into the large foyer, and now from my viewpoint I could see their reflections in a mirror. Audrey, the younger, in her midtwenties like me, attractive in an assembled way, wearing a T-shirt and jeans. Her skin was overbronzed and her nails an electric pink. She'd been the one driving the Mercedes ahead of me. The other woman, Holly, wore yoga clothes—soft, unstructured linen pants, a tight sleeveless shirt that showed her toned arms. She was the attractive blonde I'd seen in the family photos.

Now Audrey hugged her, and wow it was awkward. I watched in the mirror and I could see the annoyance, for the barest moment, flash on Holly's face. Her lips tightened, her gaze flared in controlled temper. I stepped back before she could see me in the mirror, hidden in a nook of the den, leaning against the cool of the brick. I heard more muttered farewells and then the door shutting. Silence. Then the sound of a car on the front drive revving into life.

I took several steps back into the kitchen, still holding the photo of Holly and her kids.

18

Friday, November 5, morning

JANICE SAT with Barbara Scott's laptop on her lap, afraid to open it.

The Portland airport was busy, and she'd snagged a seat on the next flight to Las Vegas. She'd hidden herself away in the executive lounge for the airline; she traveled so much for her legitimate business that she belonged to all premier flyer programs. She was flying as Marian Atkins, the false identity backed with driver's license, passport, and credit cards that Belias had given her, but she'd just shown the attendant her membership card as Janice Keene. Right now the lounge wasn't so busy; the early morning exec rush had already taken off, and she sat near the depleted buffet.

She debated opening the laptop.

In the corner the financial news network played. Not local news. She was dying to know what the news was reporting about Barbara Scott's fire, but she didn't want to ask the attendant at the desk to change the channel to the local news. It would be national soon enough.

And then how much harder might her job be?

Belias wanted three people dead. One presumption was that they knew each other. That together the three were a threat to Belias and to the network he'd built.

But why?

She opened the laptop, a silvery, aluminum Apple. She thought, *Well, I didn't bring a book for the flight, I can read hers.* The machine had been open and had gone to sleep when she'd shut it, and so she didn't have to worry about cracking a password. The battery wouldn't deplete for a few hours. She ran a thumb along the thumb pad and guided the arrow to the search icon and that was when she noticed the little splatter of blood, right along the edge of the screen, the smears of it on the keyboard.

She froze, her gaze locked on the blood—was that a little fleck of brain next to the stain—?

"Janice! How are you?"

She looked up past the screen. A man, fortyish, heavyset, grinning, in a dark suit and a blue tie. She blanked on his name.

And he was a client.

"Hello!" She closed the laptop, hid the blood from him. She stood. Diana worked on his account. She knew if her smile stayed in place, it would look frozen.

"I didn't know you had a client in Portland." He sat across from her. "Am I interrupting your work?"

"Oh, just writing up some thoughts," she said. *No.* She didn't want this man—Frank Laplace, now she remembered; he ran a software firm in San Francisco that sifted through social networking data to map purchasing patterns—to say to Diana, *Oh, saw your mom in Portland.* She was supposed to be at a retreat in Santa Fe with no phone. Her stomach hollowed out. "Trying to get a new client."

"Oh, you have people to do that for you, don't you?" His laugh was hearty. "You on the flight back to San Francisco?"

"No. I…" She faked a cough to buy a few seconds to think. "I have another client to go see." She said nothing more and Laplace didn't ask. He was a client and there was no escaping him as he sat down to chat. She could only hope that his flight would leave soon. He started talking about what a great job Diana was doing for him and she should have felt proud, and instead she simply thought, *You're a CEO, Frank, don't you have phone calls to make?*

Finally—an eternity, every second ticking on the wall clock feeling like a century, but it was only an hour, and he talked of what he wanted his public relations approach to be, and she forced herself to be clever and insightful and all the things people expected of her, the whole time thinking, *Just go get on your plane you idiot*—he got up when his flight to San Francisco was called. "I'm supposed to meet with Diana early next week," he said. "I hope I'll see you then."

She forced herself to stand and nod and shake his hand. He got up and he left, hurrying from the quiet of the club to the noisy pell-mell rush of the terminal. She went to the small buffet table, dampened a napkin, and returned to the laptop. Gently she cleaned off the blood—and the whatever it was, particle of brain, ugh—and she folded the napkin. She was afraid to leave it in the trash; what if someone saw it? But who would think that here? *Why, goodness, is that a fleck of brain in the trash?* This place was full of people who worked hard, were highly successful, traveled to represent their fine companies, and were anointed with success. No one would see a napkin and think there was a bit of brain tissue on it. She threw the napkin away.

He will tell Diana he saw me next week. Guaranteed. Already something had gone wrong and maybe this was punishment for defying Belias's orders. She wasn't superstitious. But when you sold your soul…then she had to be done quickly with this devil's errand. One down, two to go.

But the why of it. She had to know the why.

The cheap blue phone buzzed. Belias. No one else had this number.

"Yes?"

"Lazard. You go after a man named Lazard."

The name was vaguely familiar. "Who is he?"

"Lucky Lazard. Real estate mogul. Make it look like an accident. I'll send you details on him."

"I understand."

"Slight problem. He lives on the penthouse floor of a major casino resort that he owns. He has bodyguards. He's rarely alone."

"Then how am I supposed to get to him…"

"When you get to Vegas, there will be a package waiting for you at the Mystik hotel." He cleared his throat. "You're the best. You better prove it to me."

"Is everything okay?" she asked. He sounded angry. She thought he would be happy, the first target eliminated.

"Fine. Everything is fine," Belias said.

"You sound upset."

"We all have aggravations now and then, Janice."

"I thought you made your aggravations go away." She meant it as a joke, but the eerie, steely silence on the other end of the line took the slight smile off her face.

"That's what I do," he said. "Make this look like an accident. Someone might be getting suspicious with both Scott and Lazard dead. Each one, it will get harder for you."

"They're connected?" she asked before she thought.

His answer was a stony silence.

You might as well have said yes, she thought. "I understand."

"You're the best," he said.

"You know why I'm doing this. For her sake. You'll take care of her, won't you? I know you didn't think she could work for you, but she can."

"Oh, yes, I'm going to take care of Diana. No worries on that front."

"I appreciate that."

"It's not a problem. Call me when Vegas is done."

"It may take time given the difficulty."

"Hurry. But get it done right."

She nearly laughed. How often had she heard something similar from her public relations clients? You can have it fast, or you can have it right, or you can have it cheap, but not all of them. "I will get it done. For Diana's sake." Because if she got caught, there was nothing that Belias could do to take care of her daughter. Janice was destroying herself, both body and soul, for her daughter.

"Are you feeling okay?"

"Fine. I'm fine."

"It will be all over soon," he said. "And I'll make sure Diana has every advantage in life. I promise you that."

She hung up. She didn't want to hear any more about promises she wouldn't be alive to see if he kept. The cancer would claim her soon enough, and she had miles to go before she rested.

She typed on the dead woman's laptop, considering a search on her own name, if Barbara Scott knew who she was. She opened up a search field for the hard drive and she typed in her own name.

No match. She breathed a sigh of relief.

She typed in *Belias*.

No match.

Holding her breath, she typed in *pact*. It was most likely the term to be used to describe the particular relationship Belias had with...people. It was always the term he'd used with her: *the pact we've made*.

Two results: nothing to do with her or Belias.

She didn't really need to search anymore. But she kept her fingers on the keyboard and typed in *The Network*.

No match that had anything to do with Belias.

She pulled her hands from the keyboard and rubbed at her cheeks. Okay then. If Barbara Scott didn't know about Belias and his people, then why had she needed to die? What was the connection between a best-selling author and a real estate mogul in Las Vegas?

She went to the laptop's Recent Files option and looked at what had occupied Barbara Scott. The writer had files on several famous people, loaded with articles and news clippings: a rising actor in Hollywood; a financial guru who hosted his own cable show with a devoted following; an economic adviser to the president; a New Mexico senator who was a leading contender to be appointed vice president—she had become a political celebrity for her outspokenness and wry humor that managed to charm both sides of the aisle; a file on her husband as well; another on a former senator who'd become a well-known author, trying to be the modern answer to Mark Twain. Nothing to connect them or to indicate that there was a pattern between them. All these files were just kept in a folder called RANDOM RESEARCH IDEAS. In each folder was a Word document with Barbara Scott's notes in it.

In the file on the vice presidential contender's husband she read:

*how does a spouse help a politician or hurt a politician? What is
the level of influence they can actually wield? Is this a liability or a
drawback... consider historical antecedents—is there a book in this?*
Every file either began or ended with that same kind of question,
Barbara Scott challenging her brain and writer's instinct to shape a
story from these bits of information, dramatic questions, and fact.
It was just a clippings file, the kind any writer might keep.

Could any of these accomplished people Barbara studied have
made the pact with Belias, be part of his network? There was
nothing in the files to indicate this was true or that Barbara Scott
suspected this. No outlines, no damning documents.

There was nothing specifically on Belias, on the pact, on his network with its secret reach into the corridors of power and money
and influence. She searched for locked or passworded files and
found none.

Janice closed the laptop. The search was fruitless. She should re-
format the laptop, erase the information, throw the system away.
She was walking around with a laptop used by a dead woman,
whose death was at this moment a major story on the national news.

But she didn't destroy the hard drive. Information was here; this
was what Barbara Scott was working on and surely her work was
why she died. There was an answer in this laptop; only she did not
know the question. She had to focus on the second target. Lazard.
She...

She stopped. She opened Barbara Scott's laptop again, went back
to the search field for the hard drive. She typed *Lucky Lazard*. No
hits. She just typed in *Lucky*. Many hits, as any mention of the word
in an e-mail or a PDF document or a spreadsheet or a Word document returned a positive result. She scanned through them and she
found one. Not from Barbara Scott's main e-mail account, but from
another account, one hosted by a large search engine, the kind of
account you open and you throw away when you don't need it anymore. The kind you open to protect your main account from spam-
mers, the kind you use to sign up for a newsletter or mailing list.

Or maybe the kind you open when you want to be more anonymous.

Lucky: I think all of us are about to live up to your name,
aren't we? The payoff is here. Think about how best to
profit. We should work together, not apart, so we don't go
to the wishing well at the same time and exhaust the gen-
erosity. Hope you are well. Behave or I'll put you in a book,
ha-ha-ha. I kid. See you soon on even-easier-street.

Dated a week ago.

The receiving e-mail address was not one obviously connected to
Lucky Lazard's businesses; it was another throwaway account. But
how many guys were nicknamed Lucky?

She searched for more messages from that account, but there
were none. And no further exchanges between Barbara Scott and
Lucky Lazard. Would he be running scared now that Barbara Scott
was dead? They'd been in contact. They'd been planning something
that would profit them both. What could profit both an author and
a real estate tycoon? And now Barbara was dead and Lucky Lazard
should be glancing over his shoulder. This e-mail meant her job was
now a hundred times harder. He would be on his guard. Although
the news accounts had not said murder yet, it was only a matter of
time. The fire wouldn't burn the bullets away.

Maybe they knew about Belias. Maybe they knew about his secret network. Maybe they thought they could blackmail Belias.
There was a reason why they needed to die. And she had to decide
now if she was going to find out what it was.

The airline called her flight. She slipped Barbara Scott's laptop in
her carry-on and wondered if she could find out that truth from
Lucky Lazard before she killed him. Because she hadn't much liked
the tone in Belias's voice when he spoke of Diana. Maybe she could
find some extra insurance to protect her daughter.

19

Friday, November 5, morning

CONFRONTING SOMEONE in their own home is an extremely risky proposition. It's a violation to stand in their space, unexpected. It can cause panic.

I turned the photo of Holly and the kids from the mantel and held it, facing her. Most burglars or rapists or murderers — however she classified me on first sight, unwelcome in her home — didn't hold family photos.

Holly was talking to herself. "I am so going to need yoga today." Holly walked into the living room, her hands folded together and pressed up to her lips as though lost in thought.

She saw me.

Holly froze. She kept her folded hands close to her face. She didn't scream; she just froze, watching me. In her expensive yoga pants, and blonde hair pulled up in a simple ponytail, and her T-shirt for her kids' school with an uplifting motto about teamwork on it, she looked like soccer mom the same way I'd thought of her ex-husband as suburban dad. The roles I'd loved for my parents to play when I was a kid, but that wasn't meant to be. But she was staring at me like I was here to shatter her sweet life. She didn't shriek or run out of the front door or dash to the alarm system to key in a distress code.

She just looked at me.

I played it just like when I did undercover work for Special Projects. Kept my voice calm and quiet. "Holly Marchbanks? I'm very sorry to intrude. I'm not going to hurt you. I need to find your ex-husband, Glenn."

She said, "Who the hell are you?" Voice calm, steady. Me holding the picture threw her off; I wasn't supposed to be in her house, but burglars didn't hold up photos and ask to talk to ex-husbands.

"Where is Glenn, Mrs. Marchbanks?"

"He's…he's not here. I don't know where he is."

"So I heard you telling his new wife."

She paled slightly.

Surprise her with approach number two. "Who's Vivienne Duchamp? I understand that she lives here."

Her calm evaporated. "Get out of my house!"

"Vivienne Duchamp's car was used in a crime last night that your ex-husband was involved in, and if you don't know about it, then I need to find her."

She stopped her scream and studied me. "Are you a police officer?"

"No, I work at the business where the crime happened. Is Vivienne Duchamp here?"

"No, she used to be our au pair. She went back to Switzerland over a year ago."

"I guess I'll just take my concerns to the police."

"Why haven't you already?" she asked. "Why are you here instead of going to the police?" Stopping me with a question after ordering me out. She was panicking, showing her hand. *This might be easy*, I thought.

"I haven't told the police all I know. I thought maybe I could make a deal with your ex-husband." *This is a card*, I thought, *to be played carefully*.

"A deal? What, blackmail?"

Let her think what she wanted; she might talk some more. I kept my face neutral.

She did. "This has nothing to do with me or Glenn; you're mistaken." She pulled a cell phone from her pocket and showed it to me like it was a weapon. "Get out or I call the police."

"I can e-mail the cops his picture. Bet I can find one on the Internet or on a social networking site. Ask them to show it to the other witnesses. He matches the police description."

I heard the slide of the automatic gate closing; Audrey's Mercedes had pulled out.

"Or maybe your ex-husband and I can have a talk about what happened last night."

"My hus—My ex-husband is a respected businessman. If you'll leave now, I won't call the police on you, all right? The Tiburon police have little patience with trespassers…"

"Did you drive the getaway car? I thought I caught a glimpse of blonde hair."

Now there was a rage shifted into her eyes. "Get the hell out of my house."

"The man who was with your husband is a Russian for-hire mercenary. I wonder if his friends might want to know where your husband is. Why he left their buddy to die and ran."

Every jab made an impact, even if she didn't want to show it. Reading people is difficult, no matter how easy the books and movies make it sound. Her bottom lip barely trembled, but it was enough to convince me she knew about her husband's doings.

And I was holding a picture of her children. All that was at stake without a word spoken.

"Glenn's here. He's in the other wing." She gestured with her head toward the patio door, toward the other wing of the storybook house. "He's hurt."

Delicious honesty. And Prince Charming down for the count in the castle. "Show me, please."

"You won't hurt him?"

"I just want to know why he came to the bar."

"I have no idea what you're talking about. He came here, he was hurt, he wanted me to hide him." It was as much confession as I could hope for. I supposed the weight of what I knew made arguing pointless.

"Let's go, then, please." I gestured toward the hallway and she hesitantly moved forward.

As she reached me, she slammed her elbow hard into my collar-bone. It wasn't a shove; it was the kind of brutally efficient move I learned in Special Projects training class. If she'd caught me a bit higher, it would have broken my larynx. I staggered back, cough-ing, fighting for breath, and I hadn't taken four steps when I heard the whistle behind me.

I ducked, and if I hadn't, she would have fractured my skull. She'd grabbed the heavy, tall candlestick from the mantel, the one the photo I'd grabbed had rested against, and swung it straight at the back of my head.

It went over me by less than an inch, the speed of her blow show-ing she aimed without hesitation. I leaned in under her arm and dodged past her.

"Mrs. Marchbanks—" I yelled.

She didn't swing the candlestick back in a return arc. No. She pivoted, recalibrating her energy behind it, and powered the heavy blunt end right toward my face. Admirable economy of action. Clearly with a mind to drive the metal base into teeth and nose and mouth.

And Holly Marchbanks was being completely silent. There was no hysteria of the frightened soccer mom facing an intruder. No panting as she fought. Just cold, relentless calculation.

I dropped below her blow and hit the floor. She tried to adjust, now raising the two-foot-tall iron candlestick to power it down into my head like a pile driver, but I kicked out her legs. She fell. And she rolled off her back, springing back to her feet as I scram-bled to mine. She could have crushed my windpipe with the blow. She could have killed me, gasping my final moments on the stone floor of her storybook house.

Some soccer mom. She hadn't learned this at yoga class or book club. She was trained.

The iron candlestick—or I should say, her fighting stick, because that was entirely how she was using it—came at me again. I danced back. She stopped, feinted; I didn't buy. She stopped again.

"So," I said. Recognizing one of my own. A peer I hadn't ex-pected.

"So," she said. "You came into my house. Law is on my side." Every muscle of hers was taut, coiled like a cat's.

"So let's call the police," I said. "Maybe they'll protect me from you."

She didn't answer. "You're not armed," she said. Not a question. An observation. I would have gone for a weapon by now.

"Mrs. Marchbanks…" I started. I'd rather negotiate than fight.

"Tell me who you are or I will beat your brains in." She moved the heavy candlestick again, as if testing me for a weak point. "You're the infamous bartender. But more than a bartender."

"More than a soccer mom." I stayed low, ready to parry her next attack. I couldn't go hunting for a weapon, so I'd take hers.

She swung the candlestick again and I grabbed the base; it smacked hard into my palm, stinging. I was going to wrest it from her, but she was fast, darting like a viper, and she shoved the candlestick hard into my chest, leveled a kick that caught me in the groin.

She let go of her weapon. Voluntarily, I realized, as I staggered back, went over a leather ottoman, lost my sure footing.

You only surrender one weapon to get a better one.

She scrambled to the mantel, past the other heavy candlesticks, and grabbed at one of the framed photos hanging in a collage above the mantel. It was one of her daughter Emma, smiling, front teeth missing, happy in summer. Behind the frame—which opened on a hinge, I saw, resting on its hilt, a Glock 9mm, capped with a suppressor.

Her hand closed on it.

And I ran into the kitchen.

I heard the hiss of the bullet go right above my head, the deadly cough of the suppressor, heard brick chip in the wall.

She was trained beyond fighting. She was trained to kill.

The kitchen was huge. Granite countertops, custom cabinets, a heavy door that lay open showing a large walk-in pantry. I grabbed a chef's knife—nice long blade—from a high magnetic rack. I picked up a huge, heavy skillet, ringed with dried egg, that Nana must've used for cooking her own breakfast.

She didn't turn the corner into the kitchen.

I listened for her. I was a few years younger and physically stronger. But she had a gun and I was on her home turf. Her children's turf. I know what it is to fight for your child. I'd stupidly underestimated her.

"Bartender," she called. "Look. I aimed low. Not a head shot. I want to talk."

"Yeah, you would have hit my spine. Thank you." On the west side of the kitchen was the large breakfast nook; then the kitchen proper, with a cooking island and a refrigerator and the big pantry door; then the kitchen led off to a back exit mudroom to the driveway, the door the Marchbanks children had exited with their nana; and then another doorway that led to a butler's pantry/serving area, where a buffet of food could be set; and beyond that I could see a slice of a rather grand-looking dining room table. Paired with crimson upholstered chairs and a modernist painting.

Not my usual battleground.

"Bartender?" she called. "I'd like to place an order."

Mocking me. She was overconfident. I wanted her to show herself. I had the skillet and it would stop a bullet. I hoped. And I know how to throw a knife, although I'd never had to in a fight—it's not terribly accurate or reliable. Miss and you lose your weapon. She wasn't going to throw her gun at me.

"Holly," I said. "Do you think you can kill me and clean up the mess before Nana gets back? Or even before your kids get home? It might be a challenge."

I kept the skillet covering my face from nose tip to chest. I moved toward where I'd bolted into the kitchen and out of her sight. Instinct would have her believe I would have retreated farther.

Maybe she'd try to cut me off via the living room.

Or maybe she was standing in the den, waiting to drop me with one shot. That's what I would do.

I turned into the breakfast nook.

She wasn't there. I moved into the den. Here her insanely expensive stone floor was my friend; no creaks in hardwood, no rustle against the carpet. I hurried to the next corner, close to the entryway, where she'd stood talking with Audrey, the second wife.

I stood where I'd stood before. The mirror showed me her, low, crouching. Listening for me.

I bolted straight for her and swung the skillet as she turned. I cease being a gentleman when a woman tries to put a bullet into me or smash my face in with a blunt instrument or shatter my trachea. She turned and her arm caught the brunt of the metal swing and the Glock, with its suppressor, dropped from her hands. I powered a kick into her chest, and crouching low, she didn't have maneuvering room to evade me. She flew back into the wall but landed, even stunned, on hands and fingertips, ready to spring back.

I grabbed her gun. She crouched, watching me, then clutching her arm. I didn't care if it was broken.

Four beats of silence.

I realized she was waiting for me to shoot her.

"You and I," I said, "are going to have a serious chat, Mrs. Marchbanks."

I gestured at her with the gun and I herded her into the kitchen. I kept a respectful distance.

"Now. Last night. Explain."

She stared at the counter, not looking at me. A cookbook lay open to a recipe, with a photo of a luscious plate of chocolate chip cookies next to the instructions. I guess she'd thought she'd make them for her kids later. The world that she lived in—toys in the driveway and children in prep school—and what she truly was jarred me.

Because was I so different from Holly? She had a secret life. Was she me five years from now? I thought of the future, the likelihood of a gun hidden in my house (very), Daniel heading off to an Episcopal school (very) or a French-immersion école in New Orleans (just short of very). He'd wear a uniform like the Marchbanks kids, and maybe one day he'd come home and find out my secrets.

I pushed the thought away.

"I don't know anything," she said. In the same tone she might have given me her name and rank and serial number if she was a soldier.

"Why is your ex after Diana Keene?" I asked. "What's this video everyone wants?"

"I don't know anything."

"Last night I met a man in black, he likes to offer people whatever it is they want most in the world. Who is he and why is he involved? Does he work with your husband?"

She just stared.

"Well, Holly?" I asked.

"I have one piece of advice for you," she said, her gaze direct. "Leave town. Forget helping Diana Keene, because if she truly understood her situation, she wouldn't want your help. Walk out of here and forget what happened last night. You'll be exonerated in the death of the Russian; it was self-defense. You have witnesses. But forget everything else. Or he'll obliterate you. You can't even imagine how far he'll go to ruin you."

"Who is he?"

"If I answer your questions, he'll kill me. Rule number one."

Time to try a different approach. "I'm deeply curious as to why a person like yourself is involved in activities best left to street thugs."

"A person like me."

"Who has everything." I gestured at the grand kitchen and beyond, the stunning house filled with photos of her beautiful, bright children.

"Everything." Holly shook her head. "Yes, I have *everything*. I earned it."

I'd worked undercover jobs for three years for the CIA, playing people who only existed on paper: money launderers, arms buyers, smugglers. I normally was thoroughly briefed on the people I had to deal with, had to question, had to capture. Here I flew blind. I couldn't see how the fragments of the puzzle fit together.

"So I guess you're not going to kill me," she said.

"You're going to tell me who I'm up against."

"When your bank accounts are gone, when your reputation has been destroyed, when the innocent people you love have been ruined and they don't even know why, remember that I warned you." She crossed her arms. "If you leave right now, I'll tell him that you're leaving town. This is your one chance."

I smiled at her; it takes guts to issue ultimatums to the person holding the gun. "Has it occurred to you this is *your* only chance?"

"You're not going to kill me," she said.

"I would rather trade information," I said.

"Why do you think I have anything more to tell you?"

"Because you have kids. Nice kids."

Her mouth trembled.

"And if this boss of yours threatens your kids to keep you in line, don't you want them someplace safe from him?"

"You assume," she said, "there's such a place. Ask her if that's true."

"Her."

"Diana. Whatever you're getting out of protecting her, it's not worth it. Give her to us, and you'll be safe."

"That doesn't seem like a fair trade. Her life for my safety."

"We don't want her dead. Last thing we want."

"You just want the video she has."

"I know nothing about that."

"Your boss—I don't know what else to call him—seemed very interested in me."

"He collects people." She let those words hang in the air. "I'm sure he'd like to add a humble bartender who can defeat a Russian Special Forces vet to his collection." She laughed and then she stopped herself.

"Collection. That includes you and your ex. And who else? Janice Keene?" I remembered Diana's words to Glenn, *You're just like my mother.* The phrase had made no sense to me. "What is this, a gang of rich people?"

Holly bit her lip, shook her head. "Yes. I've fit it in between book club and parents' association."

"You don't answer my questions, I'll take you to meet a friend of mine, and she won't be nearly as gentle as I am. Why are you all after Diana? I know she has a video. What's on it?"

For a moment she studied my face and then she saw the truth that had escaped the man in black. "You really *don't* know her," she said in a dead tone. "What sort of fool are you? You say I risk it all? You're doing it for…a stranger."

She had a point. "I'm doing it because your boss is not going to leave me alone. It's me or him. Simple. And it's not going to be me."

"Bug versus windshield."

"You were driving the car last night," I said slowly. "An accomplice. You'd lose your kids if you were convicted."

Her lips formed a circle, as though she were about to give breath to a word. As if finally meeting a moment she'd long rehearsed.

The moment the truth comes out.

"I have to do what he says. Or my kids…my kids…" She repeated the words and gave a little choked cough. "I'm going to be sick." She clutched at her stomach. She staggered toward the metal sink, leaned over it, jetted water against the steel. Made a retching noise and spat.

I stood and watched her. I kept the gun trained on her. There wasn't a weapon nearby; I still had the gun and the knife. She wiped off her face.

"I'm not telling you anything more," she said. "If you're going to kill me, then do it somewhere else. I don't want my kids thinking of their home as where their mom died." Her calm was eerie. And I didn't buy it. She was gaming me.

If interrogation fails, try searching for evidence.

I came toward her with the gun and she fought me, driving a hard punch toward my shoulder, trying to seize my throat. I wrested free of her grab and shoved her own gun hard against her temple. I pushed her to the ground. I glanced up, looking for restraints. The big walk-in pantry. I pulled her inside. Fancy metal shelves lined the walls, filled with pasta boxes and high-end olive oils and multigrain cereals. I spotted a box of trash bags, industrial strength ones, with the black plastic ties. I fastened one around her wrists and pulled it tight.

"Stay put," I said.

Holly Marchbanks gave out a raw, howling scream of rage. She leaned back and levered a kick toward my groin. I took the blow in my hip and simply shoved her back into the pantry. I bound her ankles with the plastic grips. I slammed the door shut. It was a much heavier door than usual for a kitchen pantry, but I didn't think about the implications of that and I barely got it closed as she rolled herself against the wood; I could hear the muted thump.

I hooked a chair from the kitchen island's bar with my foot and positioned it under the doorknob. She was trapped.

"Let me out!" she screamed. I wish I'd gagged her.

"Calm down," I said. "Since you won't talk, I'm just going to have a little look and see around the house."

"You can't know! You can't!"

"Know what, Holly?" I tried to keep my voice calming and smooth. "Know what?"

"He will kill us, he'll kill my kids! Please!" Her voice melted into a harsh scream. "He'll kill the kids, he'll kill me, he'll kill you. You can't hide. Please."

"What's the man's name?"

Silence.

"I can help you. Does this video Diana have, does it expose his crimes? He can't kill anyone—you, me, her, your kids—if he's in custody."

Her laugh on the other side of the door sounded jagged. "Of course he could. He can do anything. If you are protecting this woman, it's a death sentence. He doesn't want her dead, but that won't apply to you."

"Tell me what I want to know and I'll go," I said.

"No," she groaned, with all the pain of a world ending. "Nooooooo."

She fell silent as I left the door and began to search the house.

20

Friday, November 5, morning

Rₒ𝐆ₑᵣ ₛₗₑₚₜ—out late disposing of Glenn's body in the bay—and Belias sat at the kitchen table. His laptop was open, the screen showing an interface to a cellular phone company. Someone in his network had been given access to a service-testing application, and he'd turned that into a way to eavesdrop on specific conversations. He wished he'd had this in the old days back in London and Moscow; life would have been easier. He turned up the volume on the earphones so he could hear the conversation. He was quite sure the FBI would be interested in some of the comments being said in Russian. His Russian was rusty but good enough.

He heard the words *Sam Capra*. He'd heard Sam described as the bar's owner, not just the bartender, on the news this morning. The Rostovs in New York, the family of the dead brothers, knew Sam's name, too.

The Russians discussed travel plans for two more minutes, then hung up.

Belias closed his eyes.

The Rostovs were coming to kill Sam Capra.

Even if the two Rostov brothers had been kicked out of New York and banished to the West, they were still family. Vengeance was a blood affair best carried out by relatives. A cousin named Viktor would be dispatched to San Francisco. Belias could monitor the airline reservations databases and see what flights Viktor Rostov would be boarding.

Belias wondered what Sam would do if he called and said, *I'd like for us to be friends. A man named Viktor Rostov is coming to kill you. I can make sure he never hurts you.*

Would Sam want to make a deal with him then? Was safety his price? He had not been so intrigued by a potential recruit since...well, since the project that Janice Keene was even now protecting for him. Sam could be a game changer. He had heard his name and spent the last hour seeing what the Internet could tell him about Sam Capra. It wasn't much; it was enough to intrigue.

Sam Capra was the son of Episcopal relief workers who roamed the world. He'd been an English and history double major at Harvard. He'd had an older brother who was one of the unfortunates murdered on video by Islamic extremists in Afghanistan, a do-gooder killed as a political shock statement. Sam Capra's name was tied to his brother; he'd given a couple of cable news channel interviews about his brother's death, and then he'd fallen off the media map. Cracking the job placement database at Harvard indicated Sam Capra had taken a job straight out of school for a consulting firm in London called CVX.

The hairs rose on the back of Belias's neck when he found CVX no longer existed. The building CVX was housed in was badly damaged in a London bombing blamed on extremists, and apparently the company had gone under.

A murdered brother? A bombing? What a rich life Sam had led so far for a man in his midtwenties. And now Sam was a bar owner who could take on a former Special Forces soldier and had the cool nerve to come to his victim's house to find out more about him.

You are something secret, Sam, Belias thought. *CIA, maybe, or NSA or Defense Intelligence. I can smell it on you. But not anymore. They're done with you, or you're done with them.*

I could use you.

Especially since Glenn might have gotten other people to decide the network doesn't need me anymore. The possibilities almost made Belias dizzy.

Ten minutes later he got an e-mail ping alerting him that Viktor Rostov was booked on flights from New York to San Francisco, with a connection in Denver.

Denver.

Belias reached for his phone.

21

Friday, November 5, morning

I WENT UP THE STAIRS of one of the stone turrets of the house. Passed a bedroom that clearly belonged to Emma—surprisingly pinkish door but walls decorated with posters of champion athletes, all women, from soccer, tennis, and basketball. One large photo was Emma with her dad, a better, more honest picture than the one downstairs. I studied Glenn's face. Glenn Marchbanks was tall, built solid like a former soldier, salt-and-pepper hair, a strong nose, a jutting jaw. *Mr. Business Deal*, I thought. *Mr. Kidnapper. Mr. Guy Who Was Going to Shoot Me Point-Blank.*

Peter's room was full of Star Wars toys, as though the floor were the battlefield of the films. A Spider-Man bedspread, a Superman poster. Heroes. There were no pictures of his father in here, and I remembered the pain in Peter's voice when Emma mentioned the divorce. Of course he'd taken it hard. Every kid does.

The other rooms were guest rooms. Tidy and empty of any sign of recent use. One in the back corner of the house appeared to be Nana's. An e-reader and a stack of celebrity magazines lay on her bedside table. One wall was covered with photos of Holly, Emma, and Peter. Holly smiled in every photo, but she still somehow managed to look pained.

The master bedroom was huge. The large bed was unmade, but clearly only one side had been slept on. There were very few personal possessions out other than yet more photos of the Marchbanks children, their mother's hands on their shoulders, standing over them like a sentinel. A shield.

It was as if they had to keep their happiness on constant display. Look at us. Behold a perfect life.

Not perfect at all. A life out of joint, the pain hidden.

I checked the bedside tables. On one side table I found a stack of recent hardcover fiction; a bottle of cough medicine; a notebook she used to track her eating, exercise, and sleep. So ordinary.

The closet was huge and half-empty, and I wondered how long it had been since Glenn Marchbanks moved out. His side of the closet looked forlorn in its vacancy, and I thought it must have been an unpleasant reminder each morning for Holly. Maybe she liked unpleasant reminders. Maybe it was like a hair shirt on her heart.

I searched through Holly's closet. I wanted something, anything, that could lead me back to this boss of hers or give me a clue as to why the Marchbanks were being complicit in crimes. It had to be blackmail, some hold that the man in black had on them.

But blackmail at what level? Holly Marchbanks fought like an experienced operative and so had her ex-husband. Did a black-mailer train his victims? Not likely. Their skills implied continuing work, not a onetime job to win their children's safety. So where had they learned to fight? What was their past?

I hurried but was thorough, and in checking one of Holly's jew-elry boxes I found it: a silver necklace with a symbol on it that matched the one I'd seen on Glenn. Maybe Holly and Glenn had these as cute matching jewelry when they were married, but they weren't married now so why would he wear it?

And the man in black had worn the same ring, a symbol of spaces and lines.

I pocketed the necklace.

I didn't find anything else of interest until, beneath a bureau that had been awkwardly pushed into a corner—it was on wheels—I groped and found a loose slip of carpet. I wheeled the old bureau out of the way and lifted the carpet along its edge.

Embedded in the concrete was a floor safe. The kind, I thought, that was mostly designed for the really good family jewelry. High-end. I studied it for a moment. The keypad's keys were white plastic.

I went to Holly's bathroom and started digging through her makeup. I found some dark eye shadow. Here's how you improvise. I carefully and slowly dusted the keypad with the powder. On four of the keys, the powder bonded to the grease left over from a fingerprint. The numbers were two, four, six, and nine. That meant twenty-four possible key combinations.

Most combinations are chosen to be meaningful and easy to remember. I could just start entering and work my way through the possible twenty-four passwords, but with some safes you enter enough bad combinations, either the keypad shuts down for a period of time or an alarm can sound. I didn't want that.

I went back into the bedroom. Searched along the shelves. I knocked down sweaters, shoe boxes, a wedding album with GLENN & HOLLY MARCHBANKS stenciled in gold along the leather front. The wedding date wasn't a matching combo of the safe's numbers.

I walked past the kids' rooms and back downstairs.

"Holly," I said, my mouth close to the pantry door.

"What?"

"What's the combination for the safe?"

"I don't know."

"Come on."

"It's Glenn's safe. He left it here when he left me. Couldn't exactly take it with him. I have no idea what's inside."

"I know the four numbers. Just not the order. Now, I can stick your mother in there with you the moment she gets back. I could still be here trying combinations when your kids get home. Might be hard to explain to Emma and Peter."

"Glenn kept it. I don't know the combo."

"Holly, stop lying. The numbers are two, four, six, and nine. What's the correct order?"

She took a long enough pause where I believed she might be trying to remember. "No."

I left her, and she didn't call out to see if I was listening to her on the other side of the door. I started exploring the house, looking for something that would reveal the meaning of the numbers.

At the end of one hall was a study. It was simple and masculine, the desk heavy and plain, adorned only with a laptop and a few file folders. The window boasted a spectacular view of the Golden Gate Bridge. The bricked walls were covered with framed magazine articles, often cover stories, featuring photos of Glenn Marchbanks, looking serious and smart in a suit. A few of Peter's train toys were scattered around the floor; he spent time playing in this room, with photos of his dad watching over him. Glenn's old study, I guessed, but not repurposed yet by his ex-wife. What did it say about him that he'd left this behind and her that she'd allowed him to leave this tribute to himself?

Maybe she was still in love with him. They were, after all, still committing crimes together. Bonnie and Clyde from the rich part of town.

I stopped to scan the articles. And read them with a rising sense of dismay.

Glenn Marchbanks was a venture capitalist with a respected Silicon Valley firm. He'd been an original investor in three of the biggest technology companies of the past decade. Lauded in the fawning business press as a man savvy enough to see exactly where the next hot tech trend would rise and to back the winning company. That was where I'd heard his name; I must have read it in a business article in the past few years.

And more pictures of his family. I noticed a photo of Glenn with a Super Bowl–winning quarterback. It was the top photo in an arrangement of them on the wall, and above the picture's frame, I noticed a series of scars cut into the room's molding.

Someone had taken a knife to the wood and slashed eight savage notches into the clean white molding.

Eight. Eight what? Why would you mar the room? I wondered.

Like a prisoner chalking his days on the jail wall.

But no jail was ever this nice, no cage this gilded.

I sat at the desk. I picked up her cell phone, scanned the numbers. It appeared to be calls to other moms and to stores and her kids' school. She wouldn't use her own phone for mischief like last night. There was a paper planner on the desk, a fancy leather Filofax. Electric pink, so I guessed it was Holly's; she must use this as an office for herself, even though she was surrounded by reminders of her husband's glories.

I flipped through her calendar pages. Holly kept a busy schedule supporting her kids' numerous extracurricular activities, lunching with friends, volunteering that put her close to the powerful not just in San Francisco but the entire West Coast. I went to last night's entry. *Glenn: dinner with Peter* was crossed out in a red-inked slash of annoyance. Glenn had plans with his kid that he had canceled. Maybe at the last minute. I went back downstairs; I hit the answering machine.

"You have no new messages, nine old messages..." the machine intoned.

"What are you doing?" Holly called through the closed door.

The messages began to play. A boy calling for Peter, wanting to set up times to play a new video game. A girl calling for Emma to invite her to a movie this weekend. Other moms and friends calling for Holly, someone calling for Holly's mother, Sharon, to let her know a prescription was filled and ready for pickup. Then the final message, a man's voice, "Hi, Holly. It's me. I have to cancel dinner with Peter tonight, and I'm so sorry, but it cannot be avoided. Duty calls. It calls us both. I'm going to need your help and now." Glenn Marchbanks cleared his throat. "Give him my best and tell him I'm sorry and call me back immediately so we can meet—"

And then Holly Marchbanks had picked up the phone. The recorder kept going.

"You cannot cancel on him."

"I have to."

"No, Glenn."

"I. Have. To." As if the words were going to nudge her, prod her, make her understand.

"You can't."

"I have to. It's for Belias. He wants you, too."

"What? No."

"He needs us both…"

Then a voice booming, "Mom!" Emma calling for her, panicky about something. Holly's voice hushed to a whisper. "I'll call you back."

She hung up the phone then. She must have forgotten to erase the message before she called her ex back. Maybe she and Glenn had to move with urgency. Pick up the Russian thug, find and capture Diana.

I went back to the pantry door again. "Holly?"

Ten beats of silence. "What?"

"Who is Belias?"

Five beats of silence. "I don't know that name."

"Wears black? Has a funky silver ring? I think he's the man who called me last night. I think he's the guy who scares you."

I heard a low clicking sound, punctuated by the soft knocking of something against the heavy cypress of the pantry door.

Holly Marchbanks was pounding her head against the door. She wasn't going to answer me.

I went back to her pink Filofax planner, to the beginning of the year.

Two-four-six-nine.

Two might mean February. Nothing of note in February on the fourth, sixth, or ninth. I jumped to the fourth month, April. April 9. Emma's birthday: 4-9. I skittered ahead to the sixth month, June, and looked at the remaining number for a date, the second. June 2 was Peter's birthday: 6-2.

Emma was older. I would try 4-9-6-2 as a combination.

I went back upstairs. I punched the Marchbanks children's birth-days into the keypad, Emma's first: 4-9-6-2.

The electronic display gave off a satisfying click. Then a long second beep. Odd.

The screen read: ENTER SECONDARY CODE IN TEN SECONDS.

I had a second code to enter. No other numbers on the keypad showed fingerprint traces, so it must be the same four in a different sequence. Or the same sequence, perhaps, because that would be unexpected. Which?

Five seconds left.

I reentered the first code in reverse, not knowing what else to do. I'd have to sort out what was the most likely combination or find a way to force Holly to tell me.

The screen went blank, then read, DESTRUCT IN PROGRESS.

I knelt and put my ear against the safe's door. And jerked my head back. The heavy metal was getting warm.

I let a few minutes pass. I tested my fingers against the metal. Hot now. I could smell crisping papers, the sour-on-your-tongue sharpness of incinerating plastic.

I'd heard of fire safes, but this was the opposite: fire burning inside the safe.

Not at all what I was expecting in this lovely quiet suburban home, the grand dream made real.

Who were these people?

I knelt, listening to the answers burn.

22

Friday, November 5, morning

Denver

THE CELL PHONE RANG, and instead of a name and a number for the caller, the screen showed a symbol.

Barton Craig glanced up to make sure his office door was closed and answered the phone. Listened, watching the Denver skyline from his corner office. Then he hung up and went out to his assistant's desk.

"Please clear my schedule for today," Barton Craig said.

His assistant glanced up at him. "Is everything okay?"

"I need to go deal with one of my kids."

"Um, okay. You've got a meeting with the marketing team and also a phone conference with a supplier in Korea."

"Reschedule for Monday." And Barton thought, *And if I'm dead, then don't reschedule at all.* He went back into his office, and behind the framed painting his children had done for him—a watercolor nightmare he'd insisted on hanging so anyone who came to his company could see how much his family mattered to him—he opened up a safe. Inside he took out an ID and a credit card that were in a name other than his and closed the safe. He walked out of his office and down to the parking garage.

At his car, he took out a small suitcase he kept packed in case of emergencies. Next to the package in the trunk was an umbrella. He inspected it for one moment and then he put it back in the trunk. He pulled out a small silver chain, holding a charm that had the same symbol that had appeared on his phone. He put on the chain, loosened his tie, slipped it under his shirt. It was like putting on armor for a knight, he thought, or a badge for a cop. It was time to get to work.

He stopped, and at an Internet café he booked a ticket for a flight from Denver to Los Angeles in the name of the false ID. He returned to his car and drove home. His wife was at the fitness club; his children were in a private school. Barton Craig had grown up in a far rougher neighborhood. He still felt a rush of accomplishment every time he walked into his own house. In a back corner of his bedroom, he opened up a box hidden in a back corner shelf. Inside the box he found a small box of gel caps. He took them and slipped three into a separate bottle that had once held vitamin D supplements.

He didn't have much time. He hurried down to his car.

He had a flight to meet.

23

Friday, November 5, morning

I WALKED BACK DOWNSTAIRS. I could spend the hours before Holly's mother returned tearing apart the house. But I thought it would be a waste of time. You didn't keep your dark, interesting secrets lying about if you had a vault with a self-destruct mechanism. It sort of defeated the purpose.

I thought about the Marchbanks. Highly successful. Perfect family. Big dream house. And inside, weapons, secrets, lies. I thought of the little lies that had been in my own home. My brother, who I loved dearly but wasn't quite as perfect as he seemed to the world. My father, mercurial, who didn't always live up to his own high standards. My mother, the doctor, who worried more about the children of strangers than her own. My foster siblings around the world who kept their own secrets and their distance and watched the Capra family move off to another country to help a different set of people, leaving them behind. Everyone thought the Capras were such a good family. Noble. Kind. But our fault lines were just less obvious. Like the Marchbanks.

I went back to the pantry door and knocked.

"Holly?"

"What?"

"You keep saying you are being coerced because of your kids. Tell me what is going on and I'll protect them." Mila, I thought, would agree with me making this offer.

"I don't believe you."

I took the chair away from being wedged against the knob. I couldn't reason with her through a door. I twisted the knob. It wouldn't budge.

Who puts a lock on a pantry door? From the inside? There was no sign of the lock on the outside knob.

On the other side, I heard a soft laugh. "Not very smart of you to stick me in one of our panic rooms. You can't get to me now, but I can get to you."

Then I heard the patio door opening.

Holly had somehow summoned help.

I turned the corner from the kitchen to the back den that faced the patio. I held the Glock I'd taken from Holly.

Him. Standing in the doorway on the other side of the long living room. The man in black. He held a gun with his unusually pale fingers. Aimed at me.

"Hello, Sam."

He knew my name.

Stalemate if no one shoots. But I'd now been surprised by him twice. I wasn't going to surrender control again.

"Hello, Belias," I said as I raised the gun and fired. He dove behind the heavy brocaded sofa, me retreating into the kitchen. As I stepped back I saw another man, muscled and bald, entering the den from the patio. Also armed.

I had no idea how many backups he had with him. And I'd learned what I could from the talented Mrs. Marchbanks.

I ran. My new life—the several weeks of traveling to my bars around the world and eating New Orleans food and playing with my infant son—had left me rusty and thoughtless. She'd been perfectly safe in there, free to cut her bonds loose, call reinforcements, and she'd played me for a fool.

A bullet socked into the doorframe, maybe four inches above my shoulder as I went through it into the dining room. Belias, unlike Holly, was giving chase.

I skidded across the table back first, knocking down a bowl of decorative golden apples, firing back at him twice. I saw the wood right by his chest splinter when he showed himself. I'd almost hit him.

Squeezed the trigger again; the magazine was empty of rounds. Thanks, Holly. She must not have reloaded after practicing.

I rolled off the table, onto the floor.

I heard a spray of bullets from behind me, and when the gunfire ceased, I heard the tinkling of a broken chandelier, glass tears weeping and shattering on the floor. The bullets hadn't been aimed directly at me; the shots were designed to pin me down.

He wanted me alive. To talk.

The closest exit was the front door. And the front was on the entirely opposite side of the house from the back driveway and my car. I'd have to circle the house, running in front of windows, a clear target.

Across the dining room floor, with the heavy table's ornate chairs between me and him, I saw Belias's nice shoes. He didn't know my gun was empty. Right? Where was his partner? Probably getting Holly. Three against one.

Belias stepped back behind the wall.

"Sam," he called. "This fighting is senseless. We should talk."

"Belias, what should we talk about?"

"Your future."

I heard the pantry door opening, him calling back, softly garbled, to Holly. And I had to presume she was armed again.

Belias said, "I've been studying you. Fascinating how there are these gaps in your past. After Harvard, after your brother was slaughtered. What could you have done with yourself? I don't think you went to bartending school."

A chill prickled my skin. He couldn't find out about Daniel and Leonie.

"So you've decided to take Diana under your wing. This is a very poor decision. Because you will lose, and Sam, you're so not a loser. You are a winner, and I only deal with winners. Come out and we'll talk. We won't harm you."

If he winged me, I was at his mercy, and I figured that was exactly what he wanted.

"Sam. Every person has his price. I want to know yours. What is it you want most? Because, believe me, I can give it to you."

Part of me wondered if there could be any truth to this claim. Look at the home of the Marchbanks. Look at Glenn's runaway success. But how could it be managed?

"We know who you are, Sam," he said. "And unfortunately so do the Rostovs. They have a man headed to San Francisco to kill you. I am going to protect you. As a sign of good faith. So stop shooting at me, please."

My chance was the stairs. If I could get upstairs, I could get out. Too many of them down here, too many wide-open spaces where they could corner me. Upstairs was more likely hallways and smaller rooms and windows that led to the roof.

Or I could trap myself. But I didn't have a chance with all three of them gunning for me across the lawn.

"Now, you could have brought the police here; you didn't. So you're not interested in law, per se," Belias said. "Diana needs to know it's all going to be okay. I'll need you to tell her that. I can give you everything. I can give Diana everything. She just doesn't know it. But she doesn't want her mother hurt, neither do I. I know you can convince her we can all work together."

I had a whole different motive, but Belias was thinking that my police allergy was out of loyalty to Diana. He must know she didn't want the cops involved. So he thought her reason was my reason.

"You want to become the biggest celebrity bar owner in the world—book deals, reality TV show, grosses in the millions, playing host to the rich and powerful? I can help make it happen. You just have to do a few favors for me now and then. And I think you could do them brilliantly."

He was insane. Wasn't he? What had he promised to the Marchbankses? The house around me was proof he could deliver.

"I could build you up, Sam. Build you up as high as Holly and Glenn. Make the world easier for you. Predictable, all in a good way. You just reek of potential. But sometimes"—he took a deep breath, almost of regret—"you have to break something before you build it. I would prefer not to break you too badly."

"Something's getting broken; it's not me." Where was the bald guy who'd followed Belias into the den? I had to be ready for him to charge me from the foyer. But no sound, no indication he was there. He might be Belias's bodyguard. He might stick close to the boss. Which would give me a chance.

"We just need to make a deal," Belias said. "A pact. It's the simplest thing in the world."

He wanted me to keep talking to him, listening to his soul-selling babble. So do the unexpected.

"Fine, let's deal," I said as I stood and swung a chair and flung it, with all my strength, at the open doorway where Belias lurked, half-seen, just as he stepped forward to talk again.

I turned, hearing the crash of the chair into the doorway and hopefully into him.

"This is an unfortunate choice, Sam!" Belias yelled at me.

I stormed for the stairs instead of the front door. As I reached the mezzanine at the top of the curving stair, I glanced down and saw him, hurrying toward the front door. Followed by Holly. She held a fresh gun. They thought I bolted the house.

What a good, prepared mom. But where was the bald guy?

I knew once the front door was checked they'd see I hadn't gone for the obvious route of escape across the yard. Probably one would head across the front yard, to be doubly sure, and the other would run back into the house to check the other exits.

Upstairs led to a long hallway. I hurried past the shut doors. I had to find a room that exited onto the less-steep section of the slate roof. I could let the three disperse across the lawn, scale down the side, take out whoever was closest to me, and run…

Behind me I heard a door open.

"Clever lad, you," the bald man said. "You did what I would have done." He stepped out into the hallway. No gun in hand, which surprised me.

I raised the gun.

"It's empty," he said. "Holly counted your shots and told me when I let her out of the panic room." His accent was English. I'm not good enough to know which area he came from, but it wasn't

London. He was bigger than me, taller and wider, but also ten years older. It remained to be seen which of us would fight dirtier. Don't bet against me.

"Maybe Holly's bad at math." I kept the gun centered on his chest.

"If I'm wrong, shoot me."

I lowered the gun. He knew his stuff. I hate people like him.

"My partner wants to talk to you."

"I don't think I'm interested in his offer."

"He wants to talk…but I find talking is overrated." He took a step toward me. "Now, I don't think his honeyed words are going to sway a lad like you. I think what sways a lad like you is knowing who's the boss. And it's not you."

"It's not me," I agreed.

"Diana. Where is she, Sam? I'm going to ask once and then I'm going to hurt you a bit. Then I'll ask again, and if you don't tell, I'll hurt you some more."

"Goodness," I said. "Please don't hurt me. I wouldn't like that."

"Now, I'm not going to kill you. We don't want that."

"No, we don't want that."

"The hurting, though, will be an entirely fresh experience to a snot-nosed pup like yourself."

I pretended to wipe my nose with the back of my hand.

The bald man crooked a smile at me. "I told you I'd just ask the once. That was the once." He charged at me in the hallway, hands raised, certain of the power of his fists against my smaller frame.

For a big house the hallway was a little more narrow than you'd expect. They'd given the space to the rooms. I didn't have a lot of room to dodge him so I didn't try. He slammed into me, and instead of running, letting him catch me, I took the tackle and the clubbing punch to the jaw. It hurt. But I wrapped legs around his wide back and arms around his throat. I buried my face close to his shoulder. I was a starfish. He tried to slam me back against the wall. He did once.

My fingers dug for his carotid artery, trying to grip and pinch the flesh. Cut off the fuel to his brain. He felt my fingertips probing and he growled in realization, and he tried to slam me into the wall again as my two fingers closed hard around the arterial feed. But he staggered and missed the wall and we burst through a closed door.

It was Peter's bedroom. The pile of action figures I'd noticed before lay on the floor, Star Wars and Star Trek characters and superheroes, mute witnesses to battle. We landed on Peter's bed, with the Spider-Man covers. The bald man tried to pull free from me. I punched a fist into his face, once, twice, felt his lip tear against his teeth. I let him go because I didn't want to be barnacled to him if Belias or Holly raced into the room and opened fire. They had to have heard the ruckus by now.

The bald man launched a series of sharp, sudden blows at me: face, solar plexus, throat. I blocked them and surprise creased his face. But when I threw a second blow, he dodged and powered a hard fist against my shoulder, and I landed by the action figures. I grabbed one, a bald superhero with green skin and a blue cape. But made of hard plastic.

You can do a lot of damage with a piece of hard plastic.

I jabbed it forward, like a dagger, and the superhero's head caught the bald man close to his Adam's apple. His face purpled with shock and pain. He clawed up at his throat, and where the tears tried to leak from his eyes, I stabbed with the action figure, left eye, right eye. He howled in rage, levering up an arm to protect his face. I pressed forward and then he shot a kick into my gut that sent me stumbling. I dropped my superhero, desperate to find another weapon.

He fell back against the wall, and then he grabbed a corkboard from above Peter's bed and drove me back across the room with it. The metal edge of the board caught my throat and I hit the wall. Pain rocked my neck; he aimed just a bit low, catching more collarbone than larynx. But he couldn't see so well after the blows to his eyes, and he pressed on the opposite side of the corkboard, not realizing he wasn't crushing my throat.

I popped a fist through the cork, upending Peter's perfect attendance certificate and his crayoned drawings of family. I hooked a thumb toward the bald man's eye. He yanked his head back and eased up the pressure. I grabbed what was closest—a small Superman desk lamp—and heaved it into the side of his head. Superman shattered against his temple and he retreated one step, and then I spun and hammered a thundering kick into the bald man's chest.

He went out Peter's window with a shattering crash.

I glanced behind me. Holly in the doorway, gun raised, staring at the wreckage of her child's room.

Our gaze met. She fired, her hand wavering. The bullet hissed past me and hit a Han Solo poster, and I was out the window.

The slate roof was steep here, and as I slid toward the bald man, I saw he'd managed an unsteady grip on the tiles. I slid toward him and kicked him again in the face, and he went loose, clambering for a grip as he slid toward the edge.

I was more nimble. I got to my feet and ran past the windows before Holly could shoot me.

I heard a muffled cry from the bald man. Maybe he'd gone over the edge. I didn't look back.

I skittered to the other side of the roof with care, because the slate roof canted at a steep pitch. If I slipped and fell, I might well be dead, and if the fall didn't kill me, then I'd be hurt and at their mercy. Belias and his bald partner would love that and the thought chilled me. I'd trained as a parkour runner—vaulting walls, running on edges, leaping—and my sense of balance was strong.

I could hear the bald man grunting, crying out for someone to get him a ladder.

I studied the drop—two stories, the side wall broken only by a pair of window ledges, and then another wider window, then a row of prickly hedges. I eased myself off the roof without hesitation. First lesson of parkour was how to fall, and there I'd had plenty of practice. In my head a clock ticked the seconds away.

My finger and toe tips caught the edge of the upper-story windowsill as I slid. It was not a silent descent. I held for just a moment—

Six.

—until I could see and shift slightly, aiming my feet at the first-floor edging of brick about the lower window.

Five.

My left foot hit the window with the skill for which I am rightly famed. My right foot missed.

Four.

I tottered out into space, not even trying now to balance—I knew it was wasted effort; I aimed for the shrubs, trying to hit them to spread the energy of the fall.

Three.

I smashed down into the shrubs, a bright pain slicing along my ear. I rolled parkour-style to the soft green lawn, spreading the impact and energy from the fall from right shoulder across my back to the left hip to buttocks and my leg. Momentum carried me up onto the balls of my feet and I started to run.

Two.

The bullet impacted the window above me, a thump in the morning quiet. The glass was bulletproof. A momentary advantage for me.

I ran. I didn't do parkour so much anymore, but I still was fast and I tore the opposite direction, heading the long way around the wings of the storybook house. I saw a line of tall, narrow pines along the edge of the Marchbankses' property. I glanced back. The bald man was at the edge of the roof, laying flat above the gutter, pressing himself to the roof, trying to slide his way back toward the broken window.

I didn't see Holly or Belias.

I glided up the greenery, thrust myself over the fence as the top of the branches above me exploded in a burst.

A bullet hit me.

I felt the projectile slam—ricocheting off a trunk or branch—and skim against the tender back of my neck. Hot finger between collar and skin. I fell, back onto the Marchbankses' property, and I clambered to my feet and bolted down along the stone fence. I had to get out of the angle of the shot first and hope they weren't each closing in on me, catching me between them.

I guessed Holly Marchbanks's worst nightmare was being exposed to her neighbors as a gun-wielding socialite/homeroom mother. If I was heading for a neighbor, they'd be desperate to cut me down before I could speak.

I ran a long, hard straight run, hoping no bullet found me, doing a *saut de chat* over the river-rock fence, hands vaulting me over the rock, legs pulled in tight against chest, landing on my feet and running down across the back neighbor's yard to my car.

The final shot, as had been the bald man's crash through the window, was audible; if any of the neighbors were at home, the police would surely be summoned. How would Holly explain that to her mother and the kids? *Mommy tried to kill the intruder, kids; go watch some cartoons while I clean up the mess in your room.*

I glanced at myself in the rearview mirror. Blood touched the collar of my shirt, dirt smeared my face. I pulled along the turning streets, turning and turning, no idea if I was heading back to the main street. Finally I exited at the bottom of the hill, drove back toward the highway. I went past the Tiburon police station, no cars blasting out of the lot.

Maybe no neighbors at home? No one to hear the noise of battle. Maybe it hadn't been as loud as I thought.

I got back onto the highway, thinking, *Just get back to the bar*, but I could feel the blood pulsing along my collar. My driving grew unsteady, and behind me I saw a highway patrol car. I couldn't risk being pulled over and seen as injured. I jabbed the phone.

"Yes?" Felix.

"I need you now; bring a medical kit. And a change of clothes for me. A suit."

"Where are you?" His voice was calm and steady.

"Sausalito." I took the exit, headed toward the harbor, turning into a section of piers, driving past an armada of colorfully painted boats. I gave my location to Felix.

I found a spot to park, a narrow stretch of road next to the water, a line of houseboats along a pier. And on one of the boats an older man watched me park, watched me not get out of my car. I put the phone to my ear and after a moment he turned away.

Hurry, Felix, I thought.

24

Friday, November 5, morning

THE MAN ON THE BOAT sipped coffee and watched me. I stayed on the phone. To a point, a cell phone against your ear is a camouflage; you can stop anywhere to make a phone call. I poked at the injury on the back of my neck. The wound wasn't deep. A thick splinter of pine pierced my flesh like a thorn. I eased it free.

My arteries didn't empty, but it was a messy wound and I clamped my hand over it. My breathing steadied. I'd gone about this the wrong way. Felix had been right. I kept the phone up to my ear and after a bit the man on the boat went inside.

I thought of Peter Marchbanks's room, a child's haven turned into a battleground, the shocked look on Holly's face. As though she hadn't ever expected the secrets and the violence of her hidden life to come and invade her child's space.

I thought of Daniel. I closed my eyes and kept the cell phone by my ear and thought of my son and him having a room full of superhero toys and drawings he'd made for me, and I would keep that room safe and untouched.

Felix arrived twenty minutes later, parallel parking a van in front of me on the narrow road. I got out of the rental and eased into the back of the van.

He shut the doors and hung a battery-operated light on a wire. He opened a first aid kit. I stripped off my shirt. Felix inspected my neck and began to clean the wound with antiseptic.

"This looks worse than it is. A bit deep but only requires four stitches."

"Can you handle?"

"I'm trained as a field medic. That's a Jimmy and Mila requirement." I could feel the cold comfort of Felix cleaning the wound: the antiseptic, then a chilling swab of local anesthetic. "So did you find our young woman?"

"I learned Glenn Marchbanks is not your typical venture capitalist and his wife is a cross between a soccer mom and an assassin. As a plus, I was offered the world in exchange for joining them."

I explained. Felix finished stitching my skin and covered it with a bandage.

"Like Faust," he said when he was done. I started wiping all the blood and the cleanser off me. My hands felt steady and I sipped from a bottle of water.

"Faust?"

"Did you not get an education wandering the world, Sam? Faust. Star of poems and operas and novels. The brilliant but insanely ambitious man who wanted to know everything, so he sold his soul to the devil. Twenty years of bliss and complete knowledge in exchange for an eternity in hell."

I remembered the story now. "This isn't the same. It can't be."

"He offered you a similar deal, right? You said he calls himself Belias. That's an old term for a devil. I'm guessing it's not his real name. Look at the people he controls. One of the most powerful VCs in the country, a man who could break promising companies with a snap of his fingers. A man who if he backs you can make you a fortune. And then there's Janice."

I'd started an Internet search on the word *Belias* on the smartphone and Felix was right. I looked up at him.

"Janice and I never talked much about her business. We talked about being sick and how to cope with it. She'd made reference to being a CEO, but I didn't ask how big her business was," Felix said. "So I looked her up online. She is the sole owner of one of the most respected and influential public relations firms in the country.

Strong ties to lobbyists, to leaders of industry, to celebrities. People beg to become her clients. She can help make or break a celebrity, a brand, a product launch, a proposed law."

I finished drinking the water and swallowed some ibuprofen.

"Maybe Janice and Diana didn't find out something bad about Glenn." I put down the phone. "Maybe Janice is like the Marchbankses—under Belias's thumb."

Felix began to put up his medic's kit. "Janice struck me as a very capable, confident woman. Why would she need someone like Belias?"

"Maybe she wasn't always so confident, so capable. Glenn Marchbanks is one of the kings of investment here, and he needs Belias."

"You think the Marchbankses and Janice made a deal like Faust. Success in exchange for helping Belias with his crimes? And what crimes would those be?"

"Kidnapping at least. And Holly would have killed me. So maybe murder."

"That's just…" Felix didn't finish.

"Diana said no police in the middle of an attempted kidnapping. She must know now her mother is involved with Belias. Maybe this video they want is a confession. She's sick; she might want to wrap up her affairs…or warn her daughter. If Diana goes to the police…"

"…Her mother could face criminal charges," Felix finished for me. "She's running and trying not to implicate her mom. That's brave."

I started getting dressed in the suit he'd brought for me, wincing against the pain in my neck.

Felix said, "But he *couldn't* affect their fates. He couldn't give them what the devil gave Faust."

"Not their fates. Their fortunes," I said.

"How?"

"Think about our lives. A series of conscious decisions, a series of chances. Maybe he puts the odds in their favor."

"How?"

"I don't know yet. Through information, through blackmail, through threat. Coercion of a subtle sort."

"But how does he even have power over anyone?"

"We find that out; maybe we find out how he does it and who he really is."

Felix bit his lip. "Janice is on an extended leave, according to her office."

"So we have to assume that Diana will keep hiding from Belias and keep looking for her mother. We need to find them. Now." My hand touched my pocket. "Oh. This." I held up the necklace I'd taken from Holly's closet. "This matches the ring Belias wore last night. Does this symbol mean anything to you?"

"It looks like a building," I said. "With a window. A house of sticks."

"I've seen it before," Felix said slowly. "But can't place it. Never mind symbols. We should head back to the Marchbanks house, guns blazing, and put these jerks down."

"No, you were right this morning. We find Diana. Her safety has to be the priority."

"But…"

"We have zero idea what resources Belias has." I shook my head.

"Let's say he does own the Marchbanks and Janice Keene. Do you think he stopped at three people?"

Felix started to speak and then fell silent.

"I went in blind, that was a mistake. I don't make mistakes twice." I pulled on a shirt and began to button it. "Your initial strategy was correct, Felix, and I should have listened to you. We find Diana, we find what he wants. She stole something of his. Something that can expose him. The only reason she's not using it is because of her mom. If we can protect them both, then she'll give us the information. Simple."

"Not so simple," Felix said. "You'll have to convince her that you won't turn in her mom."

"Belias will be expecting me to come after him," I said. "Because he already thinks I'm protecting Diana. So let's do the unexpected. Let's find Diana Keene. Have you been to Janice's house before?"

"No, but I know where it is. I doubt Diana is hiding there."

"But maybe we can find where she is hiding. The Marchbanks had a safe full of secrets. Maybe Janice has the same." From my pocket I pulled the symbol necklace I'd stolen from Holly. "And this. This means something. I need to find out what."

25

Friday, November 5, morning

HOLLY MARCHBANKS STOOD, shaking, aware of a hard painful knot under her foot, and then she looked down to see a broken action figure, its decapitated head under her heel. She'd bought it and several others for Peter last Christmas. He'd played with it for hours, ignoring the video games that Glenn gave him that were probably too advanced for him and the books he'd gotten from Nana. She knelt and picked up the pieces.

She'd missed. Two shots at Sam Capra—one through the window, the other as he went over the fence—and both times she'd missed. Maybe, she thought, I don't want my home to be a killing ground.

Belias had gone out on the roof and pulled Roger back inside. Roger looked beaten and both his eyes were bruised, and he huffed and breathed in what she recognized as a barely controlled fury. "He's dead when I get him. He's dead."

"No, he's not," Belias said. "Your neighbors, Holly, they might call the police." Belias didn't look at her; he looked at the distant stone wall where Sam Capra had vanished.

"Ones on the left are in Europe for two weeks. The ones on the right both work in the city. The other neighbor's house is for sale, it's vacant." She managed to pull herself together, and when she spoke again, her voice was maternal steel. "This is my son's room. His *room*. You said the trouble would never, ever come back to us. You promised…"

"The gunfire wasn't loud. Or long." Belias gestured to her. "But if the police arrive, you'll have to answer questions. You have bullet holes in the house and a broken chandelier and a shattered window. We'll have to create a plausible explanation."

Holly imagined trying to explain this to her mom or to the kids. Even if no one reported shots, Peter's room was a wreck, the chandelier downstairs was a ruin…It would be in the papers if she filed a police report, so obviously she would have to lie to the kids on that front…She must send them and Mom to stay with her aunt in Alameda until this was over. Yes. Not at Glenn's. It might be dangerous there, and she didn't want Audrey asking more questions.

"He beat you," Belias said, glancing at Roger.

"He did not. He ran." Roger's gaze flared. "But he's trained. Either CIA or another intelligence service. He went for my carotid to subdue me; that is decidedly an intel service approach. But if he's owning bars, then he's former service. He wasn't armed with a weapon he brought here."

"He's in his midtwenties. He must not have had a long record with any agency. I wonder why." Belias absently plucked at the bullet hole in Han Solo's face. "Young and maybe already a career ended due to a setback that can be blamed on others. That's who I look for."

"Who cares?" It made Holly uncomfortable to hear Belias analyzing Sam Capra, to think he might have said similar words about her and Glenn long ago. "Get out of here before the police arrive. Why are you still here?" She stayed on her knees, gathering up the broken toys, the shattered lamp. Trying not to cry.

Belias cocked his head. "I hear no approach of sirens."

Holly said, "Just go." Then she blinked. "Who's taking care of Glenn?"

"Holly. About Glenn." Belias came closer to her, and he put one of his hands—always cold—on her shoulder. He brought her to her feet. "I have terrible news. Glenn died last night, Holly. I'm sorry."

The words seemed to hang in the air before his blank face. She heard the wind in the trees, the caw of birds, and the words made no sense. The broken action figures slipped through her fingers.

"No, that can't be right."

"The head wound Sam Capra inflicted on him…it was worse than we thought. A brain hemorrhage. It was very sudden. He did not suffer."

Holly Marchbanks pressed her fist to her chest in a shuddering gasp.

"He did not suffer," Belias repeated.

She was not going to collapse in front of him. She could stop the sudden tremble in her jaw. Glenn. Gone. Her whole life with him—dating, marriage, happiness, worry, fear, danger, the children, him divorcing her when she convinced herself he still loved her and his fling with Audrey had to be temporary insanity—spun through her mind like a breath of madness. He might have left her and she didn't love him the way she had once, but he could not be…he could not be gone.

Belias and Roger watched her.

She sat slowly among the toys, picked up one, twisted it in her hands.

"It's a loss for us all," Belias said. As if he could feel grief. She wanted to slap him.

"The hospital…we should have taken him to the hospital," she managed to whisper.

"They could have done nothing. Roger did everything possible."

That was a lie. Roger knew more about fighting and shooting than helping an injured man. It had to be a lie. She thought for a second, *Kill them. Kill them, free yourself.*

But Belias now had a gun in his hand, and she didn't. She held a toy. And killing Roger was no easy feat. He'd trained her to fight, to steal, to shoot. If she tried and failed, they would kill her, and her children would have nothing.

She dropped the action figure, stood, and moved past him, back into the hallway, as if sleepwalking. Belias followed her.

"What can I do for you, Holly?"

She took a step toward her bedroom. "I just need a moment…alone. Please."

"Your grief, I get that. But time is short; we have to act now or we'll all be undone."

Her hands began to shake, but she clenched them into fists. She just wanted him to leave. But that wasn't going to happen. If he thought she was a risk now, he would kill her. For her sake, for her children's sake, she pushed the swell of grief under control.

He took her hands gently, and she forced herself not to flinch. "We say you were gone, running errands. But then forgot something and came home, were surprised, tied up, put into the pantry; you cut your bonds, heard random gunshots, escaped to find the house vandalized. And we will make that tie into Glenn's disappearing. We'll invent an enemy for him."

"Invent? Throw this Sam Capra under that bus." A bolt of anger rocked her body. The bartender. Coming into her home, going through their belongings, talking about her kids, supposedly offering her a way out of this nightmare—and the whole while, he had killed Glenn. She found herself tamping down the grief with rage. She was going to kill Sam Capra. She knew it with certainty in her heart.

It was as if she hadn't spoken. He cocked an ear against the breeze. "Still no sirens. We must keep the story simple…The police will not find his body, ever. I will arrange that." Belias's voice was soft, sympathetic, like he was a funeral director highlighting the amenities of the nicer coffins.

"His…his kids should have a grave to visit."

"And I so wish they could. Now. Sam Capra. Did you tell him my name? He knew it."

"He found a phone message from Glenn that I hadn't erased." Holly suddenly found it nearly impossible to steady her voice. Her entire world was breaking, as it had before when Glenn told her he was leaving her, snapping, crumbling to dust like ancient walls caving in during an earthquake. She told him what had happened: Audrey's visit, Sam Capra's arrival.

"I know you've had a shock, but I need you to go to Glenn and Audrey's house and clean up after him. Make sure there is nothing about me or you or any of our activities there."

"But he told me he didn't want anything about his work for you near her. He kept all that stuff in a safe here. In my closet."

He seemed to study her. As if measuring the truth of what she said. *Glenn, what have you done?* she thought. *Something else has happened.* "Do you doubt me?" she asked.

He studied her face and she almost wished that she would hear sirens in the air, so he'd leave. "No, Holly, I don't doubt you. Never give me a reason to, please."

Belias went down the hall to the safe and she followed him.

"Capra asked me for the combination. He figured out the numbers but not the right order. But there was a second code. Same numbers, different order."

Belias knelt by the keypad. "He improvised fingerprint powder. Very smart."

"He also improvised on weapons," Roger said, following them. "Which meant he was trained to fight at any moment, when a gun might not be at hand. I'm telling you that he was CIA."

Belias entered in the two codes that Holly told him, using the tip of a pencil. He opened the door and smoke and heat rose from it. Inside were ashes of paper, contorted plastic. "I wonder if this was where Glenn..." and then he stopped.

She wondered what Glenn had kept inside.

He went to the bathroom wastebasket and scooped the safe clean.

"I can't lie to the police. Can't I just clean up the mess? Send my mom and the kids away, give them a reason..."

"Holly, you don't have the luxury of grief right now. Diana and this bartender are trying to destroy *us.* Destroy *you.* He's already killed Glenn. Do you want him to take away the rest of your life? Take your children from you?"

A weird calm poured into her. "No. I understand. All right." Time later to mourn. Time later to curl up in a ball and let a part of her die.

"We can't have Audrey calling the police and asking about Glenn yet, Holly, not for a few days."

What's in a few days? she wondered. *Why then?* Belias's lips went tight and she thought, *Maybe to do with whatever Diana's mother is doing for him.* "He could go straight to the police."

"He didn't call the police before he came here. I think not. He must have a reason. That is why he is fascinating to me."

She turned on him, shoving him hard across the floor. He staggered back, shock on his face. "You…you can't think of recruiting him. He killed Glenn."

Belias raised his hand toward her, the one wearing the silver ring, and smoothed her hair with his fingertips. "I just want to draw him close to us, Holly. Then we'll get rid of him."

That was a lie. Belias could recruit Sam and she might never know. She didn't know anyone else he had recruited into the network, but there had to be more, many more, and that meant Sam Capra would live and have a good life all while Glenn moldered in a forgotten grave and the children missed him every day. *I'll kill him before I let that happen. I will kill Sam Capra.*

She could not stand to look at either man. "I'm done. I want out. I'm done."

"With Glenn dead, the debt is fully yours." He gestured at the grand house, the stone fence, the cool grass that her children rolled across, laughing. "None of this was free, Holly. You owe me, and I need you more than ever right now."

"You want me to leave my kids while their dad is dead?"

"I believe the word you are looking for is *missing*."

"Whatever! No, Belias, I won't."

"Holly. I remind you we have a deal. You don't want to dishonor our arrangement the moment the going gets tough."

Glenn is dead, she thought. *The going is well past tough.*

"Of course," she forced herself to say.

"You're the best, Holly." So much for his grief, she thought. Glenn was dead, and this sick jerk they'd sold their souls to was patting her on the head. Somehow this was worse.

"I have to go, Holly. Roger and I rely on you completely. I trust you'll be very convincing to the local police."

She looked at him through her tears. He and Roger left, and she watched them from a window. He cocked a finger at her, like it was a gun, before he turned and headed toward his car.

26

Friday, November 5, late morning

JANICE KEENE'S TOWN HOUSE occupied the top floor of an elegant building in Russian Hill, one of the toniest neighborhoods in the city. She had a marvelous view of the bay. And we were inside her town house in roughly five minutes, thanks to an electronic master keycard for the elevator and Felix's skill with a lockpick for her front door. The Round Table's resources sometimes make me uneasy. I wonder, *Who are these people?* And then I decide not to press the question, because they've always been on the side of right. That's what I tell myself.

The town house itself was magazine beautiful and tasteful. There was no sign of Diana; this was too obvious a place to hide.

In Janice's home office we found a wreck. A splintered cabinet door, the lock shattered, files spread around the floor. I knelt among the mess. I flipped and dug until I saw the logo of a cancer center on a set of papers: diagnosis, follow-ups, prescriptions to help manage the pain and the other symptoms, but no record yet of chemotherapy or surgery. "She's going untreated," I said.

"Sam," he said. "Sam." His voice sounded like ice. He'd picked up a folder I hadn't noticed as I squatted among the files.

I opened it up. Inside was a veritable dossier on Dalton Monroe. Bio, press clippings.

The Round Table member and billionaire who'd nearly been poisoned at the dinner a few nights ago. Where Mila and I had stolen the security film.

"What…what is this?" His hand shook.

"Maybe she was interested in getting him as a client."

"It can't be coincidence. She used me. *She used me.* I was at the reception. I took her as my guest. She poisoned him. She did it." Felix's face purpled in rage, in shock.

"We don't know that, Felix," I said, but my mind was insisting this was not a coincidence. *This Belias, does he know about the Round Table? Is this an attack on us—first Dalton Monroe, now me?*

Felix stood and dropped the file. "Maybe she's not even sick. Maybe she's faking her cancer. Maybe they found out I'm part of the Round Table and she got close to me as a lie. To find out more about us."

"Felix, I don't think these medical records are fake."

"They could be. It's not like we can go ask her doctor. When you worked for the CIA, didn't you have fake documentation to back up your story?"

I did but I didn't say anything to him. If Belias had aimed Janice at Dalton Monroe—if she had indeed been the one to try and hurt him—then was this something I didn't suspect, an attack on us?

"A trap, Sam. They know we exist, they want to draw us out."

"Maybe." But couldn't they then just have kidnapped Felix and interrogated him? And how would someone like Belias find out about the Round Table? Too many questions, not enough answers. So maybe what was on this video Diana had was directly related to the Round Table. Perhaps Felix was named on it and that was why Diana sought him out, even if she didn't tell him what the video was about. Perhaps she was afraid to.

Felix shook his head. "I thought…it was stupid. Stupid."

I put my hand on Felix's shoulder. "What?"

"That she and I could be a comfort to each other…if our cancers, you know…No one who's healthy understands what it's like to be sick. No one…" And then he turned away from me to look at a picture of her on the wall, with her daughter, smiling.

On the floor was a torn envelope—FOR MY DAUGHTER DIANA ONLY IN CASE OF MY DEATH. The package was torn at one end. It was empty. Whatever had been inside was what Belias wanted. Janice gone, Diana found this and opened it. It was big enough to hold a DVD or a portable drive—Belias said Diana had a video.

"Search everywhere," I said. I started to go through her desk drawers but found nothing of interest. Felix took the bedrooms.

We found nothing else in Janice Keene's town house—no hint where Diana might hide, no hint where Janice could be. Felix was broken, miserable.

I couldn't fall into the trap of guessing. The stakes were higher now. We had to find the video, not just to help Diana, but help ourselves.

I called Mila's number. But instead, a man answered with a British accent that oozed money and education.

"You must be Jimmy."

"You must be Sam. Haven't you kept us busy today?"

"How are my son and my friend?"

"Fine. Enjoying room service. I'll be sure they're protected."

"There may be a continuing threat against a Round Table member." I explained what we'd found about Dalton Monroe at Janice's house.

"Thank you for the warning. I'll take care of it."

"So this is more than a threat against a woman who just came into the bar," I said. "It's a threat against us."

"And you've uncovered this in one morning. Very good."

I thought he might be sneering at me, but then he said, "Mila thinks the world of you, you know."

"I think the same of her. She's been a good friend to me."

"Ah. Well, yes. She has her charms. So who is this man in black then, and what's he got against us?"

I felt like James Bond answering questions from M. "We're working on that." I hesitated to tell him about the morning's events at the Marchbankses' house—he might try and stop me, given the danger of exposure if I got caught.

"Mila's on her way to see you. Her plane was due to land ten minutes ago."

I welcomed the idea of her help, but not of her telling me what I could and couldn't do. And I wished she'd stuck close to Daniel and Leonie. "I'll hope to have answers for her soon."

"Take care, Sam. Be careful. And know that I will do everything to keep Daniel and Leonie safe."

"Thank you."

I hung up the phone.

"Jimmy's a good guy," Felix said. "Mila can be overcautious sometimes. Jimmy will totally back us taking the fight to Belias."

I wished I could be sure it was a fight we could win.

Technology makes our lives easier. It also makes deception easier. For example: most people use electronic calendars in the workplace. This advance has made it so much easier to fake appointments.

We headed back into the city, driving east until we got to the Embarcadero Center. Felix was silent, his mouth set in a tight frown. He parked the car in a garage in the building where Keene Global was located, and then he opened his laptop and began typing and probing the firm's electronic firewalls.

"Hey, I know you're upset. But maybe this isn't what we think…"

"She was at the party with me. I dislike being used, Sam." He tapped at the keys. Conversation over. He didn't want to talk.

After fifteen minutes, he wormed his way into Keene Global's server; they had not installed a recent software patch for a known security hole. Boom. Felix was accessing Diana's workstation, scanning and searching her e-mails and calendar appointments.

"According to an e-mail sent to all employees, she's not there today. Called in sick," he said. "So her calendar's clear. How would you like a noon appointment?"

"Perfect."

"And I have control of her e-mail account. I can e-mail the receptionist, say she'll come into the office for the noon appointment but is running late, ask to have you wait in her office."

"You're evil," I said. "I love it."

"Don't joke about evil, Sam. It exists in this world."

"I know." I watched his pained glance in the rearview mirror as he typed.

"Okay, Sam, you're in."

A top-grade public relations firm's office is all about selling the perception, so the walls were covered with photos of Janice Keene posing with prominent clients. Leaders of industry, politicians, stars. Prospective clients needed to know they were getting the best. Janice Keene was a striking woman, with a reserved smile that suggested determined intelligence. Her smile was gentle but there was a hardness to her eyes.

The receptionist (who looked like he might double as a supermodel after work) smiled and got up and led me down the hallway to an office with DIANA KEENE on the nameplate. It was small, with a narrow window of glass next to the door, presumably so everyone could peer in and reassure themselves you were working.

"Diana was out of the office this morning, sir, but she'll be here momentarily. She asked that you wait for her in her office. May I bring you coffee or tea or a soda?"

"No, thank you, I'm fine." I sat in the office's single guest chair. The receptionist, clearly unused to leaving potential clients in offices rather than conference rooms, hovered for a moment. I smiled, took out my phone, and pretended to read e-mails.

The receptionist lingered for another moment and then vanished.

I waited two minutes, then checked the hallway. Empty, the lunch hour had started. I headed down the hallway. A few doors down, in a corner, was a grander door. Either a conference room or an owner's office, maybe. I kept my phone glued to my ear. In a suit and with a smartphone you are invisible.

The door was marked with a simple plaque. JANICE KEENE.

Across from the door sat a squat, tidy cubicle with the facing wall half gone so the assistant could see Janice's door and manage access to the queen. The desktop was tidy and a screen saver played across the computer monitor. Not here. But not here like Janice was not here or just gone for a few minutes?

I'd have to risk it. I opened the door. Closed it behind me and, after a moment's hesitation, locked it. Corner office, marvelous views. Her desk was a grand antique. Right now it was dotted with a rainbow of sticky notes, written pleas for attention when the boss returned.

I moved to the desk and a piece of artwork caught my eye. It was on the wall facing inward toward the rest of the office. It was a set of pictures, line drawings. Like the one I'd seen on Belias's and the Marchbankses' jewelry that looked like a house of sticks. But this was—I counted them quickly—sixty-four of them. The one most like the ring and the necklace I'd seen on the Marchbanks and Belias was on the bottom row, in the fifty-seventh position.

Filed away for later. Back to the now.

I glanced down at the array of notes. All written in different hands. Reminders, urges to call. Had these people not heard of voice mail or e-mail? I nearly didn't read them but then was glad I did. One of the messages was dated three days ago: CAN'T BELIEVE I CAN'T CALL OR E-MAIL YOU. IN CASE YOU COME BACK EARLY CALL ME RE CORDOVA FILMS ACCT.

So Janice was gone and not reachable via phone.

Imagine. A public relations exec without a phone.

So where was Janice Keene? Maybe hunting down Dalton Monroe for a second try at murder? Jimmy already promised me Dalton would get more protection.

I began to search the office. Surely if she was traveling there was an itinerary, a receipt. No laptop stood on the desk. Odd.

Her desk drawers revealed nothing but a very organized collection of pens and stationery. In one drawer was a leather notebook. Inside were notes and strategies relating to clients.

I quickly flipped through pages. Nothing about her daughter, nothing about Dalton Monroe, nothing about Felix, nothing that sounded like it could connect to Belias.

I'd been in here two minutes. At any moment the receptionist could come looking for me to offer coffee or apologies that Diana wasn't here yet and notice my absence.

I shut the drawer. This woman had secrets, and they might be tied to her business. Would she keep them close? You'd be surprised. I'd found cooked books right in the offices of an Ugandan warlord and an Italian money launderer during my CIA days.

A secret kept close is a secret kept safe to some.

I searched under the desk. The chair, the sofa. Behind the credenza. Time ticked away. I stood and regarded the odd painting again. I touched the frame and the painting opened like a door.

Behind it, in the wall, was an electronic safe. Not the same one that I'd seen in the Marchbankses' house. This one had a keypad but also had a backup key entry. So a leading venture capitalist and a leading public relations expert, both with secrets to keep and hide.

I peeled off the camouflaged front of the key override—you don't have the lock exposed for the casual thief. The lock was only there in case you forgot the combination for the keypad, and my experience said people who were changing the keypad often were the most likely to forget the new combination. If you forgot, you could use a key. But it made the safe more vulnerable.

Then I slid a pronged lockpick deep as I could into the keyhole. Worked it, felt it grip tumblers. I inserted a thinner lockpick, twisted. No go. Tried it again from the opposite direction, carefully. After twenty seconds of fiddling it was open.

I held my breath as I pulled the door. No alarm sounded. No fire erupted to crisp the contents.

Inside was an envelope. Marked FOR DIANA'S EYES ONLY. But big and bulky.

Maybe a duplicate of what Janice had left for Diana in her file at home? I didn't stop to open it. I took it and stuffed it in the back of my pants, under my suit.

The other item was a passport. Canadian. With Janice Keene's face, but not her name.

Interesting.

And a gun. A Beretta and ammo. The gun would be easy to disassemble for travel; there was a permit for it, in the same name as Janice's fake passport. A wallet with the same ID, credit cards, and a driver's license.

This was a run box. I'd had one when I was working undercover. You needed documentation and maybe even a weapon if the CIA could not extract you quickly from your assignment—if I needed to vanish and run for home under a false name.

So if Janice hadn't run—and one presumed she wouldn't leave behind her daughter—then where was she?

The doorknob of the office jiggled. Someone trying the door to leave yet another sticky note.

I left the gun and the passport. I closed the safe and relocked it and closed the painting back over the safe. The thick interoffice envelope of papers lay wedged in my back, concealed by the suit jacket.

The doorknob had gone still. I listened. Had opening the safe triggered a silent alarm? I wondered how big a public relations disaster it would be to fight my way out of a public relations office.

I waited. Presumably the door would be unlocked in a few moments and I would confront an outraged subordinate and maybe a security guard. I was not worried.

Silence. No one coming to the door.

I eased it open. A fresh, new sticky note adorned the door. I guess such messages got transferred to her desk over the course of the day. I shut the door and walked back down the hallway, past open offices and a now full conference room, and back into Diana's office. I sat. Waited five minutes.

Got up and went out, past the receptionist. He shrugged. "I'm sorry, sir, I haven't heard from her."

"That's all right. I'll reschedule." I gave a most understanding smile and didn't want to look like an annoyed client because if I did he might try to foist some other account exec on me.

I got onto the elevator just as a swarm of interns got off.

I hurried toward the van. Felix already had the engine running. I got in. He pulled out of the garage, made turns, started heading back toward the Haight and The Select.

"I broke and entered," I said.

"I'm so proud," he said.

"Maybe this is a duplicate of what Janice left for Diana." I opened the envelope. It wasn't a video. Inside were news articles organized with binder clips. News accounts, and all bad news. People who had been arrested. Or fired. Or had some calamity befall them. At the bottom of the stack was one piece of paper with one word written on it in thick black ink:

DOWNFALL.

Were these clients that Janice had somehow failed? People that had harmed her? Or people that she had harmed for Belias? This was meant for Diana—but what did it mean?

Felix's phone rang. He studied the display. "I don't know this number," he said.

"Answer it."

Felix clicked on the phone. "Hello?"

His eyes went wide, and he mouthed one word: "*Diana.*"

I leaned close to hear, my forehead pressed to Felix's.

"I'm sorry for what happened," she said. "Are you in trouble?"

"Not me. Maybe the bar owner. Where are you?"

"There are some people after me. They have really major resources. I think they just altered my work calendar. I was checking it and my e-mail and saw an appointment there that isn't supposed to be. A text message on my phone that I never wrote."

Me weaseling into her office.

"Turn your phone off," Felix said. "Call me on another line."

"I need your help, Felix. If you care about my mom, you'll help me."

Felix made a face. I nudged him with my finger.

"What is going on, Diana? You nearly got my boss killed. And he's the best boss I've ever had."

"I am so sorry," she said.

"What does this mess have to do with your mom?"

"She's in bad trouble, and I have to help her. I have to get her out of it."

"And these people are after you..."

"Yes, they're in trouble, too. But I can't expose them without getting Mom in serious trouble. Please. I know you care about her...She told me she cares about you."

"I'm not going to be an accessory to a crime," he said.

"You won't. You won't. But just help me help her."

Felix bit his lip. "We should call the police."

"Absolutely not, Felix," Diana said. "No. You cannot. You cannot. You've kept your mouth shut, haven't you?"

"Yes, because I didn't want to get you in trouble. I knew it was you that came in; I saw the security tape. I wanted to discuss this with your mother, but I can't reach her."

"No one can. That's the problem." Tears tinged her voice.

"Um, okay. All right. Where can I meet you?"

"Can I come to the bar?"

I thought that was a dumb request. The bar was the last place Diana should be, with an active police investigation centered there. Desperation must be keeping her from thinking straight. I shook my head.

"No, the police might come back. A man died there, Diana."

"Okay. Okay. If I meet you, you'll come alone? I can explain."

I nodded.

"Okay," Felix lied. "I'll come alone."

She fed him an address in the Marina District. "No police, Felix, no one else. You do this for me and I promise you, Mom will be safe." She started to cry.

"Okay," he said. He hung up. He looked at me. "Maybe I should go alone."

"No," I said. "I'm coming with you."

"She said to come alone. We can't risk losing her trust."

"We can't risk losing her. You know Belias and his people are still hunting her." I climbed up to the driver's seat. "Let's go. We get her, this is over."

27

Friday, November 5, early afternoon

DETECTIVE ANITRA DESOTO preferred face-to-face interviews over phone calls. She also preferred the element of surprise. Unfortunately she got the surprise when she knocked on the front door of The Select, and instead of Sam Capra answering, a petite woman, with blonde hair and cold blue eyes, stood in the doorway.

DeSoto flashed her badge. "I'm looking for Sam Capra."

"He is not here," the young woman said. DeSoto guessed she was about thirty, maybe a bit younger. She wore black jeans and a dark sleeveless sweater and her accent sounded Russian or Eastern European.

Dead Russian on the floor. Dead Russian's brother dead at their house. Capra spoke Russian. Now attractive woman with similar accent. *I believe we call these connections*, DeSoto thought.

"And do you know when he will be back?" she asked.

"I do not know where he is. When I arrived at the bar, he was not here." The woman leaned against the door. "You are investigating the incident last night."

"I am. And you are?"

"Mila. I am Sam's business partner."

"I thought he was sole owner of the bar."

"I am more like an investments adviser."

"Ah."

"Would you like to come inside and wait for Sam? I suspect

he will be back shortly. I will text him and let him know you are here."

She hadn't planned on waiting but a Russian woman here intrigued her. "Thanks."

DeSoto entered the darkened bar. It had been tidied since last night, but it still smelled of spilled drinks and cleanser and underneath that the scent of death, a bare whisper against her nose.

"You live here in San Francisco?" DeSoto asked.

"No," Mila said. "I am in Los Angeles, on other business, when I get the terrible news. So I come here to help Sam in his hour of need."

"And where are you from originally?" *Smooth*, DeSoto thought. *You have a future in this detecting work.*

Mila glanced at her. "You are asking because the man killed last night was Russian?"

"Yes."

"You do not know your accents. I am Moldovan."

For a moment DeSoto thought that might be a species on *Star Trek*; then she remembered a country named Moldova. Used to be part of the Soviet Union. Poor by European standards. And a hub for international crime, she'd heard it mentioned on a panel at a police conference she'd gone to in Miami last year.

Sam Capra just kept getting more interesting.

"Would you like a drink?" Mila asked.

"Sure, a Coke. But I have to pay. Rules."

"Of course." Mila fetched a glass, put in fresh ice, poured a cold can of soda she'd retrieved from the refrigerator instead of from the drink nozzle. She put it on the bar. "A dollar will do."

DeSoto slid the dollar to Mila.

Mila said, "It must be so interesting to be a police investigator."

"Yes."

"I suspect you see the worst in people."

"Yes."

"Most people cannot imagine the depths that others can sink to," Mila said. "Until they see it."

"How does a woman get from Moldova to Los Angeles?"

"I have my papers if you are worried I am an illegal immigrant."

"No, just curious."

"I wanted to see the world. Not much to do in Moldova. I feel the entire country is small town."

"And how did you connect with Sam?"

"We met at a friend's party," Mila said. "Baby shower."

DeSoto sipped her soda. She suddenly did not like this woman, not at all.

Mila leaned on the bar. "So. This man who died. You know who he is now so you can figure out why he shows up here at our nice bar?"

"What has Sam told you, if I might ask?"

"Sam told me he was a stranger who spoke Russian."

"So that's why Sam speaks Russian? Because of you?"

"No. We speak Romanian in Moldova. Although many of us do know Russian."

"So why does Sam speak Russian?"

"He grew up with parents who worked all over world; he was always learning new languages quickly. He owns a bar in Moscow, so him knowing the language does not mean he knows this dead man."

DeSoto decided to fish. "I wonder if you might know the name of this man."

"Since we do not know him, no, I am not terribly interested in his name."

DeSoto was sure that last part was a white lie. "His name was Grigori Rostov."

Mila pursed her lips, sucked in her cheeks slightly, gave the matter five seconds of thought. "I do not know a man with that name."

"Do you know his face?" She pulled a photo from her jacket and passed it to Mila. She studied the dead man. She studied it for much longer than DeSoto thought she would.

"No. I don't." She handed the photo back. "I see what you're trying to do, Detective, and I understand it. You seek a connection. There is none, and I know Sam very well."

"How about his brother, Vladimir?" She produced another picture. Another dead face.

Mila stared and studied it. "His brother?"

"He died last night or early this morning. Shot in the chest. At a home he shared with his brother in Outer Richmond."

"How awful for their parents." She handed Vladimir Rostov's picture back to DeSoto.

"Two brothers dead in the same night, Mila, and Sam won't return my phone messages."

"He is always forgetting to charge the cell. And I promise you he was quite shaken by last night's events. He has nothing to do with this brother. I would suggest you look carefully at their associates."

"The hard drive is missing from their computer."

"Ah. Then this was about some shady business of theirs. Nothing to do with Sam."

"I'd like to know where Sam was late last night."

"I assume he was here. You'll have to ask him."

DeSoto decided to push the game with this woman. There was something in Mila's stare. Like a chess player, waiting to see what DeSoto's move would be. And a smile like she was two moves ahead.

She thought she might shock the smile off Mila's face. "This man, Grigori Rostov, was born in Moscow. He was recruited into the Spetsnaz, Russian Special Forces…"

"I know what Spetsnaz is."

"And then he got thrown out. Accused of misappropriating armaments and money, but nothing proven. So he came here, and he and his brother became enforcers for their uncle, a Russian mobster in New York. The word is they fell out of favor there after a screwup and came out here to start fresh."

"California does have good job-training programs," Mila said.

"And the word here is that the brothers Rostov were muscle for hire. Grigori and Vladimir were a solid choice if you needed a beating administered. Dangerous men."

"Not so dangerous if he can't beat up Sam. Sam is a gentle soul."

Hardly, DeSoto thought. "Since you are Sam's…partner? Was that the word?"

"Yes, I believe that was the word I've used."

"Then perhaps you can illuminate some gaps in Sam's story."

"I was not here last night. I am a poor excuse for a witness."

"More in checking up on Mr. Capra's background."

"I do not understand why you are not busy typing a report about his bravery, since he protected two dozen customers here last night."

"I don't know that he saved anyone," DeSoto said. "Beyond himself."

Mila crossed her arms and gave her a wry smile that was almost pitying. "Ask your questions, Detective."

"I found a video of him talking on a morning news show about his brother being executed in Afghanistan."

"Yes. That was a tragedy."

"He said he graduated from Harvard."

"I did not know him then, but he seems to dislike Yale, so I believe him."

"And then he joined a business-consulting firm in London."

"Yes."

"Well, the firm no longer seems to be in business in London." DeSoto raised an eyebrow. "I've had people on this since early this morning, trying to find someone who knew him there. His past in London seems a blank page."

"Consultants are the first to fall in a slow economy like we've had." Mila shrugged. "Perhaps they failed because they were bad at publicity."

"And then he came into ownership of this and some other bars. I'm wondering where the money came from to make such an investment at such a young age."

Mila gave out a long, bored sigh. "And this relates to last night's events how?"

"He owns a bar in Manhattan. Grigori Rostov came here from New York."

"I believe there are daily flights between the two cities. Is there a point?"

"I'm trying to get a picture of Sam."

"Sam's actions speak volumes. He saved a customer. You think there is a connection to this Grigori Rostov? I am telling you there is not."

"I found a record of a marriage in Virginia between him and a woman named Lucy Collins. Then this year, a record of a divorce."

Mila said nothing.

"And yet Lucy Collins Capra seems to have vanished off the face of the earth. No record of any credit activity. No death certificate. No taxes paid. She doesn't seem to exist anymore."

"Lucy left him," Mila said. "Where she is now is not of interest to him."

"His past is an odd jigsaw," DeSoto said. "I just want to know the whole truth."

"You have been told truth. You do not listen to it."

"This young woman." She slid Mila a grainy photo of the woman who had been the apparent cause of the fight. A young woman, African American, moving quickly past The Select's bar. "Do you know her?"

"No, I don't. But it's not a good photo."

"She's not the missing Lucy Capra. Is she Sam's girlfriend?"

"No. He told you he did not know her."

"Maybe she was dating both the Russian and Sam. He lies that there is no connection. Maybe he panics. Maybe he has to shut up the brother to keep him from coming forward."

"What a nice collection of maybes you have."

DeSoto took the photo back. "You see the position I'm in. Mr. Capra has some blanks in his background."

"I do not see what that matters. He is an honest businessman who protected himself and his customers."

"Do most bar owners have the skills to single-handedly disarm and kill a Russian Special Forces veteran?"

"Maybe Rostov is former soldier because he was incompetent soldier. There was another man with him. There was this woman who brought the trouble into the bar. Yet you worry about Sam."

"Sam is the one who killed someone last night."

"Detective, I am starting to believe the only reason you are here is because you want to make a headline. You want to stretch out a simple case and attach your name to it."

DeSoto felt a slow bolt of anger rise in her chest. "I'm sorry, what was your last name?"

Mila stared at her for a moment with a half smile. "Court. Mila Court."

DeSoto frowned for a moment. "Court? Is that a Moldovan name spelled some weird way without vowels?"

"No, it's not. Court, like for tennis. It is my married name."

Mila's phone buzzed. She said, "Excuse me, Detective, but I have nothing further to say and I have work to do. I will tell Sam what you told me and that you are looking to speak with him. Thank you for your concern." She glanced at her phone. From Felix. A text message:

WE FOUND HER.

And an address. Mila clicked off the phone and showed Detective DeSoto to the door with a smile.

28

Friday, November 5, early afternoon

Holly thought, *I shouldn't be here*. She couldn't do what Belias wanted.

She didn't call the police to report an intrusion and vandalism of her home. Instead she'd called her mother, summoned her from her bridge club. She'd told her mother to pick up the kids from school and take them straight to Alameda, where Holly's aunt lived. She'd met her mother out in the driveway, bags packed for all three of them.

"What on earth is going on?" her mom had asked.

"I just need you to do what I say, Mom, please." Holly's arms were folded tightly over her chest.

"Is it Glenn?" She lowered her voice. "Does Glenn want you back? It sounded like he had left Audrey without explanation…"

"No. Nothing like that." She wanted to tell Mom so bad, but Holly couldn't know that Glenn was dead, so no one else could. She bit the inside of her lip. Her mother looked unhappy. "He's in some trouble."

"Trouble?"

She lied to her mother about her dead ex, just like Belias had told her to do. "Yes, trouble. Financial. I don't know more than that. Please don't say anything."

"I couldn't help a man who treated me the way he did you."

Holly crossed her arms and stared at the driveway and thought,

And once it's announced Glenn is missing, you'll wonder, won't you, Mom? Wonder why I wouldn't let you in this house. But her mother would say nothing, ever. She watched her mom drive away.

And then she'd locked up the house, with its fresh bullet holes in the wall, and two damaged windows, and she'd driven past Blair-craft Academy.

From the street she could see Emma's class, playing on the fields. In the scattering of identical uniforms she saw Emma's bright smile as she and two friends kicked a soccer ball back and forth.

I did it for you. I did it for you and maybe it was the wrong choice, but you had to have a better life than I did. I had to make sure of it. Fate is too cruel.

And fate, she thought, might have finally caught up with her, demanding payment for all the so-called luck she and Glenn had enjoyed. She waited, wanting Peter to come out on the field, but she realized he didn't have recess until later. She wouldn't get to see him. She watched Emma go back inside and she choked back the tears.

Then she drove back to Belias's safe house, swallowing the grief, feeding her resolve. She wanted to know the truth of what happened after she left Glenn.

The only way to get her life back with her children was to end this. End the threat to Belias. Find Diana Keene. Kill Sam Capra.

And now she sat parked, looking at the house where she'd brought Glenn to die.

Behind those walls, he drew his last breath. And she thought of the endless days and nights where she'd laid next to him, listening to his breath with her eyes closed, feeling the rise and fall of his chest under her hand. She'd often slept with her hand on his naked chest and he joked she was trying to pin him to the bed. She'd laughed, but she wondered now, walking up the wooden steps, if even then in the early days he'd felt trapped by her.

As though he couldn't feel more trapped by the deal they'd made with Belias, by the trap of a life they'd negotiated.

She knocked on the door. Once. Twice.

The door swung open. Roger stood there.

"May I come in?"

Roger gestured her inside and shut the door. "I thought you'd be with the Tiburon police."

"I wanted to deal with this first."

He didn't argue with her. "I said it before, but I'll say it again. I'm sorry about Glenn."

Sorry. A one-word eulogy. No funeral. No memorial service. The police would be looking for him soon enough, yes. He would be missed by Audrey, by his colleagues at the best venture capital firm on the West Coast; lying texts from his phone would only buy them another couple of days or so. His disappearance would send shock waves through the economic press. She thought of all that and then, *How do I tell the kids? How do they say good-bye? They don't. Sam Capra cheated them out of their father.*

"You should have this." Roger handed her Glenn's necklace, with the symbol. They only wore them on jobs. Slowly she put it on, tucked it under her shirt, the silver cool against her skin. It held no trace of Glenn's warmth.

"Where's Belias?" she asked.

"He needed to take a call. One he didn't want me to hear." Roger made a disgusted noise. "We're under attack and he's keeping secrets."

"We'll find Diana."

"Not just Diana. Your dear ex."

She turned back to him. "What?"

"We found out Glenn hired Grigori Rostov to not only find and grab Diana and to bring her here, but to kill me and to kidnap Belias. To force him to give Glenn every name in the network."

She froze. "That can't be true…"

"Belias found out about it at Rostov's house. He found e-mails between Glenn and Rostov."

Glenn planning a rebellion. Kidnap Belias, force him to reveal the names of everyone in the network. He'd been afraid to tackle both Roger and Belias, so hence the Russian. She could see it. She sat down in the chair, her legs weak.

But did Glenn die *after* Belias found out the truth?

Roger took another sip of tea. "We wouldn't kill Glenn, if that's what you're thinking. He wanted to know who all Glenn would have rallied to his side in this little rebellion. Glenn was dead when he got back."

"Why...why is all this happening now?"

"Because Belias has something big cooking. I think Glenn discovered it. Very big. Like someone in the network rising very, very high."

"Higher than Glenn?"

"Oh yes." Roger smiled.

And Glenn found out about this rising star how? Those in the network weren't supposed to know each other's names, but rarely they had to work together on an assignment. She never had, but Glenn had worked with others in the network a couple of times. And they were not supposed to try and figure out who the others in the network were. That would bring the entire network down on you, all its power, its murderous rage. There was no profit, no gain in trying to circumvent Belias.

Until now. Until someone was getting so powerful that perhaps Glenn or others wanted that power for themselves, with no Belias as intermediary.

These thoughts flashed through her mind, and she saw Roger thought she was just stunned into silence. He'd always underestimated her. "I didn't know. I swear I didn't know."

"There is nothing to implicate you in his e-mails, Holly."

"Or else I'd be dead."

"Hardly, we'd just be having a serious chat. Belias has always had a soft spot for you." He cranked a smile, so inappropriate now that she was a widow. But she wasn't one. Audrey was and didn't even know it yet.

"So is Diana and this video connected to this, um, mutiny?"

"I don't know." Roger cleared his throat. She thought he simply did not want to tell her. "And Glenn might have been acting alone. Belias will want your help in finding out."

She changed the subject. "Where did you...hide...him?" She couldn't say bury.

"It's best you know nothing. In case you're questioned." Roger gestured her to a table. "Would you like some tea?"

"Thank you." Roger jetted water from the faucet into a teapot and began to heat it on the stove. He went to the pantry and pulled out a box of Earl Grey packets. "You're going to have to be sure you have an alibi for last night as it's most important that no suspicion be put on you. I'm sure you can rely on your mother."

Yes, she thought, and then she would need an alibi for killing Sam. And for being gone at the same time Glenn had gone missing. The police might raise a collective eyebrow. She needed to do this quickly.

She began to analyze how to deal with Glenn being missed. Tomorrow was the weekend, she thought. Glenn would not be missed so much by his coworkers at Vallon Marchbanks. Audrey was another story; she would not be put off by text messages and unanswered voice mails. So Monday, that was her deadline to find Sam Capra and kill him. After Monday both she and Glenn would be missed.

She nearly laughed—it was like trying to fit in yoga and grocery shopping and errands before the kids got back from school. She was glad she didn't laugh because she knew it would be a jagged, awful sound.

"Where is he?" she tried again.

"I won't tell you. It's bad enough you already will have to fake shock or grief. Belias and I will arrange it so that it will appear he took out money, booked a private jet, and flew to New York, where he promptly vanishes. I hope you're a better actress than the second wife. Her credits are not impressive."

"Did he go…badly?"

"Was he in pain, you mean?"

"Yes." She closed her hands into fists.

"His head had been knocked in. In my experience the pain is not bad. Confusion, shock dull it." Roger poured hot water into a mug, set it down in front of Holly. He dumped in a tea bag.

And you didn't save him, Holly thought. But there was only so much Roger could do, tucked away from a hospital, binding wounds in a Mission District apartment. Roger sat down with his own tea.

"I trained you all so you could fight if need be, defend yourselves, survive," Roger said. "I feel I've let Glenn down. He should have beaten this Capra."

You didn't either, Holly thought, but said nothing.

"I'm just in shock," she said.

"I can't give you anything for that other than tea. You need to stay sharp."

"Was he alone...when he passed?"

"No. I was with him," Roger said after a moment. "Belias had left."

He died with Roger as his only company. Holly felt the tears behind her eyes, hot. "He died in the other room? Where he was when I left him?"

"Yes."

She got up and went into the small bedroom. She stood over the bed. Roger had already put on fresh sheets and a clean blanket. A slight smell of disinfectant. And under that...

A smell of paint.

Why would there be a smell of paint?

Glenn teased her that she redecorated rooms as often as she changed dresses. It was a Thing to Do. A way to stay busy. She had the house she'd always wanted, and yet she kept changing it. Like a butterfly redesigning the cocoon. A bird regilding the cage. As if the gold bars of Belias's deal would change the fact of the deal.

She glanced along the wall. There. Drying still, nearly done, but not done. A patch of paint right next to where Glenn's head would have been. Right by the pillow where he'd smiled at her as she went home, told her to give the kids his love.

Why would fresh paint be needed? Why? She wanted to believe Roger—that Glenn died before Belias knew he'd turned traitor. He had never lied to her.

"What did he die of? What exactly?"

"The bleeding on the brain was severe, I guess. He lost consciousness and died."

"I…" She couldn't finish the sentence.

"Holly, Belias wanted Glenn alive. To tell him how he knew what he knew and to find out who else was helping Glenn. And to give Glenn another chance." Roger's mouth crinkled. "I swear to you."

Belias and Roger think your ex-husband betrayed them. Will he ever trust you enough to let you go?

"He is going to make the network more powerful than it's ever been before. We'll all make much more money. We'll have more power behind the scenes. This is a real opportunity for you, Holly."

If I run right now, he'll hunt me down. If I go to the police, I lose my kids, everything. If I stay with him…will he set me free? Or is he just using me?

But the smell of fresh paint hung in the air, like a feather under her nose. She couldn't save Glenn, she couldn't avenge him. She could only escape with their children. She could only make herself into someone new who could survive dealing with Belias without Glenn.

"Where is Belias?"

"I don't know."

"What's he doing?"

"I don't know."

"He doesn't trust you anymore?" she asked.

Roger said, "He never has." He set down his tea. "Go home, Holly. Feed that story to the police about your house getting shot up. Do what Belias asks. It always works out better that way." And he smiled at her.

29

Friday, November 5, afternoon

Near every safe house belonging to Belias was another house that Roger did not know about. An extra space, a quiet refuge where Belias could work, each rent paid for two full years. Belias called them the studios—it was where he could practice his art.

He opened the laptop and entered in the encryption code for the Exchange. On a server in distant Estonia, a computer awakened and fed him the submissions for the day. He hadn't checked the Exchange in four days, and he wanted to be sure to see there was no air of panic in the postings. There wasn't. All was calm.

An offer of military intelligence on a new weapons system being developed in Colorado.

The phone number and computer password of a high-end prostitute who was routinely seeing a prominent politician in Germany.

The secret access number of an offshore account tied to a millionaire investor who was hiding illicit funds.

A request that a rival be distracted from business concerns—with the mild suggestion that the kidnapping of the rival's child for three days might do the trick and asking that the child be released unharmed.

The list ran on, and he thought and considered the value of each piece before he made an offer to the person who could benefit the most from it. In his mind he imagined their prominent names and linking them all bright threads: black of immediate profit, green of information that could one day change a fortune, gray of violence, red of murder.

It took an hour, and he was nearly done, ready to close the Exchange, when a new message appeared:

Hello.

That was all it said.

It couldn't be. The account was not one that could be easily spammed or discovered by law enforcement. Only the network knew how to send him a message, and those had to be encrypted. This was from an address he hadn't approved, but they had his encryption key.

Belias realized he could do one of two things. He could immediately try to counterhack the message, see where it came from.

Or he could talk to whoever had dared trespass on his territory. Maybe Glenn sold access to the Exchange when he turned against Belias. It was the easiest answer.

Hello,

he wrote back.

I have a proposal.

I don't know who you are.

That's all right. We'll be good friends, soon enough. What you've done here is so clever. I want to help you protect it.

I don't know what you mean.

The network. What you and Roger have created. The deal you've made with lovely, deserving people. The way you took an old story and brought it to new life, Mr B., from how you and Roger got your start in London and Moscow. I want to help you.

Belias counted to ten, then typed:

I don't want your help.

Sam Capra.

Belias wrote:

Who?

Don't play dumb. You know who he is.

What about him?

I want you to bring him into your network.

I don't think I can recruit him.

I think you should try.

Belias waited. No new message appeared.

I don't have leverage over him.

You do. He has a son. Not even a year old.

Why do you care if he's in the network? What's it to you?

Because if you bring him inside, I'll leave your network alone. If you don't, then I'll bring you down. I have your encryption key. I'll hijack the network, run it myself. Or give it all to the FBI and Interpol. It doesn't really matter to me.

Who are you? I don't deal with people I don't know.

You don't know me. I helped you once, long ago, when you were the most hunted man in London.

Belias closed his eyes. He thought of nights hiding in alleys, pretending to be a homeless man in shelters, because that was the only place to hide. Until it had been safe to come out.

Your first enemy, he died because of me. Because I helped you out, unseen. I've been watching you ever since. You make people valuable. I've just done the same to you.

Belias got up, paced the floor. This couldn't be. Then he saw more words appear.

I know you're in trouble. I also know you're about to bring a new level of power to your network. This is your moment, John. I certainly don't want to ruin it for you. We've had our eye on you for a long while. With admiration.

Run, he thought. Shut everything down. Just end it. Take the profit he'd made off the network's information and retire to Fiji or Laos or Seychelles. Live a quiet life. But he hated the idea of surrender; he hated it with a passion.

I just need one favor, and I'll leave you alone. Recruit Sam Capra.

Belias typed:

And then what?

That's not your worry. Get him to be part of what you do and then I'll take him off your hands.

Maybe you're the police and Sam Capra is a mole.

Or not.

Then there was an attachment. A file. He scanned it, put it through a virus detection program, made sure it was clean.

He opened it. A personnel file, from the CIA, on Sam Capra. He read it with fascination.

The other party waited, not typing, giving him time.

Belias typed.

Why have you sent me this?

Because I want you to recruit him.

Why?

Just do as I ask. You can recruit anyone, Belias, I've seen your track record.

And once I let him inside . . . ?

He need not know your secrets. I just need him to be your

associate for a while. I've sent you a link to a computer that might help you convince him. Do that and I'll never bother you again.

Will you do what I ask? Or do I hand over the Exchange's database to the press and the police?

Belias took thirty seconds.

I'll recruit him.

He signed off. And he thought, *And maybe I'll recruit him and I'll use him to find out who you are and then I'll destroy you.*

He clicked on the link and watched in the window that opened, read the data that scrolled along the bottom of it, the person's name. Interesting. Then he began tracing the trail of the messages.

A few minutes' work showed him…the messages originated from his own server, hidden in Estonia.

His skin went cold. Someone was contacting him via his own machine, hidden away where he hadn't seen them, watching him. If they had already penetrated the server, then they already owned every secret of the network.

And in the next few hours, if the person wanted to destroy him, they could. And if nothing happened…then the offer was serious.

He needed to bring Sam Capra into his fold for sure now. Not only to appease this stranger in the wires, but to find out who Sam Capra's enemy was. That meant they needed to take him alive.

He and Roger were going to have to search harder for Diana—friends, associates, every place she might turn for help. She would be more desperate than ever after the incident at The Select. He'd been listening to her voice mails regularly; even though she'd wised up enough to keep her cell phone shut off, she still received voice mails that he was accessing through her provider account.

But he checked his monitoring software, and saw with shock she'd turned on her phone not twenty minutes ago for the first time in two days. The GPS gave a reading. A Marina District address. He remembered the profile he'd built up on Diana. She had a friend,

Lily, who lived in the Marina District. Glenn had reported there was no sign of Diana at Lily's when he began hunting for her.

Then. Not now.

He called Roger. "I know where she is. We need to take her alive."

30

Friday, November 5, afternoon

WE'D PARKED THE VAN a block away from the address in the Marina District Diana gave Felix. The house was small, elegant, tidy, painted a nautical blue. An ornate white gate blocked the entrance to the house from the street.

"It occurs to me this could be a trap," Felix said. "Maybe Belias found Diana and forced her to call me."

It was an unsettling thought.

"Go peek in the window," Felix said.

"I feel I've committed enough burglaries today. Now you want me to peer into windows?"

"Weren't you a spy once?"

"And a neighbor notices and they call the cops."

"I thought you were a fast runner."

I didn't answer and we headed for the gate. It was unlocked.

Softly against the front door, Felix said, "Diana? It's Felix."

The door opened. Diana Keene stood there. She started to smile at Felix, relief flooding her face, and then she saw me.

"Hi," I said.

She just kept staring.

"I'm Sam."

"I said to come alone," she said to Felix.

"Sam can help us. Sam already saved you once."

She looked like she might slam the door and lock herself in.

"I brought you something," I said. "From your mother."

Her mouth thinned. She stuck her hand out, sure I would just hand it over. I saw her hand tremble.

"Let's talk inside," I said.

She gestured us inside and closed the door behind me. We followed her back to a small, elegant kitchen furnished with high-end appliances that looked barely used.

"Is your friend here?" Felix asked.

"No, she's in Europe for another week." She looked at me. "You brought me something from my mom?"

"Yes, and I wanted to say thank you," I said. "For saving my life."

Her face, lovely, twisted like she was going to laugh. "Thank you for saving mine. I guess I've forgotten my manners. But…this isn't your problem. You should stay out of it. Just give me the…" she started to say as I pulled the package I'd taken from the safe from the back of my pants. She stopped and looked at the crumpled, thick manila envelope, with its FOR DIANA'S EYES ONLY scrawled across the front. She blinked, and I realized this wasn't what she was expecting.

So what had she thought I was bringing her?

She bit her lip and her gaze met mine. "This is for me and you opened it," she said.

"I'm the guy who saved your life, so yeah, I opened it. Maybe you can explain to me what it means. It all ties into why Belias wants you dead and why he's got a millionaire as his hired thug."

She flinched at the mention of Belias. "Where did you get this?"

"I stole it from your mother's office."

Her eyes widened. "What kind of a bartender are you?"

"The kind that's good at listening to people's problems."

She seemed to weigh the envelope in her hands.

"Diana, we can help you," Felix said. "You just have to trust us. We have resources…We can hide you."

She turned and began to prep the coffeemaker. Her hands shook slightly. "Look. I just need to find my mom. If you don't know where she is, Felix, then I don't want you involved. I appreciate you want to help. But…"

But this was a change from before when she was so eager to see Felix. Something had changed since we'd talked to her on the phone.

Felix said, "Your mother is in trouble and you're trying to shield her. Let us help you."

"Do you know where my mom is?"

"No, I have no idea," he answered.

"Did she mention going to Santa Fe to you? To a retreat where you can't be called or e-mailed?"

"No."

"Did she...did she mention cancer?" Her voice wavered.

Felix didn't answer, which was answer enough.

"Please. I know she has it. Bad," Diana said.

Felix closed his eyes. "I met her through a cancer support group. Sometimes after the meetings she'd come to the bar...so we could talk."

"I'm sorry. Are you as sick as my mom?"

"No," he said. "I wanted to help your mother. We...like each other."

"Yes, I know. But now she's off working for this crazy man instead of getting treatment. I don't understand it," Diana said.

"Working for Belias? Doing what?" I asked.

"I don't know."

"You stole something of Belias's," I said. "According to him."

"You talked to him?"

"Yes. More than once. He thinks I'm protecting you; he's offering me deals to hand you over to him."

"What?" Shock colored her voice.

"I won't obviously." I paused. "You have something that can expose whatever he's doing. A video your mother made."

"No, I don't have it," she said.

"Where is it?"

"I saw it on her computer and I erased it. It was like a confession. I couldn't risk someone else seeing it." She turned away and watched the coffee burble and drip into the pot.

I tapped the package, ran a finger along the paper that said DOWN-

FALL. "Is this what was in the video? Information about what she and Belias did to these people?"

"No—the video was her talking about how bad Belias was." Her gaze was steady on mine; then she looked away to the package.

"So is this her proof? They're just press clippings about people screwing up. It's not exactly hard evidence."

"I appreciate you want to help. Felix…" She glanced at him. "I just…I want to trust you, but I can't. I can't put my mom's fate in the hands of strangers. I barely know you and I don't know him."

"I killed a man for you," I said. It came out sounding harsher than I intended, and she looked like she might break under the tension. I made my voice quieter. "You don't want to expose your mom's involvement. I understand. You're trying to protect her. I'm not sure you can."

"Destroy Belias and you think you destroy your mom," Felix said. "Not necessarily. She could cut a deal with the police."

"My mom is not a bad person. She hasn't committed any crimes." Now Diana's voice rose. "Look, I understand you want to help me, but you can't."

"Where's the video?" I asked.

"I deleted it from her computer. And then I wiped the hard drive so it couldn't be recovered."

"She left you a package in her home office," I said. "That was the video, I think. Where is it?"

"You were in my mother's house?"

"Clearly you think we're going about it the wrong way, but we're trying to help her. And help you." I raised my hand, put finger and thumb an inch apart. "But I am this close to calling the police, Diana, if you don't talk straight with us."

She sat at the dining room table. She hugged the envelope to her in her lap. The fire in her I'd seen in the bar seemed dimmed.

"This Belias guy…he's forced Mom to do things for him. Betray confidences of her clients. He has leverage over her."

"So he's a blackmailer."

"My mother…is a really wonderful person," Diana said. "She

built her company from nothing after my dad died. She's amazing. No one works harder or smarter."

"But he has dirt on her, enough to get her to skip cancer treatments and do his bidding." I wondered how she would react to the suggestion her mother was a willing participant in Belias's work. *I can give you the world.* But that might send her over the edge. "Do you know Glenn Marchbanks or Holly Marchbanks? Are they clients of your mom's?"

"I don't know them."

"So. He wants you and me. He thinks I'm protecting you. He thinks we have a history, that it's not just coincidence you came into the bar—he doesn't know about your mom being friends with Felix."

Diana's glance slid to Felix, held, looked away.

"So what does it take for you to go to the police?" I asked.

"I have to talk to my mom before I'll talk to the police. That's not negotiable."

"He knows where we can find your mother, I suspect," I said. "Your mother would turn against him if he hurt you. He said he wants you unharmed. So we tell him we want to talk. Draw him in. Capture him."

"I have no intention of being bait." Diana's lovely face set in a stubborn frown. "The coffee's ready." She got up and we went into the kitchen. Lily's refrigerator was covered with photos of herself at parties, and Diana was in many of the pictures. Laughing, posing for the camera with an *I'm cool* stance and smile.

She handed me the coffee.

"The people in those clippings that your mom left you," I said.

"I don't know them."

"DOWNFALL. What does that mean?"

"I don't know."

I set the coffee down and went back into the living room, and I picked up the envelope. Dumped out the papers, spread them across the table. The names, the faces, I didn't know. The names. Nathan Horst. Patricia Gustavo. Jared Crosston. Mike and Cassie Muller-Prynne. Felix began to pick them up, study them, read them, a frown on his face. He held up a solitary article, pulled from the bottom of the pile: the newspaper account of Dalton Monroe's celebratory reception, where he fell ill. Our gaze met.

I turned back to Diana and tapped the articles. "You do know," I said quietly. "These are all stories of failure. Prominent people brought suddenly low or dead. Why does your mom have this?"

"*Cui bono*?" Felix said.

"What?" Diana said.

"*Cui bono*? Latin for 'who benefits?' It's a useful question to ask when trying to discern a motive." He looked at me. "I read that in a mystery novel."

I looked at Diana. "Fair enough. Who benefits from these downfalls? Your mother? Glenn Marchbanks? How?"

"You brought this to me, I don't know." She made a dismissive gesture toward the clippings.

"Is that what your mother knows? Who benefits? Is that what's on the video?"

"I don't know."

Felix said, "Ask yourself what your mom would tell you to do. We want to help you."

She looked at the floor and shook her head.

"Diana, let me make this clear to you. You have your secrets and I have mine. But Belias believes that either we join him or he has to kill us."

"You make it sound like a war," she said.

"It is. Us versus him."

"Then treat it like a war and kill him."

I didn't answer her.

"I'm sorry," she said suddenly. "I made you into a guy who has killed someone. Why would you even want to talk to me?"

"I can handle it." There was no sense in telling her I'd killed before. It's not the sort of thing you bring up in conversation. It makes people very uneasy. I held up the folder of clippings. "You cannot have it both ways. Either help us or I call the police, right now. Who are these people and why do they matter?"

She bit on my bluff, took the file, glanced through it slowly.

"Josh Honeycutt. Rising film director, he was supposed to direct *The Manager*." I remembered the movie; it had won a bevy of Oscars a few years ago. "He got canned from the project and basically everything else in Hollywood after child porn was found on his computer." She dropped the file, paged over to another one. "Deanna Shaw. Was supposed to become CEO of a major oil company. Rising star but she was implicated in an insider stock-trading schedule. She resigned and ended up being radioactive on the CEO search committee lists. She teaches now at a university. Nice job, but not the same as being head of a billion-dollar firm." She dropped another at my feet. "Mauricio Lopez. Freelance journalist in Los Angeles. He started a blog devoted to whistle-blowers in government. He was going to get a book out of it; found shot with two bullets in the head, in the back of a sleazy bar. Robbery gone wrong. No one wanted to carry on the blog, though." She looked up at me. "Are you seeing a pattern?"

"No," I said, "but I might be jumping to a conclusion."

She waited. I paged through more of the articles. The heir to a manufacturing concern who committed suicide after being accused of embezzlement, a young politician derailed by a scandal with a prostitute, a young physicist who'd been a leader in nanotechnology research and his wife dead in a car crash off a cliff. "People on an upward rise cut down in their prime. Either by scandal that they can't easily recover from or murder. This one, from just days ago, a billionaire falling ill at a party. Did your mom ever mention Dalton Monroe?"

"No." Resolve filled her face. "Maybe…my mother discovered an ongoing pattern in some of the clients she worked with. That bad luck befell their competition." Monroe wasn't a client, but Felix shook his head at me. Better to let Diana talk; she might say more than she realized.

"Belias said he hacks lives. You think their falls from fortune were engineered. *Cui bono?* Who benefits? The people like the Marchbankses? Your mother?"

She was so lovely and bright, and I thought if she'd come into the bar under any other circumstances, maybe we could have been friends. But she was never going to talk, never going to say a word that could compromise her mother.

Anger rose in my chest. "I'm trying to help you. I'm trying to save you from this guy. But I'm not going to fight this war on your terms. I'll fight them on mine."

She started to argue, like that was going to work, and looked at me. But past me to Felix. The door to the house opened. And Belias stepped through, followed by the thick-necked man. He raised a gun and fired and the gun made an odd puffing noise.

Felix, closest to them, dropped.

I shoved Diana behind me and felt a short, sharp pain in my throat. I pulled it away. A dart. Like the kind you would use to tranquilize an animal. And then my face sagged, my body sagged, and I didn't even feel myself hit the concrete, Diana's screams exploding in my ears.

3I

Friday, November 5, afternoon

Denver

In an airport, no one wonders why you're carrying an umbrella.

Viktor Rostov didn't as he walked past the man with the umbrella, hurrying toward his gate. He glanced at the monitor. His flight was now delayed an hour. He hated flying through Denver. But at least the delay meant he had time for the fancy coffee. He never could drink it at home in front of his brothers. His siblings liked their coffee black. He liked his with a bakery added to it.

Viktor walked the curve of the terminal row and he got in line at a coffee stand. He wanted the biggest cup they had, with hot mocha-flavored coffee, topped with whipped cream and every sugary option. Comfort food, he told himself, although the one time he'd gone into a Starbucks with his brothers and his cousins and ordered a Frappuccino they'd laughed at him. He hated to be laughed at. Grigori and Vladimir had laughed the hardest, before they'd gotten shamed by their incompetence and left for the West Coast to start their own operation.

Where they were now dead, both of them in a single night.

Their poor mother had gotten the phone call at 4:00 a.m. New York time and the family had rallied. They had contacts in the San Francisco police department, and an inquiry had produced the name of the man who had struck down Grigori: Sam Capra. Viktor was to go there and exact a quick revenge.

Viktor placed his order, loving the long Italian words on his tongue, and then he was jostled from behind, a sharp point hitting his leg. He glanced back, irritated, and saw a well-dressed man in his late thirties, sandy haired, an umbrella in his hand, a raincoat over his arm, a small satchel. "Sorry!" the man said. "You okay?"

Viktor just said, "No worries," like an American would, and he moved over to the counter to await his coffee with the whipped cream and hazelnut and chocolate shavings.

The American nodded and stepped up and gave the barista his order.

Viktor collected his coffee and started to head down to the gate. The first sip was sugarcoated heaven, whipped cream and chocolate and coffee. The second sip was richer, more satisfying. He felt the indulgent smile creep onto his face.

The third sip made him want to throw up.

His mouth felt numb and nausea churned up, like the breakfast he'd eaten in New York didn't agree with him. *No*, he thought. *I don't want to get sick now. I want my coffee.* But the feeling of illness washed over him hard and sudden, and he hurried into the men's room.

He thought, *Maybe I just need to splash water on my face.* It was not crowded, a lull of quiet between planes at nearby gates taking off and landing, and he jabbed his hand under the automatic faucet and flicked water into his face. He felt worse. He needed to sit down.

"Are you all right, mister?" a teenager said at the next sink.

"Fine," he said. "Just a headache."

The teenager turned away and left.

He regretfully left the perfect coffee on the counter and staggered into the toilet stall at the end of the row, away from everyone. He was going to be sick. He shut the door and then pain rumbled through him. He collapsed onto the toilet as his muscles felt soggy and loose, his heart slowing, and as he died his thoughts splintered and the taste of the coffee was the last thing he knew.

A moment later the stall next to him was occupied by a man carrying an umbrella.

Barton Craig sat and waited for another lull between boardings and arrivals, and then he shoved his bag, umbrella, and raincoat under the divider and he wriggled under the stall wall, neat and fast as a snake, pulling himself up next to Viktor. It took all of five seconds. He tucked up Viktor's legs so it didn't look like there were two men in the stall. He put on gloves and he removed the tiny pellet in Viktor's leg that was just under the skin. This he put in his pocket.

From his own bag he pulled an airport maintenance uniform, too baggy, that he put on over his own suit. He pulled a cap low over his face. He waited until a flight arrived and a number of men herded through to use the facilities, and when the next lull came, he inched back into the next stall, leaving Viktor's door locked, and he walked out of the men's room.

Barton Craig walked to another bathroom, went inside, removed the camouflaging uniform, and stuck it back into his bag.

Then he left the bathroom when a wave of men passed. He went to go board his flight. It was to Los Angeles; the police, if and when they determined Viktor Rostov had been poisoned, would be reviewing ticket histories. It was not good to have bought a ticket and not used it, even under a false name. There were many cameras in the airports. He would spend the night in Los Angeles and then fly back the next morning. The job done, he let out a soft, low sigh of relief. Belias hadn't asked him to do something like this in two years. He hoped it would be another long wait before he had to kill again.

The flight wasn't a waste of time. He was considering a takeover of a competitor's company, and he could get some work done on the plane. And this was the first investment: at his request, Belias would start a subtle three-year campaign to drive down his rival's stock price, thanks to today's twenty minutes of work. He could give Belias a wish list to put on the Exchange, and the others in the network would deliver, no matter how long it took. He could be patient in collecting his reward.

One useless thug's life to fuel Barton's future. He felt it a very fair trade.

32

Friday, November 5, afternoon

I woke up to metal cuffs lacing my wrists. I hadn't been down long because the taste of my own blood in my mouth was salty, coppery fresh. I knew this from experience. The fact that I wasn't out for hours was frightening; it meant Belias and his buddy were in a hurry, and they'd dosed me accordingly.

I looked up. Diana was in a chair facing me, terror lighting her eyes.

If you've never been under the complete power of another person, held against your will, you don't know the fear. I knew a horror novel had to be playing through her brain. I'd been shackled and tortured in a prison in Poland, left bound and awaiting execution in a basement in Amsterdam. You are helpless. Your captor can do anything to you. It is a nightmare of surrender made real.

She wasn't bound like I was, though. Belias stood by me, gently wiping my face with water. Beyond him was the bald man. Felix lay on the floor, unconscious. It was easy to forget he was sick with cancer, because he didn't seem overly frail. But I didn't know his condition, what medications he might be on, and I watched the shallow panting of his chest from the tranquilizer. Afraid he might stop breathing.

"Hello, Sam. Thank you for retrieving this for me." Belias held the DOWNFALL file I'd taken from Janice Keene's office. With a dramatic flick of the match he lit the papers on fire. The flame caught, coursed up, blackening the faces of the shamed and the fallen. "I'm impressed with your resourcefulness."

I took his compliment in silence.

"This is really how much they mattered," Belias said, as if to himself. He dropped the flaming clutch of papers into a metal trash can. Then he crooked a smile at me. "No one else has ever gotten close to me this way. Of course, you've been lucky…but no one has managed what you have, Sam. I respect you."

"Mr. Capra," the Englishman said. His eyes were bruised where I'd hit him with the action figure and his stare was seething. I'd made him look bad and I'd have to pay a price.

"I'd like to throw you out a window but that's not on the schedule today." The Englishman injected my arm with a syringe and the hazy dullness of the dart was gone, my heart pounding, every nerve surging, alive, hyperactive. Nothing so calming as not knowing what kind of drugs are tripping through your blood. My heart felt like it might dance past my ribs.

I looked up at the Englishman, water dripping from my face, blood from my lip and my ear. I hurt all over.

"We have questions," the Englishman said. "You will answer. Otherwise, I will be forced to hurt you without any consideration of mercy. You think you're tough but you're not. I know how you're stitched together, and I know how to pull you apart. Nod if you understand."

I gave no sign. The Englishman showed me a scalpel and moved it toward my throat. But then he knelt and placed it against the back of my leg. "Your hamstring. I don't think you'll kick people through windows anymore if I slice this, Sam. Nod if you understand."

I nodded. The Englishman stood, moving the knife away from me.

"We need to talk, Sam." Belias's voice was low and soft. "About your future."

"You mean my lack of one," I said.

"I thought you were an optimist." Belias stepped away from me. "I don't want to hurt either of you. I want us all to embrace reason." Belias turned toward Diana. "Sweetheart, your mom and I are friends. We want to help you. You don't need Sam to protect you."

"I don't know him," Diana said. "I never saw him before I ran into the bar."

"We don't believe you," the Englishman said. "Where is the video?"

"I erased it. I didn't want anyone to see it and get my mom into trouble." Her jaw quivered.

The Englishman and Belias exchanged a glance. "You love your mother very much, don't you, Diana?"

"Yes...please. Just let me go. I promise I won't talk about this. I just want to find my mom."

"But you know about us. People can't know about us...unless they're one of us, so to speak." Belias gave me a sideways glance. "I have to take it as a refusal to join us if you keep running from us."

"Please...please..."

The Englishman turned to me. His fingers closed in hard on my throat. Against the arteries, carotid and jugular. A grip like I'd used on him in the Marchbankses's house. The world hazed. Pain surged through my flesh and bones. I nearly levitated from my chair. The world went black.

He let go. "If I hold that long enough, I can destroy your brain functions," he said. "Do you understand, Diana? I can make your friend Sam here into a vegetable."

"None of us want that," Belias said. "Please, Diana."

"I deleted the video," she said in a rush. "Mom had it on a hidden drive. A little one. I deleted it, wiped the drive, threw it away."

"You might be lying. You might hold on to it until your mom's dead from the cancer and then go to the police," Belias said.

"No, I wouldn't do that."

Belias tapped a finger against his chin. "You could carry on your mother's work, Diana. Be like her. That's what she wants for you. A world with fewer worries for you. I'm impressed you've hidden from us for three whole days. You're your mother's daughter."

"If you could let me talk to my mom..."

"No. Where is the video?"

"I deleted it!" Diana screamed.

"Digital files aren't like paper, obviously. I burn the paper, you know it's gone. The file—well, how many copies could you make and hide, in e-mail accounts, on friends' computers, in the hidden vastness of the Internet?"

"I didn't copy it, I swear; I wouldn't."

The Englishman said, "Did you know how much pressure the average set of testicles can take?" And his hands began to roam down my chest, toward my lap. "They can actually be crushed by a human fist. This was common in the Bosnian war and..."

"He doesn't know anything!" Diana screamed.

"Maybe I should ask *him*," the Englishman said. "Maybe he'll tell me the truth when he watches you suffer." The Englishman straightened me up in the chair.

"Now, Roger," Belias chided, "I don't want you hurting Diana. She's on our side. She's going to be family. If she wants to keep her mother's PR firm."

"Please don't," Diana said. "Please."

I found my breath again.

"And Sam, I want you on our side. I so wish we'd met over a drink rather than at that Russian's house. If we could have a serious talk, we could understand each other." Belias's voice was cool like water on a hot day. "I know you were a CIA castoff, a brave boy they didn't appreciate enough. You have a son now, don't you? His name is Daniel..."

He leaned close to me, smiling, and I slammed my head into his mouth. He fell back, although I couldn't have hit him that hard.

Roger didn't look at me or at Belias. He kicked Diana in the chest, hard, and Diana didn't scream since the air was driven out of her lungs. She fell backward in the chair, in astonishment, her unbound hands covering her face. She moaned.

"Behave," Roger said to me.

"You behave," I said.

"Defiance from you equals pain for her," Roger said.

"Pain for her," I said, "means death for you."

He laughed. "Oh, very grand and brave. You're cuffed. You don't deal any grief to anyone."

"Window," I said and his face reddened.

Belias said quietly, wiping a trace of blood from his lips, "Where is the video, Sam?"

"She said she erased it. I believe her. She had no reason to keep it around. It puts her mother in prison. She doesn't want that."

Belias studied us both. Weighing what she said. Weighing what I'd done to him in the past twenty-four hours. Finally he smiled, and I thought it cold and unsettling.

"I need both of you," Belias said. "Diana, I can give you the world, same as your mother. Design your life, the one you want, and I'll give it to you."

"For free?" I heard myself ask.

"No," Belias said quietly. "Nothing is free. Especially not my particular genius."

I said nothing.

"Diana?"

"I swear, I promise, I deleted the video. I won't say anything…" Diana wasn't crying now, just gasping from the pain of the hood's kick. "No."

"Do you think you'll prosper on your own?" Belias said. "You're not the sharpest pencil in the cup. You need help. You need our help to shine."

His words rattled in my head.

Belias knelt before me, but far enough back where my kick couldn't reach him. "Sam, you are exactly what I'm looking for. What do you want? I can give it to you."

"Really? I doubt that."

"A better life for your son Daniel, perhaps. One free of financial worry."

My breath stopped.

"Your brother, Danny Capra, was murdered. What if I could give you the people who killed him? It would take a bit of time, but I can do it. Would you like that, Sam? You could cut their own throats in turn, just as his was cut."

I clenched my eyes shut. I could see the jerky video again: my brother, a relief worker in Afghanistan, him and his best friend, who was his translator, kneeling before a camera. Then the blades across their throats when the kidnappers' speeches were done. The horror of it.

"You have no way to give those men to me," I said.

"Never sell me short. And wouldn't you like your CIA career in Special Projects back? It's a matter of getting the right people to back you. And getting the wrong people out of the way."

The wrong people out of the way. Downfalls.

I glanced at Felix, who panted shallowly under the influence of the tranquilizer. His words: *Cui bono*? Who benefits?

"You saved the CIA from an embarrassment, twice, that could have crippled them. You exposed a traitor; you stopped a threat that would have destroyed our government."

"Shut up." How could he know? In less than twenty-four hours he'd managed to access my classified CIA file. He *couldn't*. His reach could not be that deep, that secret. I felt like vomiting into my lap.

"Now this is why you fascinate me, Sam. You have power, real leverage, over the CIA, over some of the most powerful people in this government...and you walked away from that power. You still have it. They still owe you. You know it and they know it." He smiled. "Honestly, Sam, how can you have such power and not use it?"

"Shut up," I said again.

"Use it. Go ahead and use it. I can help you. I can make it so...easy. And then you can help me."

"You'd like to own a CIA agent the way you own Glenn and Holly and Janice Keene."

"Oh, Sam, I wouldn't own you. We'd be partners. I think given your history, albeit one unappreciated, you could rise quite high. Very high. Director Samuel Capra. It does roll off the tongue."

Now I smiled at him, at his stupidity. "Would never happen. My wife was a traitor."

"Your wife's files, I understand, have been wiped from the CIA's records. She will never present a political problem to the agency. They can rewrite her history as a heroine, as an undercover agent who was grievously injured in the line of duty."

He held a computer tablet in front of me. Opened a browser. In it was a video, a live camera image. Lucy, my ex-wife, lying in her bed. Comatose, as she had been since an assassin's bullet meant for me struck her in the head. I never knew if she took the bullet for me or if it had just missed. But traitor or not, twice she had saved my life when it would have benefited her to kill me. She could have left me when she discovered she was pregnant. She hadn't.

Was that love? I didn't know.

I made a noise in my throat. A camera feed monitored her and it was available via browser. I wasn't allowed to visit her because she was in a secure location; this was the compromise. I had not looked at her in a long while.

"I watched her earlier today. See, it tells you at the bottom her name, and her stats, her respiration, her heartbeat. Very informative. If I can reach the CIA's servers to display your lovely ex—and you know, they really should be more careful—I can reach the networked medical equipment that keeps her breathing."

"No," I gasped.

Belias's finger hovered above the screen's keyboard. "If I press Delete, then Lucy is…deleted. Don't you want her dead after the nightmare she put you through?"

"Don't," I said. Lucy—I didn't love her anymore. But she was Daniel's mother. There remained a slim hope that she might emerge from the coma one day. I could not let her be killed by this man.

"I don't want to hurt her. Or Daniel. Or his babysitter, the former forger. Or anyone, really," Belias said. "You're alone in the world, Sam; wouldn't you rather be part of something greater?" He knelt close to me again. "Tell me what you want. What you really want. And I'll give it to you."

How often are we asked this? It seems to me that most of the time we push our deepest desires down, for the sake of conventionality or fear. We do what is often safe, not what we want.

"I want you to leave me alone and leave my family alone."

He raised an eyebrow. "Revenge on the secret group you worked for at the CIA, perhaps? They cast you out, called you traitor, did nothing to help you find your son or wife. They left you to die, in a way."

I would never forget how the Special Projects division at the CIA had treated me, but I had moved on. I don't hold on to anger longer than I need to. What is the point?

But Belias wanted me in his club—and if I was in, maybe I could bring him down. I loved undercover work. This wasn't the same, but I'd have to sell him on a lie. Sell it like my life depended on it. That was truth.

I stared at the floor, as though ashamed to meet his gaze. "I…I…I want them to pay."

"Pay how?"

"My whole life I dreamed of working for them, and I was only there for a few years," I said. "I knew I could go far. Now…I sling drinks. They made me untouchable. I can't explain my job history over the past few years to anyone else. My uncle left me some money and I own these bars. I'm not really good at it." I raised my gaze to match Belias's. His eyes shone with delight. "When Rostov tried to pick the fight with me, it opened up something inside of me…that I'd been smothering."

"You were angry."

"Yes."

"You want to strike out."

"More than want. I did."

"Belias," Roger said.

Belias raised a finger to his lips. "They wronged you."

"Do you know what they did to me in prison? Was that in the file?"

"No, tell me," he said, like I was promising to recount forbidden delights. "Did they take out the good stuff, Sam?"

"I could go to the major papers and news networks," I said. "I could tell them how they treated me and my family." My gaze caught Roger's frown. He really didn't like me. I didn't blame him. He was clearly the muscle in the partnership, and I'd shamed him by beating him down this morning. To him, I was nothing but a threat to be put down.

"The best revenge would be taking their jobs, wouldn't it?" Belias said. "Guilt about mistreatment can work wonders. You could rise very far, Sam, with my help."

I didn't care if I never walked into a CIA office again but I said, "Yes."

"All I need you to do is to get me this video. Where did she hide it?"

I heard a noise. Very slight. From the front of the house. I coughed. *Time for a scene*, I thought. "She will tell me if you let me talk to her."

Diana made a noise of horror or maybe pain from the kick the doctor had leveled at her chest.

"Just let me reason with her!" I yelled.

"And then you'll tell me." Belias sounded calmer now. Like he knew he was getting his way, which meant all was right with the world.

"What will you do for me?"

"You want to be back inside the CIA? I'll make it happen. Fifteen years from now you'll be director if you want, or if you prefer a position just below that where you can have huge influence but not have to worry about being replaced whenever a new president gets elected, I'll give it to you. Your enemies will be rendered helpless. Your rivals' careers will stall. Your son—he will be admitted to the finest schools if you like."

"In exchange for what?"

"You do what I say, when I ask. I'm not clingy or needy. I don't ask for a lot."

"Information." I looked up at Roger. "Or carefully applied brutality."

"When necessary."

"That is how you built up Janice and the Marchbankses." I thought of Glenn Marchbanks's history of failure, then his string of amazing successes. I thought of the ruined names in Janice Keene's file. *Your enemies will be rendered helpless. Your rivals' careers will stall.*

"They made the pact," Roger said.

"And how do you know I won't betray you?" I thought of Holly, frightened to death for her children. "Or that someone else who works for you who doesn't much like me"—I nodded at Roger—"won't betray us both to the police?" I made my voice loud, whiny.

Because I'd imagined hearing a noise at the front door. Wishful thinking.

Belias considered me with a smile. "My anger is nothing compared to the anger of a network of extremely powerful people. I think you've already felt their sting a bit."

Access to Lucy. My CIA files. And if I went to the police and said, *There's this network of powerful people who help each other...a good old boy club taken to its worst and most violent extreme...* where was my proof?

The proof was the video Diana had. What her mother had left for her. I met her gaze. She stared into my eyes. No way she'd erased it. It was her only bargaining chip, her silver bullet, the only way out for her and her mother.

"Who are these people, your...Fausts?"

He laughed at the allusion. "That's wonderful, Sam. I like that you're well-read. Fausts. Of course, that's not really the case. My little network of friends, we help each other. We *build* each other. It's all for our mutual benefit."

"And you benefit how?"

"As a broker of power, of information. I built the network. I'm its brain, its heart. I profit from it. I decide who rises, who falls. *I hack human lives.*" Belias's phone pinged. He opened it. A photo of a New York driver's license. The man's name was Viktor Rostov.

"There's a sign of my positive intentions, Sam. I saved your life. They were sending a man after you, and he is now dead. And you're welcome, Sam."

I stared at the phone's screen. He'd killed a man to convince me, to win me over. And to protect himself as well, but it was best I focus on what he was selling.

Belias said, "I keep my promises. And I keep my people safe."

"Thank you," I said. What else do you say?

"Now." He glanced over at Diana. "You seem amenable to what I offer. She does not."

I stared at her. Please let her follow my lead. Please. But terror racked her face. "Diana, they're offering us a good deal."

Diana didn't retreat from her fighting stance. "I want to know where my mom is."

"She's perfectly safe. She's doing some work for me. Work she volunteered to do so I would take care of you, Diana, give you all the help you need," Belias said.

She shook her head. "I can't kill people; I can't do what they want me to do. I can't. I can't." Kill people? Her mother was a killer? She was too rattled, and I thought of what her past days had been like: discovering her mother was part of this network; running for her life, unable to go to the police without incriminating her own mom, unable to ask for help or even shelter; facing a constant threat of kidnapping and possible death. "Just let me go. I won't talk, I won't talk."

"Diana, you and I…we can do this together." I wet my lips. *Please play along*, I thought. *Please.*

Belias looked at us. Both. "So. Moving forward. You both join Team Belias, so to speak. You're going to be taken away to a house of mine I call the Nest. Far from here, private. Where we can discuss your futures, your usefulness, and I can start changing your lives for you. You have someone who's in your way? Tell me. I can make them not be a problem for you."

"Right. By killing them." Diana's tone was harsh.

"Oh, we kill very rarely. It's much easier to derail someone. Killing invites attention." He crinkled a smile at her. "But kill we will, if we must. Your mom excels at it."

Diana made a face of sheer agony and shock. And then I realized, *He has no intention of recruiting her. She's too unwilling. She's failed the test. She's on borrowed time until her mother kills whoever needs killing. Diana Keene is the walking dead.*

If I had a hope of saving her, of saving myself, he had to believe I could be bought. "You want to know what I want gone? The suspicion that I'm somehow connected to the Rostovs because I speak Russian. The police are batting me around like a cat does a mouse. That has to stop. Rostov's death has to be seen as self-defense and it goes no further."

"Done."

Such a confident assertion. "You claim you own the police?"

"Not here, no. But phone calls can be made. Let me handle it. No worries."

I nearly laughed. It was such a bold statement to make, that he could stop an investigation.

"And Holly and Glenn Marchbanks back off from us."

He nodded.

"How do we trust you? You could take us to this Nest place and kill us," Diana said.

"I could kill you right now. A murder-suicide would be so easy. The police already think you're connected; you die together, their suspicions are confirmed once they match your face to the security tape, Diana. Don't be stupid, dear. I don't like stupid." He leaned down close to her, then glanced back at me. "Are you two a romantic pair? That would be extra convenient."

Like we could be the new Glenn and Holly. I started to answer, *No, we're not*, like it mattered, and Diana said, "Don't uncuff Sam. Don't trust him."

"Excuse me?"

"I don't know him. I'm not trusting him to stay quiet about my mom." Her voice went ragged. "He broke into her office to find that DOWNFALL file. Mom didn't give it to me and I didn't give it to him. He came here and questioned me about it. He wants to know what you are, not so he can get a job with you, so he can bring you down. Don't trust him."

She'd decided to deal. Maybe she realized she had no room to breathe. She was scared to death. Scared and she didn't know me, and I was now useless to her, a bargaining chip.

"Well, Sam, there's a dilemma," Belias said. "Who's more useful to me? Her or you? I have an extraordinary loyalty to her mom. But you. You're the prize. I could use you both. Something big is coming."

The room was so silent, and then I heard a groan from Felix, an awakening moan of him shrugging off the tranquilizer dose.

I started to speak and then the lights went out.

33

Friday, November 5, afternoon

Las Vegas

AFTER A SHOWER and a change into nicer cocktail clothes, Janice turned on the television in the hotel room and caught the national broadcast. Barbara Scott was story number five, after a profile of a new leading vice presidential contender (a senator from New Mexico, a woman primarily known as a policy wonk), her not-so-photogenic husband, and her three charming children; a suicide bombing in Moscow that killed three; an announcement of a major debt restructure for an Eastern European nation; and a congress-man involved in a one-car accident who might have been drunk but was under investigation. The announcer glanced over into the camera.

"Best-selling author Barbara Scott, known for her scathing ex-posés of corporate corruption and government malfeasance, was found dead inside her fire-ravaged home in rural Oregon today..."

And then they cut to a reporter, hair blown by wind, standing up-valley from the devastation. Janice listened to the typical re-porter clichés: "in a plot that could have been lifted from one of her books," "a woman who made many enemies," and "the twist at the end of Barbara Scott's life." It was arson; she'd been shot be-fore the fire, no clues, no suspects. Then a retrospective of Barbara Scott's life. She'd graduated from a small college with a journal-ism and English degree, then gotten a master's and a doctorate and started teaching at another equally small college. She never indicated an ambition for a career beyond academia, but then she'd written a brutal account dismantling the legacy of a former president, backed by extraordinary research. Then she'd written a book exposing three prominent CEOs and how they'd mismanaged their apparently healthy companies—scooping every financial reporter in the country and again enjoying a huge publishing success. She'd found the data to support her work, the interviews, the cold, raw facts apparently provided to her by insiders.

Then she'd gone on, the massive best seller out of nowhere, and she'd done the same to the film industry, the investments industry. A book by Barbara Scott scorched lives like an avenging fire. People became afraid of her. The news report showed a film clip of Barbara Scott saying, "Oh, I'm just an everyday person who worked really hard and caught a lucky break or two."

Lucky. Like Lucky Lazard. It gave Janice a chill.

Janice sat down. The reporter reappeared, said investigations were continuing and that according to Barbara Scott's editor she'd been working on a book discounting the idea that certain businesses were too big to fail. Then a picture of Barbara Scott, with the years of her birth and death beneath. Then the TV went to a commercial for investment services.

At least they hadn't said that her laptop was missing. Only because they were still sifting through the rubble. Maybe she had more than one laptop. Some writers did, she was sure.

She stared down the Strip from her window. She was at the Mystik, which was Lazard's newest and grandest property, but from here she could see more of his casinos: the Viking-themed Baltik, the Ekcitment (all glass and curves), the circus-themed Antik. All huge, all prosperous. He was not a loner like Barbara Scott, tucked away in a quiet, witness-free wilderness. Lazard was always in a crowd, always playing the amenable host. And there was casino security. Maybe his own personal detail.

This would be the hardest job of her life. The most challenging to do, the most difficult to survive.

She let herself think of Diana for a bare moment. She swallowed the medication the doctor had given her last week. It would only help mitigate the pain, nothing more. She felt tired. She couldn't afford tired.

Janice went downstairs to the casino. She shoved Barbara Scott and her memory of the woman's momentarily terrified face to the back of her mind. She needed to find her target and figure out how to kill a man who was very well protected.

34

Friday, November 5, afternoon

THE CURTAINS WERE DRAWN, closed at some point after I'd been knocked out, so any neighbors didn't see Belias's fun and games through the windows. Light bled along the edges but it wasn't much, the darkness soft and gray.

I threw myself backward, yelled at Diana to hit the floor.

Diana screamed.

And then Roger fell back, collapsing against a table. I heard the spitting sound of a silenced gun firing. I saw a form in the thin dark—petite, a flash of blondish hair under a dark cap, black clothes—land on Roger, wrench him around, levering an arm around his throat.

Belias jumping for cover behind the couch, aiming at the thin form. I tried to rip my hands out of the cuffs. I couldn't.

Sudden light from the window. Curtains yanked, door opened, a momentary view of the covered hills of San Francisco, the dome of the Palace of Fine Arts in the distance, then darkness again. Diana ran onto the patio and over the back fence of the shared yard.

I vaulted up to my feet, shackled to the chair by my hands. Parkour teaches you a lot but mostly how to move, even when the world is not perfectly aligned for you to be graceful. I powered my leg muscles, more of a mad dash than a jump, and launched myself over the couch, and in the dim light I saw Belias's surprised face before I crashed down on him. I tried to headbutt him—my forehead was my only weapon—but he writhed free from under me and my head hit the hardwood floor.

Black blobs swam before my eyes. Another shot rang out and Belias yelled, either in pain or terror, but he grabbed the back of the chair, yanked me up in front of him. Suddenly I was his shield.

"Stop it!" Belias yelled, and the dark figure now stood behind Roger, a gun to his head.

"I'm hurt," Roger said as though surprised.

Belias ignored him. He dragged the chair and me to the door, the gun leveled past my shoulder, aiming at the table.

"Sam," he whispered in my ear. "Sam, Sam, Sam, I did not want us parting this way."

Roger staggered, staring at the red wet patch on his chest—I could see it in a slash of light between the closed curtains. "John," he said to Belias. "John, don't leave me..."

And Belias put a bullet in his head. Roger dropped, only held up by the figure behind him.

"I'll shoot the cuff off you," he whispered from behind me, in my ear. "Come with me."

"No. We walk away from each other."

"I saved you from the Rostovs. Don't forget that." He yanked the chair into the open doorway, jamming me between door and frame. "I saved him!" he yelled back into the house.

Belias ran.

The figure bolted from the table and ran past, yanking me out of the way. Mila. She lost valuable seconds making sure I wasn't hurt. Then she ran through the gate, out into the street. I struggled and waited to hear gunfire from the street. But I heard nothing. The house was at a corner. If she turned wrong, she could lose him.

I tried to move the chair, scooting back into the town house, and I fell over onto Roger. Odd thing to lie and wait in someone else's blood and wonder which way the pendulum will swing. Live or die. Belias could kill Mila and come back for me. I always figured if I died cuffed to a chair I'd still be drawing a CIA paycheck.

I tried to kick toward Felix, who was stirring, moaning, trying to push himself up onto his knees.

"Sam," a voice said above me.

Mila.

"Diana..."

"She's gone. The man in black got away."

"We have to find Diana. She's got the evidence to destroy him."

"The only thing we have to do," Mila said, "is get you free and get you cleaned up and get out of here. What a mess you've made, Sam."

"Get me unhooked."

She turned on a light.

"Sam in cuffs. I should leave you like this. You leap before you look."

"No, I didn't. Get me out of this, please."

"And you are welcome for the saving of the life."

"Thank you."

She stood on one leg and pulled the heel off one of her boots. Wedged in the heel was a lockpick. She knelt and worked the pick into the cuffs, and in seconds I was free. I stood. Blood from Roger was on my shirt collar. I checked his pockets while she threw water in Felix's face, got him to his feet. Found a wallet, took it. The longer the police took to identify him, it might be an advantage for me.

I stood. "Do you hear police sirens?"

"Yes. Perhaps a neighbor does not care for the sounds of shooting."

"Or maybe Belias found Diana and killed her on the streets. He wants a video she has."

"Hidden here?"

"I don't know." *Where?* And we weren't exactly friends now. She'd thrown me to Belias. Where would she go? Maybe Felix would know. "We better go." I straightened up. My face was bruised from the beating; it ached, my arms hurt.

"Back to the bar," she said. "We'll get you cleaned up."

"How did you find us?"

"Felix texted me where you were."

"Diana..." Felix said. He stumbled. He'd gotten a heavier dose than I had or he'd had a worse reaction to the tranquilizers.

We headed through the shared yard, over the fence, squeezing past two buildings on a corner. The sirens were getting louder. I followed Mila to her car, Felix in between us, walking a bit like he was drunk.

A police car shot past us, sirens going. They would get a surprise, a dead man in the house. Maybe he'd knock me off the front page of the press. It seemed only fair.

"Thank you," I said as we reached Felix's van.

"You are welcome, Sam. We need to know who this man is."

I checked the wallet. Roger Metcalfe. Belias had killed his own man. And now he wanted me on his side.

35

Dɪᴀɴᴀ ᴡᴀs ɢᴏɴᴇ.

He'd overreached, trying to get Sam on his side, which seemed as necessary as recruiting Diana. You'd think a disaffected spy would be easier to convert, to buy—bars ran on narrow margins. But if he'd concentrated on Diana, perhaps he'd have that video now as well.

A mistake I must not make again, he told himself.

She'd fled the town house, and he'd seen Diana as he ran out onto the street, already driving an old BMW, and she turned onto Gough and headed south, and still on foot he couldn't give chase. He hurried toward his own car, hearing the first hint of sirens crying on the clear air. Sam's rescuer hadn't appeared—he thought in the dim light that it was a woman, and he'd eluded her on the street—she must have turned the wrong way. It had been a final bit of luck for him.

And how exactly did Sam have a helper there at the town house and a rescuer? Sam had a team. This was a surprise.

This was a costly day.

Glenn and now Roger, bad, bad, bad. Roger was special—they'd been together for so long—and he felt a knot of grief tighten in his chest. But Roger wouldn't have wanted to be captured. He knew Roger well enough, he told himself, that shooting him had been a mercy. It was the fault of that woman, the one who'd come to Sam's aid.

He stumbled to his car and got in and willed himself not to be sick. He felt weak, but the grief for Roger would come soon enough, then the mad, red rage of frustration. He had to be ready for it, prepare for it, steel for it. That was when he might make a mistake and there were no mistakes to spare.

He drove. Aimlessly. The safe house in the Mission District, off Valencia; he should go there. Figure out a way to fight back.

The decision calmed him, and he started to think again.

Possibilities. One was that someone with Sam Capra now had come to his rescue. A very competent someone who did not balk at attacking two armed men in an unfamiliar, darkened space, who had accessed the house without him noticing, in silence and stealth. But Sam Capra was *ex*-CIA. He did not have colleagues with agency skill sets; he had bartenders and waitresses and bouncers.

Or did he? What if he had...something more? Maybe he had just a friend, also ex-CIA, who had decided to have his back? The thought frightened and thrilled Belias. Two Sam Capras would be even better than one. And maybe the anonymous person who wanted Sam recruited would want Sam's friend. Possibly. He would have to get past the anger over Roger's death.

He slammed a hand against the wheel.

So who was Sam Capra's rescuer? And where would Diana go now?

He called Holly on his cell phone. "Holly?"

"What?"

"I just had Diana and the bartender as prisoners and now I don't. Because someone interfered and killed Roger, and you and I are going to end up dead or in prison if we don't figure this out."

He could hear her swallow. "I don't know what you expect me to do. The Tiburon police are here...we've had some weird vandalism at my house. I'll have to call you later."

"You sell that story hard," he said, and turned off the phone.

Next step. He'd killed Viktor Rostov to protect Sam and Sam knew it now. Now he needed to prove to Sam he could get the police off of him, as he'd asked.

And if that didn't work, well, there was this infant son of Sam's.

He didn't care for threatening children (and it was always done subtly; to be crude about it made people want to bolt to the police) but he knew from experience that people could easily be bent when their children's happiness was at stake.

And then Sam Capra would be far more likely to listen to a necessary offer.

36

Friday, November 5, afternoon

Anitra DeSoto usually skipped lunch, but her doctor had chided that her poor eating habits were wrecking her blood sugar. She tucked into a bowl of flavorless microwave noodles and wished for butter and garlic for seasoning. She read her e-mails, deleting the ones she didn't want to bother with and flagging the ones she'd finish later. She supposed it was progress, but she hated e-mail, a dislike she felt she could never air, as her colleagues would think her crazy. The computer made everything easier, didn't it? She wasn't so sure. She'd wanted this job because she didn't want to ride a desk and she liked being out and about and she loved the city and she didn't love windowless rooms. But she spent far more time on the computer than people would suspect, dealing with the digital equivalent of paperwork, e-mailing people to get information, contacting other jurisdictions, running background checks and online research. Cops used to have flat feet; she thought she'd have flat fingers by the time she retired.

Her boss sent her an e-mail, MY OFFICE NOW as the subject line, no message in the mail itself. She got up from her desk and he closed the office door behind her.

"This man who killed at The Select bar in self-defense," he said. "Sam Capra."

"I'm not sure it was self-defense. The victim's brother died that same night. That can't be coincidence."

It was as if she hadn't spoken. "The victim pulled a knife on Capra, yes?"

"Yes, but…"

"And several witness statements corroborated that account of self-defense?"

"Yes. They also corroborated that Capra spoke Russian to the man."

"But you've not tied him to the other Rostov case."

"We haven't finished processing the scene. There are dozens of prints there; apparently the Rostovs were partyers."

He let ten seconds pass. "Sam Capra works for the government. I can't tell you more than that because if I do I will violate federal law. It was self-defense, Anitra. Do not pursue further."

"He's FBI? Undercover?"

"I am saying that I have been assured by someone in Washington, who knows more than you or I do, that Sam Capra does not have a connection to Russian mobsters, but we cannot know more about him. We cannot bring attention to him."

A bar owner, who was absentee, comes to town, trouble erupts. Undercover. It could make sense. "You have to be kidding me. Why isn't he telling us he's undercover? I was alone with him in an interview room."

"With a videotape recording his every word."

She went silent.

"I cannot say more. Finish the paperwork. I expect everything in your report will support a finding of self-defense. The district attorney's office won't be pursuing charges against him."

"The Russian's brother turned up dead. Are we supposed to stop investigating *his* death? You can't say they're not connected."

"I am assuming if there is information about Capra or the Rostovs that is salient to our investigations and the feds have it, we'll hear about it eventually." Her boss sat down. "I know this is not a perfect solution…"

"Even if Capra's undercover and comes to the attention of the Russians, are we thinking Grigori Rostov decided to kill him in the middle of a crowded bar? That's not typical. They'd grab Capra, haul him out to the sticks, kill him there, let the fish feast on him in the bay. He'd just vanish. A fight in a bar? It's too public for these guys."

"These guys, as you put it, are often idiots ruled by emotion. Grigori Rostov was a screwup in New York City, he came here. Not a genius. We're done discussing this. What part of *this is not our business* do you not get?"

"We're a nation of laws…"

"Yes, we are. And if we inadvertently expose someone working against the bad guys, then we're breaking those laws ourselves. Finish the paperwork, Anitra, then walk away. I don't want you even going to Sam Capra's bar for a drink. Give him distance."

She bit her lip.

"Anitra? Are we clear?"

"Yes, sir, very clear. I'll complete the report."

"Thank you. And obviously you know what to say to the press. Which is nothing except this was self-defense."

"I do. I'll try to be more convinced than I feel."

"The reporters will probably leave you alone now. Just heard a man was found shot in a condo over in the Marina District. Headlines never stick for long."

He nodded and she got up and walked out of the office. She went to the soda machine and fed a dollar bill into the slot and picked up the cold can of Coke that popped down the slide. She went back to her desk.

Her mind raced. If Sam Capra was an undercover agent working against the Russian mob, he should have been pulled back to safety by now. And maybe he had been. But her conversation with Mila made it sound like he'd be back at his bar at any minute. It did not quite add up. Perhaps Mila was unaware that Sam was a federal agent of some sort.

Anitra glanced around at her colleagues. Several of them, in her place, would just shrug and finish the paperwork and be done with it. Move on to the next case. Maybe all of them. They were honorable men and women, and they had a hard job to do—why waste time on a lost cause? She should, too. The Rostovs were known bad guys, and there was nothing to say that Sam Capra was a bad man.

She'd thought she was about to embark on a case that would make her name and now it was dust. Nothing. And the cutbacks and the layoffs kept coming and this had been her chance to shine. To break a case that was much more than it seemed, and how often did such cases come around?

She went back to the search engine, searched for *Sam Capra FBI*, then, just because the Rostovs were Russian, *Sam Capra CIA*. And this was what troubled her: Sam Capra wasn't an identity forged for undercover work; she'd seen his video interview on YouTube. He existed. So if he wasn't undercover, what was he? An informant?

It didn't matter. She had her orders, like them or not, and so she wouldn't push further. She would have to find another way to investigate the Rostov deaths without implicating Sam Capra.

Her cell rang. "DeSoto," she answered.

The voice was masked by a scrambler and sounded like it came from the lower pits. "What part of *let it go* did you not understand?"

"What?" She was so startled she nearly dropped the phone. Her voice was a harsh whisper.

"One minute ago, you're searching for him on the Internet, DeSoto. After you've been told to let it go, that it's not your concern. Do you want to get federal agents killed?"

She said, "No."

"Then do as you're told." The phone went dead.

She slowly set the phone back on her desk. She fought the urge to push away from her computer.

They knew what she typed. They knew what she searched for on the Internet.

A cold fire crept along her spine.

She closed the search engine. She shoved her uneaten, tasteless noodles into the trash. Maybe today was a good day to go out for lunch. Yes, get some fresh air. Get away from here. Get away from the desk.

37

Mila hurried me and Felix into the upstairs above the bar. I felt a sense of relief that Detective DeSoto hadn't camped out on my doorstep to ask more pointless questions.

But Mila, mad, is a worse nightmare than the police.

"You both look dreadful." She grabbed me, not to embrace me—she is not a hugger, our Mila—but to inspect the bandage on my neck, the bruises on my face. "A gun wound. A beating. Shall I break a leg for you to save time?"

"Never mind me, I need to check Felix." I sat Felix down on the couch, checked his pulse, the dilation of his pupils.

"They didn't hurt Felix." She seemed surprised that Felix was the medical priority. Because she didn't know he was ill.

"I'm fine, Sam, really." Felix's voice sounded steady. But he was a sick man on medications. I got him a damp washcloth and a bottle of cold water from the refrigerator and then went and washed my face in the bathroom sink. I should just stay at the bar some days. Bars are safe.

"You have behaved without restraint." Mila stood in the bathroom door.

"Says the woman who roared in, gun blazing."

"Ingratitude is ugly on you, Sam, like a bad color. You were told to discover these people," she said. *Pipple*, and when Mila's accent begins to thicken, it's like a storm cloud going dense with thunder. "I was in LA when you called and I took a plane up here immediately. This morning we agreed you to find out who these *pipple* are, nothing more. Now you have had three dangerous encounters with this man in a twenty-four period." She held up three accusing fingers.

I gently took her hand and folded down one finger into her fist. "Two's the number we worry about now. Two choices—take him down or join him."

"Sam."

"What?"

She yanked her hand away from mine. "You said you didn't want trouble yet here we are. You are trying to go inside this man's criminal ring or network. Stop."

"I didn't look for this trouble, it came here. It will come back if we don't stop him."

"Trouble came here." Her tone mocked. "You had a choice. You could have stayed away from Rostov's apartment. You could have not gone to the Marchbankses' house this morning. You could anonymously phone police and say where this Diana person was hiding and not involve us deeper. Now we have war between us and this Belias man. You have, how do the Americans say? Stepped in it. Up to your chin. Which, unlike rest of you, has not taken beating."

I didn't need a lecture. "Are Leonie and Daniel all right?" It seemed like forever since I spoke to them. "Belias has seen my CIA file. He knows about Daniel." I kept my voice under tight control.

She gave the briefest of reactions: her lips thinning, standing a bit straighter at the mention of my son. I think Mila might take a bullet for Daniel. But she lowered the tone of her voice. "We cannot have that. Since they know your face and your name, you go to your nice baby boy and you take care of him and you let me handle this mess you have made. Belias does not know me."

"He might have seen your face."

She shrugged. "Might. Room was dark, and there was his friend between us he was focusing on killing."

"And I'm the only one who can get inside and bring him down. I'm the one he wants. Jimmy can protect Leonie and Daniel. Belias can't find them."

She chose to ignore my impeccable logic. "Why did you over-reach?" The tone of voice she took reminded me she'd once been a schoolteacher, a lifetime ago.

"I told you, I had to be sure this threat wasn't Nine Suns or..."

"Flimsy excuse," she said. "This man is not what you and I have fought before. We know that now. He is his own network. Not smugglers, not slavers, not dope dealers. His circle are highly placed people, that is the theory?"

"Yes. We know of at least two high-powered, influential executives he has working for him. Both are currently missing. And one of them was at Dalton Monroe's dinner, when he was poisoned. You did want me to investigate that, remember?"

"Janice used me to get close to Dalton Monroe," Felix said softly. He told her what we'd found in Janice's home, in her office—both the file there, and the clipping about Dalton Monroe in the DOWN-FALL file. I sat down heavily in the chair and explained the confrontation at the Marchbankses' house.

Felix said, "Or Dalton is somehow in Belias's way. We could get Jimmy to talk to Dalton, to find out if there's any possible connection. And Dalton needs to be under our protection."

"He's already being guarded." At the mention of Jimmy, Mila slid her gaze back to me. "And Belias knows where to find you. Here at the bar."

"Well, you're here now to save me," I told her. "Get a gun and pick a window, and we'll make our stand when Belias and his ninja soccer mom and his high-placed gang charge the front door."

"Mila..." Felix said.

"Don't you have glasses to clean?" Mila snapped.

He stared at her. "I'm sure I do." Felix turned and went back downstairs. A few moments later the phone rang and we heard him speaking softly, probably fending off another reporter. I wanted to tell her about Felix's cancer—but I'd promised to keep my mouth shut.

Mila sighed, put her thumb and forefinger up to the bridge of her nose. "Now you have made me be rude to poor Felix. That is like kicking a puppy."

"Kick me, not him," I said. "Look, Belias isn't going to let it go. He offered me my CIA career back and he acted like he could deliver it on a silver tray. He accessed Lucy's life support and could have killed her. He claims he's killed a man for me and he can get the cops off my back here. Marchbanks and Janice Keene went from nobodies to being enormous successes." I leaned toward her. "They. Want. Power. If they see me as a threat, if they find out about you, the Round Table, do you think they'll stop? Or just back off?"

She was silent for a moment as she considered.

"You and I both know, most guys who are running a network, you tread on them, they try to scare you off or pay you off or kill you. This guy tried to recruit me."

"I will happily inform him what a mistake it is to offer you a job," Mila said.

"Mila, this is not some simple criminal gang. This is a…cabal. A secret club. Both he and Holly led me to believe it's far more than Glenn and Janice. They froze Diana's bank accounts and credit cards. They've accessed my CIA file. Do you know how hard it is to do either of those things? His reach is insanely deep." I let my words roll around in her head. "Think of a gang. They seek territory, revenue, power. But first, revenue. What would you do if you had wealthy people in your pocket?"

"One like Glenn Marchbanks? I would invest in his golden companies."

"And he never backed a loser for the past ten years. Never. That's impossible. And he masqueraded it as genius."

"Very good at his job?"

Felix stood in the doorway. Pointedly drying a glass. Mila rolled her eyes and gestured him back into the room, which was her version of an apology.

"But what made him good? Instinct? He stumbled badly in his early career. Or better information? Did he have facts that no other investor could have had?" I crossed my arms. "How did he get it? That is what makes me think this is huge or far ranging. What if Marchbanks wasn't just sharing critical information with Belias? What if other information was being shared with Marchbanks inside this group so that he never made a misstep? A constant ongoing exchange of information and favors. And the members of the network are the only ones who gain. They benefit each other. Like a private marketplace of the powerful."

I could see her rolling the idea around in her head. "How could this work?"

"Belias is like you."

"What?"

"He's the hub. I'm guessing they don't know each other's names, at least not all of them. Just like I don't know who are the leaders in the Round Table but you do. That's his power, his protection and theirs. Without him it will fall apart. They can't betray each other."

I was speaking her language—she could understand secret networks. So time for the pitch on what I wanted to do now. "The file I took from Janice Keene's office. It's got people in it who were successful and then took a long painful downfall."

"Belias burned them," Mila said.

"I remember the names, don't you, Felix?"

"Yes. We can probably find all the same articles online. And even more info about them."

I turned back to Mila. "Look what Felix asked when we looked at the misfortunes of these people. *Cui bono*? Who benefits? Maybe these people paid the price for the network's success. We find out who benefited from their downfall. *That* could give us candidates who might be Belias's people. Janice Keene's terminally ill; she's trying to protect her daughter in more than one way. The video to explain the network because maybe she wanted her daughter to be part of it after she was gone and gain all the benefits."

"And the video because she was too ashamed to face her daughter," Mila said. "Confessions are always easier from the grave."

"But I think I see what Janice is doing—giving Diana a clue to people she knew were destroyed by Belias, because that's the key to finding out who else is in the network. If Diana ever needed insurance."

"People where Janice had a direct hand in their ruin."

"Yes. If we can reconstruct the names in the DOWNFALL file," I said, "we can find, maybe, who are his people, and most importantly, who is *he*? We know that, we can own him."

After a moment, she nodded.

We split up the eleven names we remembered from the file, opened laptops, and began to search for their stories. It wasn't hard to reconstruct their sad histories. People on the rise who'd fallen, suddenly and horribly. A few had died—accidents, shot, or from a sudden heart attack. Others had been sent to prison, claiming they'd been wrongly framed. Others had lost everything. The printer whirred as we sent articles to it and began to post them on the wall, grouping them by name.

"If these two people died," I said, "did Janice kill them? We know she tried to poison Dalton."

"I'm thinking yes," Felix said in a flat tone, and I went back to work. I knew what it was like to have someone you cared for be a complete liar. To use you in every way. Listening to me talk about a similar experience wouldn't help him; there is no cure for that deep sting but time.

An hour into the work, Felix got up and stuck an index card next to one of the faces.

"Sam. Mila." I could hear anxiety in his voice.

"What did you find?" I asked.

"A Los Angeles venture capitalist named Carl Standish." He pointed at a picture of a confident, older man who looked polished and successful. "He was ruined in a series of start-ups that went sour. The last three companies he funded were all beaten in the market by companies backed by Glenn Marchbanks."

"So the person who benefited here was Glenn," I said. A thread, a connection, to prove our theory.

"In more than one way. Mr. Standish had three children. After he lost his fortune his two sons financed college through ROTC and went into the military. His youngest, a daughter, decided to go into acting. She got regular work on a cop show that shot a lot of exterior scenes here in San Francisco and she ended up meeting and marrying her dad's former business rival."

It felt like a punch. "Audrey Marchbanks."

"Yes."

I studied the photo of Mr. Standish. I'd only caught a glimpse of Audrey, but her father had been a handsome man and you could see the shadow of resemblance. "Belias ruined her dad to benefit Glenn Marchbanks…and years later Glenn Marchbanks left Holly and married her?"

"That's my theory."

"But…why would she have had anything to do with the man who took down her father?" Mila said.

And then a realization jelled. "But that's the beauty of it. Under how we think Belias's network works, Glenn Marchbanks never lifted a finger. It was the rest of the network—maybe just Janice, maybe others—but not Glenn. This list of people she had, I don't yet see a way Janice profits from their downfall. But with Standish, Glenn does."

I stood, ran a finger along the photos and the articles. "Like that Hitchcock movie where two strangers meet on a train and each decides to kill the other's enemy. They'll never be suspects, they don't directly gain. But Glenn benefits, and then he does something else to help the network's members in turn. They might not even know who benefits from what they do. Belias is the hub. The conductor. The central nervous system. The way Mila is ours."

Felix and Mila were silent, studying the photos.

"But still he must have known." I wondered, *Did Glenn feel sorry for Audrey?* Her father ruined, put out of business, his reputation lessened, his investments vastly reduced in value. It didn't seem like the Standishes had turned into homeless people, though; I had no idea. But he'd married her. Maybe he'd thought he was saving her.

What if she knew the truth about her husband?

I wondered what would happen if I told her. I might need Audrey Standish Marchbanks to not stay so loyal to her husband. But I had no evidence.

"Could we find proof of this?" I asked.

"That's the challenge—Glenn wouldn't have been anywhere near her father's ruin," Felix said. "He'll be clean."

I knew Felix was right but it wasn't the answer I wanted.

Felix gestured to the other photos. "It's hard to know exactly who benefits from their falls. Some of them are easy to identify—a major rival in business, let's say, but there's never just one rival. Some it's not nearly so cut and clear. If it's a personal or a romantic rival, that would take much more time to find. And when you're dealing with accomplished people, a downfall creates a lot of opportunity for others."

I stared at the faces of the fallen, the people that had been ruined. An agony was on most of their expressions, a surprise—*why has this happened to me? What have I done?* It was so unfair—the unfairness of it in an unfair world stung me in my chest.

"So Audrey might be a point where we can get inside and find out more about this network. That information might be in Glenn's house. I want us to think about how to get inside there."

"If he wanted to take over, he had to assess the risk," Felix said. "Not to mention consider insurance."

"You're right," I said. "Put yourself in Glenn's shoes. You've risen to the top of your field. You're successful. But the price of that success is that you have to help others succeed, and you might have to break the law to do it. You get everything but you could easily lose everything. You might want some insurance. If you go down, you point at others. Maybe they can save you. Or by naming some really big names you save yourself with the cops. Or if you get enough names, you get rid of Belias. You don't need him anymore."

"Remind me not to form an alliance with you," Mila said. "Oops, too late."

Something big is coming. Which meant someone powerful was joining the network, presumably. And did that have anything to do with Janice Keene's file or her mysterious mission for Belias? I looked at the photos on the wall. Eleven people could mean dozens of rivals in business or politics or just life. This could take time. "You keep on the people in the file, Felix. I'm going to figure out who Belias is."

"Sam," Mila said. "I think that's smart. He's just like the people you used to hunt."

And she was right. I'd worked for a division at CIA that targeted criminal elements who represented a threat to national security. I went after arms traffickers and smugglers who could sneak both weapons and terrorists across borders, along with contraband. Belias was exactly the kind of guy I used to hunt, used to go undercover to get close to and bring down. I could feel the heat of excitement warm my blood. "Okay. I'll focus on him, you focus on the network."

"Why did he do it? Belias? Build this network?" Mila said. "At some point in his life, he made this choice. That fascinates me."

"Never mind the why," Felix said. "How did he do it? Who is he that he could manage this?"

I ticked off what I guessed about him. "He's an American who spent a lot of time in the UK, judging from his hybrid accent. He said he was a computer hacker who now hacked lives. He made a comment at Rostov's that he dislikes Russians, but he spoke to me in Russian. He and Holly and Glenn wear a symbol, and I saw the same symbol in Janice's office, with sixty-three others. And he knew a Special Forces soldier named Roger Metcalfe."

Those were my starting points. I wished I still had access to CIA databases. It would make life easier.

"Show me this symbol," Mila said.

I showed her the necklace I'd taken from Holly.

"And there were ones like this? Sixty-four, you said?"

"Yes."

"I thought you were exposed to other cultures in your nomadic childhood," Mila said. "There are sixty-four symbols in the I Ching, the Chinese fortune-telling system, also called the Book of Changes."

"This doesn't look Chinese," I said.

"These are hexagrams. Solid line is yang, open space is yin. The balance between opposing forces." She went to the laptop, opened a search window.

"It was in a bottom row of a whole series of them in Janice's office."

"Ah, here. Hexagram fifty-seven. Its modern interpretation is 'subtle influence' or 'with cultivation comes influence.'"

"Subtle influence," Felix said. "Behind the scenes, with no one knowing. Sounds like our guy with his promises and deals."

"How'd you know this?" I asked.

Mila smiled. "Jimmy took me to a Chinese fortune-teller in London a few months ago. I liked it better than the museums."

She would.

"After we have caught him and made him spill his secrets," Mila said, "we will turn him over to a psychologist. It should be fun."

"We catch him, we kill him," Felix said.

"No. We find out who all is in this network," she said. "But we don't turn them over to the police."

The silence in the room was sudden.

"Mila, I want to break up this network so it can't threaten us. We're not going to turn them into something useful to the Round Table," I said. "Belias might want me, I don't want him."

"Yes, Sam, I do not mean that we keep his network alive. But innocent people—families, employees, and many investors—will all be hurt when they are exposed. And that exposing them might expose us, as well. How do we explain how we caught them? Why would they remain silent?"

"If Belias vanishes, the network dies," Felix said. "That's all we have to do."

"Felix, you care for this Janice? You don't want to see her in court or in jail, especially if she is dying," Mila said.

Felix nodded slowly. "But she used me. She used me to get to Dalton. That implies they know about the Round Table."

"It implies they know Dalton comes here for a drink every time he's in San Francisco and that you are his friend, and you might be at his event. That's rather different than knowing about the Round Table as a whole."

Maybe she was right. And yet Belias seemed...surprised by me and my skills. If he knew about the Round Table, he shouldn't be. Something didn't fit. Something wasn't right.

"Then we must take them over," Mila said, "before they take us, to put an end to them. Is like a hostile takeover in movies, yes?" She almost sounded pleased.

Felix and I exchanged a look.

I watched Mila sit back down at her laptop and connect a fresh phone to her laptop. She connected to a database servicing the various cellular carriers and started looking for Glenn Marchbanks's account.

"So we take them over and you'd be the new Belias," I said. "I knew my earlier comparison was a bad idea."

"Hardly. I'm not ruining other people for them. They have access to information, to cash, access to people. This is how they're useful. We tell them we'll expose them if they don't cooperate."

"They're fakes."

She laughed. "What do you mean, Sam?"

"They didn't earn their success."

"Okay, this is what I find amusing, and yes, it makes me a bad person. What if they were capable of success on their own? What if Belias has just made them feel like he is needed to be successful for them. He is like the—What is the American good luck thing that is gross? Ah. The rabbit's foot."

"I think it's more than that."

"Is it? Oh yes, perhaps there is a rival and he takes the rival out of the picture. How does the insecure fool in the network know he wouldn't have won success on his own terms?"

I hesitated. "They don't."

"Yes. So they feel always Belias is a necessary part of their success. It is a psychological poison. Belias is their drug. I don't want to destroy them. I want to free them from their addiction to him."

I saw her reasoning and her logic irritated me. And if we took down Belias, would someone else simply take his place? Better us than a successor. "Perhaps."

"I wonder," Mila said. "Perhaps you are like these people who put their faith in Belias and his game."

"How?" I glanced at her. "No one's done me any special favors in a real long time."

"No. But you see, they have a good life. They have all they want. Yet it is not enough."

"I don't know what you mean."

"Me, my life, I can never go back to Moldova. I would be found, killed. After what I have done, I cannot be a schoolteacher again and sit in a room full of children and mold young thoughts. I have seen too much and done far worse. But you. You could just run the bars, have your life with Daniel and"—here she made a face at the thought of Leonie—"have the forger nanny person. You could have the normal life. But you would choose to have the two lives, the public and the secret, like these people. You would be two Sams."

"That's not true."

Mila didn't reply.

My cell phone rang. I answered, hoping it wouldn't be Belias. I didn't like the question Mila now had rattling in my mind.

"This is Detective DeSoto."

"Hello, Detective."

"Our investigation finds you acted in self-defense, Mr. Capra. No charges will be filed." Her voice sounded worn, dead.

"Oh. That's great." Belias made it happen. I felt the pit of my stomach shiver.

"I suppose you have heard that Mr. Rostov's brother was killed at their home that same night."

"They must have been dangerous men living dangerous lives," I said.

"The sad tragedy of House Rostov continues."

"What do you mean?" I couldn't act as if I already knew. But this was independent confirmation.

"There's a dead Rostov in the Denver airport. He had a seat on a flight to San Francisco. Poisoned, they think, in a bathroom stall." She made a small, silvery laugh. Not one of amusement.

Poison. I thought of Janice's attempt on Dalton.

"Three dead Rostovs might eventually mean one dead Capra. Be careful."

"I had nothing to do with any dead Rostovs except the first one."

"I hope your powerful friends who warned me off will warn *them* off. I'm sure it will make a great difference to the Rostovs when they're told, hands off you. They'll run home and have their three funerals and count themselves lucky they were warned. Off. You." She laughed again, bitter.

"Why?" I said. "Why are you telling me this?"

"If you're truly on the side of the angels, then good luck to you. Give my regards to Mrs. Court."

Mrs. Court? I started to ask who that was, but then I remembered she'd spoken with Mila. Odd. I'd never heard Mila use that pseudonym. "I will. Thank you, Detective." I hung up.

I told Mila what happened. "Belias said he could turn off the heat."

The idea that he could, and he had, made us all fall silent for a moment.

"He just proved to you his power. He's gotten the police off your back." She sounded slightly stunned. "He is trying to steal you away from me. Little poaching jerk."

"This is a doorway for me to get in with him."

She nodded. "We need to give him that reason. I have worked out the logic. It is very dangerous, Sam. Not just for you but for me."

"What do you suggest?"

"The stumbling block to him recruiting you is me—that you have an ally. So. I must be disposable."

I blinked, started to speak, and she smiled.

"Give me a few pieces of silver," Mila said, "and I'll betray you."

PART FOUR

SATURDAY, NOVEMBER 6

38

Saturday, November 6, morning

HOLLY RANG THE BELL and Belias came down and unlocked the gate. He looked like he hadn't slept well. She waited to speak until he had closed the house's door behind her.

"I did what you asked," she said. "The police in Tiburon don't think it was aimed at me, just random. They asked about my ex-husband, obviously, because they asked if I had enemies, or any of my family did. I told them Glenn was out of town and would call them when he got back. So. I've sold your lies." She sat down.

Belias poured her coffee. She was surprised he remembered how she took her sugar and cream. "Audrey hasn't reported Glenn missing yet."

"How do you know?"

"I have her phones, e-mails, and text messages tapped."

"Of course you do." Holly drank her coffee. "I sent my college roommate a long e-mail. Outlining how Glenn had come to the house, tore it up, fired a few shots, broken two windows. Then broke down and cried and begged me not to call the police or his wife. That he wanted time alone from her. That he was a man I didn't know. That I fibbed to the police about it. She'll keep it and have it when Glenn goes missing."

"I'm sure," Belias said, "that it was beautifully written. I wish I could write a eulogy for Roger. But it's not like I can give a speech in front of lots of people."

She didn't want to hear about Roger. "I can't be suspected in Glenn's death," she said. "Of course they'd look at me as the ex-wife. I can't go to jail, can't lose my kids." She hadn't been able to sleep last night, consumed by fear and panic and guilt.

"You won't."

"So I've done what you want and I want out." She set down the coffee mug. "I've done what you asked. This is a huge risk for me. I consider my debt discharged."

"We had a deal. You'll be free when this…situation is resolved. When Sam Capra is under my control."

"He killed Glenn. No room for him here." She said it before she thought.

"We're losing people. Glenn. Roger. Diana's mother has cancer, she doesn't have long. I need him."

She clenched her hand into a fist, pressed it to her mouth.

"What does it matter? You won't have to work with him. You'll have a very easy job. No more danger."

"What job?"

"I'll tell you soon enough. But I promise you, Holly, it will be the safest job imaginable for you."

His sudden smile made her uneasy. "How could you want to recruit him after he killed Glenn? And after Roger's death?"

"I don't have to explain myself to you…but know that I don't believe in revenge. It's messy and expensive."

She balled her hands into fists. Then let them go.

"We're going to set a trap for him, and I'm going to make him an offer. Now. It may not work. But if it does, he's mine and you're free from dangerous work and then we're all happy, yes?"

"What about Diana?"

"He can give her to us. Our problem is Audrey."

"Audrey will be expecting Glenn to contact her. Audrey will no doubt freak out when he doesn't call her tonight or tomorrow."

"Then text her," Belias said. "Pretend that you're him. You know the kind of words he'd say."

Holly rubbed her temples. She felt like she'd aged a decade in a day. "I don't think I can be that cruel, John."

"You can be if you have to be."

Holly sat down in the chair. She remembered when they bought their Tiburon house, when she furnished it with the things she liked, possessions she could love, when she and Glenn rose high in society, when the children were accepted at the best schools, and she and Glenn had more money than she could spend in a lifetime…and now her life here felt like an anchor. All that mattered were her children, getting herself out of this disaster so it would never touch them. If she had to vanish—to Canada or New Zealand or South Africa…she could live simply. The kids could, too; it would be a wrenching adjustment. But they could cope. If only he would let her go.

"I'm grateful you're still on my side, Holly. I've always admired your strength."

The tone of his words…she glanced at him, then glanced away. It was hard to think of him as a man, with wants and needs, and not just a presence that guided their lives, like a faraway god. He could not be serious. He could not be…hitting on her, not one minute after talking about recruiting Sam Capra to their cause. An easy job? What, in his bed? She felt ill.

The laptop beeped.

"What's that?" she asked, grateful for the interruption.

"Another phone call being made to the Rostov chief in New York," he said. "I'm monitoring and recording his calls…" He moved to turn the volume off. But then he heard a woman's voice speaking English, and he turned up the volume.

"Mr. Rostov?"

"Who is this? How did you get this number?" Rostov's English was heavily accented.

"A friend. I am sorry for your recent losses."

"Who is this?"

"I can give you a measure of justice."

A pause, then quiet. "Who is this?"

"The man you want dead. Sam Capra. I can give him to you."

"I don't wish anyone dead."

"Surely you do. Sam killed Grigori and Vladimir. He knows who killed Viktor in Denver. I can give you Sam and the people who killed Viktor. For a price."

"You should call the police if you know something." But he didn't hang up.

"He's not just a bartender. Well, he is now, but he used to be hired muscle," she said. "And he messed with your boys. I can make it so he doesn't see you coming. For a price. Or I can take him out for you. For a price. Never have to get your hands dirty."

"I am respectable businessman. I don't know what you mean, please leave me alone."

"Your phone is secure," she said. "I got your number off Grigori's cell. Only a few people have the number. I got it because I was with Sam when he took Grigori's cell phone and ID. Those were gone from his body, did the police tell you that?"

Belias could hear the slight suck in of breath from the elder Rostov.

"But you can call me back on another line if you like." She fed him a number. She hung up. Five seconds later, Rostov was on another call, furiously speaking in Russian.

"Sam's friend isn't much of a friend." Belias glanced at Holly. "I think we should share this information with Sam, don't you?"

39

WE WILL SOON KNOW ENOUGH for the fish to snap at the bait," Mila said. "The big fish. Now let us see the little fish." We sat in a car parked a few blocks from Lafayette Park in Pacific Heights. Glenn Marchbanks's new house was two streets away.

Mila dialed the phone.

"Hello, Audrey? You do not know me, but I am a friend of Glenn's. And I have come across disturbing information about him that might be of interest to you." A pause. "It concerns your father."

She held the phone up so I could hear.

"What about my father?" Audrey Marchbanks didn't sound like she'd had a restful, peaceful night.

"About some business dealings Glenn had that contributed to your father's downfall in business," Mila said.

The shock in her voice was clear. "My dad...I don't understand. Who are you?"

"My name is...Lucy," Mila said with a glance at me. As if she'd just plucked a name out of the ether and decided to use that of my former wife. "Glenn is out of town, yes? Without a convincing explanation?"

"Yes..." she said slowly.

"I felt as his wife, as Mr. Standish's daughter, you should know the man you married."

"I...I do know Glenn. Is this some kind of joke?"

"I will be in Lafayette Park for the next ten minutes. I am blonde and wearing a black turtleneck. I will be sitting on a bench near the children's playground. Come see me if you want to know the truth."

Audrey Standish Marchbanks hung up the phone. We headed to the park.

Five minutes later, I saw Audrey leave her house, start the hike up the hill toward the park.

"I feel bad for her," I said.

"I do not. Stupidity is not to be celebrated. Are you ready?"

Yes. I had lockpicks, I had a flash drive loaded with a decryption program.

I went my way, Mila went hers. I walked right past Audrey. She didn't even glance at me, her face full of concern and worry and fear.

40

Saturday, November 6, midday

"Holly?" Audrey sounded panicked.

"Yes, what?" Holly glanced at Belias.

"I just got a phone call... from some woman I don't know, claiming that Glenn was involved in ruining my dad." Her voice broke. "I want to know where Glenn is right now. You know, don't you?"

"Audrey, I don't. I promise you I don't know where he is. This woman, who is she?"

"She said she would meet me in Lafayette Park, and I'm going there right now."

"Wait, I can be there in a few minutes. Don't go to see her without me." Holly gestured madly at Belias for the car keys. He grabbed a gun, tucked it under his jacket, and they both hurried down the stairs.

"Wait for me," Holly pleaded.

"You know, I don't think I will," Audrey said, and she hung up the phone.

Holly got into her car, Belias in the passenger seat, and she explained to him as she roared north on Valencia toward Pacific Heights. There was little traffic on a Saturday and she blasted through two red lights.

"This woman..." Belias said. "Did she mention if she had a slight Eastern European accent?"

"You think it's the same woman who called the Rostovs?"

"We're being played. I think maybe Sam found out more than we thought he did and maybe he's being played, too."

"Kill them." The ferocity in her voice surprised her. "We have to kill them all or they'll expose us." She gripped the wheel.

"And by all do you include Audrey?" Belias asked.

A chill settled along Holly's spine. "No, you don't need to hurt her. Audrey knows nothing; she's not a smart person."

"This isn't up for discussion," he said. "You park over by Audrey's house. Wait, and when she comes back, you go inside with her. I'll call you and tell you what to do. If they're telling her about the network…"

"You can't want me to kill her!"

"She stole your husband, Holly, and if they tell her about us, she'll send you to prison. I should think you'd be eager."

"I…I won't."

"You and I made an agreement."

Holly felt sweat inch down her spine, but her hands felt chilled.

41

GLENN MARCHBANKS HADN'T DOWNSIZED after he left his wife and children. Pacific Heights homes are grand, big for the second most densely populated city in America. The house he'd picked had a gate with a lock (opened in less than thirty seconds) and a rather ornate doorway. A small plaque next to the doorbell informed visitors this home had once been a diplomatic residence for a small European country.

I opened the door. There was an alarm pad near the front but no warning chime. Which meant Audrey, just walking up to Lafayette Park, hadn't bothered to set the alarm. Excellent.

I knew he'd keep any secrets about Belias and the network away from Audrey's eyes, no matter how incurious her gaze might be.

I hurried upstairs, found guest rooms for Peter and Emma (decorated too cheerfully with photos of the unsmiling kids and their smiling stepmother, Audrey might have been trying too hard) and a master bedroom. No safe like the one at the Marchbankses' house in Tiburon. I tried the other door.

Study, hello.

Glenn's desk was a Victorian affair with locks on the drawers and a roll top that locked as well. The view looked out over the hills and the sweep of San Francisco Bay, gray and blue in the bright Saturday sun.

I pulled a lockpick and worked the top drawer. Fast. If Mila couldn't keep Audrey in her flytrap and she returned, I'd just have to run, bolt, and hope that my description never crossed the desk of Detective DeSoto.

Inside was a Glock with an attached silencer and three prepaid phones. And a laptop.

I powered up the laptop, slipped in a flash drive that would assault the log-in password until it broke.

While I tried to crack the laptop, I started checking the prepaid phones.

Nothing on the first two phones. On the third, a text discussion sent to a number with a Las Vegas area code:

YOU AND I SHOULD TALK ABOUT OUR MUTUAL FUTURE.

HOW DID YOU GET THIS NUMBER? WHO IS THIS?

I MADE THE SAME DEAL YOU DID WITH THE SAME DEVIL.

NO IDEA WHAT YOU MEAN.

YOU CAN'T BE CALLED LUCKY FOREVER WITH HIM.

There was no final reply.

The same deal. I tucked the phone into my jacket. I waited on the laptop. Mila buzzed me to say Audrey was in the park, waiting anxiously for her mysterious caller, alone.

Ten minutes later, the laptop cracked. I searched the files rapidly. There is an art to scanning a computer and not leaving a trace that you were there. If Glenn Marchbanks was dead, sooner or later this would come out and the police would be here, searching for the truth about his disappearance and demise. There would be media attention. And I had no interest in tying myself to that attention.

I found the e-mails between him and Rostov, but I already knew about those. I deleted them.

No list of people in Belias's network. And no reference to Belias.

No, if he was planning a rebellion, then there had to be something. Some trace of his actions. He was trying to reach out to a scattered network of the powerful and influential, only united and linked by one man...

One man. Belias was the hub, much like Mila was for the Round Table.

What had Belias said in the dark of Diana's friend's house: *I hack human lives*. It was an odd, grandiose boast to make, and it stuck in my mind because at least with Glenn and Holly Marchbanks it seemed true. I did a search for *hack*.

The result was a file called HACKERS. A list of hacker names, people who had not been caught by the authorities. CyberPeasant. Dragon44. Venjanz. Newspaper clippings, profiles in technology magazines, speeches at hacker conventions about these unknowns. They were suspected of being responsible for powerful computer worms, destructive viruses, and more. CyberPeasant was dead, thought to be a suicide in Kazakhstan or murdered by someone who'd found out who he was and didn't like him. Dragon44 and Venjanz—vengeance, was that what it was supposed to sound like?—remained at large. Authorities suspected Dragon44 was based in Russia, given the IP addresses of where he had launched a serious attack against Swiss banking servers.

Venjanz's file only listed a name: Vasili Andreivich Borodin.

I thought again about Belias saying he didn't like Russians. This was a Russian name.

Was Belias one of these hackers? If he was, then I was dealing with probably the smartest adversary I'd yet encountered. One with very grand ambitions. Who'd moved from taking control of computers to taking control of people and perhaps more.

42

Saturday, November 6, midday

Lafayette Park stood on the crest of a hill. The "sides" of the park were a gentle rise from the surrounding streets. A playground, a large grove of majestic trees, people giving their dogs a bit of sport on the grass.

Mila watched Audrey sit down on a bench near the playground, glancing around. Clutching her phone.

"Sam, are you in?" she said into her own phone.

"Yes. You're not with Audrey?"

"I am making her wait so you have more time. She looks upset. I think she's about to run."

"Then talk to her."

Mila hurried up the incline of the hill toward the park. She waved at Audrey; Audrey caught her eye and stopped a few feet away from the bench.

"Hello, Mrs. Marchbanks," Mila said. "Thank you for meeting me. I'm sorry I was late. It is so hard to find a parking spot in this city."

"Who are you?" Audrey asked.

Behind Mila, Belias got out of Holly's car. He watched Mila and Audrey begin to speak, and the car that had let him out pulled away and turned onto Pacific Avenue, heading toward the Marchbankses' house.

He knew Audrey Marchbanks; he'd posed as a guest at her wedding, claiming to be a former coworker of Glenn's, but he'd made sure not to meet Audrey. It had been a rather large affair for a second wedding; the bride had gotten what she wanted. He'd felt sorry for Holly the entire time, who would no doubt hear of the affair's grandeur, and even worse for Peter and Emma, who looked like they'd rather be anywhere else than feting the woman who'd helped shatter their family. Audrey, from his observations, struck him as not very bright, and he wondered why Glenn had taken such a step down from Holly, who approached perfection.

The other woman. Petite. And almost as if she sensed danger, she turned as he approached them, a smile wide on his face. He wished he could shoot her in the head. She had been the one that forced him to kill Roger. He hadn't gotten a clear look at her face in the darkened room, but he was sure it was her.

"Hello, Audrey." He nodded at the other woman. "Is this woman bothering you?"

"Who are you?" Audrey asked.

"I work with Glenn. Security consultant." He slipped her a business card; being a security consultant was a steady cover for him. He nodded toward the smaller woman. "This woman has been attempting to blackmail various executives at Vallon Marchbanks. Go home, Audrey, I'll deal with her."

The smaller woman looked like she was about to speak, but instead she smiled. "I would be very careful with this man, Audrey. Don't be alone with him. He turns on those he's supposed to help."

He felt a tickle of rage at her words. *You made me kill Roger*, he thought. *You made me kill my first real friend.*

"I'm going to call the police now." Audrey pulled her phone from her jacket pocket.

"Do that and you'll never learn what your husband did to your father," the woman said.

Audrey froze.

"You suspected, didn't you? That he somehow had a hand in your father's ruination? Yet you married him. People are so complicated. At least the selfish ones are." Her voice was a knife.

"It's not true, what you're saying; it's not true." Audrey turned and ran away from both of them. The moment she was out of the picture it was as if she had never been in it, the first pawn taken off the chessboard.

"I bet she doesn't call the police," the woman said. "She's worried about him but she's more worried she'll lose her golden life."

Belias thought, *Her voice. She called the Russians in New York. She's betraying Sam Capra. And saying she can give me to the Rostovs.*

"I think you're right." A ball rolled between them, rescued by a toddler who picked it up and held it close to his chest, blinking up brightly at the two of them. His apologetic mother pulled him out of the narrow gap between them, smiling, cooing, saying she was sorry, he was just so fast.

Neither spoke until the mother was ten feet away.

"Nice touch to have the business card handy," the woman said.

"What do you want?" Belias said.

"You, walking away. Leaving Sam alone."

"Ah. Me away from him. Not offering him a job."

"You killed your last partner. Odd you'd want to offer Sam work."

"I didn't want to kill Roger," Belias said. "You forced me."

"Are you going to try to kill me?" The woman looked almost amused.

"In a crowded park? No. Plus, I find revenge to be quite overrated. If I kill you, it will be for a better reason."

"Then perhaps we walk away from each other, and neither endures further losses. I stay away from Audrey, you stay away from Sam. He has a job."

He could not help but smile. He was going to enjoy destroying her. "And you are what? A charity?"

"No."

"Hired muscle?"

"You could say."

"Sam is useful to you, isn't he?" Belias said, a knife in the tone that the woman couldn't miss.

* * *

Mila could see Belias wanted to kill her. He could try. She thought
she could kill him with a single blow to the voice box—deliver the
punch and run. He'd stumble, clawing at his throat, choking, and
people wouldn't think it was murder. They'd think he was having a
seizure. She could walk away very quickly, vanish.

But she needed him alive right now. If he was dead, then the network was lost. And there were too many people around. Everyone
had a camera these days. So annoying.

Belias almost smiled at her. And then he turned and walked away.

Mila's earpiece crackled into life. "Umm, she's trying to kill me,"
Sam said evenly.

43

Saturday, November 6, midday

I RAN TOWARD THE INTERSECTION, away from the park and Audrey Marchbanks's house, heading toward our car two streets over, when all hell broke loose. I was tapping my earpiece to reconnect with Mila, to tell her to leave Audrey and go, when I heard the surge of an engine behind me.

I turned and saw Holly Marchbanks in a Mercedes, fury discoloring her face, jumping the curb, ramming all that German horsepower right toward the small of my back.

I ran. The streets of Pacific Heights are normally quiet, and the roar of the engine broke the Saturday hush. Dead in front of me was a garage with a townhome's patio atop it. I scrambled up a brick wall that went halfway up the garage as the Mercedes dodged, going past me. I jumped, yanked myself to a balcony, pulled myself over.

Brunch goers stared at me; I was interrupting a private party. One man, big and burly enough to be a former 49er, started toward me.

I ran across the patio, past a table loaded with egg casserole, fruit, and croissants and the makings for Bloody Marys and mimosas, and vaulted back down onto the street.

The Mercedes had shot past my position, cars careening to avoid it. Honks filled the air. The Mercedes wheeled back hard in full reverse, Holly readying her aim at me. To my left was the rise of a straight, steep hill, nowhere to easily dodge her; she could corner me and shoot me as easily as run me down. To my right, the

Mercedes. Ahead, a wall of a large building, with fifty windows looking out like eyes, and two fire escapes running down the side.

I ran for the fire escape as Holly aimed at me again. Vaulted off the wall, hit my foot against the windowsill of the first floor, seized with fingertips the bottom of the metal grating making up the escape.

I swung my legs up as she barreled the Mercedes beneath me.

Here I was an easy target. I scrabbled out from under the grating, running up the side of the fire escape, feet clanging on the metal. I glanced down, and below me she'd gotten out of the Mercedes, her hand buried in her jacket, weighing the costs of shooting me in public. In the movies it's always gunplay first; but here there were witnesses, and there could be evidence implicating her and Belias in my pocket from her ex's house. If she shot me dead on the stairs, she couldn't necessarily reach me before the police did.

Windows and curtains flashed open as I ran past them; I was interrupting the Saturday morning calm. I reached the red-bordered roof, yanked myself up the sloping territory. I heard Holly yelling, indistinct to me.

I ran to the other side of the roof. The drop to the neighboring building was far too much to make. I found a maintenance door on the roof, picked the lock. I didn't hear a cry of sirens yet; I figured the brunch host was at least calling the police.

I got inside, found the elevator. This was a risk. She could be waiting on the first floor, she could be outside. But I had to get out of the building; staying here was a trap.

I took the elevator down to the first floor. Exited into a beautiful art deco lobby.

I went out the front door. A barred door with an ornate grate marked off the entrance from the street, and I went through it.

She stepped from the corner. Hand in her jacket. Not there because the day was cold.

"I told them you threw a bottle at my car..." Her voice was a slicing whisper. "Give me what you took from Audrey's. And I'll let you go." Her voice was strained wire and she regarded me with a fresh hatred.

"Come with me," I said. "I'll hide you and your children from Belias. He'll never find you. You'll be free."

The color drained from her face. "That's not possible."

"I have friends who can hide you. I can give you your freedom right now, if you're brave enough to take it. He can't touch you, your mom, your kids. We can go get them right now, before he knows."

It is not often you have to decide your whole life in one fiery second. She bit her lip, torn by indecision. "I can't trust you. You...you...my husband..."

"Holly?" Audrey Marchbanks, in sight over Holly's shoulder, hurrying down the sidewalk toward her.

"Now or never. Or are you going to gun me down in front of her? I'm sure she'd love to see you in jail."

Holly said nothing. Offer rejected. I turned. I ran. Our car was parked another block away. When I got there, I remembered Mila had the keys. I touched the Bluetooth earpiece again; gone. It must have fallen from my ear, and in the excitement I hadn't noticed.

Police lights flashing. I saw a police car pull up by the brunch patio, people with mimosas in hand calling down to them, pointing at me, Holly's accused car vandal.

I ran.

A block away I saw a young man wearing jeans, an oversized fedora, and a T-shirt from one of my favorite bands getting out of a small black car that made me think of a little bug, a Fiat Abarth. I knocked him aside, grabbed the keys, told him I was sorry. He started calling me names and screaming and I drove down the street, downhill.

Rearview: the police car, taking the turn fast, staying behind me. They wouldn't engage in a high-speed chase. This wasn't *Bullitt*. It would endanger people and it wasn't necessary. The maze of streets in San Francisco would make it easy for them to trap me as soon as other officers responded.

But I couldn't not go home to Daniel.

I roared down the hill, hoping Mila was okay, wishing I hadn't lost the earpiece. Behind me the sirens took on a harder, brighter sound. I veered right, veered left again. Right now all I had to do was get away. I powered the Fiat down the next hill, spun it out by shifting and slamming on the brake. The Fiat spun neatly in a 180-degree turn, serenaded by the horns of the cars that had stopped, and I blasted straight at the police car. The driver tried to veer to stop me, and I plowed onto the sidewalk, shot past the cop car, and heard the crash of the police car. Rearview mirror told me the police car had been sheared on the side by a big SUV with a construction logo on its side.

I'd bought myself maybe two minutes. I had to get out, ditch the car, vanish. I wheeled up the hill, powered hard over to the left. Another police car responding. I shot past it. Clearly the officers had been given the car's description. The police slammed on brakes as I careened the Fiat down the street.

The cop car revved hard behind me. In front of me I saw cars ahead of me slowing, trying to figure out how to get out of the way. Along the opposite side stood scaffolding, stretching along three houses being redone. I veered across all the lanes of traffic, roared the small Fiat under the scaffolding, past the stopping and slowing cars. Inches to spare on each side. One miscalculation and I'd wreck, likely bringing three stories of scaffolding down on me. I bulleted out at the end of the scaffolding, out back into the intersection, horns blaring as I blasted through a red light.

Suddenly, I was hit. And spinning.

I'd been nailed by a cab as I ran the light. It caught the back edge of the Fiat, and I got to see the nice view of the neighborhood, all 360 degrees, in three seconds. The Fiat fought for purchase on the road, and I straightened it out, the police car's sirens echoing hard through the narrow streets.

But the cab was a momentary block. You think in terms of seconds in a chase, seconds bought, seconds lost. I shot past the trendy shops and boutiques along this stretch of road. The Saturday crowds were only at the coffee shops, not the bars or the clothing shops or the spas. But too many people, too many witnesses, too many cell phones that might snap my picture.

I had to ditch the car now, disappear into the crowd.

I took another hard left, saw a large home under construction, marked with emerald-green wrap covering the front and the side of the building. I drove the Fiat straight across the small paved yard, into the curtain of green. The moorings tore down behind me, draping the car. Again, thinking in seconds—would it be seconds after the cop car veered past me that they would notice the wrap was partially down?

The house was empty and I bolted from the car. I'd managed to smash into paint and drywall and the floor was now painted a tasteful forest green. I didn't want to step in the paint—it would leave quite a trail. I lowered the driver's window, pulled free the wrapping that had cocooned the car, stepped on the wrapping to the windowsill. I dropped down twelve feet to a small backyard that was full of construction equipment and supplies. I bolted over a fence, ditched my denim jacket, pulled my long sleeve shirt straight. I went back over another fence, the sirens loud now, and walked out onto a neighboring street. Down half a block was a café, and I sat outside in the nice bright sunlight, ordered a cup of herbal tea, and watched two more cop cars race by while I texted Mila.

ON MY WAY, she said.

OUR FRIEND B? I said.

HE WALKED AWAY FROM ME.

He had? That surprised me. I don't like being surprised by what bad guys do. Bad guys should be consistently predictable. He wasn't.

But was Holly giving my name to the police right now? I might not be able to go back to the bar.

I didn't even know if that was Mila answering my text. What if it was Belias? He could have killed her and taken the phone, and here I'd just given him my location.

I sat, drinking my tea, wondering which of them was going to show up.

44

Saturday, November 6, midday

Las Vegas

SINCE HER ARRIVAL in Las Vegas yesterday, Janice had watched the man they called Lucky. He routinely walked the floor of his casino, greeting gamblers, posing for pictures. There were always two guards with him. She accidently drew attention to herself when she stared at him, four tables away, and forgot to place a bet. He would leave the casino floor via a private exit, or he took an elevator to his penthouse apartment.

That Friday night he went to dinner at a new restaurant off the Strip, and she followed him. The limo drove to a high-end apartment complex, where Lucky picked up a lovely young woman. The two of them sat in the back, the bodyguards in front, one of them driving. She'd had to drive past the limo; simply hanging back would have drawn attention. She was able to trail him, though, to the Thai restaurant.

The bodyguards ate at a different table. They kept their gaze wandering the room. She decided she could not follow Lucky to another dinner; she was afraid the bodyguards would notice her, remember her face. She ate at the bar, risking glances over the crowded room when she sipped at her mineral water.

The bodyguards were going to be a serious problem. The two were big, young men in suits who looked like they might have been football players. They made her think of panthers, all coiled muscle and no mercy. She knew she couldn't outfight them, and trying to shoot three people when she only needed one dead offended her idea of economy. Plus, Belias wanted Lazard's death to look like a suicide. She needed to either find a way to get them out of the way or find a way to get close to Lucky Lazard while the bodyguards weren't around. The thought of killing the young men was repellent to her. No one should die just because they took a job.

Lucky liked to eat and she made a note of that; she still had the bottle of poison in her purse. He'd brought last night's dinner companion back to the Mystik; she'd followed them back from their meal, and seeing him surrounded by a large, boisterous party in his nightclub, she'd abandoned the night's pursuit, furious that he didn't seem to be alone often.

Now it was Saturday. She stopped at a computer store, bought the latest operating system disk, and she installed it on Barbara Scott's laptop, which overwrote all the previous data. If she was caught or arrested, she couldn't have the police finding that she had the dead woman's laptop. She'd learned all she could from it.

She missed Diana. One of the bodyguards was just the kind of guy that Diana liked: big shouldered, short haired, tall. She thought of the insanity if Diana was here with her; she would have chattered about the guy, while her mother thought about how to kill the white guy in the corner. *Hmm*, she realized, *Diana could have distracted the bodyguards*. She thought that, then felt ashamed.

She resisted the urge to call Diana and see how she was doing. She was supposed to be where there was no cell phone access and she had to stick with the lie, but knowing that she couldn't talk to Diana made her want to talk to Diana.

As the laptop finished its wipe she picked up the promotional Vegas magazines on the desk. The cover story had caught her eye before. LUCKY LAZARD: THE KING OF VEGAS REAL ESTATE, the caption read, under the plain face of a well-built fiftyish man, smiling for all he was worth, arms spread, the backdrop of the sprawl of Vegas behind him. Arms spread as though for crucifixion, she thought.

And I've got the hammer and nails.

She opened the package that had been waiting for her at the bell desk at the Mystik.

A Glock 9mm gun. Three magazines for the gun. A Canadian passport in the name of Catherine Bonheur with her picture inside, in case this very difficult kill went wrong and she had to run fast under a new name. Five thousand in cash. And a passcard to Enchant Club for Marian Atkins, the name she'd used to register at the Mystik.

Thank you, Belias, she thought.

She put the goods in the bottom of her purse. Next to the poison, hidden in an eyedrops bottle. She went downstairs.

She sat at a slot machine and, bored, fed it coins. She'd lost a fair amount of Belias's money when she spotted Lazard, walking through the lobby, a thick-necked man walking behind him. It was the bodyguard she thought Diana would like.

Lazard smiled, nodded, spoke to several of the casino employees. The man with the common touch. Enchant, the hotel's private club, lay in the far back corner of the Mystik, and she saw him enter, nodding and laughing at the bouncer at the entrance. The club wasn't busy; she knew the private club served brunch to the casino's VIPs.

She walked over to Enchant. She showed her membership card to the bouncer, who scanned it, presented it back to her with a smile, and she stepped inside. The interior was that of a four-star nightclub. Beautifully upholstered chairs in crimson and gold, tables with built-in ice coolers for bottle service. There was a simple but elegant brunch buffet set up in the corner. A chef making eggs to order. A bartender serving pomegranate mimosas and fancy Bloody Marys with applewood bacon slices for stirrers, with bits of cold, grilled tenderloin and fat olives on skewers. Not crowded, quiet. She took a newspaper from the counter and ordered a pomegranate mimosa and sat and watched Lucky Lazard.

She hadn't had a drink since her last drink with Felix at The Select. She suddenly missed him, missed The Select. She liked talking with him, the sound of his voice, the shape of his mouth, his kind eyes. Of course she'd meet a nice man when she had no time left for romance.

Time. No time left. She wanted this done and to go home, and she cautioned herself not to rush. If she rushed, she would die sooner than the cancer could claim her or she would be caught.

Lucky Lazard talked with another man at a table, the bodyguard standing a respectful distance away. Presumably it would be insulting to the club's members to be accused of being a danger to Lucky and so the guard let his gaze roam politely over the small crowd—a dozen or so. He met Janice's gaze, and she smiled and returned her attention to the newspaper. She didn't want him catching her looking again, but surely Lucky Lazard got stared at...at least in the casinos he owned.

"Is your drink all right?" She glanced up to see Lucky Lazard, smiling, impeccable in a gray suit and a silver tie. He'd gotten up from his confab and was playing the host, making a genial circle of the room.

For one awful second she thought she could pick up her purse and fire a bullet right through the thin leather, into his chest. But she had to escape, and that wasn't a possibility if she killed him in plain sight.

"Oh yes, it's delicious. Just a bit early for me still. I'm a slow sipper." The calm in her own voice stunned her.

"Then you should go play some poker, you'll have an advantage." He laughed at his own joke and Janice smiled. She couldn't quite bring herself to laugh in the face of the man she was here to kill.

"Lucky Lazard." He offered his hand and she hoped hers wasn't slick with sweat. "I own the Mystik."

"Oh, wow! I'm Marian Atkins." She made herself put on an impressed smile. *In real life I would have thought it was fascinating to meet you. To maybe recruit you as a client. But this isn't real life. This is what lies under my real life.*

"I hope you'll enjoy your stay at the Mystik, Marian." He gave an automatic smile to the automatic wish.

"It's a stunning resort. You are indeed...lucky."

"I am. I endorse what Thomas Jefferson said. 'I am a great believer in luck. The harder I work, the more of it I have.'"

"That's very true," Janice said, knowing that for her it was a lie. Her luck had been bought and paid for. She could remember Belias's words to her, smooth as silk in her ear: *What would you do for a perfect life, Janice? One where the major obstacles just don't exist anymore?* That was luck, she thought. Luck that was made for you.

"Please do let me know if there's anything you need." Smile and nod, a practiced combination move.

Over her shoulder the flat-screen TV fed a bottom line that read: THE INVESTIGATION OF DEATH OF BEST-SELLING AUTHOR BARBARA SCOTT CONTINUES. She tried not to let her eyes drift to the words. She needed an excuse to see him again, to get close to him again. She turned on her brightest smile. "Do you visit this club in the evening? Maybe we could have a quick drink. I am fascinated by how you wove in so many cultural references to magic here in the casino. How did you decide what to include? It's spectacular."

"You're so kind. Unfortunately I won't be here this evening. Perhaps another time?"

"Yes, of course. Thank you for introducing yourself."

He nodded and moved on to the next table, where two television stars—Janice was sure she'd seen them on a cable drama about two mismatched cops—were doing wiggly-fingered waves, delighted to see Lucky. Janice returned to her paper, thinking, *This doesn't seem like a man who would commit suicide.*

After Lucky said his hellos to the television stars—who did not seem inclined to let him leave—she saw him gesture to the bodyguard. "Go bring her down."

The bodyguard nodded and left. *Missed chance*, Janice thought. If she'd asked him to join her for coffee, she could have poisoned the cup. Now she couldn't get close enough to him, not without good reason. He must be heading out again with his girlfriend.

"A girl other than us?" One of the starlets made her voice a mock complaint.

"Absolutely. Spending the weekend with her."

"Incorrigible you." The starlet swatted at his arm.

Janice got up and left Enchant. She edged through the crowds and she saw the bodyguard enter the penthouse's elevator. Lazard, she knew, had one of the penthouse suites on the top two floors of the building. She took the next elevator up; hurried to her room; taped the Glock to the small of her back, under the blouse, under the suit jacket she wore. She got her purse and dumped the cash and gear into it. She wanted to be done. She knew she was hurrying and possibly making a mistake but she wanted to be done. She'd shaken his hand, hid in plain sight like Belias suggested, and it was a mistake. She didn't want to chat with him; she wanted to strip away his luck and end him and then leave town, go on to the final target. And get home and see if the doctors could give her an extra six months, an extra year, maybe longer.

She dialed the valet parking service and told them to bring her rental car to the front.

She could follow him and the girlfriend. Maybe the bodyguard wouldn't be around, not if Lucky wanted to romance the woman. It might be her best chance. Spending the weekend together, he'd said. She'd have a chance then, perhaps if he and the girlfriend wanted a bit of privacy. A girlfriend would be much easier to handle than two bullnecked bodyguards.

She hurried back to the elevator. She pressed the button, waited for the cab. The penthouses had an express elevator; she hoped she wasn't too late.

She stepped out of the elevator and Lucky Lazard stood five feet away from her, talking to another man in a suit, listening, nodding, then giving instruction. She walked slowly toward the front of the casino. She knew what kind of car he drove and where the exit ramp was for the resident penthouse. She could wheel the rental around and follow him and his date…

"Daddy!"

Weird, she would think later, that a child's voice could slice so neatly through the jangle and laughter and noise of the casino, through the chiming glory of the slots, the brayed laughter of the surprised winners, the sheer buzz of the room.

She glanced back and saw a young girl, maybe ten, dashing into Lucky Lazard's arms. She was spare as a bird, pretty, brown haired, brown eyed, dressed in jeans and a purple shirt, hair pulled into a casual ponytail. He ruffled her hair, nodded at the bodyguard. Then he and the girl walked toward the back of the casino. Probably to where his car was.

The bodyguard stayed behind.

Now, she thought. *No bodyguard.* The voice in her head wasn't hers, it sounded like Belias.

Are you going to kill a man in front of his daughter, Janice? That voice sounded like hers. *Are you going to let that little girl see your face?* She stood, a shiver touching her flesh. The gun, strapped to her back, felt heavy as iron, felt like it was piercing her skin like a doll's turnkey.

She watched Lucky Lazard and his daughter amble out of sight. Then slowly, she walked toward the front, where her car waited for her, decision made.

45

Saturday, November 6, afternoon

WHAT ON EARTH is going on?" Audrey's voice wasn't at its usual dramatic whine; it had deadened to a whisper.

Holly stood in the entrance of her ex-husband's home. Her purse felt heavy, and once it had been loaded with everyday mom stuff: water bottles, snacks, chocolate melting in its wrapper, her cell phones, including the one that was used only by Belias. Now it was heavy only with the gun she could have used to kill Sam Capra.

The blood pounded in her ears.

Belias. Where was he? Still in the park?

"What is going on?" Audrey's voice sounded thin, like a mosquito's, behind her.

"It's all about Glenn," she said quietly.

She watched the confusion pass over Audrey's face. *Oh, I thought of killing you before*, Holly thought. *Then I saw you were too selfish and stupid to hate; you weren't worth the energy.*

"Tell me what is going on with my husband!"

My? Ours, Holly thought. The pact she and Glenn had sworn to Belias outweighed those flimsy vows in the church. They were bound like blood.

"Glenn is in trouble. You cannot help him, and if you go to the police, you will just make it worse."

Her earpiece buzzed. Belias. She clicked it while Audrey frowned.

"Are you with the new wife?" Belias said in her ear.

"Yes."

"She knows too much."

"That's an overstatement."

"Explain to me what is going on," Audrey said. "Get off the phone now."

"Kill her if you must..." Belias said.

"I cannot do that." Holly hoped her voice sounded firm enough.

"Then sell her a workable lie. But there is no point in explaining if you have to kill her."

"Honestly!" Audrey said. "Do you have to take a call right this minute, Holly?"

The man who was just here? He killed your husband. You kept me from avenging the man we loved. She had to sell this, though. "Glenn asked me not to involve you."

"That woman said this had to do with my family..."

"Because if you know details, you could go to jail, Audrey. Glenn is in trouble and wants to keep it far from you."

"You're not telling me just to punish me."

I'm trying to keep you alive, you little idiot, Holly thought. "Glenn has gotten involved in a very bad investment with some people. That woman wanted you to tell her where Glenn is."

"And that security consultant?"

"He's trying to keep Glenn safe, find out who these people are. That's why you must keep your mouth shut."

Doubt made Audrey frown. "Why?"

"Because Glenn doesn't like to make a mistake. He doesn't want you to think less of him."

"He needs me."

"Yes, he does, but he doesn't see that right now. Give him some alone time."

"So he didn't go on a trip?"

"Apparently not. But I think you give him some time, maybe a few days, to fix this. If you call the police, it will just be a bigger mess." *Deep breath,* she told herself. "Does Glenn have a laptop here?"

"Yes."

"Give it to me."

"I don't know…"

"Do you want these people coming back here? Glenn needs it; I'll make sure the security guy gets it to him."

Audrey shivered. "I should call the police. I should."

"Glenn will be crushed if you make this public. He'll be humiliated. Please let him handle it."

"Can't you even tell me who these people are?"

"No, Glenn will tell you when he can. Right now you need to go about your normal business. Yoga class, volunteer work, a reality TV marathon."

Audrey shook her head. "It's not right you know more about Glenn than I do. I'm his wife. You will tell me right now where he is—"

Holly slapped her. Hard.

Audrey blinked at her in shock, her hand to her cheek.

Holly said, "I will tell you *nothing*. I am doing what he's asked. I'm doing it because doing what he says is going to keep him out of prison. Do you understand me?"

Audrey lifted her chin, like a defiant martyr tied at the stake. *Oh, that's right*, Holly remembered. *Strike a pose. You were sort of an actress once.*

The Bluetooth clicked in her ear. "If I tell you to," Belias said, "shoot Audrey in the head. And don't pretend like you haven't wanted to in the past."

"Prison," Holly repeated. "Did that word get your attention? Good, because if you help him right now and this goes wrong, you're going to prison, too."

That shut Audrey up. Sullenly, she rubbed at the cheek.

"Now. I need any phones, any computers he has here."

Audrey went upstairs, Holly following.

What if she couldn't kill Audrey in cold blood? There was no Glenn to win back. Was she going to kill a woman who couldn't hurt her anymore because Belias said so?

Are you keeping her alive because you're a good person or because you don't want to have committed something as awful as murder? There's a difference, she thought.

Holly opened up the study door. She opened the desk. A laptop. It was still warm, sleeping. Presumably Glenn hadn't left it asleep two days ago. Which meant someone—maybe Sam Capra, he'd been on this street for a reason—had turned it on. She typed in the password Glenn used when they were married; it still worked and the screen popped to life. Maybe Sam Capra had gotten to the laptop, but he'd been stymied by the password.

Wrong. Then he just would've taken the laptop, not left it behind. He'd gotten in, she was sure with a sinking heart.

"And when will you deign to give me some news on my husband?"

Holly stood up from the computer. "Audrey, stop it. Why did you make yourself look like a Barbie doll? Why did you chase a married millionaire? Why don't you have a job or any interests beyond yourself? You *want* to be shielded. You've built your whole life around being taken care of and protected. Well, I'm giving you exactly what you want."

Somehow Audrey's look was more shocked than when Holly slapped her. "I'm not some weakling, Holly." Audrey turned and flounced down the stairs.

She actually stomps her feet, Holly thought.

Audrey pouted in the kitchen and Holly told her good-bye and left. Audrey didn't turn around or acknowledge her. Holly walked on to the street. From the opposite direction came an Audi. Belias driving. She got in the passenger side.

"Are you sorry I didn't have you kill her?" Belias asked. "Isn't that the first wife fantasy, get rid of the interloping second wife?"

"Not mine. I've never killed anyone in my life." But she would. Sam Capra. She would not waste another chance.

He drove in silence back to the safe house in the Mission District. They went inside. "I listened to the police bands. Sam got away."

"What now?"

"Sam thinks he got something valuable from Glenn's place. So he'll be in touch, and then I'll spring my surprise on him. You look like you could use some fresh air. Go get us some coffees. There's a place down on the corner."

She did want fresh air. The apartment stairs led down to the street, and she walked in the cooling breeze. In the coffee shop, she ordered three black coffees—she wanted two for herself; she'd hardly slept the night before—got them in a cardboard tray that held the cups into fitted slots, filled the middle with sugar and cream packets and stirrers. She walked out, and next to the coffee place was a small hardware store, the kind that shook its fist in defiance at the chains and the online sites and managed to eke out an existence on the kindness of the neighborhood.

She held the coffees and stared in at the windows.

Poison. They probably had rat poison in there. Would it have a taste? Could she douse it into Belias's cup? Just end all this?

But he's finding the man who killed Glenn.

The smell of paint above the bed where Glenn died. It wouldn't leave her alone.

She stared at herself in the window's reflection, realizing she was contemplating murder for the third time that day.

Belias watched Holly from the window. She acted like she didn't want to come back to him. That troubled him. Glenn had openly defied him in hiring the Russian. The web he'd built was fragile; what kept it tight and functioning was fear. Fear of exposure, fear of loss, fear of what would happen if one tried to break away. Fear of him.

Was she not afraid of him anymore?

He watched her, watched the soft breeze stir her hair. Glenn was a fool. Belias had done a careful and thorough vetting of Audrey when Glenn started dating her. He worried she might be a plant from the FBI, or other law enforcement that might have stumbled into his secret, or from even the CIA or a foreign intelligence service. Sadly Audrey was exactly what she seemed to be: a talentless actress who'd set her goal to seducing Glenn Marchbanks into a marriage that meant comfort and security. But if Holly had asked him to kill Audrey, to eliminate her rival, he would have. Although murder was always a last resort. He didn't care much for murder. But only murder would do sometimes.

He watched her. She stared at something in the hardware window. She smoothed an errant lock of hair back behind her ear. He wondered what her hair felt like, what the skin of her ear would feel like against his tongue. He bit his lip. It had been so long. Women did not care for his cold hands. Except Svetlana, who laughed and whispered, *cold hands, warm heart*. But his heart wasn't that warm and he knew it. He thought of himself as a priest of sorts, a man who troubled himself with the troubles of others and took none of the baser pleasures of life. He had felt bad for her when Glenn left her. It wasn't something that he could say because he knew his sympathy would scald her.

But how would she feel now? Glenn was gone. She was alone.

But she didn't have to be. He didn't have to be. Couldn't he put on a new name, not be John Belias, live in the sunshine rather than the shadow? He'd do it for her. Belias could be a mask, a name that just existed on the computer and phone screen when he issued orders and rewards. He could be…someone else. For her.

He went to the mirror, smoothed his hair. There had not been a woman as a constant in his life since…Svetlana. Glenn had been handsome and he was a bit plain, except for his blue eyes, which women always said they liked. Did Holly like black hair? Did she like her men thin and lean? He felt suddenly stupid for even harboring such hopes.

He went back to the window to watch her.

Belias would wonder why she was taking so long. The coffees would get cold. She turned back toward the street and she saw Belias, standing at the window, watching her. She hurried back to the house.

"Was there a problem?" he asked.

"No. Just lost in thought." She handed Belias his coffee. He took a long slurping sip and now she felt relief she hadn't poisoned it. He was a horrible man, but this Sam and Diana were the real and true threat to her children's happiness. She wondered if she was losing her mind.

"What's wrong with you?"

"I was married to Glenn once, and he's dead, and I don't think I've quite processed that, John."

"Of course not." Belias put his cold, pale hands on her shoulders.

"Haven't you ever lost someone you loved?" she asked suddenly. "Don't you remember what it's like?"

"Yes, I have. I loved a woman once. I loved Roger, in a way, and I think I'm going to miss him more and more as the days pass. Are you surprised I could have ever loved someone?" he asked.

"No, John, of course not." But her voice betrayed her.

"I know I am asking so much of you. I have asked before, but never like this. We're fighting for our lives here, Holly." Like they would have a life together. He wished he'd chosen different words.

The pause became awkward and she turned away, sipping her coffee.

He turned back toward the computer. "Here's what I want you to do. Watch the bar. I'm going to call him and I want to know if Sam comes alone or if she comes with him."

I could kill Sam then, she thought. *I could kill him then.*

"All right," she said.

46

Saturday, November 6, afternoon

He knows I called the Rostovs to strike a deal." Mila shifted gears as we headed back to The Select. "You were right, he has their phones bugged."

"How can you be sure?"

"He wanted to kill me. He needs me alive because he'd rather show you I've 'betrayed' you. You deciding what to do about me will be a test."

"A test."

"One you have to pass. He has to believe that you feel completely betrayed by me and are open to dealing and working with him now."

"He's already gotten the police off me and killed a man who would have killed me," I said. "Isn't gratitude enough?"

"But you have to break from me. If you want to get inside with him, I have to be tossed aside."

"I don't like this." I looked at her. "What if he decides tossing you aside means you dead?"

"I'm quite sure that is exactly what he means." She turned off Haight, turned onto the side street, pulled up into the lot behind The Select. "Allow me to state the obvious and say that's unacceptable."

"Well, I agree. So here is my idea…"

47

Saturday, November 6, afternoon

JANICE WATCHED LUCKY LAZARD stroll through Sunset Park with his daughter. She cursed herself for allowing him to talk to her at the casino, to register her face. A park. Who knew that Las Vegas had parks? A tourist could forget that starting a few blocks off the Strip there was a relatively normal city, like any other—a city with schools, hospitals, churches, and shopping centers. And here was a park near the airport, with a huge pond and a disc golf course and several sports courts, people walking their dogs, families out enjoying the Saturday. After all, did you want your child at a casino all the time? No. Of course not.

She didn't really want to see this side of Lazard. For five seconds she'd debated after picking up her car at the valet whether she could simply rev up close to Lazard's car, fire a bullet into his brain, and roar away. Even with the difficulties of a moving target, firing through glass, she knew she could do it. But then he would have died in front of his child, and what if she'd missed, what if the ricochet hit innocent flesh inside the car? Or the driverless car then crashed?

And this was supposed to be a suicide.

You're a really sorry excuse for a hit woman. Hit person. Whatever you are. She sat in the car, parked facing away from where Lazard and his daughter began to toss a Frisbee between them, and she picked up the blue prepaid phone. She dialed.

When Belias answered, she said, "You didn't tell me he has a child."

"His daughter is in boarding school in Montreal."

"She's in Vegas and he's spending the weekend with her. Poison becomes riskier with a child around, and I'm not going to kill him in front of his kid with a gun. So much for suicide."

"Perhaps," Belias said, musing, "he would kill his child and then himself."

"I'm going to pretend you did not say that," Janice said. "Forget that right now. It will never happen."

"If you can't make Lazard look like a suicide or an accident, then just kill him," he said.

"Let me think." Janice watched Lazard and the girl awkwardly toss the plastic disc. He was coaching his daughter quietly, gently. She laughed as she made a strong throw and her father missed the catch. How much money did Lazard have? How much had he built in the city of pleasures, and yet only here she could see his genuine smile, broader than the one he offered at the casino, the simple joy of time with a child. "Why does this man have to die?"

"It's not like you have a lot of time to worry about niceties, Janice."

"It's hard to watch him with his daughter."

"You're thinking about your own daughter." And there was a steel in his voice she didn't like.

"Yes."

"Don't waste your time being sentimental. That's time you're losing with Diana."

The Lazard girl jumped up high, fingers just catching the flying disc. Her father clapped.

"I love how you cut to the bone."

"It's how I've made you all successful, Janice. Get it done." He hung up then and she wondered why he sounded so cold. Colder than normal.

She sat and watched and after a while, as the sun began to climb higher in the desert sky, Lazard and his daughter headed for their car.

Janice followed them back toward the casino, inching the car closer, rehearsing the shot in her mind. But then she thought of another idea. A better one.

She pulled into a parking lot so she could hunt on her cell phone's browser for the closest hardware store.

48

Vasili Andreivich Borodin." Felix stood up from his laptop and took a big gulp of coffee.

"Is that Belias's real name?" I asked.

"No, as Mr. Borodin is dead. But he was briefly famous. In Russia." He hit a button on the laptop and pages began to furl out from the printer. "Go get me some more coffee, Sam, please, and I'll explain."

I went downstairs. Mila was on the phone, speaking softly. Then singing. Wordlessly she held out the phone to me. I took it.

Daniel, on the other end, gurgling, laughing. Like sunshine if it could have a sound. "Hey, baby, it's Daddy." And I like to think that Daniel laughed then, that he responded to my voice. I made baby talk to him, not really something I'm good at, but I was apart from him for so long that every thread of connection matters. Leonie came on the phone as I cranked up the coffeepot for Felix.

"He's okay. I'm okay."

"How's Jimmy?"

"You mean, how is it that you've entrusted our safety to a man you've never met?" Her voice was wry.

"Mila says he's the best."

"Oh, well, if Mila says it."

"Leonie, please."

"He's taking excellent care of us. He read Daniel a bedtime story last night. But you should be doing that."

I should. I closed my eyes. "I am particularly positioned to bring this bad guy down. I have to for all of us to be safe."

"Keep telling yourself that, and I'm sure it's true."

"Leonie…"

"Every time you get the hunger for your old life, do I have to go into hiding?"

I could tell her that Belias had acquired my CIA file, but that might only frighten her.

"No."

"So this is a onetime thing."

"It will be over soon."

"That wasn't an answer, Sam. I think you better decide what you want from your life."

"If you want out, Leonie, just go." She had no claim on Daniel; it had been out of kindness that I'd let her stay in his life after we survived a harrowing experience, and she'd been like a mother to Daniel.

"I'm the only mother he's ever known," she said. "I won't leave him."

"I'll call tonight."

She hung up.

"I told you," Mila said, "to not let that woman stay in your life. I was right, you were wrong. We should have made a bet."

"She said Jimmy is taking good care of them."

"Of course he is. He knows I will kill him if any harm comes to Daniel or pseudo nanny. Or if pseudo nanny disappears with Daniel."

"She won't run."

"She is an expert forger who used to help hunted people hide. If anyone could run far, it would be her."

"She won't." I poured a fresh mug for Felix and went back upstairs. Mila followed.

Felix had done very fast work delving into the name I'd found on Glenn's laptop. On one wall he'd taped up photos and news articles, like we had in re-creating the DOWNFALL file. I handed him his coffee.

"You're a bullet," I said. "This was fast."

"I'm desperate." He smiled. "Okay, Vasili Borodin was a Russian businessman. One of those who successfully grabbed resources when Soviet industries went private. He made millions, bought a soccer team in France, lived in London." He pointed to a picture of a heavyset man with a broad smile but a cagey, knowing stare. "Now, all stereotyping of the Russian mafia and its ties to Russian business aside, Borodin was legit. There were, of course, reports of muscle being used to intimidate rivals among Russian business-men, but he was never accused of that. In fact, he started using the profits from the selling of his Russian-based companies to buy firms in western Europe. And here's where it gets interesting, be-cause there's a pattern." He pointed at a list of companies: German, French, Belgian, British. "Each of these companies suffered a severe setback right before Borodin acquired them. Thriving companies that suddenly suffered a loss…"

"A downfall," Mila said.

Felix nodded. "I think Borodin was either waiting to swoop on any company that suffered a loss, or he engineered it himself and then took advantage."

"Did any of these companies claim to have been hacked?"

"Yes. One of them had an entire credit card database compro-mised repeatedly, their stock sunk. After Borodin bought them there were no further incidents."

"Belias," I said. "Borodin had his own hacker."

"Private hackers have often been thought to assist the Russian government in bringing down people they consider subversive, and we know during Russia's short war with Georgia that the Russians used private hackers to tear down Georgia's Internet capability," Mila said. "Glenn Marchbanks must have figured out some connec-tion between Belias and Borodin."

"But there's no hard proof?" I asked.

"Not yet. But Sam, look here." He pointed at a photo. "The opening of a big nightclub in London that Borodin owned. That's him." I peered at the picture, which looked like it had been printed in a lifestyle section of a newspaper. Next to Borodin, who wore a tuxedo, was an attractive young woman.

"That's not arm candy, that's Borodin's daughter, Svetlana. Borodin was a widower who never remarried, Svetlana was his only family. She was studying at the Royal Academy Opera in London. Very promising singer."

"She's lovely," Mila said.

But my eyes had already gone on to the next photo. Another of Borodin, at the same party, hoisting a glass of champagne with another man.

"He looks like Belias." Felix spoke my own thought aloud.

"He does resemble him, but he's noticeably older. Who is he?"

"His name is Martin Raymond. An American investments counselor, an adviser to Borodin."

"You said Borodin was," Mila said. "Past tense."

"Borodin killed himself nine years ago. Murder-suicide. His companies had suffered serious setbacks, started to unravel, all to the benefit of his rivals." He stared straight at me. "It almost seemed like his companies were suffering the same fate as those he'd acquired on the cheap. The karma of it was even discussed in the European financial press. But it was suggested the companies were flawed, and he simply hadn't addressed their problems."

"He got hacked himself? By his own hacker?"

"Maybe."

"You said murder-suicide," Mila said.

Felix nodded. "Borodin apparently killed Svetlana and Martin Raymond in his home outside London. Then he killed himself. E-mails found afterward showed that Svetlana and Raymond had been having an affair and that Martin Raymond had been lifting millions from Borodin's investment accounts. The money was never recovered." He cleared his throat. "Open-and-shut case, it seemed. He killed them for the betrayal, then killed himself." He crossed his arms. "Svetlana had been in rehearsals for an academy performance of Gounod's opera *Faust*."

I put my hand over my mouth. "That was where Belias got the idea. Do for several individuals what he'd done for Borodin's company."

"The bodies were found by Borodin's head of security. A former

UK Special Forces soldier named, wait for it, Roger Metcalfe." He pulled a photo from the printer. It was Belias's partner.

"Belias is maybe ten years older than me," I said. "Did Raymond have a son?"

"Yes, Kevin Raymond. I called Jimmy with this; he's working to find out where he is, what's he's been doing." Felix pointed at the papers on the wall. "This was what I could find in a couple of hours of dedicated Internet searching, focusing on the British press. Nothing at all yet on Kevin Raymond. He had no ties to his father's business, so he wasn't suspected of being part of the embezzlement. He worked as a software designer for a number of different firms, but he couldn't hold on to a job. Then he dropped out of sight."

"*I hack human lives*, that's what he said." I stared at Svetlana Borodina's lovely photo.

"We are dealing with someone who may have killed his own father," Mila said, and we let the awful words hang in the silence.

I have friends in both high and low places. One such, on the low side, is Fagin. Yes, named for the king of the pickpockets from Charles Dickens's *Oliver Twist*. My Fagin used to be a high school computer teacher who went to work for CIA Special Projects using teenage hackers to create mischief against our enemies and sometimes our friends. All off the records, all highly deniable. Fagin was a genius when it came to computer hackery, and I was one of the few who had his home number in Manhattan.

I dialed, he answered, and I said, "Hey, Fagin, it's Sam Capra."

He hung up. I have a complicated relationship with my former coworkers.

I called back. I could imagine his rather roomy apartment in Manhattan: one room set up full of computers, teenagers (in Special Projects we'd nicknamed them the Oliver Twists) with more brains than sense sitting at the keyboards, planting bugs and viruses in software that ran Russian gas pipelines or Chinese servers that choked information off from their citizens or maybe snooping without a warrant for financial records. The last time I'd been there he'd had two teenagers leaving logic bombs in another country's power grid, and he'd stepped out to get them refills on their sodas.

The phone rang twenty times before he answered. "What?"

"Fagin. I have a trade to offer."

"I am not interested. You are no longer an agency employee."

"You are, though, and I could make you look very good."

Fagin paused. He is nothing if not self-serving. I mean that in a good way.

"It's very shiny and bright and will probably make you a national hero. Secretly, of course."

A pause, no doubt while he instructed the Oliver Twists on duty to figure out where I was calling from.

"I'm listening."

"I have a lead on a very important bad guy, a hacker."

"Aren't you supposed to be serving cocktails for a living?"

"Yes, and the martinis are on me next time I'm in New York."

"I can't even be seen near you, you know that."

"I won't be at the bar, and you'll have an open tab to abuse. Kevin Raymond. Do you know that name?"

Fagin kept a database of every known hacker. He used it to recruit those young enough to be Oliver Twists and to keep an eye on his competition.

"He would be an American who was based in Britain," I said. "Midthirties now. Might have done work for Vasili Borodin, a Russian businessman."

"Corporate espionage?"

"Yes."

"I don't recognize the name."

"Can you check your database? Please?"

"Just a minute." I could hear the click of keys. "He's not in my files."

"What about names like CyberPeasant or Dragon44 or Venjanz?" Those were the nicknames listed in Glenn's hacker file. "Or Belias?" I spelled it for him.

He checked. "Nothing on Belias." More clicking. "CyberPeasant is dead. Dragon44, not active for the past couple of years, so probably using a different code name or retired or in jail."

"And Venjanz?"

The sound of the keyboard. "Huh. That's a pointless crime."

"What do you mean?"

"Several years ago a hacker by that name broke into a database at the Royal Academy of Music in London. He downloaded, then erased a digital archive of student voice performances from ten years ago. The whole thing. Defaced the site and signed that name to it, erased the voices, the database, and the off-site backup. Any performances that survived would have been in private hands."

"Did he ever do anything else?"

"Not under the name Venjanz. He's only in the database because Scotland Yard investigated, given it was the Royal Academy, and we share information with them."

Svetlana Borodina. Ten years ago. Her life erased, then her music. How long had he had the network? Nine or eight?

And then I thought of the eight slashes in the molding in Glenn's old home office, like years ticked off in a prison cell.

His voice lowered. "Sam, why would you care about a prank hacker? A guy who erases music archives at an academy is just a jerk, not a threat."

"Profile a hacker for me. Psychologically."

"We come in all shapes and sizes, movie stereotypes aside."

"Hypothetical, Fagin. A hacker who makes another man very rich and successful. Maybe who has a father who works for said rich man; maybe the hacker has made the rich man more money than the father."

"Entitled," Fagin said immediately. "I mean that in a good sense of the word. He would want to be credited for his role in building up the rich man. And he should be. Especially if his methods were more effective than legitimate ones."

"And how do you reward such a hacker?"

"Money. Respect. New technical challenges. Women are always nice."

"Women. A relationship? Or just sex?"

"Look at every hacker bio. Most of them are always wanting to be in a relationship. Hacking is lonely. They like a regular partner that they can show how smart they are. They need someone to consistently impress."

"And if the woman leaves them or maybe takes up with the father? Or if the rich man disrespects him?"

"Oh. Well. That would be bad. Hackers hold grudges, often because they can actually wreak revenge. If he had made those people wealthy, and they rejected him or made him feel unimportant, he would burn down the house if he could."

Venjanz, I thought. He picked the right name. Maybe he'd been in love with her, his father had taken her, maybe not even knowing how his son felt, his boss maybe hadn't rewarded him. A toxic mix.

Fagin kept talking. "They don't feel the impulse to let the situation go. I'm speaking very generally here and certainly not about myself. I do yoga now. Very calming for the temperament."

"You are a beacon of sanity, Fagin." I paused. "This hacker told me he'd moved from hacking computers to hacking lives," I said.

"Arrogant, then."

"But he's doing it. His system is working. He has muscle behind him, or he did. The muscle got killed."

"Then he's very dangerous," Fagin said. "He has a system in place, and he's lost part of it. He'll want to replace that muscle."

Me, I thought. *Me.* Mila had read Belias perfectly. We'd proceed with her plan.

49

Saturday, November 6, late afternoon

DIANA KEENE WONDERED, *Do you think this is going to work? You're delaying the inevitable. You don't even know if your mother is still alive.*

Diana drove through the western half of San Francisco, pondering her options. She'd slept in the car and it smelled of musty person and cheap food. She headed north toward Sutro Baths. It wouldn't be so busy; most tourists never knew about it. She needed the comforting whoosh of the ocean pounding against the rocks. The sea breeze would make her feel clean.

She parked at the top of the hill. Steps led down to the ruins of the baths, a long ago San Francisco attraction that sat in a bowl of land next to the bay. Once it held pools that could accommodate hundreds. The Sutro Baths had burned down in the 1960s in a suspicious fire, never rebuilt. Now there were just stone edges, flat land, and a large cave close to the baths where you could walk in the near darkness. The wind was a constant stream, the trees misshapen and bent. She walked down the sand-covered steps, past two older women who were negotiating the incline with caution, past the ruins of the pools. She went inside the cave, thinking of the times her mother brought her here, and they stood in the near dark, watching the ocean rush in below through a slot in the rock. No one else was in the cave—it would be busier in the afternoon—and she could pretend she was the only person left in the world, watching the slice of ocean and sky and rock.

She thought about the deaths she'd seen. Her mother dying. The lipstick case that she needed to get back from The Select bar, but knowing Sam Capra would do nothing to help her now. She closed her eyes and let the nurturing quiet wash over her.

I'm sorry, Mom. I'm so sorry.

She remembered a friend telling her there was an old pay phone, one of the few left, up above the baths, along Point Lobos.

She walked to the phone. Then she took a deep breath and dropped in the quarters. Called the San Francisco Police Department; she'd memorized the number the night before, at Lily's, in case she changed her mind.

"SFPD."

"I need to speak to whoever is in charge of the investigation of the death of the man at The Select bar in the Haight. I have information."

"One moment." Then a new voice. "This is Detective DeSoto."

Suddenly Diana's mouth felt as dry as the sand in her shoes. "I have information. On the guy who died at The Select bar."

"I'm listening."

"The woman he was…bothering…I'm her."

"What's your name?"

"I'm not sure I want to tell you that quite yet. Let's see how the conversation goes."

Silence for a moment. "All right. Why was he after you?"

"I have something he wants."

"And."

"And it *could* be evidence in a criminal investigation."

"Evidence against Rostov?"

"Look, I'm not telling you anything more. Because the evidence…it implicates someone I care about. Someone who can give you the biggest case of your life."

"Let's just have you come in and give a statement. What's your name?"

She kept glancing at the steady traffic along Point Lobos, waiting for a police car to materialize. How quickly could the call be traced? Instantly, she would think. "I need the deal first."

"What deal?"

"I need to be sure someone is immune from prosecution."

"You?"

"Someone else." She almost hung up. This was the biggest decision of her life, she realized. If she made the deal for her mother, if her mother revealed the role Belias played in her business's success—what then? Keene Global could be shut down, sued into nonexistence. People wouldn't believe that Diana didn't know—she could be charged as well. Maybe she'd never work at all again. How would she support herself?

It's a neat little trap of loyalty, Diana thought. It was a tough, economically hard world, and she was about to rip away her comfort zone.

"Hello? Are you there?" DeSoto's voice rang out.

"Yes. I'm thinking."

She began to cry. *You will be sending your dying mother to prison. What kind of daughter are you? You don't know they will make a deal.*

"I won't back out on any deal I make with you right now. I will support that."

"But I don't know you."

But she still might have one friend at the bar. Felix. Felix would have a key to the bar, and Sam Capra couldn't be at the bar *all* the time. If she could get the flash drive back, she could edit the video and make a deal, now that DeSoto had promised to negotiate in good faith with her.

DeSoto said, "Let's make a deal now. Tell me what you know. Tell me why they're after you. I'll get a DA on the line, we can see what we can work out."

Don't go against this, Diana, her mother had said toward the end of the video. *You would be going up against some very powerful people, here and abroad. Trust me, sweetie. It's just better to join the club.*

Thanks for making that decision for me, Mom, she thought bitterly. *Thanks, but I think I have to make my own decisions now.*

"I'll call you back."

"No, wait, let's meet now. Please. Let's..."

And Diana hung up. She turned around. No police cars in the lot, but soon enough DeSoto could trace the phone call back to this pay phone. She headed for the car.

If Sam wouldn't take mercy on her, then maybe Felix would.

50

JANICE GOT WHAT SHE NEEDED from the hardware store, and then she drove back to the Mystik.

In her hotel room, she took two small cans from her bag. She went to the bottom of the large, heavy curtain by the window, and she sprayed a foamy epoxy onto the wall, in a thin sphere behind the curtain. Then she took a green foam block and carefully broke bits onto a cotton swab and decorated the smear on the wall lightly. Now the goop was greenish black. She hid the spray and the foam block in the recesses of her purse. She let her handiwork dry. Glancing into the hallway, she saw the maid's trolley and was glad she didn't have to call housekeeping.

"Ma'am," she called out to the maid. "There's an issue with my room, please."

The maid came forward. "Yes, ma'am?"

"It's easier to show you." She led the maid into the room and hoisted the bottom of the curtain to show the thin arc of green black where it grew from up the wall toward the floor vent. "Mold."

"Oh, goodness," the maid said.

"Obviously a health concern…" Janice gave the slightest of coughs.

"Yes, ma'am, one moment." The maid called a manager in housekeeping. Janice kept a patient smile on her face. She did not want to be remembered as the angry lady.

It took about two minutes. The housekeeping supervisor, a woman about Janice's age, arrived.

"Ma'am, I'm so sorry about this, we'll get you moved to another room immediately," the supervisor said, staring at the "mold."

"I don't think it's real mold," Janice said.

The supervisor inspected it. Janice knew an experienced eye and a quick chemical test would see her vandalism wasn't actual mold. Better to look helpful. "I just wondered if it might be a prank. It looks sprayed on."

"Regardless, we certainly will get you moved to a clean room."

Janice waited for the supervisor to head for the room's phone, and she carefully ran right into her, as though heading toward her own closet to gather her belongings.

"Oh, ma'am, excuse me," the supervisor said.

"My fault, my fault." Janice laughed. "I'm just in a hurry to wash my hands now that I touched it." The supervisor gestured for her to walk first. Janice went into the bathroom, cupping the passkey she'd lifted from the supervisor in her palm. The housekeeper would call downstairs to reservations, get a new room assignment for Janice, and then take Janice to the new room or send a bellman upstairs with a new key.

If the housekeeping supervisor realized her own keycard was gone in the next couple of minutes—well, she'd deal with that then. A supervisor, her passkey should open every door in the whole building. Including the penthouse level elevator, if not the penthouse itself.

One problem at a time.

She could hear the supervisor hanging up the phone, murmuring instructions to the maid.

Janice stepped back into the room.

"Ms. Atkins, we have a new room for you. One floor up, so not far. I will have a bellman come and move your belongings. Would you like assistance in repacking?"

"No, thank you." Janice smiled at her.

"I'll have the bellman bring you up a key for the new room. It's 4545."

"Thank you," she said.

The supervisor smiled and shut the door behind her.

Janice's smile faded and she packed quickly. The gun and the poison were both in her purse. She had no idea how often the keycard's combinations were struck and replaced. She had to act quickly.

The bellman was quite prompt and he moved her to her new room. It was nice and fresh and airy. Once he was tipped and gone, Janice pulled the supervisor's passkey from her bag.

If this couldn't get her into the penthouse, then she'd have to come up with a whole new plan.

A knock at the door. Probably housekeeping to make sure the new room met with her approval. She opened the door.

One of Lazard's bodyguards. She started to speak and he punched her hard in the face. She fell back. The bodyguard reached toward her, and she scrambled away, trying to evade his reach.

The poison. She couldn't be caught. She was dead anyway. She grabbed at the bottle, sitting in her purse, yanking it out, but then the bodyguard was in the room, the door closed behind him. He yanked the vial from her hands and slammed her head down toward the desk.

Agony. Then darkness.

51

Saturday, November 6, late afternoon

HOLLY WORE DARK GLASSES and a 49ers cap pulled low over her face. She walked to an artsy shop and bought a fancy journal and a nice pen. Then she figured out that a small coffee bar gave her a view of both the back lot and the front door of The Select. She perched at a table away from the window, ordered a small espresso, and opened the journal. She was half-tempted to write; she felt like she could pour out all her disappointment in herself, and in Glenn, on the paper. All the pain of the bad choices she'd made. A long confession. But if she stared at the paper too long she might miss Sam coming out of the bar.

She watched the people of the Haight walk by: the omnipresent stoners; the kids, purposeful in their hippiedom; the older rebels, softened by time; the tourists, a near constant stream.

And she thought of shooting Sam cold in the street.

She sipped coffee. She drew pictures of Peter and Emma. She drew pictures of Glenn.

The night began to fall. Holly watched the bar, the weight of murder on her mind.

52

Saturday, November 6, evening

Hello, Marian Atkins."

Janice opened her eyes.

Lucky Lazard leaning over her. She lay on a bed.

She screamed.

"No one can hear you," he said. "The room's soundproofed. My parties get too loud for the paying guests a floor below."

She stopped.

"You've been shadowing me. I want to know who you are."

"You've made a mistake...I'm a guest here."

"A guest with two passports in her purse. Marian Atkins and Catherine Bonheur."

"I talked to you this morning at Enchant. At breakfast...why have you hurt me?" She made tears spring to her eyes.

"You have two passports and a gun with a suppressor on it and a passkey you stole off a staff member," he said. "Do you think a man important enough to have a private security detail doesn't pay any attention to his surroundings? I've had you watched since you were at the park this afternoon."

"My name is Marian Atkins. I'm an accountant from San Francisco. I'm just here on a vacation. Please, Mr. Lazard, please. Let me go and I won't tell anyone. I won't."

"Stop the lying." Then he held up her pills and shook the vial. "You're a cancer patient. Now, why is a cancer patient trying to kill me?"

"You've made a terrible mistake."

"Don't. Just don't. Who sent you?"

She gritted her teeth.

"You tried to grab a vial of eyedrops out of your purse. I'm guessing it was a weapon although I'm not real inclined to test it. Poison, maybe? I could stick it on your tongue and see what happens."

She shook her head.

"Lady, whoever you are, you're messing with the wrong guy. The wrong people."

He leaned close to her, and the kindness and joy she'd seen in his face when he was with his daughter was gone. "You will tell me everything. Who you are. Who sent you. What you want."

"This is a mistake. The gun is mine, for protection. I'm a woman traveling alone."

"Explain the two passports."

"Please let me go. I'll just leave, all right? I'll just go."

"Go? I don't think I'll make it easy for you to go anywhere." And he took her IDs, took out a match, and lit them on fire. He dropped them into a steel wastebasket and she watched them burn. "Hard to go anywhere without an ID," he said. "So you don't have to be in a rush to leave."

She stared at the smoke curling up.

"You came here from Portland. You had a ticket receipt in your purse," he said. "You said you were from San Francisco."

She blinked. "Yes, I went to Portland first. Business trip."

He studied her face. "Because you're an accountant."

"Yes."

He went to a laptop on the desk and typed. Then he glanced at her. "There is no search result for a Marian Atkins, an accountant in San Francisco. Your business must be way down."

He held up the blue prepaid phone he'd taken from her purse. "This phone. Only has calls to one number. Whose number is this?"

"Call it and see." What would Belias do if he knew she was in trouble? Write her off? Send someone from the network to help her?

"I think I will."

He tapped a button and raised the phone to his face. They both waited for the ring to be broken by an answer. And waited and waited.

53

Saturday, November 6, evening

"ARE WE READY?" I asked.

"We are," Mila said.

I dialed Belias's number.

"I have something of yours," I said as soon as Belias answered the phone. In the background I could hear opera. A soprano singing. I thought of Svetlana Borodina. Maybe it was her. Maybe only he got to listen to her lovely voice now.

"And I have something I want to play for you," Belias said. He turned the music down.

"What would that be?"

"Your friend. The attractive woman I met today. Is she with you?"

"Naturally."

"That woman is selling you out to the Rostovs."

I let five seconds pass. "Is this really the angle you want to play?"

"I can prove it, Sam. Listen." He played a recording then, Mila speaking with the Rostov boss in New York, promising to deliver me for a price, the Rostov boss weakly protesting that he didn't know what she meant. I listened. I stared at Mila, who nodded.

"That...is interesting," I finally said.

"If you work for her, you shouldn't. You should work for me."

"I had something to offer you in trade for leaving me alone. I know Glenn Marchbanks was trying to screw you over. I know who he was working with."

"See? Our interests align."

I counted to ten, as though considering the risk. "We should talk. Face-to-face. Palace of Fine Arts. Be there in an hour."

"It's rather public."

"Safer for us both."

"Is little Miss Moscow coming?"

"She'll insist on coming along. She wants to sell you the information we have."

"I think I just bought the information, Sam. I just bought it by showing you she's going to get you killed by those Russians."

"I understand." I hung up.

"He bit," Mila said.

"He bit," I said.

"Then let us go reel him in," she said. "It is like these hunting shows on TV. The monster is on the hook."

"Good luck," Felix said. "I'll keep seeing what I can find out on Kevin-slash-Belias."

"I'll be back soon," Mila said, and she gave him a kiss on the cheek. Felix didn't look convinced that our plan would go smoothly.

We headed to the car, Mila talking to me, rehearsing the plan, me silent. My nerves jangled as we reached the car—I felt watched. I glanced around. No one. But something made me say, "Get into the car, quick," to Mila. She did.

But there was no threat, no danger, at least not here. Just nerves.

I headed north, turning out of the gate, knowing I was about to go into the devil's den. I drove and put the speaker on my phone and called Leonie.

The whole way over, I listened to my son's laughter and gurgles, my hands gripping the steering wheel as though I might crush it.

54

Saturday, November 6, evening

JOHN BELIAS LIKED the Palace of Fine Arts. It was designed to look like old Greek ruins—ruins built fresh, which fit his view of the world.

Something that wasn't exactly what it seemed.

The ducks moved across the vast pond that edged the false ruins; the wind was a gentle caress. Strollers walked along the pathways on the other side of the water, photographing the fake temples to creativity and artistry. He frowned; he could end up on someone's camera. He saw why Sam Capra had insisted on this as a meeting place. A small wedding party—bride, groom, two attendants, and a friend with a camera—snapped shots at the other dome, and he made sure he wasn't captured in their camera. The palace would probably get busier after dinner, with couples taking a romantic stroll.

Hopefully his business with Sam and the woman would be concluded by then. He disliked brides, he disliked romantic couples. He saw them and they always reminded him of Svetlana. The sting hadn't faded; he knew it was unhealthy. He needed to forget her. But when he tried he could hear the rich sound of her voice, singing, laughing, begging for her life.

His phone buzzed. "They're on their way." Holly sounded disappointed. "What do you want me to do?"

"The bar is still closed?"

"Yes."

"See if you can get inside and find if they have any information on us and get rid of it. Then go back to the safe house."

"I understand." She hung up. Then he saw that four voice mails were on the phone he used only with Janice. He had forgotten to look at his phone again in the madness of dealing with the bartender. Probably Janice asking for instructions. Or reporting that Lucky Lazard was dead.

The first: "I have the woman you sent to Vegas. Call her on her phone."

His mouth went dry.

The second: "I'll try again. I have the woman you apparently sent to kill me or follow me. Call her on her phone."

The third: "You must not be interested in your hired gun's safety."

He took a deep breath and put the phone back in his left pocket. Then he pulled another phone from his right pocket.

He checked another voice mail number for the second phone. Another set of messages, also from Lazard. He called him back on this second phone. He listened to Lazard shriek about the danger he was in.

"Don't hurt this woman," he said. "I'd like to be able to question her. I'll be in Vegas very soon, and I'll deal with her."

He hung up, shaking, and slipped the second phone back into his right pocket.

The meeting with Sam was now perhaps the most important meeting of his life. He waited, trying not to sweat, his racing mind considering angles, possibilities, approaches, while the ducks danced and paddled and the laughter of a bride echoed across the water.

55

Saturday, November 6, evening

HOLLY HUNG UP, slipped her journal into her purse, and hurried out of the coffee shop. She hurried to the back of The Select. She pulled the weapon from her purse. She listened at the heavy steel door. She knelt and inspected the locks with a penlight. She opened the flap on the belt and began to reach for her tools.

Then the doorknob, an inch from her face, began to turn.

Holly leapt back, her hand going to her weapon.

The door cracked open.

She fired the Taser needles through the opening. The needles and the wires hissed into a man's body.

He knew even before she thumbed the charge. He tried to slap the wires free—if he'd slammed the door shut, he might have prevailed. But she thumbed the charge and he jerked back. She slid through the door, hitting him again as he jerked along the concrete floor.

Third blast and he was gagging. She leveled a kick at the back of his head and he sprawled into stillness. She searched the man: fortyish, slight. Driver's license: Felix Neare. He was armed, a gun wedged in the back of his pants, knocked out by his Taser convulsions. She took it. She found a cell phone and a ring of keys in his pocket.

She opened a door into a storeroom, stacked with boxes of wine and cases of beer. She propped him up against the boxes.

And then she put the barrel of the gun against his forehead.

Let Sam Capra know what it felt like to lose someone.

Her finger squeezed on the trigger. A little drop of drool inched from his lip.

She lowered the gun.

No. This wasn't who she was.

Holly noticed something on the concrete floor, where he had convulsed—little plastic cuffs, like you'd use for a prisoner. He must have intended them for her; perhaps he'd seen her kneeling by the door on a security camera. She took the pair and snapped them on his wrists. Found a rag in a box and carefully stuffed it in his mouth. She made sure his nasal passages were clear, nearly laughing, since she had been going to kill him not a minute earlier. She was gentle with him.

She locked him inside the storeroom.

She made a fast sweep through the bar. It had been cleaned since the fight. Heavy curtains closed off the windowed front from the street; no one could see inside. Upstairs she found a locked door. She tried keys until one worked. It looked like a small combination studio apartment/office.

Names and faces taped on the wall. She didn't know who any of them were—until she saw the picture of Audrey's father. She scanned the notes. People who had been brought down.

They were trying to figure out who was in the network. Her skin prickled. A separate section of papers about a Russian businessman she'd never heard of were taped to an opposite wall. She wondered what they meant.

She left the papers in place. Tried another door, locked.

She tested the keys again. Inside was a small room. Stocked with weapons. Rifles, handguns. A small assortment of knives, of night vision gear, cheap prepaid phones. Ammunition.

She moved past the weapons. In a bureau drawer she found neatly stacked papers—the kind of paper used only for passports, with the appropriate watermarks. Entry stamps for countries. Tools for forgery: special printers, pens, photo equipment. Blank bank credit cards awaiting numbers.

In another drawer she found a finished passport with Sam Capra's photo in the document. But the passport was Belgian. Another one for Guatemala. Same face. One of the petite woman, in a UK passport, her name was Mila Court. A French passport bore her face but a different name.

Who were these people?

Some sort of organization to rival Belias's?

She could see a security camera feed on one of the laptops. She erased the last ten minutes of footage and turned the cameras off. She unplugged the laptops. She found a bag to carry them. Belias had ordered her to destroy the hard drives, but maybe he could crack them open and find data that would tell them who this new enemy was.

A knock rapped on the back door as she came back down the stairs. She froze. Another knock, less timid, more insistent.

The front. She could go out the front door. Felix's key ring should unlock it.

The knock again.

Boldness took her. She went to the door. Maybe it was Sam Capra, returned. And she could shoot him in the privacy of the bar.

Holly Marchbanks opened the door.

At first in the dim gleam of the alley light she couldn't see the woman's face, turned to glance toward the street. Then she turned.

Diana Keene.

"Yes?" Holly heard herself ask. *Get her inside*, she thought. She forced an uncertain smile. "I'm afraid we're not open."

"I...I...I was looking for Felix. I called him and he said to come over."

"You must be Diana. Sorry, we've had a lot of people wanting to know when we're reopening. Felix stepped out for just a moment. I'm—Emma." She said the first name that came to mind, then felt bad, sullying her daughter's name as a deception. "He should be back in just a minute. He just went to get dinner for you. I'm a friend of his."

"And a friend of Sam's?"

"Sam is trouble. Felix is a good guy. He thought we could...hide you at my apartment. He probably hadn't told you that yet. But he has a plan to get you away from all this mess, until we can find your mother."

Diana stepped inside.

Holly shut the door, then locked it with the key ring. A little but important detail to make her look like she belonged.

"Felix doesn't like to leave the door unlocked when we're closed." She set down the bag containing the laptops by the door.

"I understand." Diana stepped into the back of the bar from the rear hallway, toward the open areas, with their neat tables. Her gaze scanning the room.

"Are you all right?" Holly pulled her shirt free, with a deft yank, to cover Felix's gun she'd tucked into her jeans. The Taser was in the pouch with the laptops.

"Yes. Just strange to be here."

"Do…do you want something to drink?" Holly asked. "The bar's open. Even when we're not." She forced an awkward laugh. *I can give her to Belias, and then I really will be free. Me and the kids, we'll be free of him forever.*

"A drink. No." Diana crossed her arms, walked toward the bar. She stopped at a spot where bleach had been poured on the concrete. "The Russian man died right there. The blood is all gone."

"Felix…and I…cleaned it up when the police were done." Holly's voice sounded flat. *What if she realizes I'm lying?* She'd have to force Diana into the car. Or knock her out, and get her into her Mercedes, which was parked down the street, without anyone seeing. Kidnapping wasn't so easy, especially on your own. Or convince her that Felix wanted to meet her somewhere else and that they'd have to drive. That would be easier…

"I left a message here," Diana said. "Felix put it by the cash register."

Holly went toward the register, but in the mirrored bar back she watched Diana step away from where the Russian died and stroll along where the tables and chairs sat, back in the proper and orderly positions. She didn't speak, shoulders hunched. Dropping to one knee, looking under the tables.

She didn't want me to see her do that, Holly realized. "Are you looking for something?"

Five seconds ticked by. "No." Diana stood. "I was looking for...the blood. I dreamt about it."

"You sure you don't want a drink? I could use one." Maybe she could get her drunk. That would be a help.

"Okay," Diana said.

"What would you like?"

"Wine. Whatever's open." But Diana kept glancing around, as though she expected to find something, see something.

Holly went behind the bar, glanced along the wall till she saw the squat glass-fronted double refrigerator, knelt, grabbed an already open bottle of Riesling. She put it on the bar. She pulled down two wineglasses but she could feel the weight of Diana's stare on her back.

Did I take too long? Holly thought.

"How do you know Felix?"

"I used to work with him at another bar. We're old friends." She forced her hand to be steady as she gushed the golden wine into the glasses.

"Really? He and my mom are friends."

Holly recorked the Riesling, slid one of the glasses toward Diana. She left the bottle out.

Diana didn't touch her wine while Holly took a long sip. "My message?"

Holly set down the wineglass. "You said he put it by the cash register?" She ran a finger along the edge of the register. "It's not here."

"What did he tell you about me?" Diana took a fortifying sip of the Riesling.

"Just that you were a good person who needed help."

Diana took another gulp of wine. "Doesn't this bar serve food? Couldn't Felix have cooked something here?"

"Well, yes, but that food belongs to the bar. Sam watches the food expenses like a hawk."

The mention of Sam seemed to upset her; Holly watched Diana

take another long sip of wine. "The Russian...did the police tell you who he was? The news reports didn't say."

"His name was Rostov. Felix told me." Holly leaned forward like they were gossiping. "He used to be Russian Special Forces."

"And Sam killed a guy like that?"

"Yes."

"Huh," Diana said. "I guess he didn't need my help."

"What do you mean?"

"When the other guy was going to shoot Sam, in the alley, I stopped him. I'm glad I didn't have to stop the Russian."

A chill touched Holly. "You stopped him?"

"I hit him in the head with a board." Diana almost sounded proud. "I hope that still counts with Sam. He might not be very happy with me right now."

"That was very brave of you." The words felt molten in Holly's throat.

"That jerk was going to shoot so I hit him. Hard as I could, but I guess it wasn't hard enough because he ran and it said on the news there were no arrests yet."

Holly nodded as though her head were moved by a string. Roaring pounded in her ears.

"He hasn't come back here?"

"I don't think so." Holly stared at the woman who'd killed the father of her children, the love of her life.

Why had Belias lied to her? Maybe Glenn lied. Or was confused as to who hit him. His injury...Diana had killed him. She had just admitted it.

"Could you please call Felix? And tell him I'm here?"

"Of course I can call Felix." Holly went to the bar's phone. She dialed the first six numbers, not a seventh. "Felix? Hi, your friend is here." Paused, flexed a smile at Diana in the bar's mirror, still cracked by the bullet from the night Diana'd come into the bar. "She's understandably anxious, yes. All right." This was her chance, say that Felix needed them someplace else. If she asked to talk to Felix, though, then that was not going to happen, and in the mirror she saw Diana's hand reaching toward the phone...

And then a pounding noise.

Not at the back door or at the front.

It was the storage room door.

Diana turned toward the noise, then back to Holly, and Holly slammed the Riesling bottle into the young woman's jaw. Diana fell, terror in her eyes, hands clawing against the concrete floor and the mahogany of the bar. She nearly sat on the old-fashioned brass footrail that circled the bar, a few inches above the floor.

Holly vaulted over the bar.

"No! No!" Diana cried out in terror, kicking out at Holly. She wasn't a fighter, but she landed the kick square into Holly's flat stomach.

A cold, hard rage filled Holly. "You killed him! You killed him!" she screamed.

"Please don't, don't!" Diana screamed back. Holly powered a fist into the girl's nose—she felt blood spurt against her fingers.

"You killed him!" She grabbed Diana's hair, clenched a fist down to the scalp, hammered her head back against the side of the mahogany bar worn smooth by elbows over the years. Once. Twice. Three times.

Diana was silent. Holly let go of her hair. The woman's head lolled back, as though she'd crept into sleep. Her mouth and jaw hung slack, her eyes open.

"Wait, wait," Holly managed to sputter. Her fingertips—her manicured nails broken on two fingers—went to the younger woman's throat.

The edge of the bar. Unyielding, hard wood. She'd struck Diana's neck against the edge…too hard. The wrong angle.

I killed her.

She thought she would be sick, bile roiling up in her throat like heat.

But she killed Glenn.

The two thoughts tore at her as if they were razors.

Behind her the pounding on the door grew louder.

She crabbed away from the dead woman's body, hurried to the phone. Dialed Belias.

No answer. She glanced at the clock—the meeting with Sam Capra was on now. She hung up the phone. She grabbed a rag off the bar back and wiped the phone, then wiped every place she had touched. The railing. The bar. The refrigerator.

Then she knelt again by the body.

The pounding on the supply door ceased. The sudden quiet frightened her. Diana didn't carry a purse. Maybe she'd left it in her car. She searched the woman's pockets. A small wallet with thirty-odd dollars. A set of BMW car keys attached to a pepper spray that might have saved her if she'd used it fast enough. A cell phone, the screen cracked and broken.

She stood and stared down at the young woman's body. "You shouldn't have hurt him."

The storage door began to shudder in its frame. Felix had found something inside to use as a ram. He must have cut himself loose from the cuffs. The knob began to rattle.

She ran. She forgot the bag with the laptops and bolted out the back door. The key for Diana's car was a BMW and Holly ran down the street until she saw one. Tried the key. Nothing. She ran down and saw another BMW, an older model. She got inside, shut the door, began to search the car.

No disc to hold a video. No flash drive, nothing. A bag with some clothes, nothing else.

She forced herself to slow down. To search more carefully.

She jumped at a knock on the driver's side window.

"What?" she half screamed.

"Are you pulling out?" A man, smiling, hopeful he'd found that elusive San Francisco prey, a parking spot.

"No!" she yelled and the man retreated back to his car.

The video wasn't in here.

The trunk?

She got out of the car, stood, and she saw Felix bolting down the street, scanning, searching for her and his eyes locked on hers. He held a battered fire extinguisher in his bloodied hands.

She dropped back into the BMW, locked the doors. She revved the car out of the way just as Felix reached her. She floored it, the tires gripping on the incline of the hill, her laying on the horn.

The guy who'd wanted her parking space blocked her five spots up, turn signal on, waiting for a slot to open.

The fire extinguisher smashed into the passenger window. Starring it into a broken galaxy of rings.

Holly floored the accelerator, took off, wheeling around the stopped car, headfirst into oncoming traffic. Horns blared. Headlights dazzled her eyes. She levered the wheel over, blasting back into the correct lane.

She stared at the rearview. Felix Neare stood in the street, watching her run.

Holly pulled off the road when she got closer to the safe house. She carefully searched the car. Inch by inch. No sign of a flash or portable computer drive that could have held the video Diana had. Nothing. A cheap bag with one pair of jeans, underwear still in the package, a couple of new T-shirts. The girl on the run, trying to make her dollars last so Belias wouldn't find her. Waiting for her mom to come home, not wanting to send her mom to jail. A blanket on the backseat.

Diana Keene had been running and hiding and sleeping in this car.

But the video about Belias and his network, the nuclear bomb of evidence that could vaporize her life, was still somewhere out there.

She drove the BMW back to the neighborhood off Haight where she'd left her own car. Locked it up and wondered how long the starred window would hold or if someone would soon steal the BMW. That would be a bonus. She left the keys in the ignition and she found her car and she drove away.

Holly's hands weren't shaking now.

56

Saturday, November 6, late evening

THE PALACE OF FINE ARTS was illuminated, soft glows of light kissing the statues of the goddesses, the pillars. Belias stood and waited and watched us approach.

Mila stood in black pants, a dark turtleneck that rose to her elegant jawline, dark jacket. A dark wool cap, folded once, covered her hair. She had been careful to tuck in all the loose strands.

Belias wore a dark trench coat. The kind that could hide a weapon. I was unarmed, so was Mila. You don't walk around in San Francisco, in a place where innocents could gather, hoping to start a firefight.

"I hope you brought money, big man," Mila said to him. "What we know will cost you pretty pennies."

"I asked you to come alone, Sam," Belias said.

"We are never alone, Mr. Belias," Mila said. "We have many friends in high places."

It was a knife under his skin, under his ego, her saying that, and he smiled a coldly wicked grin. "I made the high places, little girl. I put people there. The secret is in choosing the exact right person for the exact high place. Do you know how grateful they are? How frightened an insecure person is, who thinks he or she doesn't earn their success? They're clay in my hands." He laughed and gestured with his pale hands. "You get rid of the obstacles for them, they're like children. Slightly insecure children who'll do what you ask because they don't know how to get up if they fall down."

"You profile them; then you approach them," I said.

"I profile them; then I give them a break and then they're mine."

"Like Sam. You think you want Sam," Mila said. "Silly rabbit."

"Whatever you and your bartender friend are," he said, "mercenaries—hired security—adventurers—whatever…"

"You didn't guess," Mila said. "I am so disappointed."

"Whatever you are," Belias said. "You're done. Your partnership is dissolved." He glanced at me.

She raised her hands and snapped her fingers. "Threats over. We have the information from Glenn Marchbanks. Names. Proof of your network. Pretty pennies time, right, Sam?"

I stayed put and she threw me a glance of surprise.

"She's only here because I felt she should face her accuser." I glanced around. No one close to us. A few people on the opposite side of the huge pond. Not crowded. The concrete columns were wide. A lot of places to stand unseen.

"What?" She turned toward me. "What does that mean?"

Belias said, "You called the Rostovs, sweetheart. I've been monitoring their phones. That's how I knew they were coming after Sam. And that's how I knew that you called them and offered Sam on a plate. I hate women who pretend to care." Sudden venom in his voice.

"Sam…this is not true."

"Shut up." I took a step toward her.

"We know what you are, Mr. Belias," Mila said. "If anything happens to me, you will be exposed. You, your entire network of the wealthy and successful. I will see to that."

"No, he won't," I said. "I will see to that." I took another step toward her.

"Sam, he is lying." Desperation tinged her voice.

"I heard the tape. I heard the call." I took another step toward her. She retreated one step, behind a pillar.

"Sam," Belias said. "She can draw the Rostovs into a trap we set, yes?"

"No," I said. And I pushed her up against the pillar, my arm encircling her throat, her eyes wide with fright. I jerked her hard against me and the soft crack of her neck was loud in the hush of the pillars. Over her shoulder I saw Belias flinch. He was used to weapons and the distance they gave you from death. She sagged against the stone, and I held her in place and yanked the dark knit cap down, over her face, over the collar of her turtleneck. It covered her head, no skin showed. I tucked her hands into her dark coat and I eased her into the water, calling to the ducks as I did. She hardly made a splash as I shoved her toward the center. Belias thoughtfully tossed bread from his pockets to the ducks, who scattered. To those across the expanse we didn't look suspicious, I supposed. No one screamed, no one hollered. Mila, silent, gone, drifted into the black. But it wouldn't be long until she was spotted in the night gleam of the water.

"Let's walk," I said. I didn't wait for him as we stepped from the lit glow of the pond and began to hurry in the darkness along the curving arc toward Baker Street, out from under the arches and the mosaics.

"I didn't expect you to bring her," he said.

"I wanted to make a point," I said. We walked, not glancing back at the pond.

"It's awful at first. The betrayal of a good woman."

"Like Svetlana Borodina?"

I thought he might fall out of his skin. And if we hadn't been hurrying away from a murder scene, he might well have stopped to stare at me. But he kept walking and he recovered his expression of neutrality. "Well. An equal."

"I'm more your equal than Roger was." I so wanted to call him Kevin. But if I was wrong, if that wasn't his name, then there was no point. "But I understand why you don't like Russians."

He cleared his throat. "So. You were CIA and now you're not."

"I made some interesting contacts in the course of my work. Underground, around the world, mostly in Europe. Mila was one."

"And the bars are a front."

"It gives me legitimate cover for my income. Mila was good at finding information that people will pay for, the highest bidders. I helped her."

"And Diana Keene came to you?"

"A friend of a friend."

He studied me. "So Mila's partners won't be happy with you."

"She had a junior partner. The man you saw at the Marina house. He's very sick with cancer. Money will keep him happy. I'll take care of it."

"But you'll need a job now."

"I forgot," I said. "You're in the business of granting wishes."

"I've already done you a big favor by getting rid of the Rostovs."

"I'm sure you enjoyed sticking it to another Russian."

I held up the I Ching necklace I'd taken from Holly March-banks's house. "Subtle influence. Your specialty."

Then I put the chain on, tucked it under my shirt. A sign binding myself to him.

Now for a moment he stopped. He laughed. "I've never quite re-cruited someone this way."

"You lost Roger," I said. "The situation requires speed."

"Lost is one way to put it."

"Mila would have killed him. You did him a favor."

He turned his face away from me for a moment. "I had to kill him."

"Just as I had to kill her."

It was a fearful symmetry, joining us in murder, and Mila had seen it immediately, the way to tie to this man. "You're in trouble. You need someone good in a fight right now."

Belias let that pass and said, "What else do you know of my trou-bles?"

I gave him the phone I'd taken from Glenn Marchbanks's house. "Glenn was conspiring against you. He was trying to ID the rest of your network of golden boys and girls, and he was trying to find out about your and Roger's past in Britain. This guy in Vegas Glenn contacted, is he one of yours?" We were past Baker Street now, and behind us I heard a cry, a woman scream something about a body in the pond.

"This is my car here," Belias said. "Let's find a better place to talk."

You say you hack lives now, Belias? I thought. *You just got hacked yourself.*

We got in and drove away.

57

Saturday, November 6, late evening

THE WOMAN STOPPED SCREAMING, "There's a body in the water," when Mila, floating on her back in the broad pond, drifting back into the sheen of the lights, arose from the water and waded to the shore. Then Mila bowed dramatically to the four corners of the compass, as though acknowledging an invisible audience.

"What on earth are you doing?" the woman's companion asked.

"Performance art," Mila said. "I thought the pond was for swimming with the muses." She pointed up at the statues of the goddesses. "Now I have my inspiration, I take my leave."

Once the brief screaming stopped, and people saw the woman in the pond was fine, the scant crowd lost interest. Bizarre behavior was a given in San Francisco.

Mila ran to the car. When she was inside, she stripped the plastic bottles she'd cut open and hid underneath her turtleneck. Her throat was bruised slightly, but the crunch of the plastic had made a nice substitute for the sound of bone breaking.

She called The Select. "Felix? It worked…What's the matter?"

58

Saturday, November 6, late evening

IN A HOUSE OF GLASS it was hard to keep a prisoner. But somewhere in Lucky Lazard's penthouse there was a room with no windows and a locked door. Janice Keene lay in that room, in the dark, arm tucked under her head.

I am never going to see Diana again. Ever. This would have been easier to bear from a cancer bed. She might never see anyone again. They'd take her out in the desert and kill her. Once you got a ways past Las Vegas, you could forget that civilization and buffets and European acrobatic acts and female impersonators were a few hours away. Out far from the glitter the wind and the sand would scour your bones.

She was dozing, exhausted with fear and worry, when the door opened again. Lazard stood there alone. But he was a big, thick man with ex–football player written all over him. He had hands that looked like they would make hurtful fists. His eyes were cruel now. Except when he'd looked at his daughter. Love changes everything. She knew that truth.

He studied her face. "Do I know you? Have I wronged you?"

She shook her head. "No."

"Have I wronged someone you love?"

"This isn't a grudge," she said.

"You see, I think it is," he said. "Maybe you got a reason to dislike me, like you might have had a reason to dislike Barbara Scott."

She kept her face implacable. "I don't know who Barbara Scott is."

"Bull. You look like the type who might be in a book club. Everyone knows Barbara Scott's name."

"She's a writer," she said after a moment.

"Very good. You have a brain. Who sent you?"

She was silent.

"Look, I'm under orders not to hurt you."

She was unsure what to think. "You take orders from someone? That surprises me."

"It surprises me, too, but I do." He cracked a very soft smile.

She said nothing.

"You see, either you're someone who hates me, or you were sent by someone who hates me." He let a meaningful pause fill the air. "Or maybe you and I have a mutual friend."

A mutual friend. What if she said, *Yes, we might*? What if the mutual friend was...Belias?

He held up the necklace. The I Ching symbol of Belias's subtle network. She'd forgotten to put it back on after she got up in the morning. "I didn't find this right away when I searched your luggage. I have one, too, but I don't wear it often. Only when I have to do special work. Even though I live in Vegas"—and now he smiled—"I dislike jewelry."

"If I tell you the truth, what will you do to me?" She hated the whisper in her voice. She normally spoke with assurance. But just as she'd found when she got the cancer diagnosis, she didn't want to die. She wanted to see Diana marry and have children and be a success. She wanted to see Felix's smile more. She wanted to feel the sun on her face and the air in her lungs.

He squatted by her, the chain loose in his fingers. "I could toss you from the top of the roof and let you fall forty-eight stories. Vegas has a regrettably high suicide rate. And someone who maybe didn't want a bad, slow death from cancer might take that long, last step. The autopsy'll turn up any old tumors eating you up, and the bruising from the punches will be buried under fresh impact wounds."

His logic chilled her.

"Or I could give you to my bodyguards. Randy and Andy. Randy's got a mean streak in him. I've had to pull him off working girls a couple of times when he started getting way too rough. He's the kind of kid even his parents say, that boy's not right."

She stared at her feet.

"Or you could save yourself all that. You tell me who sent you, and I let you go or I give you a mercy bullet. I have my suspicions."

"It was a mutual friend," she said. Wondering if he'd say *Belias* out loud.

"Glenn Marchbanks. Did he send you?"

Glenn Marchbanks. Oh. Of course. The venture capitalist with the golden touch. It made sense now. He must have an I Ching symbol, too. She blinked, processing the thought.

"Glenn Marchbanks," he repeated.

But now he'd seen the tinge of shock touch on her poker face, her carefully crafted mask, and he seized on it. He grabbed her by her shoulders. "Glenn Marchbanks. He sent you to shut me up."

Shut you up? How could she get him to blunder a bit more, tell her what she needed to know. Glenn Marchbanks and Lucky Lazard. And Barbara Scott. She'd looked at Lucky and Barbara as victims of the network, being put out of the way. They were part of the network. Same as she was.

We all belong to him. Belias has sent me to kill his own. Why, why, why?

"Are you for hire? Or one of his special friends?"

It wasn't really another foot of his grave that he dug then, but she looked up and she could guess what he meant. She went all in. "Special friends. You mean like you and me and Glenn all work for the same guy? A guy we all made a deal with?"

The color went out of his florid face. "No, no. He can't turn on me. I told Glenn to stop, that it was stupid. I didn't side with Glenn."

She wasn't sure how she could play this, but public relations work at the highest level had taught her to improvise. "Did it occur to you I wasn't sent here to kill you?" she said.

"What were you sent here for?"

"To find out what you and Glenn were doing."

"Glenn and I were doing *nothing*. I told Glenn there was no need for him to try a takeover." He grabbed her face. "Tell me the name of our mutual friend. Tell me."

"Belias," she whispered.

He slowly let her go. His face was pale. "So who sent you. Glenn or Belias?"

She had to hope that Belias was coming for her. Lucky would have called Belias when he was under attack, so Belias had given him the orders not to hurt her. So she lied and said, "Glenn Marchbanks sent me, and you can't tell Belias." It was either Glenn or Belias, and maybe something bad was going on with Glenn. It sounded like it from the fragments of what Lazard had said.

But she and Belias were both dead if she admitted he sent her.

He stood and stepped away from her. "Oh, you're screwed, lady. You're screwed."

"I know. Please. Just let me go and I'll go away and no one has to know."

"Who else did Glenn recruit for his little takeover?"

Takeover. Glenn Marchbanks decided to slip the yoke of the debt, of the pact that had made him a success. That would *not* go over well. "I don't know. Just me."

"Glenn gets a cancer patient to do his dirty work."

"Glenn will be better than Belias at running the show," she said. She hoped she could sell this lie. *You sell lies all day long, Janice. Just do it.*

"Why would you think that? What does Glenn know?" Now his voice rose in suspicion. "What does Glenn know?"

"Belias is losing it. Some of us are close to arrest." She let the real panic she felt fill her lie with fire. "He's made mistakes. Glenn knew. He was doing it to save us all."

"Bull," he said. "Belias losing it? Never. Ever."

"He is. He's overreached. He's tried to recruit the wrong people." She fashioned the lie out of the whole cloth of her own fears. What if Belias tried to recruit the wrong person, someone he couldn't control who decided to bolt to the authorities? It had been her constant fear the first few years, one that never relented because he was recruiting new people. Her DOWNFALL file she'd left for her daughter confirmed that. She wanted Diana to have enough information to protect herself if any of Janice's old crimes came back to haunt her.

Her fear was his fear, she saw in his face. "What's your name? Who are you?" He grabbed her shoulders. "I'll go through every business magazine and website until I find your face."

He was close to her now and he wouldn't expect it so she drove the heel of her hand into his face. The pain rocketed in his eyes, and then she slammed her forearm hard into his throat. Grabbed his head and rammed it into the wall. She wrenched free of his grip and she stumbled out into the hallway.

"No, come back here!" he yelled. "You can't get off this floor."

He thought she was trying to escape. *Oh, honey, no*, she thought. *I just need a weapon.* She scrambled down the hallway, out into a large den with spectacular views of Las Vegas stretching every way. To her left she saw a breakfast table, an opening that showed the kitchen. Lots of sharp, lovely items in there.

Lazard lumbered after her. "I'm not gonna hurt you; would you listen to me?"

Where are the guards? she thought.

She yanked open a drawer; utensils clattered in it with the force of her yank and no knife inside. She flung the drawer at him, backed up, fingers fumbling for the next drawer.

Then her hands closed around a knife. She pulled it free from the slot in the drawer. Black handled, sharp edged, suitable for cutting meat.

Janice held it up.

"Come on. I'm bigger and stronger than you and I'll just take it away from you."

"Roger taught me," she said. As if that were a threat.

"He taught me, too."

She feinted to one side, he didn't buy it. Knives weren't her thing. She preferred the subtlety of poison or the quickness of the bullet. Knives were messy.

She heard a chime of elevator doors opening. Then she saw Lazard's face contort in shock. The guards. She turned and ran toward the sound. *Strike fast*, she thought, *like a snake*. Stab one immediately, get his gun.

"Daddy?" a voice called. "Dad?"

She froze. From the entryway, the sound of the chiming elevator, came a girl. The girl she'd seen with Lazard the previous times out.

"Baby!" Lazard screamed. And the noise jangled in her head.

Was she going to kill this man in front of his own daughter? Was she going to have to kill a child?

She hid the knife behind her back. Lazard ignored her, barreled toward the girl, scooped her up in his arms. "Baby, baby, what are you doing here? I sent you back to your mom's for a reason."

"I got Jose to drive me over," she said. "I wanted to see you."

"You know you have to call Daddy first." His voice was taut as pulled wire.

"But you didn't answer." Lazard had interposed himself between his daughter and Janice. She had stopped. The knife stayed behind her.

"Daddy…Daddy wants you to go downstairs. Is Jose waiting with the car?"

"Yes."

"Then go downstairs and go home. It's bedtime."

The girl looked at Janice. "Who's she?"

"Just a friend…" He kept his gaze locked on Janice's arm that held the knife, that concealed the blade from the child.

"Sweetheart," Janice said, "your daddy is right. Why don't you go back downstairs?"

Lazard stared at Janice. He tapped the call button for the elevator and the doors slid immediately open. "Go back downstairs and get an ice cream at the restaurant and then tell Jose to drive you home."

"All right," the girl said and then the doors slid closed.

Lazard turned to Janice. She still gripped the knife. "You could have attacked me while I held her. You would have had the advantage."

"I know that."

"Why?"

"I'm not going to kill you in front of your kid." The words wrenched from her chest.

"But you will now?"

She had to lure him in. "Just let me go. Please."

"I won't let Belias hurt you. All right? I swear," he said. "You just tell us who else Glenn Marchbanks turned against him. Drop the knife."

Janice didn't.

"Drop it."

She came at him with the knife, slashing the air in front of him as he ducked back, but he grabbed her arm. Slammed the knife hand down on the French table that held the big vase of flowers. The knife clattered to the floor.

Twice he slammed a fist into the side of her head, stunning her, then dragging her back toward the room, scooping up the knife, and holding it close against her throat.

59

HOLLY WATCHED SAM CAPRA enter the safe house with Belias and Sam looked at her and she tried to look at him with hate. But she couldn't manage it.

"Holly. You remember Sam." Belias's voice was dry.

She nodded. She didn't like Sam, never would—he'd invaded her home—but her blinding hate was gone because she knew the truth now.

"Hi, Holly," Sam said. He looked nervous—of course he was—and if she told Belias he'd offered her and the kids an escape route, he wouldn't be the golden boy at the moment, would he? But she kept her mouth shut because maybe that was an option she needed to keep open.

"Hello," she said to Sam. Then she stared at Belias. He'd said Sam hit Glenn. Why would he lie? Why would it matter?

Because he'd needed Diana unhurt. And if he'd told her that Diana had hurt Glenn, delivered the blow that eventually killed him...and at that point Sam Capra was a problem, not a potential asset.

Or maybe Glenn lied to both her and Belias. She tried to remember the frantic car ride from The Select to here at the safe house. Glenn had never said who hit him...she assumed it was the man capable of killing the Russian. She felt a misery well up inside her.

Belias blinked under the stare and she looked at the floor. "Did you do as I asked?" he said to her.

"I couldn't. Someone was there." No way she could admit she'd killed Diana to Belias. He wanted her unhurt.

Belias seemed to shrug this off, given his new alliance with Sam. "We have a more pressing issue. I'll need your help. And Sam's. We're going to Las Vegas in the morning."

"I...I need to go home. To my kids."

Belias knelt before her.

"Look, Janice is in trouble. And I need to go pull her out of it, and Sam is going to help me, and you are going to help me."

"And then I'm done? I'm free." She saw Sam Capra react slightly to the word *free*.

"You're too important to me, Holly. I have a new role in mind for you. One that's not dangerous. One that you will enjoy."

"But I want out." New role? She didn't like the way he looked at her. He could not think she would want him.

It was as if he didn't hear her. "I don't want Janice to know yet we've had...an issue with her daughter. I will explain all that to her when this is done, and she can call Diana, and this problem goes away."

She felt sick at what her rage had cost her. She forced resolve onto her face and she nodded.

"Go home and get packed. Sam, we'll get you some fresh clothes. I'll make arrangements for a private jet." He smiled at Sam. "I do it all first class."

"Holly," Sam said. "We're on the same side, now." Off his throat he took an I Ching symbol, the subtle influence sign Belias had given her eight years ago. "I think this belongs to you."

"Yes, Holly, you need one to wear when you're on a job," Belias said.

"I have Glenn's," she said, almost savagely, her hand pressed against her chest. She couldn't keep the hate out of her gaze and she looked away from Sam. She looked at Belias. "Let's go. Let's go and get this done."

60

Saturday, November 6, late evening

MILA SAID, "We have to get rid of the body." She was kneeling next to Diana. Mila folded the dead woman's hands on her chest, closed her eyes, smoothed her hair.

Felix nodded. His eyes were reddened from crying, his mouth bloodied where he'd bit himself during the Taser attack. He nodded. "I failed her. She…"

"Why didn't you tell me she'd called?"

"She didn't call until you guys had left…I wasn't going to call you back here. I thought she'd just wait here with me. Her mother will never forgive me." His voice sounded broken.

"We cannot leave her here." Mila rubbed her face. "Poor girl. None of this was her doing." Mila glanced at him. "Odd that she would come back to the bar. She must have had a reason."

"I offered to meet her wherever she wanted. But she insisted on coming to the bar."

"You said she and the other woman—"

"She was Holly Marchbanks. I recognized her from our Internet research."

"—talked for a few minutes. Could you hear them?"

"No. I'd woken up, cut myself free on a beer bottle I broke, then took a fire extinguisher to the lock. I never heard anything except a scream that I think was Diana."

"Where do we put her, Felix? And we must be quick. I think Sam will be taken to Las Vegas."

"Why?"

"Consider what we know. A person in Vegas was contacted by Glenn Marchbanks to help fight for control of Belias's network. Diana's mother is out on a job for Belias. I think perhaps she is getting rid of a threat to Belias."

Felix bit his lip. "So now Sam will help him get rid of this threat."

"So he thinks."

"So we go to Vegas."

Mila checked flights on her phone. "We can get seats on a flight tomorrow morning."

"I think I should go alone. They think you're dead. If any of them spot you…"

"Only Belias knows my face, and if he sees it, it will be because I am about to hurt him."

"I think you should stay here," Felix said again. "You're dead. Sam will be too if they see you." Diana's death appeared to have unnerved him.

"Felix, enough. You will not go alone. And I am not abandoning Sam. We will be careful. We check the data from the laptop and the phone that Sam stole. We simply need to find a prominent person in Vegas who could be tied to Belias." Felix was smart, but she needed him to focus.

Felix reread the phone message. "Huh. Glenn wrote 'You can't be called lucky.' It might be a literal meaning. Someone nicknamed Lucky?"

"I'll see what I can find," Mila said.

"And Diana…I will take care of her. There's a park near the bay, and I'll call it in to the police. Respectfully. This will kill her mother. I know you and Sam think Janice must be a horrible person, but…I got to know her. She's not. She's…can't be."

"You never know about people, Felix," Mila said. "You just never know."

PART FIVE

SUNDAY, NOVEMBER 7

61

It's time for honesty," Belias said.

I sat across from him and Holly Marchbanks on a private jet. Storms in San Francisco were delaying our takeoff, hard hammering rains, skies inky like it was still night. Holly looked gaunt, worn, as though she hadn't slept. I wondered where her kids were. I wondered if she'd told Belias about my offer of safety. It could be problematic if she mentioned it.

"Isn't it always?" I said.

He crooked a smile, because we had the bond of knowing each other's secrets.

"I wasn't tricking you before, Sam. I've read your CIA file."

I kept my expression neutral. "I've long thought I should sell the film rights, but it's too boring."

"You have enemies," he said. "Several."

"Yes."

"Are they still gunning for you?"

"Why do you ask?"

"I don't wish to acquire new problems through my association with you." Do you see how normal it all sounds? Like it was a business deal, the kind negotiated thousands of times a day.

"I won't tell the other kids we're supersecret buddies."

"I'd like to know specifically who might wish you harm."

"Why do you care?"

"Because I'm facing enough trouble and I don't need more."

I weighed this. Why did he care now in the midst of all his other worries? Had someone been talking about me? Who had given him my CIA file? An enemy?

"Sam?"

"You didn't get my file from the CIA. Because that would be nearly impossible. You got it from someone who doesn't like me."

He shifted slightly in the chair.

"Did you broadcast my name out into the underground and get a response?"

"Actually, no. The file was sent to me. Anonymously."

Nine Suns, my enemy, the international crime ring I'd nearly leveled to the ground, must still be watching me. Or watching Belias. Both thoughts were disquieting.

I shrugged. "Anonymously. And for free? How generous."

"Not for free. I suspect they want me to give you to them. And they won't be anonymous for long. I'll figure out who they are."

"And you're telling me this why, Kevin?"

I wondered how long it had been since he'd been called by his real name. His face paled. "We're all wrapped up in each other's secrets now."

"Kevin?" Holly said.

"Kevin died in London. Call me John." Belias cleared his throat, risked a cautious grin at me. A respectful one. "I'm telling you because I have no intention of giving you to them. I don't take orders from ghosts in the wire. But they have threatened me, and now that's a threat to you."

I'm really the new Roger, I thought. "I appreciate that. We'll solve your problem first, then mine. Deal?"

"Yes, deal," Belias said. "Because when my problem is solved, all our lives get far easier. We get rich, Sam."

"What's about to happen?"

"Soon enough I'll share. Let's deal with Vegas first."

"What about Diana?" I asked.

"I think she's badly frightened. She'll go underground for as long as she can. And I think when she and her mother can talk face-to-face, when her mother's work for me is done, that situation will quietly resolve itself."

I noticed Holly stiffen slightly in her chair, staring out of the rain-smeared window. I could imagine what she was thinking. Janice's daughter pulled into the network. Maybe she worried years from now the same fate awaited her children. You could convince yourself Belias's shortcuts to success would help your kids to a better life, and then you might be consigning them to your mistake. But the Marchbanks kids and Daniel need not worry, because I was going to burn down Belias's house.

"Your son and your friend Leonie, they're safe?"

Of course they were mentioned in my file. "You need not concern yourself with them." I am not sure I could keep the threatening tone out of my voice.

"I always worry about the loved ones of those in the network. Don't I, Holly? Holly has marvelous kids, real little winners."

Holly said nothing.

"Part of your appeal, Sam, is what you risked, how you fought, to get Daniel back. You do not hold back. Neither do I."

"Don't ever threaten my son." But I said it pleasantly.

"I think you know a lesser leader would have ordered Diana Keene killed. I never did. I never once tried to hurt her. If she'd listened to me, all this would be over with."

"She destroyed that video," I said. "She told you the truth." I'd told him this last night but I wasn't sure he believed me. "She's not a threat to you."

"Good. And we're going right now to help Janice."

"What am I doing?"

"You're going to help me rescue Janice from a rather dangerous situation. No one in my network has your particular skill set, Sam. I need you to be a secret soldier again."

My gaze met Holly's; then she stared out the airplane window at the curtain of rain.

62

Sunday, November 7, early afternoon

WE DIDN'T LAND in Las Vegas until after lunch; it wasn't until late morning when the dreadful weather in northern California broke enough for the pilot to take to the skies. In contrast, Las Vegas was bright and sunny, and I'm sure people around the city woke and arose out of beds thinking, *I feel lucky, this is the day I beat the house.* I wasn't sure I shared their optimism.

Belias had arranged a car for us at the airport, a black Escalade with reflective windows, the kind a celebrity visiting Vegas for the weekend might rent. Holly drove and he told her to head for the Mystik Casino and Resort.

She parked in the lot and we left Holly in the car. She seemed relieved, and I couldn't tell if she was simply happy to be away from me or from Belias.

Belias placed a phone call as we walked toward the Mystik. The building was a modern, glass tower, shaped in a C curve, and a spiderlike window-washing disc was moving down and across one side of it. The nod to its name and its magical theming were the wands and top hats and tarot cards decorating the entrance plaza. Cheesy. I felt sure Mila would have made a smart remark and I wished she was here with me. I glanced behind me; you never knew when she'd appear. But she had no way to know I'd gone to Las Vegas; I couldn't risk a call or a text while with Belias. I did not want to be caught texting a woman who was supposed to be dead.

"I'm here. She's still unharmed?" Belias said into his phone. "I want the camera feeds turned off now. Just while I'm coming and going. No record of me being here. That protects us both."

He listened again. "That's not negotiable. And I'm doing you a favor, don't forget that," Belias said. A pause then. "Send down one of your guys with the elevator; again, all cameras off. See you in five." He clicked off the phone.

"What are you taking me into?" I said. "We're not armed."

"A death trap, Sam." He smiled. "Trust me, I suspect it's a total death trap."

We walked through the casino. It was very new and noisy and pointless. I hate gambling. I suppose I have had enough chaos in my life that I don't need the manufactured, fleeting thrill of the thrown dice or the bouncing roulette ball.

A man stood waiting for us near the main elevator. He was taller than me, thick necked, looked tough except he was wearing these nerdy black-rimmed eyeglasses. His lips were thin and pale, and they contrasted with the slightly instant orange tone of his skin. Fake tan. Did you need that in Vegas?

"Mr. Lazard is expecting you," the orange man said. "Who's this?"

"A friend."

"It's only supposed to be you," the orange man said in a low voice.

"He carries my casino chips for me." Belias gestured his head toward the elevator. The orange man hesitated, but then he slid in an access card and the private elevator opened. We stepped inside. I was relieved it wasn't one of those glass-sided contraptions.

The doors slid shut and the orange man frisked us both, carelessly. Then he keyed in his access card. The penthouse floor lit up and the elevator began to rise.

I glanced up at a small camera in the corner. Where there should have been a green light indicating activation, there was none. Lazard kept his word.

"Is the hostage unharmed?" Belias asked.

"Yes. Banged up a bit. She's kind of hot for a cougar."

"How charming. Did you hurt her?"

"Not much. Not more than we had to."

Belias folded his hands behind his back, studied the counter that showed the elevator rising. "Sam, would you be so kind as to kill this man?"

The orange man and I both froze. Belias stepped back, away from us, waiting, his words heavy in the air. You can either believe the words someone says or not, but you threaten someone with death, they react.

The orange man went for his gun.

There's not a lot of room to fight in an elevator. The key to victory in an enclosed space is brief, savage blows delivered to whatever vulnerable spot you can reach. You have no room to re-treat. So you have to overwhelm quickly.

The orange man was bigger than me and thickly muscled. But I thought his power might be derived from a gym (where he no doubt acquired his sunset hue) and not from fighting.

Often, I'm wrong.

He had his hand going for the gun in his jacket holster and I slammed the heel of my foot hard into his chest and pinned his hand where it was. Against the gun. Do the math and he still had one hand free. Which he used to upend my leg, piledriving me back into the other side of the elevator.

Belias stood there, unmoving, watching the floors tick by as we zoomed toward the penthouse.

The orange man grunted, pinning me against the wall, which hurt, but now I wasn't off-balance for one second. That took the weight off my free foot so I kicked upward, catching him in the armpit. He stumbled back, releasing me to go for his gun and I knew that was a tactical mistake. You already have a weapon; it's called a hand.

The gun caught in the holster, jammed between us. I powered the heel of my hand hard into his throat. He choked but didn't ease up. He still had his one hand free, hesitating on how to punch me. I closed my fist around his and powered it back, forced his fist back into his own throat. That really hurts. He coughed hard, a wheezy, broken noise, and for one second I thought I'd cracked his trachea.

But now he yanked the gun free of the holster—easier to do since we weren't tangled up together.

"Just a few more floors, Sam," Belias said.

I closed a hand on the gun. It was capped with a suppressor so that gave me more gun to grab. You never think of that as a short-coming of a suppressor, do you? It is. He had his hand on the handle but I had the rest of it. I slammed the gun upward into his chest. Now if he pulled the trigger, pressed against his own chest, he'd shoot off a chunk of jaw. But he controlled the trigger, not me.

I didn't want to kill the guy. Not that he knew or believed that even if I'd announced it. He used his strength to push himself off the wall, launching me back into the other side of the elevator. But I kept the gun pressed hard against him, pushing its shape into his hard chest.

Then he took a chance. He slammed a fist into my face. It hurt. But it meant he wasn't pushing back against me with both arms. He sacrificed half his strength on the risk of a punch. Mistake. I took the punch and didn't block it because I kept my hands on the prize, the gun.

I got a finger on the trigger. "Let go," I said. "Or I'll pull the trigger."

"No!"

"I won't kill you. My friend is overly dramatic."

He grappled and I turned the gun down and pulled. The bullet hit his foot, punching a neat bloody hole where his big toe was. He screamed and let go and I slammed a blow hard into his throat, then another into his jaw, then two more into the back of his head. He crumpled.

I glanced up at Belias, who studied the orange man's injuries, as though evaluating my work.

"I told you to kill him."

"You seem to have mistaken me for your attack dog," I said. "I decide when I kill someone. Not you."

"When those doors open, you may not have room for so many morals."

The elevator chimed, and the doors to the penthouse slid open. I raised the stolen gun.

63

Sunday, November 7, early afternoon

IF LUCKY LAZARD is in this network, they'll either meet in his penthouse or elsewhere in the casino. No other public spot." Felix's voice had a confidence that Mila had not heard before. He and Mila had flown commercial to Vegas. They'd driven to Sam's bar in Las Vegas, The Canyon Club, and Felix called Jimmy, then gave the phone to Mila, who stayed in the car, while he ran in to pick up needed equipment—a generic maintenance uniform, electronic passcards, a smartphone wired to scan alarm entry codes, and weapons. He took a shotgun and ammo, packed in a canvas tote, a Glock in a holster, and Mila took a telescoping baton he bought her. She hid it in her boots, under her jeans.

They parked at a bar, a few streets away from the Mystik. Felix said, "I don't want our license tags on the lot's security cameras."

"Jimmy is unhappy we're here," Mila said. "He is not convinced this is worth doing."

"He'll get over that." Felix checked the shotgun, then zipped up the canvas tote.

Mila frowned. "We go in shooting to save Sam? He wants to get in close to this man, learn all his secrets."

"If Lazard is one of his people, we might learn enough of his secrets right now to bring him down. We only need one person willing to cooperate. And he and Belias are cornered here."

Mila nodded. "But penthouses have keys."

"The security company that runs the private floors' elevator access, we have a master key code for their systems." He held up a card. "This should get us access via the private elevator or the stairway."

"Or the penthouse must have a service elevator."

"That's the better choice," he said. "And I've got a maintenance uniform."

"Get dressed then."

He ducked into a men's room and emerged two minutes later. He carried the canvas bag to hide the shotgun and a spare for Mila, and he had the master key clipped to him, along with an ID that approximated the look of the Mystik's employee badges.

"You are certainly prepared," she said.

"I work fast."

"So, the service elevator."

"Service entrance back here," Felix said. "Let's see if our master card works." He ran it along the scanner and the door clicked.

They stepped inside the service entrance. Like an amusement park, most of the necessary work of the casino is hidden from tourist eyes. They saw a trio of maintenance personnel, a woman in chef's whites pushing a tray, another woman pushing cases of beer on a cart.

"This way," he said. Mila followed him down the corridor, sticking close, since she wasn't in uniform and didn't have a badge, but they walked with brisk certainty and that is half the trick to a disguise. She saw a sign for a service elevator: PENTHOUSE ACCESS—CLEARANCE REQUIRED.

"There," she said. They followed the arrow down an empty, small corridor. They were alone. "We can take it to the floor below, and then if Sam needs us…"

Felix turned and hit her, hard, in the side of the head. She was stunned and she fell back against the wall. He hit her again, in the stomach, then at the base of her neck, and she went down, nerveless. He took the baton from her boot under her jeans, and he slid the key and shoved her into a storage room.

"This is for your own good," he said. She tried to stand and he hit her with a brutal, precise punch in the throat. She slammed into the shelves, dazed. "Forgive me, Mila."

She gasped, choked, coughed, managed to breathe. He took her phone. "I need you to do what I say. Stay here for the next hour or Sam may well die. Do you understand me? Stay here."

She managed a nod.

"Don't raise a fuss. But stay here. I'm so sorry."

Felix shut the door.

She lay on the floor, anger blinding her. Her own good? What did he mean? She slowly got to her feet. She couldn't believe he'd taken her down—she was better than that. And he'd been so…polite about it.

Sam. She had no way to reach him, no way to access the elevator to the penthouse.

She reached for the door and the knob turned, and Mila started to put the lie in her mouth that she'd taken a wrong turn, or just push past whichever custodian was standing there.

But it was Holly Marchbanks with a gun leveled at her. Capped with a suppressor.

"You made a mistake," Holly said. "I never did think your boyfriend came over to our side."

She fired.

64

THE ELEVATOR DOORS OPENED. A man stood on the other side, looking bored, until he saw the unconscious thug in the elevator and me aiming said thug's gun at him.

His hand moved toward his own holster and I said, "Don't," and he didn't. He froze, staring at the orange man sprawled on the elevator floor. He looked at me with pure hatred. He was taller, even bigger than the orange man, thicker in the chest, broader in the shoulders.

"You killed Randy," he said.

"He's not dead. Keep your hands where I can see them." The private elevator wouldn't go back down without being summoned by someone with a penthouse card, but I thought it best Randy's journey be at an end. "Drag him out of the elevator," I said.

The other guy moved past me slowly, watching the gun, and took Randy by his shoulders and pulled him out. The blood from his foot left a smear. The elevator door slid closed but the elevator stayed in place. He pulled the shoe off Randy's foot, the blood gushing from the wound.

"Do you have something we can staunch it with?" I asked and he glared at me.

"Leave him, it's not fatal." Belias fished the key off Randy and nodded politely at the second man. "You might get to live if you cooperate," he said. He stepped close, relieved the man of his gun, frisked his leg. He found a long, wicked stiletto. "My goodness, we were expecting trouble. All this for me."

He pushed the man along past the hallway that led to the elevators and out into the main room. Las Vegas spread out beneath us, grand towers close and in the distance, a bizarre landscape of Eiffel Tower and pyramid and castle and glass towers, a medley of toy buildings pressed close together.

Lucky Lazard stood in the middle of the room, surrounded by a giant square of leather sofas gathered around a huge circular marble table. I knew his face because you couldn't own a bar in this town and not know who he was—he owned bars, casinos, apartment buildings. A king of the desert. A woman—Janice Keene, I presumed, because her daughter looked very much like her—sat on the couch. Her hands were bound but she wasn't gagged. She had a busted lip and her cheek looked bruised. But she was lovely, like Diana.

Our gaze met for a moment; then her stare went to Belias.

Lazard saw the guns. "What's the meaning of this?"

"You know, Lucky," Belias said, "if I order you to turn off the cameras so there's no record of my coming and going, then I sure don't expect you to have…guests."

"These are my security guards."

"You don't need guards with me."

"Don't I?"

"They shot Randy in the foot!" the guy volunteered. "In the elevator!" As though that compounded the breach of etiquette.

"She lied to me. *You* sent her. I didn't want to believe it, Belias. I've been good to you." He sounded incredulous.

"You've been the best."

"I know what this is about," he said. "I know. Put Randy in the other room. Andy, it's going to be okay. I know why this is happening."

"Okay? Okay? No, it's not okay. Randy's shot. Nothing is okay," the second man said.

"If you don't want things to get worse, go into the other room."

"No, stay put. I don't want him making phone calls," Belias said. "What is this about, Lucky? I'm curious to hear your, no doubt, brilliant theory."

"She's like me. One of yours. Now I think you sent her, since you've come in with muscle."

Belias said very quietly, "Why would I do that?"

"Because Glenn Marchbanks wanted to revolt against you. He wanted to grab control. I told him to forget it. I told him there was no reason."

Belias looked almost amused. It made me uneasy. "How did you even know about each other?"

"He was trying to figure out who you are and who all you've recruited. He figured out me."

"And what? Just asked you?"

"No," Lazard said after a moment. "It was coded. A couple of things he said to me when we met a couple of times at business conferences. We were both keynote speakers. He said something about deals with the devil. Then he showed me his I Ching necklace. The visual password. I told him we weren't supposed to know about each other, I wasn't interested."

"So he wanted you to join his little project."

"Yes. And I said no."

"And didn't warn me."

"He was feeling me out. He was worried what would happen if you got caught or arrested or sick with cancer"—and he glanced at Janice Keene—"or if you just got hit by a bus."

"Glenn was disloyal. You should have called me the moment he contacted you." Belias seemed to notice Janice. "And, Janice, you fumbled this, but that's a separate conversation. How badly did he hurt you?"

"They hit my head against a desk and a wall. Hit me hard. But I'm okay."

"She does, in fact, have cancer," Lucky said. "Did you know that?"

Belias smiled. "I'm not here to talk about her. I'm here to talk about you."

"What is it you want from me?"

"I want you to untie her and apologize."

"After you sent her to *kill* me?" Lucky's face reddened with rage.

"I sent her to spy on you," Belias said. But he looked at Janice as he said it. She met his gaze without blinking.

"Spy on me with a gun."

"Glenn is dead," Belias said. "Not by my hand, either."

Now I flinched because I thought, *He can't tell Janice what's happened with Diana. She'll know he's after her daughter.* I was more than willing to tell her—as soon as I got her out of here. She was the key. I didn't care about Belias and his squabbles with his gold-plated underlings.

"Glenn…I told him he was foolish, that he shouldn't do this…" Lucky began.

In the midst of their bickering, I could feel the weight of the thug's stare on my shoulders. "You shot Randy," he hissed. "He's gonna lose a toe. I hope you like to dance, because I'm going to shoot off all ten of your toes, one at a time."

"Randy was armed and I wasn't," I said. "Think about that for a minute."

He shut up.

Lazard kept pleading his case. "Look, I told Glenn to settle down. I didn't tell you because you'd kill him and you'd lose a valuable man. It was a temporary insanity with him. If he recruited anyone else, I don't know about it…"

"Anyone else," Belias said.

Lazard wiped his mouth. "Barbara Scott is dead. Did Glenn get to her?"

"That must be why Barbara is dead, then," Belias said. "No other good reason." I thought he was going to laugh for a moment.

"What do you want? I'll make this right." Now I could hear the undertone of fear in Lucky Lazard's voice. Now I was seeing the man he was without his master behind him. Standing on his own.

"What is it you want?" Lazard asked again. "You want me to prove loyalty to you? What do you want?"

"First off, apologize to Janice. Hitting a cancer patient? That's low, even for you."

"I'm sorry, Janice."

"Now. Take a knee."

I saw Lazard's face flush red. Who kneels to anyone anymore? An ancient custom, one stripped of purpose unless you're being knighted. It's degrading. It reminds us that we haven't come that far from the days where people owned each other or owed their lives to liege and lord. It's not so many turns around the sun since those days.

"Belias, this is silly…"

"Kneel. Or I'll send Janice or Sam over to your daughter's house."

Lucky's jaw worked.

I didn't appreciate him offering me up to kill an innocent kid. "I thought you didn't make threats." I made my voice cold. My hands tensed. I couldn't let him kill Lazard in cold blood, but if I made a move, the angry guard would go for me. I had to wait and see what deal they struck.

"Promises," Belias said with a smile. "Not threats. Kneel, Lucky, and I'll let you live."

"You'll let me live." Lazard laughed. "I mean, this is all very grand-sounding language. I can bring you down is the plain way of putting it. Anything happens to me, the truth about you comes out."

"I expect a Vegas man to be a better bluffer. If you do that, your estate loses everything. It'll be tied up in court for years, people you stepped on suing you. People you cheated, people you wronged. Your daughter will never see a penny of it. Hurting me is hurting her."

And then I saw the truth of it in Lazard's eyes: he was bluffing. *Because what a neat little world Belias builds for his network*, I thought. He lifts them up the ladder but they can never step off it; if they do, those that follow—their kids, their families—fall as well. Look at the Madoffs. Look at the corrupt executives who get exposed. The wealth and the power vanishes with the truth.

You never, ever got out of Belias's debt.

So Lucky Lazard knelt. "I swear I don't know of anyone else Glenn recruited."

"That's what I needed to know," Belias said softly. "But that's not why you're going to die, Lucky. It's because…you and Barbara know too much. And I think you know why."

I saw a dawning realization shift across Lucky's face.

And, impossibly, behind us, I heard the barest chime.

The elevator doors opening.

65

Sunday, November 7, early afternoon

AND AROUND THE CORNER came Felix.

I felt my chest heave in relief. He and Mila must have followed me. I knew they would. They'd figured out Lazard was the target in Vegas from Glenn's cell phone text.

I heard Janice say, "Felix?" in surprise, in shock.

He was in a dark maintenance suit, and he carried a shotgun.

"Freeze," he said in a voice more like steel than his own.

"Glad you're here," I said, stepping toward him. He looked at me like he didn't know me and he smiled.

"Sam. Sorry." And he slammed the butt of the shotgun into the side of my head.

I fell across the leather ottoman. Stars dancing through my eyes, thinking, *No, that's not right.*

I heard a scream—Janice—the booming blasts of the gun, a horrid wet sound, the answering fire of a pistol, screams again, someone begging. I was sprawled on the leather, no one aiming at me, trying to bring my brain back to focus.

I raised my head.

Carnage. The second thug was dead, felled by the shotgun. Janice was…gone. Belias was gone. It's unnerving to have a room full of dangerous people and misplace two of them. I felt a trickle of blood on the side of my head where the edge of the gun's stock had struck me.

Lazard had taken cover behind the couch. Firing at Felix, who blasted back.

I rolled off the ottoman and then Lazard was shooting toward me, tufts of stuffing dancing in the air like pollen as the bullets tore the leather. I rolled up into a ball under the marble table. I was hurt, didn't know how much, and people were trying to kill each other.

Then the shooting stopped.

"I don't want to kill you," Felix yelled and I hoped he was yelling it at me. The gun I'd taken from Randy. I'd dropped the gun when he hit me. Where...oh, Lazard had taken that gun. That was unfortunate. I stayed under the marble table.

"I want information," Felix yelled. "I'll let you live for information."

"What?" I yelled.

"Shut up, Sam," Felix said. "This has nothing to do with you."

I begged to differ, but I don't argue with shotguns.

"Why does Belias want you dead?" Felix asked. "Tell me and you live. Lie and die."

"I think he wants to silence us," Lazard said, his voice shaking badly. "Me and Barbara Scott. And..."

So Felix wasn't on my side anymore. He'd destroyed my attempt to get information out of Belias. Let's deal with the new reality. I inched under the marble slab of the table, looking for a way to get to Lazard. If he shot Felix and killed him, he'd kill me. He owned the casino, and one assumed he could get more Randys to help him clean up the mess. But Felix, Felix could be reasoned with, right? I knew Felix. At least I thought I did.

Then a chilling thought occurred to me: Where was Mila?

"And? Is there a third one?"

"If I tell you...you'll just kill me."

"Stop shooting at me and at Sam, and come out and let's talk," Felix called to Lazard.

"No. You shot Andy."

"Andy would have shot me. Forget Andy. Focus on your future," Felix yelled.

Andy and Randy. You can't make this up. "Belias!" I yelled. "You two are missing the point. Where's Belias?" I didn't care about the garden snakes in the room, I wanted the cobra.

"Sam, stay down," Felix ordered me. "Stay out of this, please."

At least the shooting had stopped. I wondered if either of them had run out of ammunition.

I thought Lucky Lazard might respond to negotiation. "Lazard, I work for some people. We can hide you, hide your daughter until this is over. You don't have to be afraid of Belias. I need you to stop him. It's over now, you can see that. He's over."

"He's far from over. He's..." And he stopped.

"What's he planning? What's going to give him so much power?" I said.

"I shouldn't have helped Belias...We shouldn't have helped *her*..." Lazard's voice, earlier a bullhorn, went soft. "Me and Barbara Scott and Rawlings..."

Rawlings? And Belias wasn't a "her."

"I won't hurt you. Tell me what he's doing," Felix said. "Tell us where he and Janice will go."

Well. Felix had his own agenda. And if I got out of this alive, I'd give some serious thought as to what it could be. He could have shot me dead, first and easiest. He hadn't. So he might be willing to talk to me. "Tell us," I said, like we were still working together.

"Sam, shut up. This has ceased to be your problem."

I shut up. I looked out from the table. Lazard stood. He'd run out of bullets and he'd tossed the gun on the couch. Felix stood, the shotgun across his arms. I recognized the shotgun. He must have gone to my bar in Vegas, The Canyon Club, and armed himself. I pulled myself up from the floor very slowly. My head ached.

"Sam, sit down, or I'll kill you," he said.

I sat. "Belias?"

"He took the elevator down with Janice. They got out in the cross fire when I took out the muscle."

"They're running," I said. "Where are they going?"

"Chicago. But it won't matter. Rawlings will run now. I'll call him and tell him to run," Lazard said. His hands shook in relief that the shooting was over.

"Felix, you've been keeping secrets," I said.

"Shut. Your. Mouth," he hissed at me.

I shut up.

"What is Belias doing? What's his scheme?" Felix said.

"You act like you already know," Lazard answered.

"I already suspect."

"He's going to own the president."

"President of what?" I asked.

Lazard looked at me and laughed.

"Outside, both of you," Felix ordered.

"Felix, where is Mila…?"

He gestured at me again. With the shotgun. "Shut up. Outside. Now."

"Why outside?" I said.

"Because you're not the boss anymore, Sam."

He followed Lazard and me out onto the patio, gesturing us forward with the shotgun. Las Vegas lay before us in the desert sprawl. I would have liked to have seen the view at night.

Lazard turned to face him and Felix asked, "Can you expose Belias? Did you leave anything behind that can incriminate him?"

"And have my daughter lose her fortune? No. Just the stuff in the bedroom safe."

"I'd like the combination, please."

"No."

"I will shoot off your arm. The combination, please, Lucky."

"Seven-three-six-eight-zero."

"Sam, go get the safe open. Bring me what's in it."

I hesitated.

"Sam, please. Do as I ask and I'll tell you where Mila is. She's perfectly fine."

I obeyed. I found the safe in the floor of the bedroom closet. Entered in the numbers. No burning smell this time, no heat against the metal. The door clicked open. I pulled open a closed folder of papers, one of those kinds of folders that has a fold-over top and a brown elastic band to secure it. I opened it.

"Sam. Doesn't take that long," Felix yelled at me.

My head throbbed but it was clearing. Faces on the paper. Barbara Scott, a famous writer, I'd read one of her books. I hadn't

heard she was dead. Other faces I didn't know. And then the face
of a senator from New Mexico and her husband, a woman who'd
been mentioned as a replacement for the recently fallen vice president. I'd seen her multiple times on the news this week, but only
when I was checking to see if *I* was on the news myself.

This was it. If this woman was named the new vice president...and then something happened to the president...

Shock twisted in my chest. Belias owned her. That had to be
the explanation. But why start killing off the other members of the
network, why rid himself of the powerful people he'd built and cul-
tivated?

"Sam!" Felix said. "Out here, now!"

I closed the envelope. No time to go through it all, although I
wondered if I locked myself into the room how long it would take
him to reach me. Annoyingly there was no weapon inside the safe.
Or in the closet. I just had the envelope that he wanted, nice and fat.

I walked slowly back out into the den, one hand holding the envelope, the other pressed against my bloodied head. I'd borrowed
one of Lazard's shirts for a bandage. "I don't feel well," I said. The
two men were glaring at each other—Lazard sick and raging about
being backed into a corner and Felix desperate to get the information that I'd been here to collect.

"I'm sorry, Sam," Felix said. "I'm not one who has anything personal against you. Give me the envelope."

I said to Lazard, "I can't believe you knew this about Belias." And
while looking at Lazard, I threw the package right at Felix's face.

A weighted object, thick with paper, can do damage, thrown correctly. The envelope—heavy, worn—caught him right in the face.
He staggered back, just a step, but by then I was launching myself on and over the patio table. I hammered my foot into Felix's
chest. He staggered back, and then Lazard threw himself at Felix,
knocking him back. Lazard looked like a former linebacker and
Felix looked like a thin tree, all wire and muscle. Lazard tried to
wrench the gun out of Felix's hands.

If I'd had sense, I would have run. If I was still CIA, I would
have grabbed the package and run. And there would have been a

Special Projects extraction team ready to pull me to safety, to a de-
briefing room with medical staff and bad coffee and quiet and a
nice, warm feeling of safety before I went home and curled next to
Lucy's warmth. But all that was gone. And Felix had questions to
answer for me.

I grabbed the package and I ran to the edge of the patio. Below
was the smooth glass drop, the artificial canyon, down to the curving driveway. Forty-eight stories below. To the driveway that led
up to the Mystik and the permanently green, desert-defying acreage
below.

"I'll throw it off," I said.

They ignored me—so much for shock value—and fought over
the gun. Fine. I timed it as they spun together, leveled a kick into
Lazard's head and he stumbled, dropping, blood welling from his
mouth. He staggered away. Felix levered the gun back at me, and I
slammed my hands into the barrel, knocking it to the left.

The gun fired.

Lazard didn't scream. There wasn't a mouth to scream with. He
was shredded and the blast threw him over the edge, out into the
blue, and I didn't see him tumble and spin forty-eight stories down
to the driveway below.

Because Felix wrenched the gun free and shoved me with it. He
hesitated. Deciding whether or not to kill me.

"Don't," I said. "Don't."

He threw the gun at me—so therefore it was empty—and I
caught it, and while I did that he drew a Glock from a holster under
his shirt. "Sit down, Sam, or I'll blow your brains out."

I sat. "We have to get out of here; the police will be on their way."
The casino's owner having plummeted from the roof? The casino
security guards would be here in moments.

"Yes. They will. And you're holding the shotgun that killed him.
I suggest you tell them that you are CIA and get your old masters to
hold your hand again. Maybe they'll get you out." He scooped up
the package and stepped back. "You're done following Belias and
his network. They're no longer your concern. I'll take care of them
from here."

"Why?" I said. I had no idea why he had betrayed me, what his agenda was. "Why?"

Sorrow, I thought, twisted his face. "I'm letting you live, that's enough. Call the CIA when you're arrested. They'll help you, I think."

"Where is Mila?" I yelled.

"Back in San Francisco. She wasn't going to risk being spotted by Belias since she's supposed to be dead. She's not your concern anymore."

The elevator doors slid closed.

I ran, pressed the button again. The elevator continued its descent away from me. Randy was dead, a single bullet in his head. Someone had killed him exiting and I figured it was Belias.

Stairs. There had to be stairs. A fire escape. I found a door tucked in the back. Locked. Of course. Lazard had been keeping Janice a prisoner here; he wasn't going to risk maintenance or anyone else coming up the stairs and surprising him during this meeting. And I had an awful feeling the keys were in a pocket forty-eight floors below me.

I hate feeling trapped.

I glanced over the edge of the patio. Small crowd gathering below, around the broken body of Lazard.

And on the side of the building to my left, moving, a circular sled type of contraption, blasting the windows with water.

An automated window washer. I'd noticed it on the way into the Mystik. The cables attaching it to the building were thirty feet to my left.

I could stay and explain the two dead men and the dead multimillionaire at the base of his casino, and then I'd be spending plenty of time in a Nevada jail and maybe Leonie would take off with my son forever and maybe the CIA wouldn't come and help me after all, no matter what I said.

I ran through the penthouse. I found the cables for the automated washer gently banging against a window. I grabbed a heavy teak chair and smashed against the glass. It cracked. I hit it again. The chair shattered the window and sailed out into the void. I looked down, worried that I could have hit bystanders below. But this curve of the building looked out over the rest of the Mystik complex, so the chair and the glass plummeted onto the rooftop of the casino that extended out from the building.

I needed protection for my hands. I still clutched the shirt I'd taken from Lazard's closet for my bloodied head.

And heard the elevator door chime. I figured Felix got out on a lower floor, and the return trip of the elevator was bringing—

"Security!" a voice bellowed.

No time to think. I could only pray that the automated washer's cables could hold my weight. Surely they would have tensile strength to hold me? Right?

"Security! On the ground!"

I did not care to make new friends among the Mystik's security staff. Maybe they were buds with Andy and Randy.

Holding the shirt across my palms, I jumped.

You can't run parkour and be afraid of heights. However, my parkour runs usually only took me up a couple of stories. Not forty-eight. That is a gulf that chokes the human brain's processing power and I forced my gaze to stay on the cable. I grabbed it, both hands, but the shirt made the grip feel slick.

The slide down the cables, I began to pick up speed. Too fast. I looked down and nearly folded in blind terror. I felt the muscles of my arm loosen in shock and fear. I reflexively closed my fists. Didn't stop. The shirt's fabric began to heat under my palms. I kicked against the glass, trying to slow my descent. It worked.

Twenty stories below me, the disc wobbled, spewing concentrated water and foam, the cables bouncing hard against the glass canyon side of the casino as I slid.

Ten more stories.

Below me shocked screams drifted upward.

I lost my grip, fumbling with the cloth beneath my fingers. I would hit the disc too fast, perhaps tearing it off its moorings or bouncing off it, past the cables, plummeting the remaining twenty stories. Terror filled my body, and I hugged at the remnants of the shirt, closing arms around one cable, kicking hard into the glass, anything to slow myself.

I hit the disc, not going as fast as I had been seconds ago...

And stopped. Water misted above me, beside me. The disc was slick and wet, soapy. Not what you wanted to hang on to twenty-something stories above the earth.

Upward I looked and saw faces peering at me from the shattered penthouse window. Someone had to be controlling the washer or could gain control of it, and they'd just lower me to the ground or hoist me to the roof and I'd be arrested. I seized the cables, I kicked against the glass. The disc reared back from the building, slammed into the glass. Again. Again. The disc wasn't heavy, but it still packed a punch as it slammed into the side of the Mystik. Water soaked me, cleanser hit and stung my eyes. Agony.

Suddenly the water shut off. Someone was going to reel me in.

I kicked again, and the disc careened back into the window. The glass shattered. Jagged, artery-slicing blades of glass remained mired in the frame. But there was a curtain, and I seized it and pulled myself into the room.

A floor beneath my feet. I'd never been so grateful.

A naked woman, sheets pulled up to her chin, was screaming into the housephone for security, and a naked man squatted on the bed between her and me, as though he thought I might impinge upon her virtue.

I scrambled to my feet and hit the hallway. Room numbers started with twenty-three so I knew which floor I was on. I was sopping wet in full clothes—that marked me instantly. Security would have seen which floor I entered and the woman would tell them the room.

I ran. For the stairs, looking for the FIRE EXIT sign.

An alarm began to sound. A woman's voice piped onto the intercom. "Guests, attention, we are asking for everyone to evacuate the building." Of course they were. There were bodies up in the penthouse, and the presumed gunman was still in the building and clearly crazy. I hit the stairs, and coming down from a floor above was a security guard, young, looking scared but intent. He stopped dead when he saw me, sopping, and he knew who I had to be.

Ten feet away from me he pulled the gun. I could hear more footsteps behind him.

"On your knees, now!" he yelled.

I charged him. Slammed the gun downward toward the steps, it spoke, concrete chipping around my knees. I threw an elbow into his throat and he sagged. I smacked his head against the metal railing just hard enough to stun, not to kill.

Another one coming fast after him. Older, salt-and-pepper in the hair, thick chested. I put one hand on the railing, the other on the wall, and he ran into my sudden kick. I slammed my foot back down against his face and cracked his head on the stair. He was unconscious but okay. I took his radio off him and put the receiver in my ear.

The security teams and now the Las Vegas police were swarming on the hotel. And onto the twenty-third floor. I ran up to twenty-five, past a few hurrying evacuees. I listened to security teams begin to head toward twenty-three. In the hallway a few guests were leaving their rooms and I hung back. Two business types, in khakis and polo shirts with the logo of a software company on it, were exiting a room. Both tapping at their smartphones, lost in their own world. I stepped behind them, stuck my foot in the room's door before it could shut.

They walked on.

I ducked into the room. In one of the suitcases I found jeans that were a bit too big on me and another polo shirt with the turquoise swirl of their software company. I toweled off my hair best I could, but nothing could disguise the rising, cut bruise on my face from Felix's shotgun or the injuries to my hands from the long cable slide. I looked like I'd been in a fight. No matter. My shoes were sodden but I left them on.

In my disguise I went back out the door. I headed for the elevators. There wasn't a line; it was the middle of the day, so reasonable to assume most guests were out and about, down in the casino proper or down by the pool or out enjoying Vegas's sundry pleasures. I waited for the elevator. I didn't want the stairs.

The elevator stopped. Two people were aboard, an older couple who looked deeply annoyed. The intercom kept repeating the evacuation order. I turned off the buzzing security earphone and put it in my pocket and stepped on board.

We dropped down two floors to twenty-three. The elevator stopped. *Uh-oh.*

"We're gonna hit every floor," the old man said, as though it were a personal slight.

"We'll get there," the old woman said.

"You're supposed to take the stairs in an evacuation," he said.

"She didn't say not to take the elevator. My legs hurt anyway."

A security guard got on the elevator. Down the hall I could see a crowd of them at the room where I'd smashed the window-washing machine into the naked couple's hotel room. He stepped in.

He glanced at us all, but it was an old couple and a traveling software businessman. *See? I'm wearing a polo with a logo. A turquoise logo. Clearly I am no threat.*

The elevator dropped. I could hear the buzz of status reports coming from the security guard's earphone.

"What's going on?" the woman asked him.

"I can't say, ma'am," he said. "Sorry."

"Terrorists," the old man said. "Probably a bomb scare. How much money the casino lose every minute it's closed? It's economic warfare."

The security guard glanced at the man, and because the man was standing next to me, he glanced at me again. Then he stared.

The cameras had been turned off by Lazard's orders. I was sure that must violate all sorts of Vegas gaming laws, but there was no way that the cameras weren't still off, now that he'd fallen forty-eight stories.

I put my gaze back to the guard. He'd turned back to the front, but in the reflection of the closed door, he was watching me.

"Son," the old man said to me kindly. "Did you walk in the swimming pool? Your shoes are wet."

The security guard should have just started yelling into his mike. Instead he looked down at my shoes, and when he did I hit him hard, hard, twice, his head snapping back into the wall. The old woman screamed and the old man drew her close to him.

The guard slumped. The elevator said we were past four and the mezzanine was the next level, and I hit the button just in time; the elevator slowed.

The guard had a gun and a baton. I took the baton and left the gun.

Chime. The door opened and there was a spill of crowd beyond, mingling, some waiting for the elevator. A convention of some sort, full of people wearing software shirts and logos. Purple crescents/ swoops appeared to be popular. I walked out of the elevator and through the crowd with purpose. Behind me the old couple started to yell, and I moved toward the stairs that led down to the main casino floor. There was a service stairway and I took it. It spat me out into the kitchen that was already deserted.

I went out the exit. The police were looking for me as a murder suspect, and they'd have a description. At the airports and at the bus stations. I had to find a way out of Vegas, and now. My prints would be in the penthouse, although it might take a while to process that crime scene.

I should just run, I thought. Gather up Leonie and Daniel, wherever Mila and Jimmy hid them, and run.

But Felix had turned against us for an unknown reason and now Belias was running. And he would just keep on manipulating the world, wielding power he didn't earn or deserve, unless someone stopped him.

The crowds of the Mystik's casino were thick and heavy on the grounds, the police sirens glowing where Lazard had fallen to his death and I'd put on a show at the side of the building. I saw an ambulance, sirens blaring, blasting out of the lot. Sirens? He couldn't have survived.

It wasn't hard to make my way through the crowd. I heard someone say, "There was a shooting," and I thought news travels fast from the penthouse on down.

And then I saw him. Felix. In his maintenance man's uniform, forty feet away, the shifting, moving crowd a divider between us. He was staring up at the building. He could put it together. I'd gotten out. He frowned.

Felix turned and walked away. And hanging back, I followed him.

66

Sunday, November 7, early afternoon

"WHAT...WHAT IS HAPPENING?" Janice began.

"Shut up," Belias said. "I got you out. They'll kill Lucky."

"They will?" She leaned against the side of the service elevator.

"If we're...lucky."

"Who is the other man? Sam's friend?" Belias said.

"I..." She touched her bruises.

"You said his name. You said Felix."

The service elevator chimed and the doors opened. Chaos. People running, rushing in the hallways and Janice thought, *How do they know it's a war zone upstairs?* And then she heard a man shouting, "She's been shot," and she realized there was a wholly separate crisis going on down here.

"Come on." Belias grabbed her arm, steered her out of the elevator cab. No one noticed them, and she could see people swarming around an open door down the small hallway from the elevator.

They pushed the other way, hurrying out. They stumbled out a service entrance into the bright Vegas sun. "This way," he said. On the air they could hear the fast approaching scream of an ambulance.

They worked their way to the side of the casino, toward the parking lot where employees parked. Beyond it lay a public lot.

Belias pulled out a phone, selected a number.

And behind them Janice heard screams.

"Dear Lord," she said as she glanced over her shoulder.

She just caught a glimpse of a man falling. Lazard plummeting from the penthouse patio.

"I told you they'd kill him," Belias said.

Janice felt horror climb her spine.

"Come on, let's go." He turned and spoke into the phone. "Holly, where are you and the car?" He listened. "Meet us down the Strip. At the Carnivale Resort, it's just a few blocks away."

Who was Holly, Janice wondered. Another member of the network.

It was a dangerous thing to be in the network right now.

"He was one of us. So was Barbara Scott," she said quietly. They were a block away when they turned back again toward the Mystik. On the side away from the street they could see a man using the automated washer's cables to rappel down the side of the building toward the wide disc of the automated washer.

"Insane," Belias breathed. "Oh, he's crazy. In the best way. Wish I could have kept him but when his buddy showed up, there's just no trusting him."

"He'll fall. He'll fall." Janice didn't want to watch—seeing Lazard tumble from the top of the Mystik was horrifying enough—but she couldn't tear her gaze away.

They watched Sam Capra nearly fall, get control, smash his way through a window.

"Extraordinary," Belias said. "He might actually get away. We need to hurry."

"We need to get out of here."

"Yes." They hurried two resorts past the Mystik. An Escalade pulled up next to them when they reached the Carnivale. Belias and Janice climbed into the car, Janice in the back, Belias in the front.

A woman Janice didn't know—presumably the Holly he'd just called—sat in the driver's seat. She was in her early thirties, blonde, slim but strong looking. Her mouth was a twist. "Sorry," she said. Her voice shook and she trembled when she glanced at Janice. "When all the police arrived I didn't want to be trapped in the lot."

"Understood," Belias said.

"Where's Sam?" she said. She inched back into traffic. Sirens were approaching from all sides.

"Sam got left behind."

"Good. Good. Sam's little friend was here," Holly said. "She's followed us. He didn't break her neck like you said."

"Ah," Belias said. "So best then I left him behind." He managed to sound both sad and furious.

"The Russian girlfriend," Holly said. "I shot her. In a storage closet in the employee area."

"Dead?"

"Yes," Holly said. Her voice was steady. "Can we leave Vegas, please? I would really like to leave now."

"Tell me details."

"I saw her and a man dressed in maintenance worker clothes. They went into the back and I followed them—I flirted with a young guy, told him I was a hostess and had forgotten my pass. I saw him push her into a storage room, and then he left and the way he was shaking his hand...I knew he'd hit her. So I shot her and left her in the storage room. Then I ran."

"He'd hit her? Interesting. He hit Sam as well." He stared back at the Mystik. "You just shot her once?"

"Once is enough."

"You may have been seen. The person who let you in will remember your face."

"Then let's go home."

"No. No home yet. We have more to do, Janice. Two down, one to go. In Chicago."

Janice shook her head. "I...I want to go home. Please. I'm done."

"You want me to take care of Diana, to make her one of us? This is the price. One more. Chicago."

Janice hung her head.

"One more. One more and you're done."

"Can't you do it? Can't she?" And Janice touched Holly's shoulder.

67

Sunday, November 7, early afternoon

I KILLED YOUR DAUGHTER, Holly thought. Earlier this week she'd thought she would spend the weekend taking Peter to his friend's birthday party, going shopping with Mom and Emma, and maybe stopping by the bookstore and buying the new novel her book club had selected. A normal weekend. Now she had killed a young woman in a hot rage and she'd shot another in cold blood.

And now she was going to look a mother in the eye, a mother whose daughter she'd killed. *I didn't mean to. But she killed my husband. She…*

"I…" Holly glanced back. Janice was looking right at her. *Right at her.* Like she knew. "I don't know what's going on."

"You're Glenn Marchbanks's wife, right?" Janice looked at Belias for confirmation. "Seen you at fund-raisers."

"Holly, this is Janice Keene," Belias said. "No point in pretending you won't know each other's names."

"I am not getting on a plane to anywhere until I know what is going on, John," Janice said. "Are we driving to the airport? Just stop. Stop right now."

Holly turned, went down two side roads, pulled into a shopping plaza. They were in a strip center: a Thai restaurant, an old vinyl record store, a Mexican-themed cantina. Belias turned to face them both.

"Janice, Holly's husband is dead. Killed by Sam Capra. Sam is the

man who has proven himself so adept at high-rise escapes. He's an
ex-CIA agent who crossed our paths."

The smell of paint, odd, sudden in her nose. How far did Belias
go to get his confession from Glenn?

"But you brought him with you," Janice said. "But..."

"I thought he would be useful to us. Well, he was, but he tried to
trick us. Now he's just a dead man walking. Or dead man climbing
as the case may be."

"So Glenn Marchbanks is a dead network member. So are the
two you sent me after." Janice turned and looked at Holly. "He's
killing his own. He's killing us."

"Glenn was mounting a revolt against me. Holly didn't know it."

"And Barbara Scott and Lazard were part of this? Bull!" Janice
yelled. "You just... You just... you're lying. What is this really about?"

He took a deep breath. "You know about the unfortunate death
of the vice president."

Silence. Holly watched Janice nod. Holly wanted out of this car
so badly—it was like a coffin. She couldn't stand to be near this
woman. She couldn't breathe, she couldn't look at her, she couldn't
be expected to speak to her, to act like a nonmurderer around her...

"And, well, he has to be replaced. He is going to be replaced by
a senator from New Mexico. Who is...one of us. I smoothed every
path for her. There were three big obstacles in her political growth.
Barbara Scott and Lucky Lazard eliminated two of those obstacles.
There is one more who helped her rise, who sealed the deal. They
all know she's ours."

"And you need him dead."

Holly thought, *You need everyone who knows you're going to
own the woman a heartbeat away from the presidency dead. But
you just told me and Janice. And I'm not terminally ill.* She opened
her mouth to speak but nothing came out.

Belias said, "I need the people who elevated her dead now. Any
one of them could expose what they did, prove the connection between us. The stakes are now too high. Glenn was already rebelling
against me, like Satan against God." His voice had a sudden cold
creak to it.

You're insane, Holly thought, but she stared out the window. *I let you turn me into a killer. I let you ruin me. But that's done, and now I just have to get back to my kids.*

She still had the gun. She could just shoot them both. End it here. Belias had told her Janice had cancer, she'd be dead soon. And Belias…Then she'd be free.

"I'm the only thing standing between you and Capra, Holly," Belias said. It shook her out of her reverie. Could she shoot them here? In the middle of the city? He had a plane. He had a pilot. She could just walk to his plane and say, *Take me home.* Would the pilot, if Belias wasn't around? No. Okay, forget his airplane. She'd wait until they parked in the airport lot. She'd shoot him and then the woman, Janice. Who was so worried about her daughter…And now she wouldn't have to worry anymore. Shoot them and walk away. There were probably security cameras in the parking lot, but there had been cameras in the casino although Lazard shut them down under some pretense when Belias came to see him…The cameras would catch her. Maybe she should wait. Somewhere less public…

I'm sorry, she thought. In the rearview mirror she saw Janice watching her as if she could hear her thoughts.

She put the car into drive and took the side roads to avoid the traffic.

They were now ten minutes from the airport.

"So you own the vice president. Then what?" Holly said. "Wait for the president to die?"

"That is an option. I think having a spy deep inside the government is going to be good for all of us. People can be appointed to positions of influence. Get massive contracts. Ambassadorships. There are many ways for us to profit. To secure our futures."

The two women were silent.

"I need to go meet with the senator. It won't be easy for me to get access to her but it must be done, given this situation. And I want the two of you to go to Chicago. To deal with the last person who knows."

No, Holly thought in horror. *No. You can't ask me to travel with this woman. You just can't.* She stared at her hands on the steering wheel. Was that blood on them? No. Just a trick of the desert light. Diana's blood. The Russian woman's blood.

Her hands shook. How could she look at her children?

"Holly?"

"I killed that woman. I...I have never killed anyone before." Her voice sounded like her own but the words might have been in a foreign language.

"It gets easier after the first time," Janice said. "A little."

Holly swallowed bile at the back of her throat. *The first time was your daughter; do you really want to talk to me about ease?*

"I don't want you to worry about your families," Belias said. "I have them being watched, so they're safe."

The threat was implicit. He'd dispatched someone to watch her kids and her mother and probably another one to find Diana. Not that she could be found. What would Felix and the little Russian have done with Diana's body? Left it in the bar? Left it for the police to find? It could be on the news. What if Janice decided to check San Francisco news websites or broke her radio silence to call her daughter? What if people in San Francisco got desperate to try and reach her? She might call Diana the moment the Chicago hit was done.

And she'd be with her. She'd be facing a mother like herself, who'd been willing to accept the moral compromises and shortcuts, all the advantages. Someone just as ruthless when needed. And if they failed? Would her kids pay the price?

Maybe it was a lie. Felix knew she'd killed Diana. And Felix had his own agenda, apparently, if Belias was to be believed.

"Sam's friend...Felix...he was in my cancer support group," Janice said. "Felix must have targeted me. He must have known about me."

Belias stared at her.

Janice kept talking. "And if Lazard told Sam Capra who the third target was...would Lazard know?"

"Yes. He would have worked once with Rawlings."

"Then...Felix is maybe heading toward Chicago as well."

Belias said, "You're in a race, ladies. Don't lose it."

"Do you warn this Rawlings guy?" Holly asked.

"I'll warn Rawlings that there's a threat to him. I'll have him meet you both someplace private. He'll think it's for protection. It will make your job much easier."

They pulled into the airport parking lot. Holly glanced around. The only place more observed than a casino under the constant glare of security cameras is an airport. *You can't kill them here*, she thought. *It's too public. Wait until it's just you and Janice. Then Belias. Then you're safe.*

Holly said, "So this Felix guy, what is his story? He knows about us? That means Sam knew about us before…" Before Diana came into his bar asking for help. But that didn't seem to make sense. There was more to the story.

"Let's not speculate, Holly," Belias interrupted. He wrote down an address. "You'll find what you need in Chicago here. Guns, cash. Leave your weapons you've got here with me, we don't want attention from the TSA today. Here's the name and address of the man. I'll tell you where to meet him." *Wade Rawlings*, the note read.

"And when this man Rawlings is dead, what then?" Janice asked.

"Then come home," he said. "And enjoy the time with your families. Janice, given your medical situation, perhaps it would be best if first I met your daughter with you. We could do a meeting as soon as you are home. You can…introduce her to me. And me to her and help her understand why she should be part of what we do."

Holly watched Janice's reaction, which would have done a poker player proud. "All right."

He'll kill her, Holly thought. He's used Janice up. Diana will be gone and she'll know he had something to do with it. *Janice Keene is not going to die from cancer after all*, she thought, and a hysterical bubble of laughter nearly erupted from her chest.

And now that you know the truth about his most powerful puppet, he'll kill you, too. She had wondered how far he would dare go in his recruitment of those who wanted his special brand of help. He would have a person he owned a heartbeat away from the presidency. Would he dare an assassination? Yes. He would. He had nothing to lose and everything to gain. He wouldn't use a network member to kill the president—would he?—but he would be sure his pawn made it into the Oval Office.

The thought frightened her. Where would he stop? What if Belias thought a war would profit him?

She felt dizzy.

But…there would have to be some way for him to communicate with his pawn, and how? Everything the president and the vice president did was archived, every e-mail, every phone call…There was so little actual privacy in the office. How would he work it? She was sure he would have figured it out. The thought, unbidden, as to how he would make this work, tickled at the back of her mind.

"Do you need a doctor?" Belias asked Janice.

"Between the beatings and the cancer? No," she said. "Let's just get this over with." She sounded resigned.

Belias gave Janice a replacement ID for the third leg of her trip. Belias booked them their Chicago flight, seating them in first class, and arranged for the jet that had brought him to Vegas to take him to Washington.

"I'm going to go wash my face," Janice said. "Freshen up a bit." She went toward the ladies' room.

Belias watched her. "You don't tell her a single word about her daughter. Not a word."

"I wouldn't dream of it," Holly said.

Belias drew Holly close to him and she was so surprised her mouth fell open. His lips came very close to hers. "I know you think you want out, Holly. But think what I can do for you now. Think of the life I can give you. Everything. You could be a very special help to me—a special job only you could do."

She thought of the smell of drying paint, the bed where the one man she'd loved died. *Haven't you done enough to me?* she thought. She'd shoved away the realization that he was attracted to her. It wasn't something her brain could process, not in all the horror of the past few days.

She swallowed and she didn't pull away. His lips brushed hers, a tease. He didn't want their first kiss to be in an airport, she figured. Men were that way.

She nearly laughed. She was wondering if he'd killed her husband and now she was getting on a plane with a woman whose daughter she'd killed. This was one bloody circle she was trapped inside.

Janice returned. She and Janice headed for the security line, and on the TVs in the terminal, the stations were showing smartphone-shot footage of Sam Capra on the side of the Mystik; the feed headline said, SHOOTINGS AT MYSTIK CASINO; MAN AT LARGE, and she thought, *Sam got away. Sam got away and he will be hunting us now.*

68

Sunday, November 7, afternoon

BELIAS HAD TAKEN my phone from me. I had a hundred dollars in my wallet and a credit card that would alert anyone looking for me that I was on the move.

Chicago. Rawlings. That was all I knew.

The key was Felix, who clearly knew more.

Felix wove his way through the crowd, and I followed. Sirens still howled at the Mystik.

I started to run toward him as the crowd thinned out. I couldn't do that before—I would have been shoving people left and right and I had to get out of the area. If I was caught or recognized, I'd be the prime suspect in three murders.

He walked four casinos away from the Mystik, turning onto a side street. I hung back, hiding behind cars as we went across the lots. If he saw me he gave no sign. He hurried to a parked black Navigator, parked in front of a dive bar, got into the car. The Navigator began to pull away out of the lot.

I had no way to follow. He'd betrayed me, and so I'd had to assume he'd betrayed Mila and Jimmy and the Round Table...

Parked behind the bar I saw an old motorcycle, vintage, but not restored. It looked like it needed work. I cracked the case, jiggled the wires. Spark. You can only do it with the old ones and I had found some spare luck.

The motorcycle cranked to life.

I zoomed after the Navigator, weaving into the Vegas traffic. As we got farther away from the Mystik and the Strip, the traffic jam thinned considerably. What I did next would depend on the following possibilities: Mila was inside the Navigator, a prisoner, or unaware that Felix had left me to die; Mila was a hostage somewhere else. Mila was perfectly fine and had been left behind in San Francisco, just like Felix said; maybe Felix never told Mila where he was heading, and she wasn't even here in Vegas.

I had no weapon on me, just the bike. If I attacked in traffic, he'd either shoot me or run over me or I'd draw police attention.

But Mila. If Mila was in trouble…

I revved the motorcycle close up behind the blacked-out windows of the Navigator. Every impulse told me to try and run them off the road, do anything to stop them; but I couldn't draw attention to myself.

The Navigator accelerated, heading away from the Strip into suburbia. Then he started whipping through traffic, either panicking or certain that he could lose me. It is hard to lose a motorbike. His advantage was that a collision is much less risky in a heavy SUV than it is for a helmetless rider on a junky old stolen motorcycle.

He kept on his course away from the busiest part of the city. I followed. He had to have seen me. I had no helmet to hide my features, and as the traffic got sparser there was no place for me to hide. So be it.

He took a chance then, accelerating through a red light, horns screeching at him. I peeled around a car that had wisely stopped, blasted through the intersection, narrowly avoiding a Jaguar that screeched to a stop. It slowed me for ten seconds as I had to pivot the old bike around the stopped car and then power back up to speed. Now Felix had floored it, gunning the engine up toward eighty. A light ahead started to gleam red and he steered the Navigator up onto the sidewalk, screaming past the stopped cars. He hit a fruit display at a market; fruit and wood exploded up over the Navigator.

But it slowed him for a minute.

The motorbike coughed a choking noise I did not care for at all. But I just had to get close enough…

The Navigator slewed around the traffic, laying hard on the horn, and I revved the motorcycle harder, dodging an apple-red pickup truck and an SUV. Both honked in loud, braying cries. I flew between them, head down, intent on Felix. I heard the squeal of brakes, the chunk of a crash. I glanced back—I didn't want to get anyone hurt. The truck and the SUV had bounced off each other's sides. They looked drivable. I put my attention back on the road ahead of me.

As we both roared down a stretch of road that wasn't so busy, me hoping the sputtering sound didn't mean the motorbike was about to die, I heard an engine driving, surging behind me. I glanced back. The bright red pickup truck. Apparently the Navigator or I had pissed off the driver and he'd decided to join in the chase.

I hate vigilantes.

The red pickup drew close to me. Very close. In the motorcycle's cracked rearview mirror the bumper must have been scant centimeters behind me; if I slowed or turned, he'd run me down. Then he cut over to my left, his window sliding down, and I could see a guy my age, midtwenties, baseball capped and screaming at me. He didn't have kind words.

I pointed hard at the Navigator.

He didn't care. Apparently I was the one who had angered him or dented his truck, and I was the one to pay the price. He kept gesturing me to stop.

So I did. Not entirely. I dropped back and he arrowed over again, intent on forcing me to stop. I had nothing to fight him with but my fists and those were useless while I was on the ancient motorcycle.

So. This jerk was going to cost me Felix. Maybe Mila if she was a prisoner inside the Navigator. Ahead I could see the Navigator powering up fast, racing toward eighty again. He was on a straight outshoot from the city. At this speed and playing road hockey with the jerk, I would lose him.

I revved the bike up close to the pickup's back bed, and the jerk thoughtfully headed over toward me again, closer. I threw myself off the cycle and grabbed hold of the truck's edge. I started to pull myself over the edge, and the jerk blasted into an abandoned shopping center lot, nearly scraping me off a light pole at the entrance. The pole missed hitting me by inches.

Now I was really mad.

He slammed to a stop and I dropped off the edge, racing toward him. He stormed out of the driver's seat, smelling of beer, with the arrogant air of a football player who was used to intimidating people.

"You little—" His breath reeked of afternoon brews and those were the only words he ever spoke to me. I slammed hands into his throat, his face, his chest and he was folding before he knew what hit him. I dug the keys out of his pocket—they were the electronic kind—and I wheeled out fast, back on the street, leaving him choking and half-conscious in the parking lot.

It was a sweet truck, and I was grateful for his indignation and happy to get a drunk off the road. I plowed ahead, blasting the powerful engine. But the Navigator was gone. I'd gone four miles, no sign of it. I backtracked on the roads.

Two police cars shot past me, looking for whoever had caused the wreck three blocks back. One of them suddenly slowed and I remembered I was driving a truck that had clearly taken a hard hit.

He'd probably want to question me, the driver. No, thanks.

I wheeled the truck hard about in a circle as the police car U-turned back toward me. I floored it, racing back into oncoming traffic. Horns blared. I leveled the truck across the median strip of grit and desert dust, blasted onto the correct side of the road. The police car revved past me and then sluiced around, blocking the road.

Only a dummy T-bones a police car, at least with the front of the truck.

I spun it hard, putting the truck bed between me and the police car. I veered to the right at the last second, hammering the cop car's trunk rather than the engine, bursting past the supposed blockade. The cop car whirled past the median and into the opposite lanes, where cars honked and slowed and stopped.

I drove the truck away as fast as I could, zooming across another parking lot, revving behind a small shopping center. I could hear the pursuing whine of the other police car. In my rearview I saw the police car, lights flashing, shoot past the shopping center. It would barely buy me a minute's time. I ditched the truck, jumped over a fence. I found myself in another parking lot for what looked like a slightly seedy office complex.

Felix was gone. And maybe Mila with him. I'd failed. And I was currently the most hunted man in Las Vegas.

So I did the only thing I could do. I walked. I headed for a bar.

69

Sunday, November 7, early evening

My bar in Las Vegas, The Canyon, was not a place where I'd spent a lot of time. I'd only been there once before to meet and detain the woman who'd taken my missing child (she thought I was someone else), but none of that had gone right and my major contribution to the bar was evacuating it before a bomb hidden there could detonate.

I'm pretty sure if The Canyon was a person, it'd want to punch me.

My sorry neglect of it aside, The Canyon is a lovely bar. I would be walking a good ways across town. I didn't know if the police now had an ID on me, if they knew my name and would be waiting for me at the bar. Early in my hike I stopped at a local drugstore, bought what I needed to mend my temple. My clothes were dry from the motorcycle ride and I just looked like a disheveled type, and those aren't that unusual in Vegas. I walked from there toward the bar, past an electronics store, and in the window I saw the television coverage of myself descending the Mystik's side. I watched the entire footage. My face was hidden by the shirt; you could only see my back side. The footage replayed twice and you couldn't know it was me.

So unless Belias gave the authorities my name…and that was suicide for him. I'd spill all with nothing to lose. I knew too many of his secrets.

By the time I reached The Canyon, it was early evening, opening time, surprisingly busy—I remembered The Canyon started its happy hour at four. It is hard to stay hip in Las Vegas; it was a very different kind of bar from The Select in San Francisco or The Last Minute in New York or Adrenaline in London. Those were bars with a regular clientele. Tourists were far more easily distracted.

The bouncer looked at me like I was gum off last year's shoe.

"Dress code, sir."

I was still in the clothes I'd stolen from the room at the Mystik. I looked like a grimy, filthy dork who'd been in a fight. Bouncers do not like people who look like they've already fought in the evening or have the dust of a crosstown walk on their shoes.

"Understood, but I'm Sam Capra. I own the bar."

I didn't know the bouncer. But he pushed me with his thick finger in the chest. "I have my doubts."

"I'm Sam Capra. I own the bar. Go get Gigi. She'll vouch for me." Gigi was the manager of The Canyon.

He started to shove me, going for the wrist, clearly with a mind to steer me away from the door with a minimum of force. I didn't have time to spare him the humiliation. He was taller than me and wider than me, but in three seconds he was facedown on the pavement, his wrists in my grip, and my knee on his back. I fished the earpiece out of his ear and said into the mike, "Gigi, it's Sam. I'm here in town. Would you please come to the front?"

Gigi arrived at the door in about forty seconds. She stopped, stared, and said, "Oh, Sam. This is Michael. Michael, this is Mr. Capra, the owner. Sam, would you please let Michael up?"

"Hi, Michael. I apologize. I need to speak to Gigi now, but I'll be happy to review bouncer protocols with you at a future time." Yeah, I can be a jerk.

"Yes, sir," he said. I let him up and I made him shake my hand although I thought he didn't enjoy it.

Gigi hurried me inside. "Oh, that's great publicity, wrangling with the employees. He could sue you."

"I have worse publicity problems." I shut the door to the upstairs office, cutting off the thrum of remixed dance music below.

"What's the matter?"

"I need your help badly. First, I need to get in touch with Mila. I need you to call every number you have for her, start with the bar in San Francisco. See if she's there. If not, then I need to talk to a higher-up at the Round Table."

"They don't exactly have a directory," Gigi said.

"There must be a number to reach Jimmy."

"Mila's our sole contact," she said. "I honestly do not have another way to contact them. Compartmentalizing protects them."

"Give me a phone." I called the number I'd been given to reach Leonie.

There was no answer. I tried her cell phone.

She answered on the third ring. "Yes?"

"Are you okay? Is Daniel okay?"

"We're fine."

"Where are you?"

"Still in Los Angeles. Still at our hotel. I wish Daniel was old enough to appreciate Disneyland, I'd take him there…"

"I need to speak with Jimmy."

"I've not seen him since this morning."

"How do I reach him?"

She fed me a number. I spoke to Daniel for a minute; then she came back on the line.

"Leonie, is there anyone there to protect you?"

"Yes. Jimmy has a guy in the next room for us."

"But you don't know where Jimmy is."

"No, Sam, what's wrong?"

"Maybe nothing." There was no point in worrying her. I told her I'd call back soon and I tried the number she'd given me for Jimmy. No answer. I tried Mila's number. No answer. I tried the number for The Select. No answer. I left messages in the voice mails.

I clicked off the phone. "The other problem is Felix Neare."

Gigi made a face. Gigi is short, strongly built, with an angelic face. She was once a Marine, and one year after an honorable discharge an ex-girlfriend of hers tried to talk Gigi into murdering the girlfriend's parents for all the goodies in the will. Gigi refused and so the girlfriend framed her for the murders. The Round Table, with some subtle work and behind-the-scenes maneuvering, got her wrongful sentence overturned, and now Gigi, like many of the other managers, offered the Round Table an extraordinary loyalty. "I don't much like him."

"Why?" I stopped, reaching for the fresh cell phone she'd tossed me.

"He's just a pill. Asks a lot of questions that don't pertain to his work. I mean, we're a tight group. The managers talk. We're friends. But not Felix."

I told Gigi a very abbreviated version of what had happened at the Mystik. Her cherubic face paled. "I saw the news at the Mystik," she said.

"What are they saying?"

"At least three people dead, others injured. There was a rush in the evacuation and some other folks got hurt. Most of the news has been about Lucky Lazard, he's famous here. Like this was an organized crime hit or something. They haven't given more details. The police tend to be very tight-lipped here. They don't like to panic the tourists."

I paced the floor. She said, "Let's get you to Chicago, you have to get out of Vegas. You can't stay here. I will find out where Mila is."

"Felix must have come here first," I said. "He was equipped."

"I don't even get here until three," she said. "I don't know how he would have a key."

"Mila would," I said. "Check the video history."

She did on her laptop. "It's Felix."

I watched the video feed. He came in, using a key, stayed for less than four minutes, left with a bag of gear.

"Where would Felix have gotten a key to this bar from?"

"Mila has a key to every bar," she said. "So does Jimmy, although I've never met him."

"I haven't been to the Chicago bar yet. Who's the manager?"

"Benny. You haven't met him?" I heard a shift in her voice.

"Is he good?"

"Well, yes, he's just a bit different."

I couldn't worry about idiosyncrasies right now. "For some reason, Felix Neare has betrayed us. I don't know if he wants to destroy Belias on his own or what his motive is. But someone in the Round Table, whoever vetted him, is going to tell me everything that he knows."

We went into emergency mode. Felix would know that I had other bars, other resources, but he would be running. I didn't think he'd come after me at the moment; he was a man on a mission against Belias. Belias must know by now I was alive and coming after him.

Gigi arranged for a private jet for me to Chicago; again I tried every phone number, every e-mail account. Nothing.

"Sam," she said from behind the laptop.

"What?"

"Every one of your bank accounts is frozen," she said. "I was just looking to move some money for you into a Chicago account tied to the bar. It's locked. I can't get a response from the bank."

Belias was tightening his grip on me, pinning me so I couldn't move.

What else would he do? I felt like my head would explode.

My only hope was that Belias didn't know that I knew about Rawlings in Chicago. He'd run before Lazard shared that sliver of knowledge. He might think I'd just drop out, give up, go home to the family.

I could do that. Or I could end this threat. There was no one else, with me unable to reach Mila and Jimmy. There was only me. "Let's go."

Gigi drove me to the airport. "I'll find Mila."

"Rawlings. Chicago. I need to know every prominent person in Chicago with that surname."

"I'll get Benny on it." She surprised me by squeezing my hand. "We'll find Mila. I promise you."

"If I don't come back, you find Belias, Gigi; the Round Table has to find him and kill him. End him. He can't have a direct hand in running this country."

"I promise," she said. She watched me get onto the plane and she stayed by the car as the plane left, the phone pressed to her ear.

70

Sunday, November 7, evening

Outside Chicago, Illinois

WADE RAWLINGS PARKED the car behind the house, blinking at the scattering snow. The old house loomed up against the night sky. To a stranger's eyes it was a bit Gothic, but to him it was grandmotherly hugs and summer lemonade and winter cocoa. He felt safe here.

You need to get out of town, the voice on the phone had said. *Just go to your old family home. I'll be there in the morning. Just wait for me.*

He had learned long ago not to argue with Belias. So he went there, and he waited. He was tired. He'd just gotten back from a trip to London, and while the summons was disturbing (like a call from Satan himself, Belias scared him and would any normal-thinking person), it was not unusual. Belias needed something done and so he would do it. And then he'd benefit, and life went on its merrily predetermined course.

He was certain this meeting had to do with Marjorie Henderson. The newspapers in London had been full of the story that she was the leading pick to fill the vacant vice presidency. Oh, that would indeed be sweet. He had helped build Marjorie Henderson and now he would reap his rewards. Belias would see to that. Because power built power, everyone knew that.

Wade put on the kettle and he puttered about the kitchen. He was a small, slightly pudgy man and he felt the jet lag from his return from London. He'd stopped on the way and bought some groceries, in case Belias was hungry tomorrow. So he began to fry up two eggs and some toast, and he didn't hear the quiet footsteps over the sizzle of the butter and the frying hiss of the eggs.

But then his face slammed downward, the left side right into the cooking breakfast, and the pain was beyond imagining; it was horrific even with his head yanked back immediately from the sizzling skillet. Wade's skin was seared and his eyes were swelling. And the pain made him scream instead of answer, and the man gripping his head said, "You are going to tell me everything you know about John Belias and the next vice president."

He made a noise, not an answer, and his face hit the skillet again.

71

Sunday, November 7, evening

THE PRIVATE JET LANDED in Chicago, unexpectedly early snow dancing across the sky. The plane taxied to a private hangar, where a car with a man inside waited for me.

Benny proved to be a thin, spare bald man in his sixties, dressed in jeans and a military-looking sweater and a Chicago Bears baseball cap. "Mr. Capra."

Benny was more than double my age so I said, "Please, call me Sam."

"I understand that some of the bars have had difficulties this evening with frozen accounts," Benny said. "I have taken certain liberties. There are no cash or weapons or false ID papers still at the bar." His tone of voice was very formal, like a butler's.

As Benny drove into the night, I asked, "Have you heard from Gigi?"

"Yes. She gave me a number for you to call."

I took the phone, dialed the number. It rang twice.

"Hello?" I said when I heard an answering click. "Mila?"

"No, it's not Mila. Well. The famous Sam Capra." The voice was steely, male, English.

Jimmy.

My heart froze. "Where is she?"

"Mila is in a hospital in Las Vegas. She was shot once in the chest at the Mystik Resort. She is in critical condition."

I closed my eyes. The ambulance, the wailing of the sirens. "Is she all right?"

"I don't know. She may live or she may die. And I blame you."

I said then about the stupidest thing I could muster in my shock. "We're...we're all on the same side."

"This...folly of yours was not approved by the Round Table. Or by me. Mila gave you a little room to maneuver but you took it too far. Now the bars are under attack. Our computer systems, tied back to the bars, are under attack. You've brought a war on us and you had no right."

"It became critical. This man Belias was aware of us."

"He was aware of *you*. Not us. Huge difference."

"So I'm useful only to a point."

"The only thing you're useful for today is getting Mila shot"—and here rage tinged his voice—"and making a spectacle of yourself on the news. You left a crime scene. You better hope they can't tie your prints to it."

"I don't have prints on file anymore. The CIA took care of that." The words bounced in my head. *Mila.* Mila was lying hurt and we were worrying about my prints.

"What would happen to you if you didn't have us or the CIA to hide behind? One wonders."

"Felix must have shot her. Belias was with me before Felix came up to the penthouse..." I said. "Who vetted Felix to be a bar manager?"

Silence. "Well?"

"I did," Jimmy said. "I did."

"Your man betrayed us. Where was Mila when she was shot?"

Silence again. "She was in a storage room in the employee area."

"Felix was dressed like an employee. Felix must have shot her to keep her from coming up there with him. He considered shooting me, but he left me to create a distraction for the cops."

"Sam..."

"Jimmy, please, this doesn't matter right now. I am going to find both Belias and Felix. They're both after a guy here named Rawlings. I need..."

"I need you to stop this and to come back here."

"Belias is going to own the next vice president, and I think the odds of her becoming president are not inconsequential now. I can stop them."

"I am ordering you to stand down."

"No. I can stop Felix."

"You will do as I say."

"Only Mila gives me orders."

"Well, she gets her orders from me."

"Maybe. Maybe not. Maybe I'm tired of not knowing what the Round Table is exactly. Maybe you're as screwed up as this group of Belias's."

"You chasing them isn't going to fix Mila," he said. "You've done enough damage."

"I am going to stop Felix and Belias."

"I don't care," Jimmy said. "Mila could die. And if that happens, Sam, run. Run far and as fast as you can because I will find you and I will kill you for this. I. Will. Kill. You. Do you understand me?"

"I won't run," I said. "Are we done?"

A long pause. "Yes. I have to see how she's doing. She's back in surgery. There were...complications."

Please let her be okay. "Daniel and Leonie...look, you and I are having differences, but..."

"They're perfectly safe." He made a choked noise. "What did you think, I was going to threaten your family to get you to obey me? You are unhinged."

My heart felt blackened, like it had burned. She was my boss (as much as I could be bossed), she was my friend, she was the reason I had my son back. She could not die, she couldn't. My face felt hot.

"Why would Felix do this? Loyalty to Janice Keene?"

"I don't know. I have no idea. Sam..." he said. "But..."

"What?"

"If you're going after them...then kill Felix. Kill him for shooting her. Bring me Belias. We'll break him together."

His attitude certainly had shifted in the past minute, but I didn't care to argue. "I'll call you when I have news."

Jimmy hung up.

"His lordship feels strongly about things," Benny said. *Lordship*, I thought, *what a weird nickname.* Jimmy could sound imperious but right now I didn't blame him. "Okay. Rawlings. I need to find this guy."

"Here's a file. Gigi and I think he's Wade Rawlings, a former political strategist. We don't know where he is right now, but we'll find him." Benny handed me a tablet computer with a file displayed and I began to read as he drove through the thickening snow.

72

Sunday, November 7, late evening/Monday, November 8, early morning

IT HAD BEEN the hardest trip of her life.

Holly tried to sleep on the plane but the delayed shock of what she had done made her hands shake. Janice said sensibly, "You should have a drink," and Holly thought, *Now I have to drink with her.* It was unimaginable. But she nodded and Janice ordered them each a bourbon, and Holly tasted its smoke very slowly, careful not to slam it down and relinquish control, but to sip at it like it was medicine.

"So you have kids," Janice said after their drinks were brought.

"Yes." *Of course,* Holly thought, *moms always discuss their kids.* "Two. A girl, just turned eight, a boy, six."

"I have one daughter. Diana, she's twenty-three. She's my heir apparent. Taking over my business." She looked at Holly. "I've got less than a year if the doctors are right."

"I...I am so sorry."

"When your clock's done, all that matters is making sure your kid will be okay. It's why I did...what I did."

"Me, too."

"I want John...to take care of Diana. I think the world today's too hard without some help from him. From the others. Like us."

Shut up shut up shut up. "I can understand your concern."

"I...I think he'll take care of her. And I hope she'll understand. It's all worth it."

"Yes," Holly said, hoping the word didn't sound as dead in the air as it felt in her mouth.

"I hope I made the right decision. As a mom. I didn't really have another mom to talk about it with. You know."

Oh, please don't ask me for advice. The flight attendants slammed a galley door and for a moment it sounded like Diana's neck cracking against the mahogany bar. "I'm sure you did. I'm sure John will be good to her."

"You're right. Thanks."

She wondered how bent Janice Keene had become under those years of secrets, to think drafting her daughter into the network was a maternal gesture. *This isn't a sane life*, she thought. *We start to crack under the pressure. We can justify anything. Like bringing our kids into Belias's orbit is somehow protecting them.*

Like you're still a good person if you accidentally killed a young woman.

"This Felix guy…"

"He's a friend. I thought he was. Now I think he must have been targeting me. He must've known, you know, about us."

"How? How would he?"

"I don't know. Maybe Belias ruined him years ago, and he's been looking for us."

The thought horrified Holly. The people they'd wronged, coming back for revenge.

Janice said, "There were so many people Belias ruined. All that matters now is we have to deal with Felix. He lied to me, so I'll take care of him." And then Janice looked out the window, as though the void of night held the answers. She finished her drink. Holly did not touch hers again.

"I think I'd like to sleep," Janice said. "Wake me if I start to talk in my sleep. I don't want the world to hear what I have to say."

The text message from Belias that appeared on Holly's phone after landing read, TOMORROW MORNING AT 8 AM DRIVE NORTH OF CHICAGO, with directions and an address. Alone in her hotel room, she listened to two voice mails, one from her mom, one from the kids. Emma's voice, bright in her ear but a little worried, a little tense: "Hey, Mom, when are you going to be home? We miss you. Tried Dad's number but he's not answering. We're having fun with Nana and Aunt Martha. Love you."

She turned off the phone.

The next morning they got up early and drove to a storage unit near Midway Airport Belias had told them about. The key was taped above the frame of the unit's door, and inside it was a duffel bag, loaded with two pistols, capped with suppressors, and ammunition and a thousand in cash. Either Belias left stocks of this scattered around the country, or a network member in Chicago was helping them out.

I don't even know who's pulling my strings, she thought.

Janice drove.

"How many people has Belias had you kill?" Holly asked.

"Before now? Three."

"You say it so calmly."

"How do I know they would have had long, full lives? They could get hit by a bus the next day. They could get sick with cancer, like me. Death can come at any second for any of us. That's the box I put it into. That's how I sleep."

"And you'll kill this guy Rawlings today."

"I will if you won't. I can carry it. No need for you to."

Holly's chest ached. "And then you'll go home."

"Yes. I will tell my daughter I'm sick, and there's little hope for me. And then I'll explain Belias and the network to her, so she'll understand."

"What if we get killed?"

Janice hesitated, then confessed, "I made a videotape for her. So she'll understand. So she won't be afraid of him. Coming from me, she'll know it's true."

You really should not have done that, Holly thought. *That has ruined us all.* "You've thought about how to explain it to her?"

"Sure. Haven't you, if you were ever caught? How would you tell your kids?"

"Deny. Deny everything," Holly said.

"Children appreciate honesty," Janice said. "Maybe you could help me explain to Diana."

"Maybe," Holly said after a few moments, staring out the window.

They arrived at the house's address, but they parked a half mile away, on a side road, and hiked through a heavy dense grove of oaks. The house was grand but gray, with a wraparound porch. The snow had stopped skittering down from the leaden skies. Janice gestured her toward the side of the house.

I don't know what I'm doing, but I'll follow her lead. And then what? We call Belias, we tell him he's dead, and then what? Janice goes home to discover a missing daughter.

You have to kill this Felix guy first. Felix knows you killed Diana. Kill him first. Before he can say a word to Janice.

73

Sunday, November 7, late evening

Belias lied.

He didn't go to Washington. He flew to a small private airport outside Santa Fe, New Mexico, because as it became clearer that Senator Marjorie Henderson would be named the new VP, Henderson and her husband had come home and hunkered down. Within days it was assumed they'd fly to Washington and join the president and Vice President Camden's widow for the announcement.

Belias walked along the trail. The air was rich with the smell of ponderosa pine and snow hung in the air like little escaped fragments of light. He felt savagely glad to be alive after the horror of the penthouse, and as he waited he thought of making a snowball. Silly, insane. He remembered making them one day outside Moscow, at Borodin's dacha, a snowball fight between him and Roger and Svetlana. Pure silliness. Their laughter had floated in the air like the snow. Her beautiful, lying laughter. Throwing snowballs with him, encouraging him, while she was bedding his father. Now they were all dead, but he was alive; all was going to work out all right; and Sam Capra and this Felix person would soon no longer be a problem.

And Holly. He would have Holly now. She'd seemed a bit surprised by his overture in the Las Vegas airport, but soon she'd want the protection of his arms. Maybe he could join her. Be a father to her kids; he'd do a better job than Glenn ever did. Have a family. The network just needed to run itself out for the next few years, until Henderson's political career was done with honor, and he'd have enough money to retire wherever he pleased. With no one the wiser of what he'd done.

He saw Frederick Henderson—the senator's husband—hurrying up the trail. Alone. Good. Out of impulse he hoisted up the cool, pliable snow in his hands and lobbed the snowball at him. It dusted the side of Henderson's jacket arm on the left side and Henderson scowled at him.

"Is this a joke? Do you know how difficult it was for me to get away? And you want to have a snowball fight?"

"Goodness, you're tense. Best practice your smiles for the camera. Your wife is going to be the next vice president of the United States. It will be very hard for you and I to meet face-to-face ever again."

Henderson said, "Yes. And I appreciate how you've always been there for us, John. Helping me help her."

"When is the big announcement?"

"Two days. The vice president's widow will be joining us for the press conference. In Washington."

"So unfortunate about Vice President Camden. A stroke, yes?"
"Yes."

"And lucky that Madame Senator was an obvious choice."

"Right place at the right time. As you always say, Belias, we make our own luck." His voice sounded strained. "We thought we'd have to wait for the next election to get the VP spot. But this is better. To steal another quote, fortune favors the prepared."

"Your own luck. I make your luck. The three people that could conclusively testify in a court of law that they broke laws to benefit Marjorie Henderson are being eliminated. Barbara Scott and Lucky Lazard are already dead. The third will be dead soon enough."

Henderson paled. "No. Stop it. There's no point."

"I won't have anyone threatening Marjorie's position," Belias said. "It's been a long-term chess game and we're close to the end. No way I stop now." He knelt to gather up another snowball.

"You have to stop. Someone might figure out the connections. You have to stop now."

Belias stood, the snow in his hands, watching Frederick Henderson's frown. "Like I said, Steady Freddy, practice that smile. I wanted to tell you how we'll communicate in the future."

"There is no more. We're done."

Belias smiled at him. "What, you think you get too successful, our deal is null and void? Just the opposite."

"John. Be reasonable. Marjorie has done so much to help you and the others…who have made the pact with you."

"She doesn't get to walk away, Freddy."

"There is no way you can ask Marjorie for anything anymore. She's under too much scrutiny. You're like a lobbyist on steroids. She has a chance in three years to run for president."

"This is what is going to happen…" Belias began.

"No, John, it's not." Frederick Henderson's nasal tone turned to a growl. "You step back. After Marjorie has been president, when she's no longer in office, maybe she can help you then. She'd still be hugely influential. But we've moved beyond you. It would be far too big a danger not only to her, but to you. Be reasonable. You'd get caught trying to stay in touch with us and it won't ever work."

"Marjorie is going to make a new best friend. Her name is Holly Marchbanks. They'll meet at some fund-raiser and Marjorie will find Holly just charming. Holly will quickly become like a sister to her. Holly will be the conduit for information from me to Marjorie. There will be no files, no phone conversations, no electronic or pa-per trail. They'll have a private lunch every few weeks and Holly will tell Marjorie what I need done. She can ask her detail to wait outside so Marjorie and Holly can have private talks, the way dear-est friends do. No one will suspect."

Frederick Henderson shook his head. "This won't work. I told you, we're done. For the time she's in office. Then we'll see."

"I wonder what the rest of our friends would think, to know someone who could help them is in such high office but won't. Do you think your beloved wife is the only politician in my network? Do you think I put all my eggs in one basket?"

"Are you threatening Marjorie?"

"I always say I make promises, not threats, Freddy." He dropped the snowball, dusted his hands free. "I'll tell the others that she is a direct threat to expose us. Do you really want her targeted by some of the most powerful people in the world?"

"They won't be able to touch her."

"They can bring her down. It won't be hard. The higher the pedestal the more it can totter. I can think of about five or six scandals we could manufacture that would force her resignation. Or even block her appointment before Congress votes on it. There are no more trials these days, Freddy, just unfortunate media coverage."

"You do that and I'll expose you."

"And therefore expose your wife. Who will go down as the first vice president to go to prison." Belias cracked a smile. "Barbara Scott destroyed her first political rival and Lucky Lazard poisoned the finances of her next big rival and Wade Rawlings derailed another politician who could have brought her down. You are here, Freddy, because we are here. We put you here. And we can remove you."

"The others…they won't risk it."

"Won't risk what? There is no risk to them. You'll never tie it to them. What names can you name? None. That's the beauty of my system. And if I ever thought you were close, then I'd worry about some sort of terrorist attack on you and Marjorie. An assassination attempt. It could be financed. Suicidal fools are easily bought."

Freddy's voice shook. "We'll have Secret Service after the announcement and the confirmation; you'll never get close to us."

"What if I own someone inside the Secret Service, Freddy?" And he almost smiled as Freddy Henderson's face began to pale. "Do you think I haven't thought this out? You don't decide to make someone president and not consider all the angles. I thought you loved me for my brain."

"It won't work…"

"Marjorie is the throne, Freddy, but I am the power behind the throne, and if you ever forget it, I will kill you and Marjorie and I'll elevate someone else in her place, even if it takes me another eight years."

Frederick Henderson didn't seem to move. As though the words didn't register.

"Or option two is I get rid of you and let someone else woo Marjorie. A lot of them are very successful men, Frederick, frankly more impressive and better looking than you are. I'm sure many of them would love the chance to be the Second and then the First Gentleman, if you don't want the honor."

Frederick Henderson stared.

"Think about all the time you've invested in this, Freddy, and what a tragedy it would be to throw all your hard work away. Now. You go on back to Albuquerque. Enjoy your last night not squarely in the limelight. I'll be in touch soon."

Without another word Freddy Henderson turned in the snow and walked away. Belias watched him. He dropped the snowball, almost reluctantly, and walked back to his car. Maybe when all this was settled, he'd be able to take Holly and her kids to Canada on a nice vacation. Peter and Emma would probably like a snowball fight, he thought.

He blinked up at the night. This Felix man and Sam Capra were out there somewhere, trying to ruin things. The women had to get to Rawlings first. And then wait for Felix and Capra to show up, and make sure they could never create trouble again.

The lie that Sam had killed Glenn was a good investment, he thought. It made Holly motivated. And Holly as a murderer would bind her tighter to him. It was all going to be okay. It always was.

PART SIX

MONDAY, NOVEMBER 8

74

Monday, November 8, morning

"W E COULD JUST KNOCK on the door," Holly said.

"If Wade Rawlings is connected to Lazard and Scott and he knows they're dead, then he'll be skittish," Janice said.

"But Belias will have told him to wait here for us."

"We can't know Rawlings's state of mind. I prefer to leave nothing to chance."

Of course you don't, Holly thought. *If you hadn't made that video, my husband would still be alive.* That thought had wriggled into her brain ever since Janice confessed to making the video; her sympathy for Janice because of Diana's death kept weakening, charring.

"He'll be more worried and freaked if we break into the house and surprise him," Holly pointed out.

"Fine," Janice said. "You knock on the door and tell him Belias sent you to help him. And I'll sneak around the back. That way we still have an advantage."

Holly frowned but said, "Fine."

She kicked the snow from her shoes and waited until Janice vanished from sight around the house.

Holly stepped onto the porch and knocked. In her coat jacket was one of the guns, the suppressor removed. Out here in the countryside it didn't matter much if the gun made noise.

She knocked again. No answer. She thought she could hear the quiet buzz of a television and she walked down to the bay window. It opened up onto a den, and in the room sat a man, his face turned away from her. SportsCenter was on ESPN and next to the table was a bottle of Jack Daniel's, half-empty, a glass next to it. His head sagged.

Scared and drunk, she thought. *Men.* She rapped slightly on the glass and the man's head moved upward but he didn't open the eye that she could see. He sat in a dark upholstered chair, dark suit jacket.

Holly went back to the front door and twisted. The knob was unlocked.

It made her uneasy because she never left the house unlocked. But maybe it was a country habit, no other house for a mile.

She pulled the gun from her jacket. She thought of the Russian woman, the shock on her face as Holly fired.

She stepped inside. She could hear the soft drone of the TV commentators and she waited and she listened and she didn't hear another noise.

She went back outside and found Janice.

"He's inside. Drunk and asleep and has SportsCenter on. The front door's open."

"Good," Janice said. "I've had enough drama."

They went back onto the porch and Janice followed Holly into the den. An odd smell, like a distasteful food, lingered in the air. Wade Rawlings looked like his picture, the side of him they could see, and it was only when they stepped close that Holly saw the heavy black masking tape binding Rawlings to the chair.

He seemed to become aware of them, and he turned toward them, the hidden half of his face seared and burnt horribly.

"Janice..." Holly turned toward the other woman, but she registered Felix standing there, a cloud of pepper spray hitting her face and then her world crisped into agony. She was dimly aware of a heavy weight hitting her hard in the stomach, fingers seizing her hair and dragging her along, Janice screaming, and then steps. Falling down steps.

Water. Cool, merciful water pouring over her eyes from a bottle. The agony began to subside, and she could see Janice, her eyes rimmed in red, pouring water over her face. Janice's lip and nose were bloodied.

"Holly, it's okay, you're okay," Janice croaked.

"Oh, it hurts, it hurts."

"I know. He left us water. Here." She pressed a fresh water bottle into Holly's hands and Holly upended it over her face. The sensation of needles in the eyes began to subside, and for a moment she just lay on the hard, cold concrete, shuddering in her breath.

Felix. He'd hit them with the spray and then beaten them with something heavy. Her face and her stomach ached. She groped in her jacket; her gun was gone.

Slowly she sat up. There was a twelve-pack of bottled water at the base of the stairs, and Janice was pouring another bottle over her own eyes in a trickle. The fronts of their coats and blouses were soaked and a shiver took Holly. She blinked her vision clear and began to glance around.

A basement. They lay at the bottom of the stairs, where Felix had apparently thrown them, and she saw the junk that accumulates in tucked-away spaces: an old typewriter, stacks of boxes, a table with a tottering tower of picture frames laying on their backs.

Unsteadily Holly got to her feet. She clambered up the stairs and tried the door. Locked. A dead bolt appeared to be freshly installed.

She went back down the stairs. There had to be a window. She saw two, both small and narrow and bricked over. She ran back to the middle of the basement as Janice got to her feet. There was a laundry chute but it was a clear drop. She tested the chute's bottom. It was plastic framing and fabric; it wouldn't hold her weight. Maybe they could climb on boxes.

Janice joined her. "Maybe," she said, but doubt in her voice.

"Or maybe there's something to use as a weapon. An old gun, a knife. He'll have to open the door to feed us."

"You're an optimist. Who says he's still here or we're getting fed?"

"He wanted us alive. He could have just shot us dead while we were down," Holly said, and as she realized it, a chill took her. Not for death. For separation from her kids. She had to get out of here for them.

A gentle knock on the door. "Ladies? Have you freshened up?" Felix.

Holly felt a bolt along her spine at the sound of his voice. *Felix knows I killed Diana. What if he says something to Janice?* She started glancing around for a weapon. Janice was a killer. Fear pricked her tongue with a taste of brass and blood.

"Ladies?" the voice called again.

"Felix?" Janice went up the steps and Holly hung back.

"Hi, Janice. How are you? Have you been taking care of yourself the past few days? Getting your medications?"

"Felix, I thought you were my friend."

"I am sure you did. I'm not. And I don't have cancer. I just pretended to so I could get close to you. So I could ask you to come have a drink with me after the support group meetings. Shame, really, because I liked you. When I didn't think about you being such a dirty rotten cheater."

"Cheater?" Janice asked.

"Like all of you. Gaming the system so only you can win. Destroying lives of innocent people so you get the promotion or the hot investment or the right woman. Cheaters." He said it like someone long ago might have said *lepers* or a cold warrior might have said *Communists*, Holly thought. "I got cheated once. You'll all pay the piper for your past crimes."

"Felix, let us out. You didn't really hurt us so I know you don't want to hurt me. We had so many nice talks…"

"You bore me," Felix said. "It was so boring listening to you talk at the support group and then at the bar. Having to listen to you talk about how worried you were about your spoiled rotten daughter, your business. Your all-consuming business. I know what you do. I saw the DOWNFALL file, Janice. Ruined lives. You must be so proud. But that's all right. I used you, too."

"Felix, please. We can reach an agreement…"

Janice started to speak and Holly touched her arm, shook her head.

"I mean, have you ever thought once about the lives your boss ruins so you can do better? Do you ever think about what it's like for them? To feel like they've played fair, they've been honest, they've been good, and then some freaking hand of fate reaches down—or rather up, from hell, where Belias belongs—and ruins everything?"

Janice and Holly looked at each other, and then Holly looked at the ground.

"You didn't keep that DOWNFALL file out of guilt for what you'd done, Janice. You left it so Diana would understand what would be required of her. So she could be just like you." He managed to spit out the last three words.

"And Holly? I heard what you told Sam. That you did this for your kids. So they could have a better life. What a load. You did this for no one but yourself and that jerk husband of yours. So you could have the nice big house and the finer things and never know want or need or hardship. Not through work, but through deception."

"No," Holly said. "I did it for my husband. I did it because he made the pact…"

"And you lacked the courage to leave him," Felix said. "You two are the sorriest excuses for mothers that I've ever seen."

"Shut up! Did you leave us alive just to give us a lecture?" Janice snapped.

"Yes, I mostly just wanted you to know I'd fooled you, Janice, because you always looked down on me just a bit. The exec, deigning to be friends with a bar manager. I know it warmed the cinder of whatever's left of your heart."

"Let us out," Janice said, "and say that to my face, tough man."

Holly began to shiver.

"It's more fun if you stay locked up. I want you to listen to me closely, Janice."

Oh no, Holly thought.

"Janice, Diana is dead."

"You're lying," Janice said after a moment.

"No. And two people killed her. You are one of them."

Janice made a noise; she hit her fist against the wall, a blow of rage.

"Do you want to know what's happened or not, Janice? Every mother should want to know."

"You're lying!"

"You made that video, and Diana found it and watched it. She had no way to contact you. She found the video, and she called your personal phone, and Belias heard the voice mails she left for you."

"No...No..." Janice collapsed against the stairs and Holly grabbed her shoulders, an instinctive response.

"Of course, being a good daughter, Diana didn't go to the police. She didn't want Mama getting in trouble and she wanted to confront you with it. But Belias knew she was a danger. So. He sent people after her. She came to the bar; she left you a note begging you to call her. She thought maybe you were still in town because she knew you weren't at that retreat, she called. She needed her mama so bad and you weren't there. You were busy planning the murders of another mother in Barbara Scott, and a dad in Lucky Lazard, and well, Wade Rawlings doesn't have kids but you get the idea."

Now Janice was keening, sobbing, the awful weight of it hitting her.

"So. You sent Diana to her death. I will tell you who killed her if you'll tell me where that video is. You must have a copy of it hidden. Where is it?"

"This is a trick!" Janice screamed.

"Is it?"

Janice shuddered.

"You made a video, but Belias couldn't find a trace of it on your home computer. Or on your phone or camera. Where was the copy that Diana found?"

After a moment, Janice said, "On a USB flash drive. A hidden one. It looks like a lipstick case. Who killed her?"

"Thanks, Janice. Huh, a lipstick case. That's a good one."

"Felix, okay, I told you. Let us out."

"No, you two are staying here and I guess we'll determine who the better parent is via trial by combat."

No, Holly thought.

"Holly. Holly killed your daughter."

Janice's wail choked off. Holly froze and in the dim light of the cold basement she could see a wisp of her own breath.

"Holly killed her. Broke her neck, I think, against the bar railing at The Select."

"He's lying," Holly said. "He's lying. He wants to turn us against each other."

"Belias sent the Marchbankses after her. Diana came back to the bar, hoping you were there, and they tried to ambush her and that was when Sam Capra got involved. Diana called me for help on Saturday and wanted to come back to the bar to see me, and since we were closed, I told her yes. I just wanted the video; I wouldn't have hurt her. She was innocent. Not like you. She came back to the bar but Holly was waiting for her. Holly Tasered me and locked me in a storeroom. And then she broke your daughter's neck."

Janice turned a teary, angry face toward Holly, who shook her head.

"Good luck, Holly. Janice is a trained killer. Good luck, Janice. Holly is younger and stronger and still has children to live for. Oh, and there are no guns or weapons in the basement. And Belias isn't here to make it all easier for you." He gave the door a farewell tap. They stared at each other in silence for ten seconds, the quiet shattered by the distant sound of a gun firing.

"He's lying," Holly tried, but she knew it was futile, too much specificity in his words. Janice shoved her and Holly thought, *She's got cancer, she's weak.*

But rage can be a fuel for the heart.

It was as though whatever life was left, whatever months remained for Janice Keene surged into her body all at once. She powered a fist hard into Holly's chest and Holly staggered back one step and then Janice clocked another punch into Holly's stomach. She fell backward down the steps.

"Don't! Please, Janice! Stop!" Holly screamed. She slammed into the concrete, started scrabbling backward. Janice roared down the stairs, rage contorting her face. She threw a fist at Holly; Holly blocked it, tried to shove Janice to the ground.

You can't reason with her, Holly thought. Then her mind went blank, into survival, and the two of them fought like women have fought for centuries to save their babies, to hide their children from the marauders and the rapists, to fight for the morsel of food that staves off starvation, to fight for a space on the boat during the wartime evacuation. Reason died.

Janice hammered a fist into Holly's jaw. Holly collapsed against the table stacked with framed, forgotten photos and she grabbed one of the pictures, an eight by ten. She swung the frame hard into Janice's throat. The older woman staggered back and Holly hit her again with the frame, hard in the chest. Janice screamed; she retreated, grabbed a heavy glass vase on a bench that was crowded with ugly, dusty decor. She shattered the top against the wall. Jagged glass remained.

"You killed my baby," Janice said. "You killed my baby."

"Please, he's lying." Holly didn't know what else to say. She wanted it to all be a lie.

Janice swung the vase at her and there was a hiss like the air tearing before the sharp, brutal shards. Holly ducked, punched Janice in the stomach. The edge of the vase caught her thin coat and ripped the sleeve. Holly shrugged out of the coat, and when Janice charged her again, she threw the trench coat over the jagged glass. Seizing the vase, she drew Janice close. Janice hooked fingernails toward Holly's pepper-spray savaged eyes.

Holly screamed as the fingernails scored. She slammed her forearm into Janice's throat and swung back with the picture frame, catching the edge of it along Janice's temple. Blood, skin, and hair tore away and Janice fell. But she clutched at Holly's leg and both women landed on the cold floor.

And then no more screams. Holly's fingers closed around Janice's throat; Janice's fingers closed around Holly's. And then there was just the hard, insistent breathing of two people fighting to the death.

Outside a car started, the music turned up loud as it drove away.

75

Monday, November 8, morning

WADE RAWLINGS," Benny said as we ate a quick breakfast. "Really one of those people that you wonder, how did he get to be a success?"

"Belias is the answer to that." It had taken a while to find out about the last name on the list. Wade Rawlings was a top political fixer, a paid consultant who guided campaigns. He had a sterling record of success except for one notable fail: He'd managed the re-election campaign of the senior senator from New Mexico, one of the most popular and powerful men in the Congress, but he'd managed to squander a twenty-point lead and the seat had instead been won by Marjorie Henderson. Who was about to become, according to every news channel, the new vice president.

It would not be hard for Wade Rawlings to be fed a lie that given the deaths of Barbara Scott and Lucky Lazard, he was in imminent danger. But Belias wouldn't want to move him to kill him. He might tell Rawlings to go to some place where Rawlings had easy access but wouldn't be known to someone hunting him. Benny had finally found, digging through public records, that Rawlings owned a lake house and his family still owned his grandmother's house, a good distance west of the city.

Those were our possibilities.

"The other possibility is he's here somewhere in Chicago. Or that Belias has had him leave the city entirely."

"I'll take the grandmother's house," I said. Because didn't Belias want this guy dead? That was the lonelier house, easier for murder. "You see if you can find him here in town."

Benny gave me a truck and I drove west. City and suburbia faded in time and I was out in the countryside. Fifteen minutes later I drove past the address, then turned around and parked a quarter mile away, keeping the truck hidden in a grove of trees.

I hurried through the scattering of snow.

The front door was unlocked.

I crept through the house. There was a man taped to a chair, half his face badly burned, griddled like it had hit a nonstick skillet. It was Wade Rawlings; I recognized him from the pictures Benny had found. He was dead, a bullet through the throat. I touched him; a hint of warmth touched the body, he had been dead for maybe an hour.

I saw a sheen of pepper spray on the furniture and the rug and noticed a trail of blood. I followed the blood to a door in the kitchen. Locked.

I listened. I could hear the soft quiet of someone moving around in the room.

I unbolted the door. Slowly I crept down the cellar stairs, thinking of every movie I'd seen as a kid where the hero or heroine went down the stairs, only to find horror and death.

I found both.

I saw Holly Marchbanks lying on the cellar floor, curled up in a fetal position. But she sat up as I came down the stairs. Dark bruises marred her throat; she had a rising black eye and an ugly gash along her palm.

In the other corner lay Janice Keene. Blood spreading from the back of her head, eyes half-lidded. Dead.

I swung the gun toward Holly.

"Where is he?"

"Who?" Her voice was a broken rasp.

"Belias."

"I don't know. Your friend Felix left us here. He killed Rawlings, and when we got here..."

"To kill Rawlings yourself."

She ignored my comment. "He was bound but not dead and Felix threw us down here."

"And…you killed Janice?"

Holly glanced at Janice's body, then looked away. "She tried to kill me."

"Why?"

"You know why."

"I don't," I said.

Holly said, "It doesn't matter now. Are…are you going to kill me?"

I suspected all the fight was out of her. She looked broken. I thought of her children and wondered, Will they see the change in her? That she's a killer now?

And then I wondered, Will Daniel see the same in me?

"Where did Felix go?" I asked.

"I think he's off to find Belias."

"Where?"

"I don't know. I really do not know." She watched the gun. "Two things. I'll tell you what I know if you will let me live, Sam."

"What?"

Her mouth worked. "You offered me safety once…you offered to hide me."

"Tell me what you know and we'll see. Do you know who shot Mila?"

She bit at her lip. "Your friend? Felix shot her. I saw it. I was following them…They went into a storage room. He came out a moment later and I hid down the hallway; he didn't see me. I didn't see her again."

"You followed Felix then?"

"I started to but someone found Mila and started screaming and it got crazy. I lost him in the crowd. I think he got on a service elevator."

That was how he'd arrived at the Lazard penthouse. All right. "You said you knew two things."

"The video Janice made for Diana. Explaining Belias's network. It's in a lipstick case Diana had. There's a flash drive inside. That was the only copy of the video Janice made, and I don't know if Diana made a copy but it for sure is in the lipstick case. You can stop Belias if you have it."

"Do you know where Diana is?"

A momentary flash of surprise crossed her face. "No. No, I don't."

"Did you have to kill Janice?"

Holly pointed at her throat. "She tried to kill me."

"Why?"

"Because she's dying and she's crazy and she's been killing people for Belias for years. Killing people—it ruins your mind." She looked at me. "Is your friend dead?"

"No. Not yet."

"I hope she will be okay."

"Now that you're in dire straits."

"If you're going to shoot me do it," she said. "Just…I'm tired. I'm so tired."

I put the gun down but I kept the distance between us. I remembered too well how she fought in the splendor of her own grand house. "Where will Belias be?"

"You offered me safety once before," she said quietly.

"That offer expired. I don't trust you, Holly."

"I'm too much like you," she said.

"You're nothing like me."

"What we wouldn't do for our kids. Belias knows you broke the law to save yours."

"Where is he?"

"He would have texted us where to meet him after Janice killed Rawlings. But Felix took our phones."

I turned and went back up the stairs.

"Sam. Please. Don't leave me here." Her voice rose in horror.

"I said I'd let you live. I didn't say I'd let you out."

"Don't…"

"I'm actually curious to see how you deal with a real problem, without Belias to remove all the obstacles. You're smart, Holly, you should be able to get out of a basement."

I slammed the door closed, cutting off her words. Let her be scared to death. I'd tell Benny to let her out in a day. If I found and dealt with Belias, I'd let her out myself.

Felix shot Mila. The betrayal was complete. *Yes, Jimmy, I will kill Felix for you.*

I searched the house. I found a cell phone, tucked next to the cushion of the chair where he sat.

There was a text message, the last one sent:

WR IS DONE. FELIX WAS HERE. WE HANDLED HIM.

Felix had phoned in Wade's death using one of the women's phones and faked his own.

Then a reply:

COME TO THE NEST.

The Nest. I remembered the term from when Belias and Roger captured me and Diana at her friend's place in the Marina District and offered us a deal. I recalled his words: *You both join Team Belias, so to speak. You're going to be taken away to a house of mine I call the Nest. Far from here, private. Where we can discuss your futures, your usefulness, and I can start changing your lives for you.*

"Holly," I called through the door, "where's the Nest?"

She came close to the door, I could hear the scrape of her feet. "Why should I tell you?"

"Because I'll let you out."

She weighed my words, then decided to answer me. Hope is a lovely thing. "It's a bolt-hole of sorts. We're supposed to go there. If the network melts. He's arranged for us to be able to get out of the country."

"Where is it?"

She told me a rural route number and a town northwest of Chicago. Made sense, the center of the country, not far from a big airport where you could fly anywhere in the world.

"Did Felix ask you where it was?"

"No."

But Wade Rawlings might have told him. He might have tortured the location out of him before he killed him.

Felix and Belias had a head start on me. I wanted them both. But I didn't know where Belias was coming from, I didn't know if Felix would simply be laying in wait.

I hoped he'd be alone. I prefer to face one man who wants me dead instead of two.

Holly was still calling my name through the door when I left the house.

76

Monday, November 8, afternoon

Belias loved the Nest.

He'd gotten the idea from his favorite Hitchcock movie, *North by Northwest*. He knew he was supposed to root for the hapless adman hero, Cary Grant, but the supposed bad guy, James Mason, was just so much more interesting. Suave, smart. And he had a private chalet and a private little airstrip right by Mount Rushmore. Belias loved that. He wanted such a rural yet well-designed escape.

So he'd found and had a network member acquire for him via a front company an abandoned airstrip north of Chicago, not far from Lake Michigan. He'd had a comfortable house built there. He called it the Nest because he told every member that if the network melted, if it fell apart, they could run to the Nest and he'd prepared escape routes for them and their families.

Of course it was a lie. If the network fell apart, he would abandon them and he would tell the authorities where to find them all, waiting there at the Nest. He was their master, not their keeper, and if he had to go, then he was gone. They were on their own.

His plane from New Mexico landed. The pilot got out, said he'd refuel, do a postflight checklist and then asked when they'd want to head out. "Probably a couple of hours," Belias said.

A car was parked close to the house, and he recognized it as the one he'd left for Janice and Holly in Chicago. They'd arrived. He clicked on his smartphone.

A message from the anonymous benefactor who'd sent him Sam's CIA file appeared on the screen: DO YOU HAVE SAM YET?

NO, he wrote. BUT SOON. I'M GOING TO SET A TRAP FOR HIM.

And he would. Rawlings was dead now, and Sam, if he had sense, might be able to sniff out a trail that led here. Let him if he dared show his face. Here he would die.

The plane could take Holly home to San Francisco, back to her children. Janice could come home and reason with Diana. And he could focus on finding Sam and his friend Felix, and silencing them.

He went inside the house. The lights were off except in the kitchen and he walked into the room, drawn by the slight smell of coffee. He knew that Holly loved her coffee, she must've made a pot…He flicked on the lights, blinking.

"Hello," the man in the kitchen said. "My name is Felix Neare and we are going to have a talk." And then he shot Belias.

77

Monday, November 8, afternoon

I DROVE TO THE ADDRESS of the Nest. It was the middle of nowhere, and I had phoned Benny to say where I was heading but he was a good hour behind me. I wasn't sure how much use Benny would be in a fight. He looked very quiet and soft. Of course, sometimes those are the deadliest people.

He had brought bad news: Mila's condition had worsened.

I wanted Felix Neare's throat in my grip.

I parked on a country road about a mile away. The woods were sparse here, but I moved quickly and quietly through them. The sky spit early snow at me, a brief brisk flurry that thinned. I wished for a blizzard for cover. The snowfall here had been sparse.

And then I saw the plane. I heard it first, a low approaching buzz, and I ducked close to a tree. The snow hadn't been much here or I think the plane could not have landed, the strip would have had to be cleared. I stayed very still and wondered if I'd been spotted.

The plane landed, drove to a smooth stop. I saw Belias get out, speak to the pilot, then walk toward the house. I snuck up carefully on the pilot. Maybe he was just a paid flight jockey, maybe he was a network member. He was inspecting the engine of the plane, going through a postflight checklist to kill time, and he didn't hear me until I was ten feet behind him. He startled, surprised, but I hit him hard in the throat and slammed his head against the fuselage. Three times. In the movies they make it look easy. It is not that easy or that quiet to render someone unconscious. I eased him down to the cold ground. He was armed, a gun under his coat. So not a flight jockey, probably a network member who had a pilot's license, doing his master a favor. It would be hard for him to fly with a concussion.

I moved toward the house.

And then I heard a gunshot and a scream.

I ran up to the house. Curtains and screens insulated the interior from view but I could hear the roaring coming through the other side. They were killing each other, I guessed, but right now I needed them both alive.

I threw a porch chair through the window. The curtains fell back enough for me to see Belias on the floor, a bloodied shoulder wound, and Felix standing above him, the gun pointed at Belias, starting to turn toward me.

I jumped through the window and fired. The bullet caught Felix in his gun hand, a bright red awful blossom between two fingers. He screamed. Belias scrambled across the floor. He must have weapons he had stashed here. But Felix was the greater danger. I was blind with hatred and rage. I lost my cool. If this had been a CIA operation, I would not have allowed myself. But this was me, who'd only tried to help a poor young woman who begged, *Help me,* in the dark of my bar, scared out of her wits, and tried to make my world safe for my son, and now it was a whole chain of deaths and maybe Mila dead and my so-called friend Felix had shot her and betrayed me.

Felix could see it in my eyes. I would kill him with my bare hands.

He knew it was life or death. He'd swallowed the agony with adrenaline and switched the gun to his nonfiring hand, and if you're not used to it, the gun is practically useless. He tried to fire at me again and I kicked the gun. The weapon went flying across the kitchen and he tackled me. We staggered through the shattered window, separating as we hit the ground.

I levered the gun up to shoot, fired twice, but Felix yanked my aim away from him. He screamed like a kid who'd been cheated on the playground, hammered blows to my groin, my throat. He knew what he was doing. Mila and Jimmy had trained him. If I underestimated him, I was dead.

He tried to pin my arm and so I did a flip jump to untwist his grip. I got free but I landed on my back and he kicked me savagely in the ribs. Something broke and pain bolted up my body. He did it again and I tried to writhe away. The patio had ornamental bricks in the bare, snow-lapped flower beds.

Felix grabbed a brick and lifted it up high, his bloodied hand seizing my throat. He was ignoring the agony. He was going to bash my head into a jelly.

Belias shot him in the other hand. He keeled over, howling, both hands punctured, the hot fresh agony countering the rush from the first shot and his need, apparently, to kill me and Belias both.

"No, no," Felix bleated. "Sam, help me."

"No," I said.

"I hate a betrayal," Belias said, leveling his gun at both of us with his good arm. Blood puckered his shoulder, dotted his blanched-looking fingers. "Felix. Where is Diana's video?"

I kept my mouth shut.

"We never found it. And she's dead, so she can't tell you." His words were a broken bray in his pain, but he spit them with defiance.

"She's *what*?"

"Dead. Holly killed her in the bar. When you were recruiting Sam to switch sides." Spittle flew from his lips.

Belias kept the gun on me; there was really no need to keep it on Felix, with his ruined hands.

"Sam? True?"

"I didn't know Diana was dead. I didn't have contact with him after... Vegas." I stared at Felix. "You shot Mila."

"I didn't shoot her... I wouldn't... No."

"You shot her and you left me to die," I said.

Felix shook his head. "I let you live. I was supposed..."

"Supposed to what?" I asked; then I thought I knew.

Belias stared down at him. "Who are you?"

"The nobody who's bringing you down," Felix said, courage in his voice. "Truly and finally down."

"Truly and finally?" Belias shot him. The shot was loud and clear in the quiet. It caught Felix between the eyes and he snapped back to the ground.

I looked up at Belias. His shoulder was bloodied but he seemed in control of himself. I had busted ribs and so we might still be evenly matched.

But he had a gun and mine was on the ground, a few feet distant. About the depth of a grave.

"Kevin," I said.

"Only you get to call me that now," he said. "Sam, what a shame this is. I told you I wanted a partner. I wanted you, Sam. We could have been brilliant together."

"It wouldn't have worked," I said.

"Did you see that he set up video equipment in there? I guess Janice's digital confession gave him the idea. He told me I was going to name all my network on tape. What an odd revenge. You'd think he'd just kill me."

"I have Diana's video. The one Janice made for her. Holly told me where it is."

"Holly?" I could hear a shift in his voice toward panic. "Where is she? Did you hurt her?"

"She's alive. Stashed away. You want her back?"

His tongue worked inside his cheek. "Maybe you and I can work out another deal."

Like we could trust each other. "Doubtful. I have two things you want, and you have nothing I want."

"Wrong. Remember, it wasn't the CIA who got me your file. It was someone who wanted me to recruit you and then hand you over to them." He raised a palm toward me in surrender. "You have a very dangerous enemy. Wouldn't you like to know who it is? We could draw them out together."

The story took shape in my brain. Small bits that had made no sense before. But instead I said, "I have no reason to trust or believe you."

"But I just saved your brains from being gushed all over my patio." He smiled at me. "I mean, that counts for something. Why would you want to bring me down? My people and I, we didn't hurt your friend Mila. Felix did. You know I can give you what you want, Sam. You want power, you want money, you want to make everyone who ever hurt you pay? You know I can do it. Knowing that—it has to count for something."

"Yes, I know you can." I made my voice reassuring. Like it was a vote of confidence. Because he had. He had made his scheme work. He could do the same for me.

"Well?"

I threw the dirt from the flower bed in his face. Simplest trick in the book. He was leaning toward me and the dirt impacted his eyeball. He gasped and I scrambled to my feet, pain stitching my side, grabbed at him, catching the I Ching ring he wore, and yanked him off-balance as he fired the bullet between my feet. I grabbed and slammed the brick Felix was going to brain me with into his knees as he staggered back.

"I don't want it. I don't want anything to do with you." I yanked the gun.

He jumped back through the shattered window, stumbling into the kitchen proper, and I saw him grab a knife from the rack.

But I had the gun now and I steadied my aim.

He opened a door, it blocked my view. I thought, *He can't hide in a pantry*. But I heard a ripping noise and then he ducked out, holding a length of cable.

I could smell the sudden, rich odor of natural gas, the deadly hiss of a heater emptying into the air.

I hate smart people.

He turned and he ran.

I cut through the house, knocking over the sad little camera and tripod.

I could smell the gas flooding into the house.

I charged around the corner and Belias slashed at me. My forearm opened through the jacket and the shirt.

I couldn't risk the shot.

But Belias was used to people who gave up. He was used to those who wanted life easy.

He was not used to me.

Belias swung the knife back at me as the blood spurted from my arm, and I blocked it and powered his arm against the wall. He didn't drop the knife. The smell of gas was growing, fast, and panic flashed in his eyes. He hadn't thought about the broken window near the leak, that would buy us a bit more time, but he wanted out. He was still stuck in his trap for me.

But then he got lucky. The devil is always lucky.

Or I got bad. He slashed the knife across where Felix had hurt my ribs and the pain was blinding. I felt fresh blood spurt along my side.

"Where's the video?" he yelled.

"Where you will never get it. You kill me, I don't check in, it'll be on YouTube in a matter of hours."

How do you scare the devil? You drag his evil into sunlight. I didn't even know what was on the video but the thought of it was enough to scare him. "Sam, call your people, tell them I trade you for the video."

"They won't." I was bleeding. Badly. I fell to one knee.

He kicked me in the shoulder, and I sprawled on the floor, clutching the gun, scared to fire as the gas filled the house.

Even with me hurt he was done with risk, it was time to run. He hurried out the front door.

I thought he must be searching for my car. But no. Through the window I could see him running toward the plane.

He knelt by the unconscious pilot, kicked him out of the way.

Mila. I thought of Mila.

I managed to get to my feet, every breath an agony, bleeding badly. I stumbled out of the house, the gas smell rich as awful and unwelcome perfume, running toward the runway. Then onto the runway.

Belias started the plane, began to taxi down the little strip. Toward me, the only way to go.

I stopped, steadied, and fired. You have to play hurt. You have to take the obstacles as they come. Belias and his people never got that.

I emptied the gun into the plane and the range was barely there and I'd missed.

It was a small plane. A small target. He rose into the ashen sky and then circled back toward me and I thought, *Get to your truck*, and I tried to run but I staggered and I fell, looking toward the clear slate-gray sky.

Smoke.

The first little black finger of it curled out from the plane, and I heard a noise that didn't sound right and he was swinging back, trying to bring the plane back and land and probably run right over me as I bled out on the ground. But then it dipped and rolled, and I thought, through the clear air and the broken window of the plane, I heard him scream.

I didn't see it but he must have smashed into the gas-filled house because then the world exploded, hot and bright even behind my shut eyes, and I crawled toward the woods as the dry winter grass began to burn, began to burn faster than I could crawl and I heard Mila saying, *Samuil, you stupid, get up, get up for me and Daniel*, and I staggered across the ice-cold creek and fell down by my car, trying to remember Benny's phone number.

I think I called Mila's number instead because the last thing I heard other than the rising hiss of the fire on the other side of the creek was Jimmy's perfect voice, demanding to know what I wanted.

PART SEVEN

LAST DAYS

78

Chicago, New Orleans, San Francisco, Taos

BENNY, AFTER GETTING ME TO A DOCTOR who worked for the Round Table and could keep his mouth shut, went to go release Holly Marchbanks from her prison basement. He came back and told me the cellar door had been broken. The bodies of Janice Keene and Wade Rawlings were still there. I told him to leave the bodies where he found them.

I wondered how quickly Holly would run. Fast, it seemed. Within twelve hours she dropped out of sight, her kids vanished, and the San Francisco police began to make very unpleasant noises about the missing Glenn Marchbanks. They were already making noises about the unidentified body with the broken neck left in a park. Soon enough they would know it was Diana, and they'd be looking for Janice.

Shortly after Glenn's picture appeared in the papers, a witness at The Select reported that the missing man matched the description of one of the assailants in the bar. They found Glenn's DNA on the plank Diana used against him.

So Glenn and Diana were tied together. You can imagine what people thought—the beautiful, young woman and the powerful, wealthy older man. Audrey Marchbanks began to make a lot of noise about a conspiracy against her husband and then went silent. Maybe her family realized they had much of Glenn's money, and it was justice of a sort.

* * *

Benny got me home to New Orleans. Jimmy told me to stay the hell away from Las Vegas. I might be recognized by the police. They were treating Lazard's murder as a revenge killing for bad investments, calling it almost a savage gangland-type slaying, and looking for a man who looked like me. I might have to sell the Vegas bar, buy a new bar in a new city, give Gigi a job elsewhere.

Mila held on by a thread. Jimmy moved her to a private hospital and told me it was none of my business where.

"Felix is dead," I said. "Like you asked."

"Thank you," Jimmy said. "But it won't fix her."

Leonie and Daniel came home then, and they were good medicine. I lay in bed, recuperating, Daniel curled next to me. Leonie wouldn't let him sleep there for fear I would roll over on him and I didn't argue with her. I'd put her through enough, and him.

"A week in LA. It was sort of a vacation," she said. And Leonie fed me good food and brought me my favorites from the restaurants of the city, but the food had no taste, and only Daniel could make me smile for those first few weeks.

I rested and I got better, and I thought about what had happened and Felix's unexplained betrayal.

I went to San Francisco as soon as my strength was back.

Benny and I stepped into The Select. Still closed, still shuttered. This bar was done, under this name. I felt bad for the employees. Maybe San Francisco had gone bad for me as well.

All because of this.

The lipstick case.

Diana had hit Glenn Marchbanks in the face with her purse; it was a detail I had forgotten while fighting Rostov. And when Felix and I cleaned up after the fight...I went to the lost and found box.

A silver lipstick case. I hadn't opened it. I'm a guy. It was lipstick.

I opened it and there was the USB drive. I took it upstairs to the office and powered up Felix's laptop. For the first few minutes, I looked for answers to Felix's betrayal in the computer's data. But everything was gone. Everything was pristine, like the laptop had just come out of the box. He must've scrubbed this machine before he and Mila followed me to Vegas.

Then I slid the lipstick drive into the port on my laptop and I watched Janice Keene begin to speak, signing the death warrant for Glenn, Belias, Felix, Diana, and maybe even Mila. I watched the video twice. Twenty minutes. She laid out the whole network, crimes she herself had committed, prominent people she suspected of being involved, how Belias's exchange of favors worked, a plea for her daughter to accept this world for her own good. It would have been just enough to break them.

And I thought about what had been said at the Nest, Felix saying, *I let you live*, and then, *I was supposed...*, and then the lie I thought he'd told me. The enemy Belias told me we shared.

Then I picked up the phone.

I had some people to see.

"You're not Belias." The Second Gentleman, Frederick Henderson, stood on the trail not far from Taos, where he'd met Belias before. It had been an ordeal to get the Secret Service detachment away from him; he finally told them he had to speak in private to an old girl-friend who wanted to embarrass the Henderson family, and they were in fact waiting for him a mile back on the trail.

"I represent Belias," the young man said. He was tall, lean, dirty blond hair, blue eyes. He was well dressed in wool slacks, good shoes, and an expensive-looking navy jacket, a dark scarf. *Like the desperate up-and-comers crowding Washington*, Freddy Henderson thought. But he moved stiffly, as though recovering from injury.

"Well, what is it?"

"It's done. Belias is done. Actually, he's dead."

The Second Gentleman stared at him.

"So, if you had any thoughts that he'd help you get rid of the president so your wife could step up, abandon those. She'll be re-signing. A tragically short tenure."

Henderson began to sputter. "She will do no such thing. Are you insane?"

"According to some. I have his phone records, which showed a GPS record that he met you here, on your own property. The fact I know where to meet you, like he did, ought to give you serious pause."

Henderson wiped a trembling hand across his mouth.

The young man continued, "She resigns. Or she gets named. We have all of Belias's network. All of them. Every name. Two I've confronted committed suicide within hours." The young man's words hung in the cold air. "She resigns or she gets named along with the rest."

"But...it's not fair."

"That's what you were so afraid of. Life not being fair. You have a week."

"What if I can't convince her?"

"Then I guess you'll see what happens."

The well-dressed young man turned and walked slowly off into the forest.

79

Seattle

I HATE HOSPITALS.

Jimmy and the Round Table had flown Mila to a private clinic in Seattle. Jimmy called me and told me that Mila had asked for me, so he relented on letting me see her. I gave my name at the front desk and waited and waited and then I waited some more. I looked out the window at Mount Rainier, shrouded in gray. I read four magazines and I tried not to jump out of my skin. Then a tall woman in a suit, very lovely and cold, came into the waiting room—it was more like a library at a spa; there were no other families waiting alongside me—and asked me to follow her.

We went down a sleek hallway and then to another, where computers beeped and hummed with high-definition screens colorfully laying out the etches of life, heartbeats and brain activity and what have you.

I thought of my ex, Lucy, in her CIA hospital, mired in wires, and I thought, *Does everyone I care about have to suffer?* Daniel, kept from me for those first few months of his life. I always worried it would mar him in some way, keep him from loving me.

And now Mila. I'd followed the nurse to a room and she stepped aside and I saw Mila lying there. Tubes and wires, like Lucy in her forever bed. I felt sick. Her eyes were half-lidded in sleep. There had been multiple surgeries. A complication. A slow recovery.

The well-dressed woman stepped away as I stepped inside. I

JEFF ABBOTT

could only stare at Mila. She was alive. She was breathing. But the bullet had nearly ended her. And there would be a long road ahead of her and would she ever be the same?

She turned her head slightly toward me and I saw her smile. The ghost of a smile. "Sam," she croaked.

"Yes. I'm here. I'm sorry. And sorry it took me so long to come here." Never mind that I'd been forbidden until today.

"Is...Is..."

"Belias is dead. It's done." Jimmy had no doubt told her all this but I wanted her to hear it from me. "His network is dismantled. And you're going to be okay."

"My heart's made of Moldovan steel," Mila said. "I will be all right. It will just take a while." She lifted a hand, weakly gestured at the tubing as if annoyed with it. Her voice was thick with painkillers.

"How is Daniel?"

"He is fine. He'll be ready for you to play with him your next visit."

"I hope this clinic has good gift shop. I will bring him best toy." She closed her eyes. "Sam. What about the woman who shot me..."

"Woman? Not Felix?"

"No. Holly Marchbanks shot me." She opened her eyes.

Holly had told me one lie too many now.

"You need not worry," I said. "Just concentrate on getting better."

"Better...I think I will go back to sleep now, *Samuil.*" The Slavic form of my name. She only used it when she was upset or worried.

"Sleep, then," I said, and as she closed her eyes, I became aware of the gun pressed into the back of my neck.

"Sam Capra. At long last." The voice was quiet, steely, English, upper-class.

"You'll make a mess if you shoot me in here," I said. "Jimmy."

"You don't get to call me that. We're not friends. And as far as a mess goes, the nurses are competent. I'll tell them to tidy up while you bleed out your last."

"I told you I didn't know she was hurt. I didn't even know she was in Las Vegas."

"Then you didn't try."

I didn't have an answer. The gun left the back of my head and I felt breath return to my lungs. The man stepped around to face me. He was a bit taller than me, black haired and blue eyed, casually handsome, dressed impeccably in a cashmere sweater and dark slacks. He must have been spending nights in the fold-out at the foot of her bed; blankets lay stacked next to it. "So what do I call you, Jimmy?"

"Mr. Court will do."

Mister… My throat closed. "Court is one of Mila's aliases." DeSoto had said to me, *Give my regards to Mrs. Court.*

"Not an alias. It's her married name."

And this was… "Now that you've seen my wife, spoken to her, assured yourself that she will recover despite your abandonment, you may go."

I didn't move. Mrs. Court. She really was…

I found my voice. "She told me about you. Not that you were married. But that you recruited her into the Round Table. You found her, you trained her…"

"And I trained her not to leave anyone behind." Jimmy Court's mouth curled in disdain. "It's only because the Table wants you alive that you're alive. I could kill you and tell her that you vanished. She'd think talking to you now was a dream, morphine-induced mental blather. But she would believe me."

"Then do it if you must."

"The Round Table wants you alive. They want you running the bars. Didn't you ever wonder why she needed someone like you, Sam, to run the bars? She didn't want to travel the world all the time. She wanted to be with me."

"So… who do I report to?"

"Me for now. And my first order to you is to go. Just go. But not to New York and not to London. Not where *she* likes to go, not where I'll take her to heal. Go home to your child in New Orleans if you like. But just go."

I could take my marching orders. Turn around and leave. But I didn't.

"I know what you did."

Jimmy cocked his head, a slight smile.

"You. Felix. You knew about Belias's network before Diana Keene ever ran into The Select and asked me for help."

"I hardly see how."

"Dalton Monroe. Janice didn't use Felix to get close enough to poison him. Felix used Janice. Brought her to the event, but *he* poisoned Monroe. Not her. And he put Monroe's name in the DOWNFALL file."

"Belias easily could have targeted Dalton. Janice had a file on him at her home…"

"That Felix planted when he and I were there. That was the clincher for me that we had to go after Belias, with me leading the charge. And he planted that article from that first file we found in her house into the one I took from her office; he would have had time when we were heading over to find Diana. But Dalton was the only name in that file that wasn't dead or ruined, it didn't make sense. What the faked poisoning, and then Felix improvising and sneaking that article into the DOWNFALL file was supposed to do was to make it look like a Round Table member was under attack. So we could respond to a threat quietly without you telling the rest of the Round Table. You and Felix had been working this, but Mila didn't know about it. There's only one reason for that."

Jimmy glanced at Mila, as if to confirm she was asleep. "I didn't know you'd suffered an injury to common sense. Why would I do such a thing?"

"Maybe Vasili Borodin was a member of the Round Table—I'm pretty sure a Russian billionaire would have been an attractive target—and you'd been looking for Belias and Roger for the past several years. The Round Table worries about and deals with the threats that no one else quite sees yet. And the Table's backed by very wealthy people. If any organization was in place to notice the patterns of success and downfall created by Belias, it's us."

Jimmy's expression gave away nothing. "Theoretically, I suppose that could happen."

"And when you found Belias and Roger, found one of their people in Janice Keene, well, look what they'd done. Duplicated the advantages Belias had given Borodin many times over. A new network with great wealth and influence—and you wanted to take them over. But here's the kicker, no one else in the Round Table would know. You never told Mila."

"These are baseless charges, Sam, and I think reflective of my problem with you being a person who leaps before he looks."

I wanted to reach across her bed and snap his neck. "You weren't going to share Belias's network with the Round Table. Mila or they would have had you shut it down. You were going to run it. Just like Belias. What did you promise Felix if he helped you?"

He said nothing.

"Janice had cancer, Felix knew how to get close to her. You even moved him to San Francisco—he had only been there a few months. He was your way to charm past a weak point in Belias's network."

"Sadly, reason is on my side. Felix betrayed us all. He attacked Mila."

"He was supposed to kill me in Vegas, along with everyone else, but he balked. He even told me to call my old bosses and beg for help. He was trying to get me out of the way without killing me or me ending up in jail. But it would have been *your* order to kill me."

"One of the many reasons I find you unappealing, Sam, is that you think the worst of people. Felix loved Janice; he was trying to free her from that network."

"Maybe Felix didn't realize you had no intention of turning over Belias's network or dismantling it." I crossed my arms. "The Round Table saves people from lifetimes in prison and gives them meaningful work. Like me. And sometimes the gratitude can be overwhelming. In Felix's case, blinding. You took advantage of his loyalty, his belief he was doing right. Every manager has been wronged, it wouldn't be hard to aim someone like Felix at a group of people who routinely wrong others in unfair ways."

We stood on either side of Mila's bed, her sleeping.

"I wish you would apply this imagination of yours to running the bars at a higher profit," he said.

"I know you did it. You tried to keep Mila away from San Francisco. And I bet if I ask her, she'll say Felix tried to keep her from going to Vegas with him. Felix never would have hurt Mila, except the only way to keep her out of that penthouse was to knock her out of the fight. A fight you didn't want her in. If Mila's in this hospital bed, it's your fault, not mine."

"If any of this fable of yours was true, then I could have threatened your child to corral you. I didn't."

"Because Mila would have never forgiven you if harm came to Daniel. You took responsibility for keeping my son hidden and safe. If you failed, you'd risk losing Mila. Or maybe even you draw the line at murdering an infant."

Jimmy's handsome face didn't lose its composure. "If you care to accuse me in front of my wife, Sam, I hope you have hard evidence."

"Felix sure did track down Belias's start as Borodin's private hacker years ago very quickly. I thought Felix was brilliant. But his speed of discovery was because he and you already knew that history. Long before Diana Keene asked me for help in the bar, you'd already done that research. But you're a careful guy, Jimmy, and Felix's computer at The Select has been wiped clean, the data destroyed and overwritten. Now, why would anyone bother to do that, given everything that's happened?"

"Felix would have done it before leaving for Vegas, obviously. Your imagination, when it takes flight, it's supersonic."

"Mila even recognized the I Ching symbol for the network, because she'd seen it with you in London. Coincidence? Or maybe you'd realized that symbol was a visual password for them and took her along when you wanted to find out what it meant."

I had him, but I couldn't prove it. And he knew it. I shrugged.

"Here's the funny thing. If Diana had come in when Felix was downstairs and I was up, this might have ended all differently. But it didn't. Twist of fate."

"Life is full of such twists." Jimmy glanced down at the sleeping Mila, and for the first time I saw tenderness in his gaze.

"But I'd like to know why I was your cannon fodder. Felix was the one who played on my fears of getting involved, claiming I had to do this to protect my son. But I wasn't supposed to survive for long, even if I won, was I? You needed someone to do the dangerous work and then be lost in the line of duty. But after Mila was shot, Felix kept on his mission you'd sent him on. You tried to send me home, but when you saw I wasn't giving up you switched gears and told me to kill Felix for you. If he'd killed me, you'd have Belias's people under your thumb. If I killed him—well, then you figured your secret was safe, because a dead Felix couldn't rat on you."

Ten ticks of the quiet clock above Mila's bed. His gaze was steel. "My wife enjoys your company a bit too much," he said simply. "I don't like you."

Jealousy. The same poison that had been the black seed to grow Belias's network. In this case, unfounded. "You'll have to explain to her why you kicked me out of the Round Table."

"I'm doing no such thing. You still own the bars. You still have a job. That's what Mila and the Round Table want." He smiled. "It's a very dangerous job."

"And now so is yours," I said, and his smile shifted ever so slightly.

I looked at Mila a final time, and then I left, out into the gray day.

80

The Bahamas

IT DIDN'T WORK." A man, tall, muscled, with darkish blond hair and eyeglasses, stood at a window and watched the surf slide in over the flat of an empty beach.

"As hostile takeovers go," said the woman standing next to him, "I suppose we could have been more hostile. Gone in with guns blazing. I'm not sure that would have worked."

"Encouraging Glenn Marchbanks to take over didn't work, either," the man in glasses said. "But that network would have been a nice acquisition for us."

"Very hard to maintain without its creator. Successful people are so much more demanding than those that are hungry. I still don't think this Belias would have ever worked for us. We gave him that CIA file and he didn't know what to do with it."

"Belias was at heart a hacker, not a leader. He kept that network together through fear and guilt, not inspiration. And they were showing their hand to anyone who looked. I don't think we were the only group aware of Belias's little collection of modern-day Fausts. I think there was another interested party sniffing around them."

"We could try to duplicate Belias's approach."

"We could." The man in glasses sighed. "But it's an investment of many years to own so many successful people."

"And to own Sam Capra."

The man in glasses watched the sea.

"Because you didn't want him dead. You wanted to own him."

The man in glasses watched the sky.

"If you'll excuse me, you seem slightly obsessed with him, and I'm afraid his charms are lost on me. A CIA agent who was only there for three years and let go. They only toss out the bad apples, you know that. And perhaps if you'd just ordered him killed straightaway, he wouldn't have ruined our takeover attempt." The woman didn't bother to hide the disappointment in her voice. "We'd own the vice president now if it wasn't for your sentimentality. And, darling, you are not normally sentimental."

The man in glasses watched the beach.

"What makes Sam Capra so special?" the woman finally said.

"Someday I'll tell you," the man in glasses said, and he turned to look out at the surf.

The woman leaned against him and rubbed his arm in the cool of the night breeze. Every few seconds her moving hand covered the small tattoo below his elbow, a nine with a sunburst in its center.

81

Goa, India

THE KIDS FINALLY ANSWERED to their new names. They liked Goa; it was full of Europeans and a few Americans—hippies, students, people wanting a break from the incessant rat race of the West. There were more children than you would think and the beaches were beautiful, and for the first time in a long while, Holly felt like she wasn't trapped, chirping in a golden cage. She read good books from the library (there were plenty in English), she went for long walks along the ocean as the surf called its gentle song, she listened to the polite gossip of her landlady who enjoyed practicing her English and was trying to minimize her accent.

Her name was Rosie now, Peter was Paul, Emma was Ellie. Their last name was Grayson. She had managed to get out a lot of her money, transferring it to a Caymans bank, then on to a Swiss numbered account that steadily fed a small, discreet account in Goa. Enough to stay for a while. And then, in six months, they would go to Thailand, with new Canadian passports she would arrange, and then maybe New Zealand once they had a history established. She might get a job as a teacher. Something where she could do good.

She walked back into the cottage from the beach, the sky blue as an eye, the wind a kiss off the sea, and when she came into her dining room, Sam Capra sat at the table.

He held a gun in his hand.

She froze. She knew her new life might collapse but she thought it would be the police. She had seen that weeks ago Marjorie Henderson had resigned the vice presidency, and there had been news in the English-language papers about a spate of top business leaders resigning under sudden and surprising clouds.

"Hello, Holly," he said. "This house is much smaller than the one in Tiburon."

"Yet I like it much better." She wet her lips. "Come uninvited into my house twice and it's a habit."

"You have this habit of being a liar."

She set her bags down on the small tile counter.

"You shot Mila. Not Felix."

"Yes."

Sam raised the gun toward her.

"Are you going to kill me in front of my kids?"

"Your kids aren't here."

"They'll be home in a few minutes. The school lets them come home for lunch."

Sam looked at her like he was trying to decide whether or not to leave her body for the kids to find. She braced herself against the counter.

"I was surprised there are no weapons in the house, Holly. I checked."

"No. I'm done with that."

"If I let you go, I let a murderer go."

Her voice was calm. "I didn't mean to kill Diana. It was an accident. And Janice was self-defense."

"But I'm not here for Diana or Janice."

Holly nodded. "I panicked. You'd lied to us that Mila was dead. You'd gone to the trouble to fake it. I was sure she was springing a trap." Holly hesitated. "Did she die?"

"No. I don't think I'll ever get to see her again. All the time Belias asked me what I wanted…" Sam steadied his voice. "And it turns out you took from me the one thing I wanted, other than my son."

"Do what you must." She held his gaze steady.

Sam Capra's expression didn't change. Slowly he lowered the gun. "Your kids are innocent, the way Diana was. I'm not going to make things harder for your children. But if you ever breathe a word about me to anyone, if you ever come near me or Mila again, I'll kill you."

"I won't."

"I won't come looking for you again, in that case."

Sam Capra was giving her life. She tried not to tremble. "I won't. I promise."

"I can't make that promise for Mila's…family. They will not be so forgiving. They won't hurt your kids. But they might kill you."

Holly paled.

"You'll spend your life looking over your shoulder, Holly. But maybe that is the price you're supposed to pay. That's your downfall." Sam Capra got up and walked out into the bright sunshine on the beach, the sky blue above him.

And Holly thought, *I'm still in a cage.*

I walked away, the ocean a blue shimmer, a group of European women and small children playing in the white-capped surf. Peter and Emma Marchbanks ran past me toward home. They didn't glance at me and I didn't glance at them. Holly had done all she had because she wanted something better for her children. The problem had been her road to heaven was paved with bad intentions. Now their perfect lives were gone, but at least they might have a life full of honesty.

My road wasn't any easier. I still had the bars but Jimmy might take those away from me at any moment. I could fight him if I knew who else in the Round Table I could turn to with my accusations. I had no evidence, only conjecture.

Or, like Holly, I could try and run. Vanish. Walk away forever. Make a new life for Daniel. Leonie might run with us. Or she might resent any such attempt on my part to vanish. She wanted normalcy with Daniel as her surrogate son. If I took that away from her, what would she do?

Mila was married to a man who was capable of nearly anything. His calculations had nearly gotten us both killed. But would she even believe me if I told her? If I ever had the chance to tell her?

I was afraid of Jimmy. He was afraid of me. For now, a détente. Until I could decide what to do.

I returned to the airport in Dabolim and called home. Leonie was fine, her voice bright. Daniel cooed and gurgled and made spit noises and laughed. I cooed and made daddy noises, telling him I'd be home soon, very soon.

I hung up. Why couldn't I have both? A safe home to return to and the world to roam. This was a world where the bad guys still lurked in shadow but held more power, more wealth, than ever before. Where they wore a kind of mask of respectability to the world.

I still wanted to be the man who tore those masks free from the shadows. For Daniel, for all the kids. Holly and Glenn and Janice had made the mistake of thinking only of a better house, a better school, a better career.

I wanted, for Daniel, a better world.

I studied the arrivals and departures screen and decided.

I bought my ticket; but not to New Orleans. I owned a bar in Mumbai. I hadn't been there yet. And I thought I could use a drink.

ACKNOWLEDGMENTS

Many thanks to Mitch Hoffman, Jade Chandler, Daniel Mallory, Peter Ginsberg, Shirley Stewart, Jamie Raab, David Shelley, Ursula Mackenzie, Deb Futter, Lindsey Rose, Beth deGuzman, Siobhan Padgett, Sonya Cheuse, Thalia Proctor, Brad Parsons, Anthony Goff, Michele McGonigle, Christine M. Farrell, Dave Barbor, Holly Frederick, Sarah LaPolla, and the terrific teams at Grand Central Publishing and Little, Brown UK.

Also thanks to those who kindly helped me with my questions: Laura Lippman, Sherrie Saint (Director of Investigations, Alabama Dept. of Forensic Sciences), Commander Lea Militello (San Francisco Police Department), Bevan Dufty, JT Ellison, Tom Perrault, Karl Scholz, Marcia Gagliardi, and Ashley Schumann. Errors or bendings of truth for dramatic purposes are my fault, not theirs. Very special thanks to Leslie, Charles, and William, as always.